The Dust within the Rock

SWALLOW PRESS BOOKS BY FRANK WATERS

The Lizard Woman (1930, reprinted 1994)
Midas of the Rockies (1937)
People of the Valley (1941)
The Man Who Killed the Deer (1942)
The Colorado (1946)
The Yogi of Cockroach Court (1947, 1972)
Masked Gods: Navaho and Pueblo Ceremonialism (1950)
The Woman at Otowi Crossing (1966)
Pumpkin Seed Point (1969)
Pike's Peak (1971; reissued 2002 as individual volumes):
  The Wild Earth's Nobility
  Below Grass Roots
  The Dust within the Rock
To Possess the Land (1973)
Mexico Mystique: The Coming Sixth World of Consciousness (1975)
Mountain Dialogues (1981)
Flight from Fiesta (1987)
Brave Are My People (1998)
A Frank Waters Reader: A Southwestern Life in Writing (2000)

ALSO AVAILABLE

A Sunrise Brighter Still: The Visionary Novels of Frank Waters, by Alexander Blackburn (1991)
Frank Waters: Man and Mystic, ed. Vine Deloria, Jr. (1993)

The Dust within the Rock

Book III of the Pikes Peak trilogy

Frank Waters

With a Foreword by Joe Gordon

SWALLOW PRESS/OHIO UNIVERSITY PRESS

ATHENS

Swallow Press/Ohio University Press, Athens, Ohio 45701

Printed in the United States of America
 Published 2002

Swallow Press/Ohio University Press books are printed on acid-free paper ∞ ™

10 09 08 07 06 05 04 03 02 5 4 3 2 1

This volume reproduces the text of *The Dust within the Rock* as it appeared in Frank Waters's 1971 edition of *Pike's Peak*.

Library of Congress Cataloging-in-Publication Data

Waters, Frank, 1902–
The dust within the rock / Frank Waters.
p. cm. — (Book III of the Pikes Peak trilogy)
ISBN 0-8040-1049-8 (pbk.: alk. paper)
1. Gold mines and mining—Fiction. 2. Colorado—Fiction. I. Title.

PS3545.A82 D87 2002
813'.52—dc21

2002021794

CONTENTS

Foreword

This is a story about the West, the day-to-day reality of the men and women who came to a frontier town to build homes and businesses and to raise families. It is not the formulaic, mythic West of cowboys and Indians, although Native American perspectives about the land are an important part of Waters's story. Such adventurous stories reside on the surface of Western experience, and are the stuff of the "western" as traditionally understood by outsiders. This is the story of the West as told from the inside by a writer who was born and raised in Colorado, who experienced firsthand its land and people. This insider's vision makes all the difference, and gives Frank Waters's story its realism, poignancy, and verisimilitude.

Joseph Dozier, Waters's grandfather, arrived in Colorado Springs, a frontier railroad town at the foot of Pikes Peak, "America's Mountain," in 1872, a year after the town was founded by General William Jackson Palmer. Dozier was a successful building contractor, and many of his buildings stand in Colorado Springs today, including the house at 435 East Bijou Street, where Waters was born July 25, 1902—the same year that Winfield Scott Stratton, the "Midas of the Rockies," died. Waters grew up in Colorado Springs, attended Central High School, and dropped out of Colorado College after his junior year in 1924. He left home shortly afterward. Real people, places, and dates are the historical-autobiographical basis of this story, the physical and imaginative places of Waters's story of the West. He didn't even change the names of people and places, except for his family—Dozier to Rogier—but there is no mistaking whom he is describing.

After leaving Colorado Springs, Waters worked at various jobs in Wyoming and California, traveled extensively in Mexico, and along the way became a writer. He visited the Pikes Peak region often in the mid-1930s. By that time he'd written two novels and published one, both set on the border between the United States and Mexico. He also was writing a new novel that would become the first of three in the Pikes (Waters used the possessive form—Pike's) Peak trilogy—*The Wild Earth's Nobility* (1935). The 1930s were important years in Waters's creative life. He was going back to his roots, rethinking his past, and formulating themes that he would develop more fully in his later work. He spent more than a year in the Pikes Peak region, in Colorado Springs and the mining towns of Victor and Cripple Creek, Colorado, where as a boy he'd worked in his grandfather's mines. His return is analogous to that of another Westerner, Mark Twain, who rediscovered his past, the deep pool of his imaginative center, in the small river town of Hannibal, Missouri. Pikes Peak, the mountain just west of Colorado Springs, became Waters's Mississippi River. His next three books focus on the "Matter of the Mountain." *Below Grass Roots* (1937) and *The Dust within the Rock* (1940) continue the story begun in *The Wild Earth's Nobility. Midas of the Rockies* (1937), while not directly a part of the Pikes Peak trilogy, is closely related. It is the biography of Winfield Scott Stratton, the richest and most spectacularly successful of all the miners in the Pikes Peak region, and a friend and sometime business partner of Waters's grandfather, Joseph Dozier.

The three novels that make up the Pikes Peak trilogy can be read individually, for each book is a complete story, each focusing on a different generation of Rogier family history; however, all are related by the central, tragic story of the rise and fall of Joseph Rogier, and the impact of his life on his family. Of growing interest in the story is the life of March Cable, Rogier's grandson, who is the semi-autobiographical representation of Frank Waters himself. Read successively, the books provide a panoramic overview of the history of the American West, especially of the mining industry during the late nineteenth and early twentieth centuries.

By 1960 all three books of the trilogy were out of print. Waters felt the story too important to be forgotten, and began an extensive redaction of the books, sharpening their focus, eliminating interesting but peripheral characters and scenes, and, in general, constricting the plot. In all he cut 800 pages. The result was a single volume, 743 pages long, divided into three sections that were titled after the original trilogy, but were more tightly structured, less rambling. *Pike's Peak: A Family Saga* was published in 1971. A reprint appeared in 1987, its title modified to *Pike's Peak: A Mining Saga*. Nothing else was changed, and the book remains in print today.

This new edition provides another interesting episode in the history of the publication of Waters's story, for it returns to the original three-volume format, but by replicating the redacted version that appeared in 1971. This allows the reader the benefit of Waters's own editorial judgment as found in the single-volume edition of 1971 without the awkwardness of balancing a 743-page book.

Central to all Frank Waters's writing is his understanding of and commitment to the land, what he calls his "sense-of-place." Pikes Peak, the 14,110-foot batholith rising west of Colorado Springs, dominates the geography of the region today much as it did when Waters was growing up. This explains why the mountain overshadows the three novels in the Pikes Peak trilogy. Joseph Rogier is mysteriously drawn to settle within its shadow. Its meaning and silent power haunt him throughout *The Wild Earth's Nobility,* even as he struggles to succeed in a frontier town still visited by roaming bands of Plains Indians. The mountain is always there "from the depths of dreamless sleep to the horizon of wakeful consciousness." Rogier builds a successful construction business, maintains a household full of relatives, and raises his children. Then gold is discovered in Cripple Creek, just over the mountain.

At first, Rogier resists the temptation to join the miners, to probe the mountain's depths. However, when *Below Grass Roots* opens he is deeply involved in mining; he is not interested in gold primarily, but in knowledge—a need to understand himself by unraveling the secret of Pikes Peak. On one level, this novel includes some of the most detailed and descriptive passages about hard-rock mining in Western literature. On the human level, it is the story, not often told, of those who failed. Rogier's mission to find the heart of the mountain becomes an obsession and ends in financial disaster. The family's dreams of wealth turn to dust in the dry holes drilled in the solid granite of Pikes Peak. Family members find an escape only at the Sweet Water Trading Post on the Navajo Reservation. At various times, Ona, Rogier's eldest daughter, her husband, Jonathan Cable, and her son, March, discover a new world: an environment, a way of life, totally different from that of Pikes Peak.

When *The Dust within the Rock* opens, the family is barely surviving. Rogier is a broken man, and though he lives until the end of the book, he is no longer central to the events of the novel. The story turns to his grandson March, a deeply troubled and alienated young man. March loves his grandfather, but is embarrassed by his failure, and resents the snobbishness of the millionaires who did strike it rich, and who abandoned Rogier and his family. Most important, March is struggling to find his own understanding of the mountain, his own sense-of-place. He drops out of college and leaves home. For several years he wanders the Southwest and Mexico, returning to Colorado Springs only after he learns of his grandfather's death. At the end of the novel, March, like his grandfather before him, stands contemplating Pikes Peak. "Toward it he began his long and resolute journey."

Frank Waters's story of the West is rich in history, the details of life of the people on the frontier. It is, as Waters tells us, the saga of a family and of the most important industry in the early West—mining. Pikes Peak, the great mountain to the west, becomes a symbol of all Western land. In the end the reader must stand with March contemplating that mountain and ask: What is my responsibility to the land? How shall I inhabit it?

JOE GORDON

BOOK THREE

The Dust Within The Rock

PART I

CONCENTRATE

1

Shipments of ore from the Sylvanite were returning so little that Rogier accompanied a carload down to the mill to make sure he wasn't being cheated.

The mill was the former old bromide and hot chlorine plant at Colorado City, three miles west of Little London. Several years before, it had been changed to handle the new cyanide process and was destroyed by fire. It had then been bought and rebuilt by the Golden Cycle Mill Company which owned the Golden Cycle mine, then commonly believed to be the third richest gold mine in the United States, and a consolidation of one hundred other mines in Cripple Creek. The mill was an immense structure whose long and high dump rose against the blue mountains like a barren gray mesa.

Rogier, wandering through the roasting rooms, noisy and hot as the inside of a furnace, finally ran into the superintendent who accosted him at once. "Hello, Mr. Rogier! You got my letter?"

"No," Rogier answered sourly. "I came down to see if you're going to give me a decent control assay on my carload of sylvanite. You've been running me short."

The superintendent shook hands. "Another little carload of that stuff? Every time I get one I swear it's nothing but granite, and the assay almost bears me out."

"Never knew a mill man yet who wasn't ready to steal you blind and swear the best ore didn't run half an ounce! What're you trying to do with all those Company mines, run us little fellows out?"

The superintendent frowned. "We're a custom mill. Don't forget that. We give everybody a fair deal." Then he grinned. "What I want to know is why you've gone in for mining gravel. You haven't given up your work?"

"Why not? Last time I talked to you, you were going to call me about an estimate on enlarging the mill. That was a long time ago. How do you expect me to pay my boys' wages?"

"That's what my letter was about. Here, let's get out where we can talk."

Rogier followed him outside and listened to his quick, precise explanation. The Golden Cycle Mill was ready to enlarge its plant. The plans provided for an extension of its huge ore bins, offices, and more space for facilities to increase its capacity to handle 1,100 tons daily – based on the firm expectation of treating 400,000 tons a year. When completed, the Golden Cycle would be the largest and most modern wet chemical plant for the treatment of gold ore in the world.

"That was what I had in mind when I wrote you, Mr. Rogier. The job will be put up for bids. But the Old Man knows the work you did for us some years ago has stood up sound as a bottom dollar, and if you can give us a fair figure it'll probably be given preferential consideration on the basis of your previous work. That is," he added, "if you don't hit a jackpot in that gopher hole of yours."

"Much obliged to you," muttered Rogier. "I'll get the specifications and put in my bid right away!"

"Sure thing – but don't ship us any more granite. This job will pay better!"

Rogier's bid, as expected, was accepted. The job pulled him out of a nasty hole and allowed him to hire a man to help Abe and Jake up at the Sylvanite. Rawlings, his old foreman, agreed to boss his crew only on one condition. "I handle the men. You do everything else. But I handle the men. We ain't goin' to have any more fusses like you had with Deere and Moody."

Rogier solemnly agreed, and the work went along smoothly. The construction was no fancy piece of architecture to grace the scenic landscape of Little London, to be sure, but one in which Rogier took unusual interest. Wasn't it the mill to which Abe and Jake were occasionally sending a carload of ore from the Sylvanite? And striding along the railroad spur lined with carloads of ore from Cripple Creek, he would eye each one of them with a tingle running up his spine. Any one of them might be from the Sylvanite!

During the long days he spent at the mill, he came to know every room and every process in the plant as he followed the run of ore. Never did a long train of ore cars fail to evoke in him instant enthusiasm. He would scramble up the steep embankment to watch the cars being shunted up the high trestle above the bins. In the glint of sunlight he could distinguish instantly the grayish sulphide ores from the brown-streaked oxides and tellurides. By their feel and color and a peculiar sense developed from long familiarity, he could tell where they came from: the west or east side of the district, Battle Mountain, Bull or Globe Hill. The oxides he knew were from a depth not exceeding a thousand feet; over the others he wasted time envisioning the deep dark stopes from which they had been mined. With the tremendous roar in his ears as the cars were emptied into the receiving bins, he strode past the great crushers, watched the ore being sorted to mesh sizes and transported into the sampling works.

The cavernous roasting room entranced him most. Till his shoe soles grew hot and his collar wilted, he would stand before the great roasters. Brawny men stripped to the waist walked past him, reflecting the red glow from their grimy, sweaty bodies; the clang of furnace doors, the roar of the flames echoed in his ears. Rogier never looked up. He stood watching the ore on the hearths. It was fine and powdery, glowing red; in little ripples, like that of sand, it passed underneath the spindles and was slid to the cooling hearth to become the color of dirty brick dust.

Often he sauntered along the narrow gangway over the tops of the huge flotation tanks. Looking down, he could see the dirty spume of the concentrates sluggishly rising to surface like the gold-flaked soap suds in the washtub of the woman who had discovered the principle while washing out her husband's mining clothes. He watched the dirty red flow streaming into the ball mill, being ground in a cyanide solution. He followed it to agitators, to the slime presses where it was washed free of gold-bearing solutions. He then watched the gold being precipitated, treated in the refinery, and finally reduced to bricks of gold ready for shipment to the mint in Denver. Bricks worth $5,000 each. Day by day the repeated process, by which men refined from the great masses of mountain rock the tiny living sparks of gold, became more familiar to him.

Invariably the day's end found him standing on the long, high tailing dump outside the mill. From the flume beside him poured out a steady sluggish stream of waste pulp ore being discharged as tailings. He watched it, a reddish slime like the slow red rivers which had given Colorado its name, a vast ejecta which would harden into another layer of the powdery mesa stretching eastward toward town. A gust of wind would whip off sprays, like fine sand from a desert dune, and elite Little Londoners would make haste to close their windows to the dust, noses up to this irritating reminder of the riches which had built their mansions on Millionaire Row.

Behind him a whistle blew. Workmen – his own among them – streamed from the mill and down the trail. He could hear the jingle of their empty lunch buckets across the creek and into the rows of shacks at Colorado City.

Technically competent, a good construction and mining man, Rogier was more engrossed in an aspect of the mill seen with his own peculiar inner eye. Standing on a narrow shelf between the high wall of mountains and the plains, he could envision beyond Little London the skyscrapers and minarets, the lofty proud cities of America. All built from the gold in the mountains behind him – from that tiny area of only six square miles on the south slope of Pike's Peak which was producing as much gold as both the Mother Lode of California and the Klondike combined!

Here to this high continental plateau, to these mysterious mountains and snowy peaks, had flocked the treasure seekers of the world. This was their treasure chest, the backbone of the continent, the ultimate source of the rivers and the natural resources for centuries to come. And standing there in the twilight, Rogier could see them coming from the cities of cobwebbed steel with their swarming streets and busy marts, from the ships crawling like ants across the seas. Foreigners speaking in strange tongues, shrewd city men calculating how to make an easy dollar, awkward country youths and shy girls in gingham, bashful lads in black string ties sounding their r's with a harsh Western twang, women who enfused strength and freshness and simplicity into the stagnant pools of life for all their blushes and nervously spilled teacups.

They were all ore. In the vast mill of the yet crude West, they all went through the run. Rogier could see his own – poor Tom, Sister Molly, and Cable; Mary Ann, Sally Lee, Ona, and Boné still in their own roasters; March, Leona, and Nancy whose tests were yet to come. Some of them would assay as concentrates. The rest, for all his hopes, would be tailings cast aside.

The devil roast them all! What could he do to help them? A power greater than he had spoken.

"I have graven it within the hills, and my vengeance upon the dust within the rock."

"He who has no roots beneath him has no god."

But he! – he knew to what led his own roots down through the breathing mountains, divined the heart that beat deep inside the fleshly rock. The secret of all men's alliance with the earth would soon be his. No mill of men but would show that he, at last, through the Sylvanite, had reached the final oubliette.

If an inconsequential splatter of shipping ore had been for Rogier a significant discovery, a slip of paper found in the safe constituted a more significant one for Mrs. Rogier. The huge iron safe stood in a dark corner of the dining room for want of a better place to keep it. In years gone by, Rogier had locked in it his valuable papers and a considerable amount of currency. Of late it was unused; the door swung open whenever Mrs. Rogier's dustcloth caught on the combination knob; and occasionally odd papers fell out. So it was that she discovered a note that betrayed Timothy's investment in the Sylvanite to the tune of $5,000. Mr. Timothy! That rich, spoiled, pampered wastrel! It was all clear to her now; buttering up Boné with that party at the Deer Horn Lodge, introducing Rogier into the Ruxton Club, and then dropping the family altogether. He had got what he wanted, a share in that fabulous gold mine certain to make him another fortune!

If this was reprehensible, Rogier's acceptance of the money

was worse. Knowing him, Mrs. Rogier was certain he had taken it under false pretenses as surely as if he had stolen it out of Timothy's pockets. There was no talking to Rogier now. It was up to her own honor to be ready to clear the debt when that awful day of judgment should surely come. Five thousand dollars! It would take months of saving, scrimping, slicing expenses to the bone in ways that no one could suspect.

She began at once. No longer did her sugar bowl contain savings for a rainy day, but contributions to her honor fund.

Rogier began to be suspicious; his profits from the mill job were vanishing too fast. "What do you do with all the money I keep giving you?" he demanded, glaring across the breakfast table at Mrs. Rogier, slimly erect and indomitable in her demands.

"Jonathan's doctor bills and nurse bill, medicine and funeral expenses were all large, Daddy. And you must remember I'm not here alone any more. There are six of us now, and the three children must have milk and eggs and fruit."

"They don't eat a peck apiece. I never see them going for anything but cornbread and molasses. Didn't Ona pay those bills? And didn't she give you some money when she moved down here?"

"Money doesn't last forever," she answered calmly. "A thousand dollars, Daddy."

"A thousand! God Almighty! I've got three men up at the mine to pay and feed, and they're running into trouble. Five hundred. That's all you get, and make it last as long as you can."

Before long the argument came up again, this time before Ona. She was embarrassed. "I don't like feeling that the children and I are sponging off you. I thought that keeping Daddy's books and accounts for so long without wages would pay our way. Maybe I could get a job somewhere else. All I have left is Jonathan's lot east of town."

"It's in Nob Hill now, being built up fast. You'd get a good price for that piece of land," suggested Mrs. Rogier.

"It isn't the money, Mother. But Jonathan's land! Oh, I can't! He loved it so. Remember how he used to drive out there every Sunday just to look at it and feel the dirt in his fingers? Why, that was to be our home. He'd turn over in his grave!"

"Nonsense," said Rogier. "You'd be paying taxes on it as long as you live – with what? Or lose it. You know you'll never have a house out there. This is your home now."

The shamelessly spoken truth broke Ona's will. She sold the five-acre lot for the handsome price of $2,500. That evening she laid the check on Rogier's plate and went to bed supperless and weeping.

In the barny Third Floor she could not sleep. Oh God, she missed him so! The slim straight shaft of his body, his dark head on the pillow, the stubborn independence of that strange man whose only spot of beloved earth had been sacrificed, like himself, for a worthless mine.

Leona and Nancy in their own beds stopped giggling and whispering. The light in March's room across the landing finally went out. Ona lay listening for the creaky steps of the Kadles making their nocturnal rounds. Suddenly, about midnight, she awoke from a doze, stiff with fear. She was staring down the long dark room and across the landing at a spot of light which hung on the closet door at the head of the stairs. It was about as big around as that from an electric flashlight, so bright that she could see the polished grain of the wood it illumined. Suddenly it moved – scarcely six inches to the left, then stopped. Ona, too terrified to move, lay staring at it as if mesmerized. The light kept slowly moving across the wall of the landing and coming to rest again. It was accompanied by no sound, no stealthy fumbling of hands in the dark, no restrained breathing, no sound of steps. Then at last it wavered across March's closed door and stopped on the door-knob. With the flickering reflection of the polished knob, Ona screamed. The light vanished instantly and without a sound.

Nancy woke up, sleepily muttered, "The light? Just like I told you," and dropped off to sleep again. Ona lay sleepless, unmoving, till dawn.

Now began for her a fear-ridden existence she cautioned Nancy to reveal to no one. Mrs. Rogier would have insisted she move downstairs. Rogier would have stormed and stamped around again, doing everything but tearing down the house. And March – she trembled lest he learn of the light that hung on his door like a phantom. Her concern each night was that his door was securely closed.

The light reappeared again and again. It might appear twice within a month or it might be weeks, but it wàs sure to reappear sometime. She began to try to trace its source. There were no lights kept burning in the house at night. The only light outside was the arc-lamp suspended over the bridge at Shook's Run, too far away to cast a reflection through the one north window of her room. There were no other windows on the third floor it might shine through except the small west window at the head of the stairs. Nor was it moonlight. Like as not it would appear on the darkest night. The eerie light was round and small, undiffused and never varying in size. There was only one other possible source – the new revolving searchlight on Pike's Peak whose thin ray swept the trails and canyons to guide lost hikers. Ona knew this was a foolish assumption. People didn't hike up the mountains this late in the year, nor was the Summit House kept open except during the summer tourist season. Nevertheless she drew the blinds on the stairway window and the windows in Sister Molly's front room downstairs, even closed the door to shut off every possible source of light. And still she would awake to see the cold malevolent eye fixed on the wall before her.

She bought a flashlight, throwing it upon the wall when the phantom light appeared – and saw nothing. The doors she locked securely; no one could possibly get into the house. She began to suspect Rogier, or even her mother, of walking in their sleep. But when she jumped out of bed and rushed to the landing, the light vanished instantly and there was no one on the stairs or in the hall below.

Many a time when the incomprehensible phenomenon appeared, she was on the point of screaming out to the Kadles for help, trusting to those two old faithful family ghosts to make their nocturnal rounds and set the seal of their benediction upon the house. But in the morning sunlight, looking at the reflection of her worn and sleepless face in the mirror, she would think of this folly with amazement: appealing to ghosts for help against the supernatural!

"Am I – are we all crazy?" she muttered to herself.

She only knew that this gaunt old house on Shook's Run was haunted by specters of the unforgettable past and the dreaded future, by the ghostly flow of all time; haunted by worries and doubts and futile hopes; haunted, oh haunted, even by the aimless ancient winds forever prowling about the creaking timbers which stood where once tall slim lodge poles raised firm and straight.

2

And now it was October again, the time of change; and haunted by the ghostly flow of time March lay in the attic of his grandfather's house grieving for his father and listening to the aimless ancient winds. It was October and autumn, the season that the Americans call fall, said James Fenimore Cooper, because it was the time when the leaves fall. Of all the months of the year, it was America's month, the corn-ripe moon, when corn came in by wagonloads: Indian maize, the crop of America's soil, blue ears and black, blood red, bronze, yellow, white, and speckled. The first frost had come, "the thunder sleeps." So now to Shallow Water, from out of a desert wilderness of sage and sand, of mesa, butte, and canyon, came hundreds of Navajos in their squeaking wagons to gather for their great Sings. And the nine bitter frosty nights drew down upon the river's elbow, the muddy San Juan, upon the plain of flowering campfires.

But where was his father now, on this cold October's night when he lay alone and lonely in his bed in a ramshackle old house on Shook's Run? Not to Shallow Water had his spirit fled. Not to the mountain Utes, the desert Mojaves, the fierce banty-legged

Apaches. Nor to the mud-brown pueblo dwellers, the reverent Zunis, the Acomas and Hopis isolate on their remote high mesas, the swarming pueblos along the Rio Grande. But farther, over the last range, had fled his long-legged, lonely spirit. Back to the tall slim ghosts of arrogant warrior horsemen who slashed their wrists and were strung up by the sinews to dance, showing how they could endure pain.

Where were their lodges now? Where now the smoke-gray ghostly tepees once strung out along the thousand-mile water courses of the Arkansas and the Platte, the Arickaree and the Red, that clustered in Bijou Basin, at Smoky Hill, standing out like gray anthills against the great blue Rockies? Where did the aimless ancient winds cry to his father's ghost as they prowled across the great plains, stirring the dust in huge wallows where phantom buffalo rolled, and whipping the smoke rising from a thousand campfires of invisible tribes? Was it among the Kiowas and Comanches, the Pawness, the Shawnees, the Crows and innumerable Sioux of the Seven Council Fires? Or was it rather among the Blue-Cloud Arapahoes and the fighting Cheyennes in whose tongue he spoke to Indian Poe?

Where had fled his ghost over the long trail where the pony tracks go only one way, the ghost of that strange dark man, his father, who seldom spoke and now would never speak again? Oh sweet medicine, by the four sacred arrows I ask: "Who was my father, the strange dark man I never really knew?"

It was October, the time of change, when the great male Rockies turned blue and white, and the pines grew smoky in the haze, and the aspens turned yellow and pink. It was the crack of Jake's rifle bringing down a deer, the smell of bacon sizzling in the pan, the tall tales of ore wagons creaking up the Pass to Creede, Tin Cup, Fair Play, Leadville, and Buckskin Joe high in the Colorado Rockies. It was the time when Cripple Creek, two miles high, drew in its horns for winter and the first snow whitened the shaft houses on Battle Mountain. At night the long train of empties puffed slowly up to the Bull Hill junction under the steam of four engines and from high above, you could see the furnace-red glow from their tenders. Then when the great mines, the Independence and the Portland, the Golden Cycle, Jack Pot, Mary McKinney, the Wild Horse and the

American Eagles looked like great liners dry-docked on the mountain slopes; and miners' wives lined the insides of their shanties with the pink-sheeted front pages of the *Denver Post* to keep out the wind; and the little fellows boarded up their tunnels and drifted to town to make a stake for next year's beans.

Shallow Water and Cripple Creek, adobe and granite. And lying there sleepless in bed on a cold October's night, listening to the aimless ancient winds whipping the leaves from the trees and whining under the eaves, he stared through the darkness at the case of ore specimens from the Sylvanite, at the single eagle feather tipped with red yarn that hung from the rafter. They were symbols of things which were themselves symbols, imbued with a terrible fixity and at the same time reflecting a terrible change. Who knew what they meant? To himself he seemed unreal, worn out with the vain effort to discern what in him was the transient, what was the enduring. He knew only that he too was an eternal stranger, and that always he would be alone as now. And all that he had known and felt and loved and lost had been swept away by a current too timeless and immense to give him the sense of its onward course. For he had lost his father and something else – his childhood; he was twelve years old.

The mysterious flow of time that does not move, yet ever moves. Who am I, he wondered. The leaf that falls into the flow or the leaf that sprouts anew? Am I the mountain rock shattered by frost and disintegrated by time, or the timeless dust within the rock, carried to the sea to rise again a lofty peak with sea shells on its summit?

There is no beginning, no end. I am all that ever has been and will be, in me is rooted all that I have ever met. I am my mother's worn shirtwaist, the shining crystals of sylvanite and calaverite in their dusty cases, the deep black stopes of my grandfather's worthless mines and the fiendish laughter that pursues him, the wind that warps the pines at timberline and the cry of the wolf it carries. I am my grandmother's false pride and envy, the crumpled magnolia leaves and the moth-holed Confederate flag in her old trunk. And I am my father's dark hawk face and the smoke of a thousand camp fires in his blood.

I am the dark adobe world of my father which lies behind, and the white granite world of my grandfather which lies ahead. In me the great flow of time is a leaping fountain which will water both. For I am the feather, the flower, the drum, and the mirror of the old gods who have never died.

And yet as he lay listening now to the wheels of a milk wagon rumbling across the bridge, he wondered, What or who is in me that knows these things I do not know? Who and what am I?

Columbia School did not teach him.

There were seven public grade schools in Little London: two each in the north, west, and south, and one in the sparsely settled east section. The geographic boundaries of these sections were as definitely fixed as patented mining claims. Each of them reflected the exact, rubber-stamped social status of its residents. For Little London by now, ignoring the hoarded gold it had wrung from Cripple Creek, had completely forsworn its environmental heritage. Built on the ideal of a European spa, it self-consciously proclaimed itself a cultural oasis in the crude American West, a culture possessed by its various sections according to their positions on the rising stairsteps of distinction:

$$$$$$

$$$

$

¢

0

No liquor could be sold within town. Newspapers were prohibited from carrying funny papers in their Sunday issues. the *Odeon* and the *Princess* movie palaces were closed on Sunday. And all manufacturing within town limits was forbidden. The ore reduction mills which it ignored were restricted to the sandy mesa west of town. Here on the west side and in the suburb of Colorado City lived the brawny Golden Cycle mill workers who trooped on Saturday night to riot in the block-long array of saloons nearby called Ramona. So of course their children and the two west side schools they attended were on the lowest step.

Lowell School on the southern edge of town reflected the haphazard, listless nonentity of the ramshackle buildings and fringe-area residents. Liller School, farther in, stood just a block from the railroad yards and drew its rowdy children from the houses at the bottom of Bijou Hill and the nigger shanties of Poverty Row along Shook's Run.

The North End was the elite heart of Little London. To its wide and gracious avenues, particularly Wood Avenue, had flocked the lucky who had struck it rich at Cripple Creek. Their rococo mansions filled block after block. The side streets accommodated the mere comfortably wealthy, the leading business men, and the barnstorming social climbers. So naturally its two grammar schools, Steele and Garfield, were the best in town.

Columbia was across the tracks in the sparsely settled prairies east of town. A tidy, two-storied, red brick building, it stood beside an unfinished white brick church holding Sunday services in the basement. Around it lay a vacant expanse of prairie playground stretching eastward to the pine bluffs. But the district was clean and tidy; more and more tradesmen, professional men, and newcomers were coming in. There was even a big house or two, rows of cottonwoods, and fresh cropped lawns. It was here that March and Leona had gone to school before moving down to the bottom of Bijou Hill in the old house on Shook's Run.

"And I don't see why March can't keep coming here just one more year," pleaded Ona, seated with March in the principal's office. "He's in the eighth grade and will graduate next June. Naturally he wants to finish up with his old classmates and teachers."

"You have moved into the Liller district. That is evident," said Miss Trumble coldly.

Miss Trumble, the principal, was almost six feet tall. Her backbone was an iron ramrod, her jaws a steel trap, her eyes a pair of rifle sights that drew a bead on any youngster who showed a streak of wildness. She was a capable woman who formerly had taught school in a mining camp. Now the muzzle of her ambition was pointed at Garfield School. *Excelsior* was her favorite poem, and "Old Excelsior" her nickname among students.

"It's not Leona I'm thinking of," replied Ona. "She's young and can adapt to Liller. But March would be distressed; you know how high strung he is. And such a short walk, too. Just up Bijou to the railroad embankment, then north, and four blocks east. For only one year!"

"It's too irregular. I will not recommend it." Old Excelsior rose.

Ona set her own square jaw as she stood up. "I don't want to have to pass my simple request any higher, Miss Trumble."

"I and my pupils obey the rules. That is the spirit of Columbia. Mrs. Cable!"

Ona returned to Mrs. Rogier storming with indignation. "It's not the education. Goodness knows the boy does nothing but read, read, read. But I won't have the stigma pinned on him of being a Liller boy. With all those niggers and numbskulls!"

Mrs. Rogier laid down her spectacles on her Bible. "A Rogier is a Rogier in any company. Blood tells, always. Now if his demeanor and deportment are worthy –"

Ona whirled around to face the boy. "I'm goin' to get you back in Columbia and you're goin' to have demeanor all right! And deportment too! You're goin' to brush up on figures if I have to burn up every book in the house. I won't have you runnin' wild as a jack rabbit any more!"

Mrs. Rogier nodded. "Your father built Columbia, every other school in town. Mr. Ford is still on the School Board – one of Daddy's best friends – and if you were to ask him, casually like –"

"And there's a precedent already set!" interrupted Ona. "That pretty little girl who lives up on Bijou Hill. Leslie Shane, whose father owns the Saddle Rock Grill. She's going to Columbia even though she's out of the district too."

"What's good for the goose is good for the gander," agreed Mrs. Rogier. "But easy-like. No hard pushin'!"

It was done. March was allowed to finish eighth grade at Columbia while Leona and Nancy were transferred to Liller. The triumph was all Ona's; she didn't have to taste each day the bitter fruits of her success. For one thing it alienated March from his neighbors, the twelve Caseys and two Kennedys on either side, who went to Liller. Occasionally he played with them in the street: marbles, cricket with tin cans and baseball bats, and kick-the-can. But there was no bond between him and them, no mutual dislike or like of the same teachers and lessons, no confidences to be exchanged as they walked back and forth to school. He was there for the moment in their midst. But in the morning, a stranger, he walked away.

Many of these neighbor boys never knew his last name; to them he was March Rogier or simply the Rogier kid. His tribal affinity with the Rogiers set him apart too. For the Rogiers were different. One knew this without question early on the morning of every Fourth of July when Mrs. Rogier took out from her trunk the large Confederate Flag and hung it over the front railing of the second-story balcony. By mid-morning clumps of neighbors began gathering to point at it and protest with scowling faces. The telephone rang. The caller was a man on the *Gazette* who had received protests from people in town, and wanted to know why a good old American flag couldn't be displayed in its stead on this patriotic Fourth of July.

"And I don't see why not, Mother!" protested Ona herself. "You know hanging that old rag out there is just like waving a red flag in front of a bull. It always creates a stink and a rumpus. Damn it, Mother! Don't you know yet the Civil War's over and forgotten?"

"It is far from me to forget that many brave and true men died nobly for that old rag as you call it, Ona," Mrs. Rogier answered quietly. "The Stars and Bars is just as much an emblem of our family faith as the Stars and Stripes to other people. As long as this is a free country I see no reason to take it down."

So there it stayed all day, the rest of the family hiding as if in shame behind it. Peeking out the window, March could see neighbors putting up their noses at it or spitting on the sidewalk as they walked past, hear the firecrackers hurled at it. But when the Casey and the Kennedy kids began to throw mud balls, plastering windows and the front of the house he felt rise within him a curious stubborn pride.

"General Grant beat Lee, didn't he?" they shouted. "And we can take the Rogiers like Grant took Richmond! Come out, you little Reb, if you ain't scaired of us boys in blue!"

And then he would rush out to get his nose bloodied, knuckles skinned, and clothes muddied; and the glorious Fourth of July, as usual, would turn into another shameful, noisy, family row.

Even at Columbia he felt deracinated and alone. He was dark and thin, beginning to grow tall and skinny, with his father's small hands and feet. The Cable in him made him grave and shy, the Rogier in him too sensitive and stubborn. After long months at

Shallow Water and up at the Sylvanite with none but the companionship of taciturn men, he did not know how to get along with children of his own age. His schoolmates often seemed childish, but none were as gullible to pranks and jokes as he. He was easily wounded. A word, a look, would thrust into the quick of his being, and he was slow to forgive. Still he was never bullied by the bigger boys from outlying ranches, for in him was a cold cruelty and he could be sly as an animal when pressed in combat, kicking into the groin or jabbing a thumb into an Adam's apple.

Arithmetic was his despair, fractions his nemesis. Miss Thomas, the teacher, was a plump little woman who stood at the blackboard in front of the class, the horizontal line of her corset showing across her round posterior.

"Above the line we place four. Below the line, what? March! What do we have below the line?"

A thumb poked his shoulder. A steamy breath whispered in his ear, "Plush Bottom!"

No; he had no mind for figures.

Nor for geography. The United States of America were forty-eight. They were tidy parallelograms, properly fenced: pink, green, red, blue, brown. But really, the Rocky Mountains marched right through. You couldn't tell Kansas from the wasteland prairies of eastern Colorado on a clear day from the slope of Pike's Peak.

History, you might say, was in the same boat. The country was England's, Spain's, France's. Then came the Louisiana Purchase and it was the United States of America. But what about it when it was comprised of the great united nations of the Iroquois; Pontiac's confederacy of the Ottawas,Ojibwas, Hurons, and Delawares; Tecumseh's alliance of Shawnees, Wyandots, and Kickapoos; the mighty nations of the Cherokees, Creeks, Chickasaws, Choctaws, and Seminoles; the Seven Council Fires of the Sioux; the Cheyennes, Arapahoes, Kiowas, and Comanches; Apacheria, land of the Apaches; the combined clans of the Navajos; and the multi-storied mud cities of the Pueblos? History, like geography, had nothing to say. But the snow drifted over the bunch grass just the same, and the great mountains shouldered aside races, customs, governments, creeds. And the aimless ancient winds whispered of a mighty continent with its own spirit of place that was and would always be beyond political division.

At his desk during the writing lesson he sat like one automaton of many. Feet down flat, back straight, left arm curved above the paper, so!

"Ready now? The vertical strokes first. Very lightly. Don't move your fingers. The whole arm, remember. Ready? Dip pens! Stroke!"

Hail Columbia, the Gem of the Ocean! You can't tell one's handwriting from another's. The same slant, the same shading, the same size. Stroke! The light ovals this time! Procreation next by the Palmer Method.

March was awarded the thirty-ninth Palmer Certificate of the class with a gold seal and tags of purple and white ribbons, the school colors.

Drawing in the public schools was a negligible diversion. Miss Marion made the rounds every two weeks, coming to Columbia on alternate Thursdays. A big breasted woman with a deep and fertile voice, she wore leather gloves and a floppy coat, like a man's. March adored her. Like a plain faced daughter of Ceres, she brought the grasses, fruits, and flowers of the fields, and all the secret beauty of an earth he had never noticed before.

In the spring, Indian paint brushes, bluebells, an armful of pussy-willows. In the fall, milkweed pods, one to a child, to be drawn in charcoal. Often when the snow lay deep she trooped in with pine branches, a sheaf of barley, or merely alfalfa purchased from a feed store. Or they painted apples. But always these trivial things took on an astounding vitality; they still clung to the stem of all life.

"Let's open these windows! Let the day in!"

The boy's soul leaped up to meet it. He saw outside, waving in the wind, the brown prairie grasses, the sere weeds, the withered stalks he had blindly ignored. On his desk lay a brittle, green-gray milkweed pod on its leafless stick, and beside it his charcoal scrawl.

Miss Marion, prowling silently down the aisle, stopped beside him. "Not bad. But look!" She dug him playfully in the ribs. "You're making a submarine out of it. All iron, closed up tight against the water. Look here."

She turned it, gently pried open the narrow tapered lips, drew out the white silky spume with its enmeshed black seeds. The breeze from the window sent the tufts floating across the room, landing on desks, papers, backs. "See? It's got hinges. It opens to the wind so the parachutes can drop out. Remember, everything in nature is alive."

She sauntered on; and the boy, smeared with charcoal, began again.

But for Miss Watrous' grammar class March trod willingly the treadmill of his school existence. Miss Ruth Watrous was tall and bony, wore glasses, and maintained an habitual air of disassociation from the mechanical grind around her. Old Excelsior didn't like her. Neither did Miss Plush Bottom. But against her easy mannered immunity both were powerless. She kept perfect order. Instead of sending a pupil out to stand in the hall for whispering, or making him eat crackers in front of the class for chewing gum, she would turn around listless at the sound of any fuss.

"You might think this grammar is dull, but you need it and I'm the one to give it to you. However, if you don't want it, just quietly walk out. But remember, you don't come back. Now who is the first to leave before the rest of us diagram this sentence?"

No one ever left. She rewarded them by reading out loud for the last twenty minutes of the day. Greek and Roman mythology at first. Gradually for March the world of Old Excelsior faded away. Pike's Peak rose higher, more majestic, into Mount Olympus. The great Labyrinth yawned blacker than the deepest stope of the Sylvanite. He was in a new world watching the sowing of the dragon's teeth, the phoenix rising anew, the salamander in the flame; hearing the sea maidens cry, the crash of shields before Troy, and in the woodlands the pipes of Pan. Now, from the waters of Babylon came the sacred hawk-headed, ram-headed, and winged beasts; and from the great Nile the god Osiris and the goddess Isis, and the sacred bull with a beetle under his tongue and the hair of his tail double. And now the many-headed gods of the east, Vishnu and Siva, and all the rest, ivory and peacocks, and streets that quaked to the tread of elephants. Then the new and mighty world of the north and the frost giants, and the lusty Vikings swilling mead from great horns. It was Thor hurling his hammer, Odin seated on his throne, two ravens perched on his shoulder, two wolves crouching at his feet, and the Valkyries thundering over the rainbow bridge to Valhalla with fallen warriors. Then, late one afternoon, he was transported from the shadows of the Druids' sacred oak and mistletoe to a land he knew well, his own great continent of the hereafter, so unutterably old and unknown that men called it the New World. High above it towered still-smoking Popocatepetl, and Ixtaccihuatl, the sleeping woman covered by a snowy mantle. Below them the war god Huitzilopochtli hungered for blood-dripping human hearts torn out from the breasts of victims on top of pyramids greater and higher than those in Egypt. Yet he, Quetzalcoatl, the Feathered Serpent, the Lord of Dawn, the god of gods, had not forgotten his children. Someday he would return. And darkly, in his blood, March could hear beating the tall drum *huehuetl* and the flat drum *teponaztle*, echoing in the deep-toned belly drums and the little water drums. And he could hear again the deep-voiced singing out beyond Shallow Water. This was the altar, the high flat mesa across the desert, and burning cedar the incense. For we of America, its children, are the feather, the flower, the drum, and the mirror of the old gods who never die.

The bell rang. In a daze March walked out into the late, gray October afternoon, under the honks of wild geese passing overhead. What a wonderful woman was bony Miss Watrous! She was a priestess seated on a moonlit rock lapped by a glimmering sea. The boy knelt before her on the lonely shore. And she dipped her fingers into that sea of ethereal plasma and sprinkled his bowed head. Thus was he baptised in the living mystery. Mythology, the only true history of the soul of man!

And then suddenly he saw riding past the schoolhouse the ghost of his father. Mounted stiffly, knees up, on his old paint-peeling bicycle. Dressed in his black business suit, his handmade boots stuck into the leather toe-clips provided instead of safety brakes. And still wearing on his hip, hidden beneath his coat, that long-bladed, razor-sharp toad-sticker with a bone handle! That strange dark man who was his father, who had faced down the son of Black Kettle, peddling past like an Ichabod with his life insurance premium book protruding out of his pocket!

This then – Old Excelsior, Miss Plush Bottom, Miss Marion, and Miss Watrous, with their straggly classes – was for March Columbia School.

There was also Leslie Shane.

3

Leslie Shane! Oh magical and musical name!

He had seen her first during one afternoon recess. She had been up in Old Excelsior's office with her mother, arranging to enter school; they had just moved into town. Now they came down the sandstone steps outside. Old Excelsior pointed out the girls' playground on the left and went back upstairs. Her mother walked away. And she was left alone to look about and see her new companions.

One like her sees more than this. In a group of children one sees the whole of society: the cheat, the coward and the bully, the quick wit, the dullard, the sensitive, and the vulgar. Each has his own capacity for understanding and spiritual growth that never enlarges; it only fills. The world of childhood is not so childish as the adult world that pompously proclaims it so. It sees this immediately with an intuition not yet dulled by experience nor clouded by reason. They *are,* simply, unaccountably, they are. Tall, strawhaired Grace already superficial and cheaply elegant; Eunice, beautiful and butter-mouthed; German Marie whole-souled and stolid; Two Bit Liz eyeing the big boys from the ranches; Torchy swaggering in another new suit; the hunchback Thompson kid, smarter'n a whip. And another skinny lad leaning against a tree, fumbling with a jackknife. The casual proper pose of a boy too superior to notice a mere new girl who has entered school. But she catches the sudden tautness of his body, the furtive glance. Clear across the gravel and the strip of lawn the glance holds. A swift red stains his brown cheeks. He squirms like a grub impaled on a pin. And still the glance holds. It is a moment of strange truth that time will never alter nor explain. She knows that his soul streams out toward her like a flood, and that he mysteriously seeks to dam it, powerless as he is. A queer, contradictory boy! She simply, shyly smiles.

It releases him like an arrow. He leaps forward, grabs Torchy's cap and throws it into the drinking fountain, and dashes off as if pursued by a thousand shrieking demons.

She had seen him! She had seen him!

A mighty song filled him, a great strength leaped into him. By a single glance, like the touch of Moses' rod, the hard rock fastness of his being had been split asunder. Beauty and wonder, joy and life gushed from him. For the first time he felt whole and sound, the premonition of manhood. Out on the prairie he stopped, panting. Inside him wrestled a boy and a man. Then the two merged into one that was neither; sheepishly it crept back to where, unobserved, he could stare helplessly at her who held him in such magnificent bondage.

She was leaning against the balustrade, watching the girls playing around the drinking fountain. The wind had blown back her spruce-green sweater, played with the hem of her corn-yellow dress. She was small but well formed, with the suggestion of early maturity. Her hair was a mass of apricot-colored curls, her face pale and covered with freckles. She had large brown eyes, a wide mouth, and a stub, sympathetic nose – a face that never in childhood was childish, but only unawakened. Later he was to see and remember always her thin, delicate hands with their tiny network of blue veins. The hands that already, before her face and body, had become a woman's.

Leslie was in his class and sat in the next row. Mr. Shane, after managing Fred Harvey railroad lunch rooms for years, had just bought the Saddle Rock Grill. The family lived close to March, two blocks west, on top of Bijou Hill. Mrs. Shane impressed March as cold and shrewd; it was she who had managed to enter Leslie in Columbia, establishing the "precedent" Ona had used to insure March's own return to school. The family owned an automobile in which, on rainy days, Mrs. Shane drove Leslie to school. On good days she walked, and March longed to walk with her. Instead, tortured with his own cowardice, he straggled homeward a block behind her.

Before he could screw up courage to catch up with her, his turn came to stay after school and dust erasers. A few afternoons later he came out to see her ahead of him. Alone. Sauntering along, a step at a time. Panic overcame him. The blind urge which drove him to her, and that equal force which restrained him before they merged – this was the eternal craving and the stubborn integrity of every human soul driven by loneliness to seek that which must be found only inside itself. Suddenly she looked around. Just as suddenly he was beside her, roughly grabbing her books to clench under his own arm.

"You're awfully slow walking," she said quietly. "I've been waiting for you."

"I'm done beatin' erasers," he muttered.

"I'm glad. I was wondering if you were going to walk home with me."

She looked up at him. Her eyes were clear and unquestioning, dark and fathomless. Into them he plunged helplessly, as if into a mindless oneness that absorbed him wholly. He came up naked and clean of shame, stripped of pretense and fear.

"I am. I'd rather walk home with you than anything." Then in a rush of feeling he added. "I like you, Leslie. Oh, I sure like you!"

Lightly she laid a hand on his arm. "Yes. I know. You don't have to tell me. I know!"

And sedately, in silence, they walked on.

Bad weather set in. Her mother drove her back and forth to school. Then, late in October, Old Excelsior called a meeting of the eighth grade. "Marie is giving a Halloween party for the members of her class and its teachers on Friday night. You are all graduating next June and should know how to conduct yourselves like grown-ups. So every boy in the class must escort a girl. Boys, be gentlemanly! Agree among yourselves whom you will ask. And tomorrow after school report to me the name of the young lady who will accompany you, and for whom you will be responsible."

Boys and girls went out giggling in two groups. A few bolder boys made a rush across the lawn, then swaggered triumphantly across the street to congregate in front of the drug-and-candy store. March slunk across behind them.

"I got Eunice!" boasted one. "And didn't waste no time either!"

"That's nothin'! Didn't you see me givin' Grace the wink right when Old Excelsior was talkin'? Ferris did. He seen me!"

"Who's goin' to take Two-Bit Liz behind her old man's barn afterward?" snickered another. "Not me this time! Her old lady purt near caught me last time!"

March waited apprehensively for what would come.

Cecil James spoke first. "I asked the new girl – Leslie Shane. I guess she's pretty enough to ride in my dad's new car if he'll drive us."

"So'd I," said a lanky redhead named Bob Schwartz. "She nodded yes and didn't say nothing about you."

March's face had gone sallow. "She's goin' with me," he said quietly.

A titter went around. "Fight it out, all three of you!"

Cecil drawled, "She must think she's popular, sayin' yes to everybody. Who does she think she is?"

"Well, I asked her," said Bob, "and I'm goin' to take her."

"I said I'm takin' her," March insisted in a low monotonous voice.

A curious, cold expectancy held him as he looked at Schwartz' long rangy body lounging carelessly against the fence. He remembered the long sharp blade his father always carried on his hip, and he felt the comforting shape of his own jackknife in his hip pocket, knowing triumphantly that he really meant what he said as he had meant nothing else before.

Schwartz lit a cigarette. "Oh, the hell with anybody so far gone on a girl! But I've got a good mind to turn her name in too, just to see what she says!" He spat and walked away.

There was no triumph in March as he slunk homeward, obscessed by the fear of asking Leslie and hearing that she already had promised to go to the party with Cecil or Bob.

She had been sitting on the gutter down the street for nearly half an hour. "Hello, March!" she said cheerfully, rising like apparition before him.

They walked in silence to the railroad tracks before she asked quietly, "Are you going to Marie's party?"

"I guess so," he answered fearsomely. And then, "Why don't we go together, seeing that we live so close?"

"All right."

He was bathed now in a wonderful aura of delicious warmth and self-assurance. As always, once they were alone, he lost his fear of her. He took her books, his gaze caressing hungrily her slim white hands with their fine blue veins, her freckled face, the apricot curls protruding from her green wool tam.

"As long as you live a ways on the other side of me, why don't you just drop by on the way to the party?" he suggested casually. "I'll take you home, of course, but there's no need climbin' the hill twice."

"Sure. Why, sure I will, March. I'm glad you're going with me. We haven't talked together for a long time."

That Friday evening as he dressed in his blue serge suit, pinning to the lapel an enamel Confederate flag given him by Mrs. Rogier, March was conscious-stricken. He ought to go after Leslie, but he dreaded knocking on the door and meeting Mrs. Shane's cold, inquisitive face. So, dressed up, he lingered downstairs, waiting for supper. It was always late; the Rogiers could never pull themselves together.

"Is Leslie Shane going to be at the party?" asked his mother.

"Everybody in class," he mumbled.

"Do you like her?" asked Leona. "She's a pretty girl."

"Maybe you can bring her home," suggested Nancy.

The family finally settled down at table. What an array it was, thought March. Mrs. Rogier, Ona, Nancy, Leona, himself, and Rogier for a change. He could hardly eat. There was a sudden loud knocking on the front door. March lunged to open the front door.

By the dim light behind him he saw the figure of a burly man, grinning humorously from a considerate, benign face. It was Mr. Shane.

"Well, young man!" he roared in a heavy jocular voice. "I've brought your girl here for you to take to the party. But see that you bring her home. Understand?"

He reached around behind him, pushed Leslie over the threshold, and walked away.

March, petrified, brought her into the dining room, managed to introduce her.

Mrs. Rogier rose up in wrathful indignation. "You mean to say, March, you are escorting this young lady and didn't have the courtesy to call for her? I am ashamed, deeply ashamed. Young lady, you have my full permission to resent this insult by returning directly home!"

"March! How could you?" gasped Ona.

Leslie was not at all embarrassed. Perfectly composed, she said easily, "March and I understand each other. Here, have a piece of the candy I'm taking to Marie." She passed around a satin box of chocolates. March's eyes met those of his mother with the same unspoken guilt: why hadn't he thought to bring a gift?

Rogier indecorously was the only one to take a piece. He took two. After which he rose and put his arm around her. "Young lady! You've confronted with courage and equanimity a bastion of outmoded conservatism! You have given me some mighty tasty candy everybody else was too polite to touch. I welcome you into this house!"

It was awful, Rogier touched with port after starving in Cripple Creek. March backed Leslie hastily of of the room.

"Take care of that boy!" Rogier boomed out behind them. "You can see he's got a chicken-heart!"

"Don't you worry, Mr. Rogier!" Leslie called back as they closed the door. "We'll get along all right!"

Her mature assurance oppressed March as they walked in darkness to Marie's house. Yet all these insults and injuries to his pride, his own angry shame, were dissipated by the fragrant perfume of her proximity, the feel of her arm through his. "It's too bad we're so young and have to wait so long till we're grown up," she said.

He stopped and turned her face around, his thumb caressing her cheek. Then he kissed her on the mouth. He had never kissed a girl before and it was a funny feeling. The touch of those warm, dry, velvety lips which clung to his, and through which stemmed the indefinable essence of all that was Leslie Shane! Charlotte, sweet Charlotte, born a virgin, died a harlot, had kissed him once before. She was his first love, but the rapaciousness, the hungry loneliness of her kiss had frightened him. It had bruised his lips! This was different. It was something he couldn't understand or ever forget. He only knew, even then, that whatever became of them both, they were sealed together by a bond which could never be broken.

They reached Marie's house. The lights were blazing. All the members of the eighth grade class were there and their teachers. Blindfolded, they pinned the tail on the donkey, played blind-man's bluff, dropped the handkerchief. In the cellar they paraded through dark tunnels illuminated by ghostly skeletons and Death's heads. They bobbed for apples in wash tubs, ate sandwiches and pumpkin pie with ice cream. Through all this childish fun, the flow of ghostly time, the boy was acutely aware of Leslie's face gently smiling at him across the room. And now they gathered to sit on chairs arranged in a semi-circle around the fireplace.

"Just this one game before we leave," announced Miss Plush Bottom, holding up one of the forfeits given her by the students for the game. "What shall the owner do to redeem it? Just this one last game!"

The forfeit was March's jackknife. He sat deathly still. "Bow to the wisest, kneel to the prettiest, and kiss the one he loves best!" somebody shouted.

"And it's March's! March's!" shrieked Grace.

He was pale and shaking. It was the first forfeit in the game, and the voice sounded in his ears the irrevocable sentence he must pass before Old Excelsior, Miss Plush Bottom, Cecil James, Bob Schwartz – publicly, before everybody.

In silence and loneliness he got unsteadily to his feet. He tried to smile and the pitiful attempt contorted his dark face. To pass it off as a joke! To kneel in front of Marie or Two Bit Liz! This was his only frantic desire. And yet as if in a dream he saw her to whom he was so irrevocably committed. She was sitting head down, hands clasped, modestly withdrawn.

He stumbled across the room to stand in front of her, bowed stiffly, got down on his knees. She raised her face. He could not look into her eyes, and quickly and gently kissed her on the forehead.

Then he rose and with hands clenched at his sides stalked back to his chair.

Old Excelsior rose at once. "That's enough of that! Don't you think, Miss Thomas, that kissing games are out of place among children of this age? Like March. They are simply too intense! And besides, it's late. We should all go home."

They walked silently out of the house into the darkness, arm in arm. Through the gloom of the great cottonwoods along the creek.

"It wasn't just a game? You really meant it?" asked Leslie.

"Sure, or I wouldn't have done it."

"Thank you, March."

"That's all right," he said. "That's the way it is, that's all."

A light appeared: the single bare globe in the railroad underpass at the head of Bijou Street. Self-consciously they walked through to the street. A strange feeling followed March. This was the way he had come to his grandfather's house that other night long ago. In its feeling of aloneness and loneliness, he could hear faintly behind him a rattle that kept increasing in volume and meaning. Leslie, he noticed, was glancing apprehensively sideways at the wooden shack now haunted by the murderer and the murdered and the bloody axe that had served as the final bond between them. In silence he walked her down the middle of the dusty road, over the bridge at Shook's Run, and past his grandfather's house to the arc-light at the corner. From its aura into more darkness they climbed Bijou Hill to Leslie's house.

The porch light was on. "I think I'd better go in. They're waiting up for me," she said.

He hesitated. "Wait here in the porch light, will you, till I get to the bottom of the hill? Then I'll wave and you can run inside."

"Yes, that's better!" she agreed at once. "But run fast, March!"

They gasped hands, stared into each other's eyes. Then March ran quickly down the hill to turn, wave back, and run on home in darkness.

4

Late that November Abe and Jake, in their cabin at the Sylvanite, were preparing to go to town. It was unusually early, before noon. They put on their black suits and black string ties, rubbed their boots off, brushed their hats. They moved somberly and quietly, as if preparing themselves for a funereal ordeal rather than a weekly spree. Finally dressed and ready, they closed their duffle bags and stood looking at each other's long sad face.

"It just don't seem right to be leavin' here before we tell him, man to man. The Colonel's been mighty good to us fer a long time," said Jake.

Abe rubbed the moisture off his sweaty hands, pulled at his mustache – irresolute movements that betrayed his own reluctance. "We can't be waitin' here till he comes to tell him the hole's worked out and we're finally leavin'. You know the Colonel! He'd talk us out of it, and we'd be stuck again. That's why I say we'll meet him when he steps off the noon train. It'll be easier tellin' him there – And I reckon a drink beforehand won't hurt none."

"Well – "

They gave a last look at the cabin they had tidied up, latched the door behind them, and duffle bags over shoulder strode down the trail –

Rogier, unable to catch the noon train, did not arrive till midafternoon. Jake and Abe, with their duffle bags beside them, were waiting on the platform when he swung off the train. Rogier did not notice the bags for the knots of people, all excitedly talking. A strange air of expectancy seemed to imbue the very air.

"Well, boys!" he greeted them warmly. "Never expected to see you here! Come on! Let's have a drink at the Mint before we go back!"

Jake nodded and walked off with Rogier. Abe dallied behind to leave the duffle bags in the depot, then joined them in a comparatively quiet corner in the Mint. Rogier could not help but notice his companions' unusual animation. Cold sober, their faces were flushed; their eyes sparkled with a mysterious expectancy like those of two boys waiting for Santa Claus. Nor did Rogier fail to observe the tremor of excitement running through the men at the long bar. Occasionally above the murmur of conversation rose the name "Cresson."

"Dom me!" he said at last. "What's goin' on up here? You both look like the cat that swallowed the canary. Hit another streak of shipping ore?"

Abe leaned forward. "Colonel, it's not the Sylvanite. It's the Cresson."

"That old workin'?" snorted Rogier. "Well, tell me about it!"

Jake looked solemnly around him before he spoke in a low voice. "It's a mighty big thing, Colonel, and still secret even if it's leakin' out. But we know Luke, and he says he'll give us a peek – just a peek, mind! – if we come up right away. So we been waitin' for you."

A curious tremor of foreboding shook Rogier. "Let's go then!"

Abe and Jake strode out of the saloon. Rogier followed them. The Cresson was sunk in the gulch between Bull and Raven hills. They rode the Low Line to the Elkton and walked up the gulch to the portal of the Cresson.

What had got into these two old fools, Rogier kept wondering, to make them so excited about anything here? The Cresson had been a marginal working ever since its discovery in 1894; the government report on the district in 1906 didn't even list it. But somehow the mine had been foisted on a couple of real estate men in Chicago who periodically sold a few shares of stock and leased its working levels to different operators who could never make its low grade ore pay. The shaft was down to 600 feet and the mine was $80,000 in the red.

Then three or four years ago, as Rogier recalled, Dick Roelofs had taken over its management. He was a young man, a graduate of an engineering college somewhere in Pennsylvania, but unable to find steady work he clerked in the Green Bee Grocery on Second Street. Rogier had pricked up his ears when Roelofs, with a small crew under Luke Shepherd, began to lift the Cresson out of debt. He sank the shaft to 1,000 feet, blasted out great stopes, and by economic management began to make the low grade ore pay dividends. Ore which averaged only $15.67 a ton! Why that was no better than the Sylvanite! The Cresson however seemed to have plenty of it, but still the mine was barely making out and Rogier had forgotten it till now.

The surface plant looked tidy enough he admitted when he reached it: a great smooth-rolling drum, clear indicators, a commodious new cage. The place was crowded with men. From them stepped Luke Shepherd.

"We come like you said we could, Luke," said Abe.

"We'll have to hurry," replied Luke. "Roelof's bringin' the officials to go down, and the whole workin' will be closed tighter'n a drum. Maybe we oughtn't, but if we get out before they come – just a peek, understand?"

They stepped into the cage, dropped swiftly, smoothly to the twelfth level. A man with a sawed-off shotgun met them when they stepped out.

"It's all right, Sam," said Luke. "Hold the cage. We're only goin' to take a quick look."

He struck off into a drift, turned into a lateral, another drift, another crosscut. Behind him plodded Rogier, Abe, and Jake. "He's tryin' to mix us up," whispered Abe, never a man to be lost underground. "You countin' your steps?"

"Why? You ain't figurin' you'll ever get in here again?" asked Jake.

Rogier began to tremble with a curious expectancy.

The four men brought up short against a huge bank-vault, steel door. Luke sounded a signal, and it was opened by three guards with drawn revolvers.

"It's me," said Luke, "I'm givin' these boys a quick look. The cage's waiting."

The guards stepped aside to reveal a large hole in the back wall about the size of a doorway and just above the level of lateral. "Go on up!" directed Luke.

Rogier, pushed ahead, climbed up the platform, followed by Abe and Jake. Then Luke behind them lighted and raised over their heads his magnesium flare.

Rogier uttered one gasp — a gasp that seemed to empty his lungs and bowels — and then was silent. What he saw was a geode, a vug, a "poop hole" as Abe called it — an immense hollow chamber in solid rock nearly forty feet high, twenty feet long, and fifteen feet wide. A cave of sparkling splendor that almost blinded him, a cave from whose walls and ceiling hung crystals of sylvanite-and calaverite crystals, and flakes of pure gold big as thumbnails glowing in the light. A cave floored with gold particles thick as sand and glittering like a mass of jewels. Everywhere he looked was gold tellurium of astounding purity, sparkling gold crystals, glittering gold sands; even a protruding small boulder of quartz gleamed golden. Here it was as he had envisioned it so clearly: an Aladdin's Cave transported from an Arabian Night to the twentieth century, a treasure greater than Croesus ever took from the sands of the Pactolus, or Solomon from the mines of Ophir.

Somebody with a hand on his collar jerked him back. In a daze he was walked back to the cage, ascended, found himself back in the Mint. "We got to pick up our bags," said Jake. Abe stopped at a corral for burros. "It's too far to walk," said Abe. "The Colonel looks played out."

Voices shouted in his ears. Vague phantasmagoria flitted across his mind. Arriving at the cabin late that afternoon, he insisted on going down into the Sylvanite. "Man the hoist, Jake," ordered Abe. "I'll take him down."

They went down to the bottom level. In the darkness, lit only by the flare of their carbide lamps they traversed the drift to the crosscut, turned into a giant stope, the vug Abe had opened up. Rogier knelt on the floor, sifted blasted granite through his fingers. He got up, ran his hands over the sheer rock walls, stared up at the ceiling. "Abe! Lock off this vug. Keep out all trespassers. Nobody comes down here but you and Jake and me! Understand?"

"Colonel! There's nothin' here!" remonstrated Abe. "Not even $15 ore! That's why me and Jake were goin' to leave the old hole. That was Cresson vug we saw! Remember! Not here in the Sylvanite!"

"The Cresson! Not here!" Rogier clawed at the bare rock walls. "The Cresson! No, not here!"

Abe picked him up bodily, carried him to the station, furiously rang his bells. Once up, he carried Rogier to the cabin, laid him on his bunk.

"He's havin' a spell," he told Jake.

"What'll we do?" asked Jake.

"Cool head, warm feet," said Abe. "That's all I know."

Jake bathed his face with cold water. Abe put a hot-water bag at his feet.

"Leavin' me and the Sylvanite?" Rogier kept crying with a piteous voice. "Is that what you said, with your bags all packed? Just when what I said—"

"We were, but we ain't now, Colonel!" shouted Jake. "Everything you told us was true as all get out. We saw it! Gold crystals hangin' from the walls and the ceilin'! Gold dust thicker'n a carpet on the floor! All them riches of Midas shinin' in our faces! Just like you told us, Colonel, over'n over! We ain't leavin' you now!"

They found some whiskey, mixed it with hot water, and poured it down his throat. He stopped mumbling. His lips grew still. The old body stiffened, then relaxed in sleep.

Abe and Jake, their backs to his bunk, sat before the fireplace.

"It was just like he said," Jake kept muttering. "Everything! Just like the Colonel said!"

"The twelfth level, and we're on the fifth," said Abe. "How're we ever goin' to get down?"

Day after day Rogier sat there on his bunk or at the table, reading the newspapers brought him. Some 1,400 sacks of crystals and flakes had been scraped from the walls and ceiling of the

Cresson vug and sold for $378,000. A thousand more sacks had been gathered from the gold-littered floor, bringing $90,637. Eight four-horse wagons with armed guards had transported a shipment of surrounding ore from the collar of the shaft to five broad-gauge cars sealed and marked for the Globe Smelter at Denver, which brought more than $686,000. And then, when at last Rogier was induced to go to town, it was only to see exhibited in the window of the bank a cancelled check showing an amount of $468,637.29 for a shipment of 150 tons.

Rogier, like all Cripple Creek, the whole world, was stunned by these richest shipments of ore ever made. They raised the yearly mean ore value of the Cresson to $33 a ton, yielded an extra dividend to its stockholders of more than a million dollars, and raised the annual production of Cripple Creek to $13,683,424, the highest in a decade.

All taken from a vug in the Cresson, that worthless mine, not the Sylvanite! He could not believe it, and every day he went down the shaft to examine the bare rock walls. Coming back up, he sat for hours envisioning the rewards had the discovery been made in his own mine. The different tune of the townspeople who had ridiculed the Sylvanite, the way his idiocyncrasies would have been miraculously converted into marks of genius, the ready acclaim of the Ruxton Club and all Little London. He thought magnanimously of the money he would have wired to Boné, of the check he would have stiffly handed to Timothy, of the fortune with which he would have rewarded ever-faithful Ona. And Martha! Dom! He would have built for her at last a mansion in the North End that would shame the palace of an Oriental potentate, though to be sure she had not mentioned this old desire for a dozen years or more. And Abe and Jake, who had stuck with him through thick and thin! God Almighty!

—and all these mundane rewards, long past due, were yet but the trivial by-products of his one desire. A million dollars profit would have been but a bank account on which to draw means of continuing his search into the black chasm of the world below. At $40 a foot, say—he began to compute the depth to which he might drive.

And then into these resplendent daydreams obtruded the harsh insistent truth: it was in the Cresson, not the Sylvanite, the miracle of wealth had happened. And with a shriek of despair he would fling over in his bunk to pound the log wall with his fists.

Jake would roll him back with a brawny hand on his shoulder. "Colonel! Don't take it so hard. We never believed you, Abe and me, until we saw it with our own eyes. And there it was, just like you told us. The gold and the glory, shinin' plain as day. We seen it. With our very eyes. We ain't givin' up the Sylvanite. Why, we might hit it right here!"

Rogier sat up to listen to Abe. "Colonel, let's don't go off half-cocked. They never hit that rich stuff till they went down to below 1,000 feet. And they couldn't get down that far without the Roosevelt drainage tunnel that opened up the district to lower levels. It's that simple. Now I figure that with depth we're all goin' to open up more ore bodies."

How strange it was to hear these two old obstinate faithfuls preaching the sermon he had expounded for years! He began to come to himself, to eat a little, to sleep.

"We ain't leavin' yet," Jake assured him. "Take it easy, Colonel. Things will work out."

And shortly before Christmas, Rogier returned to Little London shaken but not shattered.

5

Mary Ann and a gentleman friend also had come down for Christmas from the small mining town of Silverton. They were a day late; the little narrow-gauge train had been blocked by a snowslide for eighteen hours. She and her friend Sam had eaten five of the fifteen pounds of candy she was bringing home, but that afternoon a new mahogany-red box phonograph was delivered from uptown with ten records.

"It's the very latest: a Victrola! I want my family and dear little girl to enjoy their Christmas present the year around!"

Mrs. Rogier did not have the indelicacy to inquire what had happened to Jim, and obligingly installed her and Sam in the two adjoining middle rooms on the second floor. Sam was a brawny, middle-aged man who for years had been a railroad man, and still wore the traditional polka-dotted blue shirts starched stiff as iron. He had been a great help to Mary Ann in Silverton and she intimated that he might continue to be a great help to her in business in years to come.

At supper she left the family no doubt of her acumen as a shrewd businesswoman, and that it was unforseen conditions which had made her Chocolate Shoppe a failure.

"No, with conditions the way they were, Silverton is no go. ABSOLUTELY no go! And such taste you NEVER saw! Sticky nougat, colored gum drops, plantation sticks – all glucose, mind you, the Greek across the street used. Did they see the difference in my pure sugar creams, my bitter-sweets?"

"Maybe the difference was the price," suggested Ona. "Silverton's a dwindling mining town isolated half the year. You didn't expect poor miners' wives to buy your chocolates at eighty cents a pound when they could get ordinary sweets at forty? Or a really nice bag of mixed candy for a quarter?"

"That's beside the point. You just don't understand business, Ona. But I'm considering a new location. Alamosa. A thriving town in San Luis Valley. Sam tells me it's just the place to appreciate quality. Perhaps in the spring – "

How difficult it was for her to find the niche where she belonged as a maker of fine candies in a shop catering only to the elite. This was where she had started, in Durgess' Delicatessen which served the North End trade. She had heard the ring of the cash register, known the self-importance of being proprietor of her own "Shoppe," and after her divorce she had wedded business. And yet within her was a streak of wildness that impelled her to one remote mining town after another in the Rockies instead of to the populous marts of the state.

She was a small, nervous, opinionated woman. She spoke sharply but with a husky voice the jargon of commerce without understanding the one hard-rock basis of its function: distribution only at a profit. Like all Rogiers, she had no conception of the value of money. She might be down on her uppers, head over heels in debt, but the dollar in her pocket came out with free-handed generosity at a moment's whim. Her judgment was usually in error, her heart never.

Nancy she loved volubly, extravagantly – and was always ready to abandon her at the next beckon of Business. Nancy, during her mother's infrequent visits, accepted her protestations with a pleasure tinged by a sense of wonder. She was small, rather chubby, with dark brown hair and a dead white skin. The antithesis of Leona, she was somber and quiet as a mouse, preferring her own little corner to the world outside. No! – never like Leona was she joyous, active, swift as an arrow. And never like March, cruelly alive with an intolerable awareness, a stranger to all men. She was always quiet, tender, gentle, a passive pool.

To Sam she was pleasant but remote, as was the whole family. Nobody could fathom Mary Ann's attraction to him. Always the first at table, he ate heartily, spoke little. After meals he wandered down to the station to watch the trains come in. Between times Ona and Mary Ann washed and starched and ironed his blue shirts.

One evening Mary Ann, for want of something more important to say, imparted a scrap of information to Mrs. Rogier and Ona that they had awaited nearly thirty years. In Silverton an old prospector with white hair and a long beard used to ride down into town on a shaggy burro for supplies. He always stopped in Mary Ann's Chocolate Shoppe for a quarter's worth of taffy "chews" to carry back. Every month, regular as clockwork, said Mary Ann. Early that winter he had failed to come. The cold was terrible; the drifts in the mountains were six, eight feet high; even the elk were starving in the high valleys.

A group of men broke trail to his solitary cabin up the gulch. The old man was in his shanty, frozen to death. He had burned up the flooring and all the rude furniture, and was lying in bed wrapped up in his blankets with a half-chewed-up slab of raw salt pork. The drifts were too deep to bring his body down to Silverton. The men had simply placed it in his tunnel and blown up the entrance.

His next-to-worthless claim was registered as the "Molly H." His own name was unknown. He had been called only "Old Tom."

"Tom Hines! Sister Molly's Tom! Our Tom!" Ona's voice rang out with all the cloying pain and bitterness of thirty years suddenly washed away. "Oh, why didn't he ever come home?"

"Maybe so," said Mary Ann. "Of course I never knew him."

There was nothing else for her to say; it was the end of a tale that needed no epitaph.

Yet to Ona, clenching her lands in her lap, it was more than this. Tom, Cable, and Rogier—each in his way had given themselves as hostages to this deep and spacious earth high above the hopes of men, close under the inscrutable eyes of a Heaven that attested the heroism of their labor, their greed and ambitions, their faithfulness or their unfitness to the futile task of its subjection. Tom was ours, she thought, and yet he was America's too. He dies, the Strattons die, and the Tabors and the Walshes, but the immense and wild and lonely earth endures forever. The earth with its haunting ghostliness, its secret terror, and the savage exultant cry that rises by night from these lofty Rockies when moonlight floods its canyons, and the cougar screams from the aspen thicket, and the tall pale peaks hunch up their shoulders to brush the frost from the stars. They die; great new cities arise from their campfires; the gleaming rails span gorge and creek and gulley; the steel bites deeper into granite. And when in a forgotten gulch, on a lonely hillside, one comes upon their bleached bones, their upturned skulls seem fixed in a derisive grin. For the earth endures forever and is greater than its masters. Yet why do men, mere men, forever and always, without stint, hurl their strength against the rock, plod on towards a star that gleams and fades and dies?

"I think, Mary Ann," said Mrs. Rogier quietly. "that we shouldn't mention this to Daddy right now. He seems a little upset. Maybe because of that excitement about the Cresson discovery. At a later time, perhaps, a marker would be appropriate. But not now! Do you understand?"

Rogier, confronted daily by a strange man in his house who wore the starched blue garb of heaven dotted with stars but who never contributed an earthly dollar for his board, stayed in his shop out back. Seated on his high stool, his frail shoulders hunched over the drafting board, he seemed bent under the burden of an invisible and insupportable guilt.

The Cresson vug, shining, sparkling, and glowing with a wealth and splendor greater than the Aztec treasure room of Montezuma or that of Atahualpa the Inca, Son of the Sun, had been too much for him. He had been betrayed by something within himself he had never suspected. Never! – no, never in all his conscious life had he craved with the greed of most men wealth for its own sake, the power and luxury it bought. Yet at one glimpse of that incandescent chamber a dormant and hidden desire, a karmic predisposition inherited from a previous existence, had leaped forth. He had ignored the golden sun within him, reflected for his edification in the chamber before him, thinking only of the mortal debts its earthly treasure could cancel. Betrayed! Betrayed in his pride by the secret propensity, that hidden increment in his cumulative character of ages past! Bowing his head, he contritely accepted the verdict of his own accusation. No wonder that luminescent vug had been placed in the Cresson rather than in the Sylvanite! To teach him, old as he was, the lesson every man must learn in his time. But he would learn it now. He would root out every vestige of inherited desire, all the shreds of false pride, envy and jealousy that embroidered it. Yes, by God! he swore not profanely, banging his fist on the board. Now he saw that chamber for what it really was: a dim reflection of that deep golden heart of the earth which mirrored the golden sun within him, a promise of his eventual self-fulfillment. Nothing would ever betray him again. He was consecrated for the last time to his search.

That search, he reflected in calmer hours, still led down. It was no longer he who constantly proposed and preached the sermon of depth. He didn't have to. Abe recognized it too. If the Cresson vug had been opened on the twelfth level, why wouldn't high-grade stuff be encountered at equal depth throughout the whole district? And the Roosevelt drainage tunnel was unwatering the region down to a thousand feet or more. So Abe and Jake were still staying on the job, at least for a time. To keep them there, Rogier had to pay their keep.

But how?

Suddenly, in a lucid moment, he happened to think of the life insurance policy Cable had taken out while trying to sell insurance. Straightway he rushed into the house to ascertain if it had ever been cashed. Ona was uptown fortunately, and it was with Mrs. Rogier he had his first battle. It ended an hour later with Rogier flinging back out to the shop in a fine rage. Mrs. Rogier sat rocking away before the front window. Not for a minute did she fool herself the matter was ended. And at the first sight of Ona coming down the street, she jumped up, threw a coat around her shoulders, and hurried out to meet her.

Arm in arm the two women walked up Bijou to Wahsatch, turned on Platte, and came down El Paso. Talking like parrots, they discussed every phase of the matter except the most important — Rogier's frantic obsession with Cripple Creek.

"Of course he's just Daddy and always will be," admitted Ona. "I'd give him anything I owned. But Jonathan did plan so much on leaving something to the children. He loved them so much! That's why I'm saving this policy to put March through college. Mother, he's got to have a chance! He can be just as big a success as Boné with an education. And this is all I have left in the world, Mother – all I ever will have. But Daddy –"

"Don't be a fool!" Mrs. Rogier told her sharply. "Didn't I tell him all that and more too? I tell you Daddy's – well, you know how he is. And he's gettin' far worse. The minute we get back to the house he's going to hit you up for that money. Don't you do it, Ona!"

"Mother! My own father! What'll I do?"–the one agonizing plea she asked over and over.

They turned through the underpass to Bijou again; it was getting late. "How much will that policy pay?" asked Mrs. Rogier.

"Five thousand dollars."

Mrs. Rogier walked a few steps in silence, then turned to Ona. "There's no use deluding ourselves. Something about women makes them all fools. They know it but can't help themselves. Daddy's going to get that money. I'm as sure of it as I am of Judgment Day. Now let me tell you what to do! Tell him it was for $3,500 and give it to him if you can't help it. Give me a thousand. I'll see it goes for a better purpose. And you hang on to the rest. Don't let a soul know you have it. Keep it for the time you just have to have it."

So it was when Rogier cornered Ona alone, begging the loan and promising rich returns, she gave him $3,500. That night was the first of many which they all passed in peaceful sleep. Ona with her conscience at rest because she had not withheld help from her father, and Rogier momentarily at ease because he could resume shaft drilling. Mrs. Rogier slept the most soundly of all. She had added another thousand dollars to her honor fund.

Early that spring Mary Ann and Sam left to open a new Chocolate Shoppe in Alamosa. Rogier hardly noticed their absence. He had gone up to the Sylvanite to encourage Abe and Jake. They had been convinced by the resplendent Cresson vug that an equal treasure might be found at depth here, or anywhere in the district. But Rogier had run out of the bulk of money Ona had given him before he had sunk the shaft to another level. So he persuaded them to open another exploratory drift on the level above with hand drills.

It was dull, hard work. But things were slow, and the remainder of Cable's insurance provided them wages. So they kept hammering away.

Rogier down in Little London could hear, like an echo, the faint tap of their hammers. For awhile it would cease. Then a rasp of gravel underneath his shoe or the sound of Mr. Pyle next door hammering nails into his fence started it again like a painful tooth or a phrase of remembered music. A faint tapping that began on top of his head, increasing into a staccato hammering on his skull that shook his whole bone structure. A devilish tattoo ceaselessly urging him to hurry down the shaft another level.

Where and how could he raise more money for shaft drilling he kept wondering. As he lay in bed at night, the loud hammering increased in volume and tempo. He could hear the hiss of escaping air under pressure, the reverberant thunder of steel drills biting down into granite, swelling into a full-bodied orchestration of musical and meaningful sound. Then suddenly, with a great crescendo, the finale was translated into its visual counterpart: the glorious spectacle of a golden sun whose facets of sylvanite and calaverite crystals reflected all colors of the spectrum. And this combined both light and sound, a music he could hear and see, in whose ineffable beauty he began to dissolve in peace and fulfillment.

And then, too swiftly, it faded. And again, like Boné's right hand fingering on a piano the few notes of the motif of the whole orchestration, there began the faint tapping of Abe and Jake's hammers.

6

Late one afternoon the Rogier's next door neighbor, Mr. Pyle, came to call. It was such an unusual occasion that Rogier and Mrs. Rogier, Ona and March, received him in the now somewhat shabby front room. The Rogiers and the childless Pyles were barely on speaking terms. Mrs. Pyle remained shut up in her house all day long, and Mr. Pyle was always out on business. Rogier characterized him as a bald-headed, sanctimonious, Presbyterian plate-passer and a sneak thief of a real-estater.

Ona, regarding Rogier's presence with trepidation, made haste to be cordial. "Why, Mr. Pyle! It's so nice of you to call. I do wish Mrs. Pyle had come too. May I make you some tea?"

"Nothing like that!" Pyle asserted. He seated himself in a rocker, carefully thumbed the crease in his trousers, and brushed his bald head. "This is not exactly a social call. I came to see why you do not join the church. This young man, particularly, should be in our Sunday School."

"I've told you before, Mr. Pyle," answered Mrs. Rogier testily. "We can't join the Presbyterian. We've always been Southern Methodists."

"But you are no longer members."

This was Mrs. Rogier's sore spot. "My husband built that church. He donated the work and lumber for it. It was I who in the early days scrubbed the floors, scoured the windows, washed all the curtains. For a quarter of a century or more our family served God in that church!" She paused to sniffle. "But then, Sir, when we suffered reverses, when our mining venture declined, we could no longer afford our large contributions. The new minister had the temerity to ask that we give up our pew to someone else. Mr. Pyle! I asked for my letter from the church! Now Sir, we serve God right here in this house, and expect God to serve us. It's His turn now!"

Pyle adjusted his cravat, frowned. "But what about the boy here? A young untried soul searching for the fold?"

"Please, Mrs. Pyle," answered Ona. "When March is older will be soon enough. When he can choose for himself. Understand?"

Rogier, figiting in his chair, could contain himself no longer. "Dom this snifflin' women's religion of yours! What are you going to dig below the grass roots of all this tomfoolery? What we need now is a man's religion, a religion with granite guts, the faith of mountains. No more Saviors will come walkin' across the Galilees. No more angels will come flittin' through the air like flocks of doves. The almighty God-power of Creation is locked in us all, in the earth itself. We've got to dig in, blast him out. The GRANITE GOD, by Jove, you keep locked up in the mountains, in the hard-rock canyons of your own flinty souls!"

March was embarrassed. Mrs. Rogier squirmed. "Daddy!" protested Ona.

"Very well, then. You refuse." Mr. Pyle got up, bowed, and stalked out.

"That skinflint!" snorted Rogier. "If I thought he'd take that boy in with his petticoat religion I'd switch his bony behind to kingdom come!"

"Enough of that, Daddy! You know he didn't come here to rile you up!" Ona whirled on March. "Nobody's making you go to church and Sunday School—although it might be good for you, the way you're running wild!"

March fled out to the shop behind his grandfather. The old man was sitting on his high stool at the drafting board. There was growing up between them a curious intimacy that dispensed with casual preliminaries. "I reckon you saw what I meant when Pyle came, didn't you boy? Sittin' in Sunday School listenin' to his stuff and nonsense. Or lettin' your mother send you to school to learn how to sit uptown in a stuffy office and do your thinkin' with a pencil, pilin' up money in the bank and whorin' after Broadmoor society trulls, and drivin' to church in a fancy automobile. It's a disease that's mighty catchin'—money-eczema, the uncontrollable itch, the national disease. You'd be better off sneakin' away from home and makin' a man of yourself."

"Yes, sir."

"But you have to learn your lessons, hey? Fairy tales, every one! Do they teach you what time is, space and the earth, and the cement that binds them into one? Bah! Look at me? Do you know who I am?"

March stared up at him wonderingly. Rogier's hat was off, a wisp of white hair stuck up above one ear like a horn. He began pounding on the drafting board with his fist.

"I'm the great eunuch, the wind between the worlds, the frost of glacial epochs yet to come. I'm the maker of seas, the destroyer of mountains, the biggest joke of Eternity and the invisible hand of Infinity. Time—they call me Time—a great worm crawling through Chaos eating up worlds and leaving in the dung behind me the seeds of worlds to come. I'm Time, boy, whose other name is Space, the unmeasured and measureless, the great uncreated without beginning and end, the nothing from which is created the all. If I can be shrunken to here"—he jabbed a pencil-point on the paper—"I can also expand to everywhere, just as I can be both now and always. Call me whatever you want. Divide me with clocks and calendars, fence me off with foot-rulers and surveying lines, and I vanish into the nameless One I am."

March crouched on an apple box before the old man's oratorical outburst. "Yes, sir."

"Get up from that box. Let's have it out here in the middle of the floor."

March obeyed.

Rogier slid off his perch and knelt under the long work bench, sliding blocks of wood out between his legs. These he gathered and stacked on the upturned box. "Come on," he demanded gruffly. "Scrape around. Let's have a stack."

Ransacking the barny shop, they stacked up a column of blocks reaching almost to the lofty ceiling. Rogier clambered down the ladder and stood looking at the faintly swaying pillar. His sleeves were covered with sawdust, shavings stuck to his coat and white hair. "There, by Jove! That column of blocks represents space-time, geologic time—the age and surface depth of this one little earth we think we know all about. Do you get me?"

"Yes, sir."

"Then tear off a piece of that onion-skin tracing paper on the drafting board." When the boy brought it, he ordered, "Now skite up that ladder and lay it on the top block. Better spit on it so it'll stick – It don't make the pillar much higher, hey?" he called as March leaned over carefully from the top of the ladder. "Well, come on down and see that it makes a lot less difference from down here."

For a minute they stood together, staring.

"Now, son," Rogier went on, "the thinness of that piece of paper you can hardly see up there represents ALL the time of the existence of ALL mankind, of all your recorded history and unwritten legends, your dom fairy tales. In the thinness of that paper is buried Nineveh, Carthage, Thebes, and Tyre. All the antiquities of Babylon and Egypt, the lost cities of Africa, and the templed cities in the jungles of America, Uxmal and Chichén Itzá, and proud Cuzco high in the Inca Andes. And more than that! The great civilizations on lands that sank under the sea ages before naked savages were roaming through the forests that grew in the streets of Paris."

He climbed up to sit on the work bench.

"Look now at that top block—that piece of red cedar about an inch thick," he demanded. "In that little time of up to sixty million years ago was formed the oldest rock here in Colorado, and the mountains and the seas began looking pretty much like they do now. Vertebrates started to stand on their hind legs. The hairy ape changed into a hairy cave man spearin' hairy elephants, mastodons with mighty tusks, and monsters seventy feet long with even longer names. A dom little time ago when what we call modern life began!

"To six inches down from the top there were great crawling reptiles a hundred feet long and weighing thirty tons, snaky-necked reptiles swimmin' in the seas, and snake-like birds flappin' through the air with leather wings. And the earth was just cooling off, coal red, making the Painted Desert in Arizona and the Great Red Valley in the Black Hills.

"And to a couple of feet down – maybe as far as that chunk of quarter-sawed oak – are fossils and the prints of insects, fish, and oyster-like things that lived in the hot mud and seas that took the place of the mountains. Everything was hot and stinky, the oceans were meanderin' through America, and plants were beginning to form and creep across the land bridges from Brazil to Africa, and from Asia to Alaska – jungle plants.

"Yes sir!" Rogier slapped his leg. "All this in just the top three feet or so in that column of blocks. Seven hundred million years or thereabouts. Below that – you see that piece of maple sticking out? A single rock stickin' up in Russia, the oldest rock in the world, two billion years old. And below that, in all the rest of the column down to the floor, no plants, no animals, nothing. Eight billion, ten billion years, who knows, nothing but the mysterious, eternal earth, the dust of the rock that endures forever. There, boy, that's time as we think we know it!"

A vacuous look crept into his eyes as he sat picking sawdust from his sleeve. Then they brightened as he lowered his voice. "I reckon you're catchin' on now to what a man might find out if he could sink a shaft to the bottom of that column, to the beginning of time, eh? Why, he's likely to discover that he's had all his work for nothing! All that time, the whole dom column, is condensed in that piece of paper on top; in a pencil point marked on it; right in himself, by Jove!" He tapped his head. "And the reason is, like I told you before, he's the Beginning and the End which meet like the ends of a great circle. Like this."

Jumping down from the work bench to go to the pillar of blocks, he raised his right hand toward the top, his left hand to the bottom, as if to bend them together.

At his touch the pillar swayed.

"Look out, Granddad! The blocks are comin' down!" yelled March.

Rogier tripped and went sprawling, as with a roar the stacked-up wooden blocks came tumbling down. He threw both hands above his head, diving from his knees to safety behind a floor post. But a piece of falling wood had gashed his forehead; he came out from the vast wooden talus with a thin trickle of blood running down his temple.

'I told you to lay them blocks on straight! That's what your education's doin'!"

March contritely held out his handkerchief. "I'm sorry, Granddad. I didn't mean to. But I got the idea. Honest."

Rogier whipped around upon him. "Who says you got the idea? That's the idea on the floor! Diastrophism. Crustal unrest, continual uplifts and subsidences. Why, these mountains have sunk under the sea a dozen times. Didn't you find sea shells on the slope of the Peak?" He kicked the heap of blocks on the floor. "They build up again, and not with your help either, to maintain the isotatic equilibrium of the whole earth. And none of these blocks are ever destroyed. Cut 'em up for kindling, make sawdust out of them. The wood's still there. Burn it. You can't get rid of the ashes. Why? Palingenesis. Eternal palingenesis. No death. Just change. What you need, son, is to get out of school and suck some wisdom from the teat of a granite outcrop!"

He stalked out grumbling to the hydrant to wash the blood off his face.

A few days later when March came home from school he saw a strange young man sitting in the front room with his mother.

"Come in here, March," called Ona. "I want you to meet Mr. Austin. Mr. Howard Austin. He's the assistant in the Fred Harvey news stand at the big new Santa Fe depot, and boards with Mrs. Jenkins up the street. We've been thinking you'd be just right for the newsboy they need. Now run upstairs and get into your blue serge suit so you can go down with him to see the manager."

"Mr. Warren is very particular about neatness," said the young man, himself neatly dressed in blue serge. He was blond, blue-eyed, about twenty-five years old. "The Fred Harvey uniform is blue serge. We furnish the cap and the brass buttons. I have mine in my pocket."

The buttons were in his hand when March came back. "See? Hollow, round brass buttons with the name 'Fred Harvey.' They slip over your regular buttons like this." He fitted the buttons on

March's coat. "Now, do you think you'll like it? Your commission will be a penny for each paper you sell, paid at the end of the week. You work the platform alone and the trains that don't have our own butchers. But there are other small duties in the news stand between trains. You open it up at six-thirty in the morning—I come down to meet Number 5 at seven. Then you empty the trash, dust magazine racks, wash the cases, jerk paper heads, and so on."

"But school?" asked Ona.

"Mr. Warren sees no problem. March will miss only the train at noon and at two o'clock. Most of them come between four and seven. Then he's through. Now what do you think, March? Maybe you can wait on customers and become a Fred Harvey clerk like I am." He was simple, straightforward, earnest.

"What about it, son?" asked Ona. "Do you want to earn money so you can go to high school? To help your mother? To learn business from the ground up?"

March nodded dumbly. If only there weren't those awful brass buttons.

"Mr. Warren is sure to take him," said young Mr. Austin. "He's really very neat and quiet."

Together, silently, they went out the door.

Ona leaned back with a sigh of immeasurable relief. March would learn punctuality and strictness, which Columbia hadn't taught him. He and his grandfather would be separated. And thank God!—there would be no more talk about mining, no more trips to Cripple Creek. He was on the safe and sane road to business!

Yet as she watched him walk past the window, she caught the quick flash of his metallic dark eyes—the same kind of a look that Cable once had given her when she had engineered him into a foolish real estate venture. And now, as then, she felt the premonition that she was losing something wild and perverse, but hauntingly precious—something she could never quite regain.

7

Still it kept up—that devilish tattoo on the top of his head, echoing the sound of the Zebbelins' hammers. He hated it and perversely feared it would stop for the simple reason he had no more money to keep it going. So he went up to the Sylvanite.

There was little to do. Abe and Jake kept up a show of work, but it was evident their brief enthusiasm had worn off. Rogier descended the shaft to add depth to depth. He would squat down, holding his head, waiting for the drills to crash through the last wall of granite to the mysterious world below. When the crash did not come, Rogier knew it was the incessant hammering on his own skull. Then Abe would touch him on the shoulder, and lead him back aloft. Rogier began to worry over his mind; there were periods now, he realized, when it could no longer think consecutively. It kept whirling him about and ever downward into a chasm of despair blacker than any stope.

A letter from Mrs. Rogier climaxed his worries. One night, without warning or apparent cause, one of the big spruces in the front yard had toppled with a crash into the other, which also had to be cut down. There was no wind and the tree looked sound, she wrote, and March had watered it faithfully. Just age and internal rot, she supposed. The trees had been Rogier's favorites; among their tangled roots, when they had been brought down from the mountains thirty years before, he had discovered his first traces of tellurium. Their sudden toppling now seemed ominously significant. He seemed to see himself in the clear perspective of time and as if at a great distance: an old white-headed man cursed with a mine into which he had emptied all his substance, without money for his dependents, too old to work, and with a mind that was beginning to wander frightfully.

All that day he lay in his bunk, refusing to get up to eat. In the evening after supper Abe and Jake sat playing dominoes. In low tones they talked about the decline of gold and silver now that the Kaiser was on a rampage with all the Frenchies and Britishers in the Old Country. Iron, copper, and molybdenum. Manganese ores for the steel plants. That was the thing now. Ain't Leadville shipped almost 100,000 tons of manganese ores to the steel mills?

The evening dragged on. Rogier lay gripping the edges of his bunk. God Almighty! Something was coming to a verge. With a queer sense of impending disaster, he jumped up and heartily wrung both Abe's and Jake's hands as soon as they had finished their games. He said nothing, although with the turmoil in his head it seemed he was emptying his heart in a rush of words.

"Colonel! You ain't feelin' sicker!? Shall I go get a doctor?"

Abe raised his hand in protest and quietly laid back the blankets on Rogier's bunk. Rogier lay down again in his clothes; he merely wanted to rest, he said. Jake and Abe, with apprehensive glances at him, undressed and went to bed.

After awhile Rogier turned over. The lamp was out, but by the light of the fire he could see they were asleep. An hour or more he waited for the flames to die down. Then he laid back his blanket carefully and sat up. For an instant he debated whether to scribble a note. Deciding that the flicker of a candle or the scratch of a pencil might waken Abe, a light sleeper, he got up and flung his coat over his shoulders. Quietly now he tiptoed across the plank floor, opened the door carefully, and stepped outside.

There was a half-moon. In its light he could see the dark ragged fringe of pines along the gulch and the gauntly outlined timbers of the Sylvanite gallows frame. He hurried to the shaft. The iron bucket was lashed securely above him to the frame, its rusty side faintly scraping in the wind against the wood.

Gathering his coat about him, Rogier kneeled on the shaft collar. Before and above him, looking down with passionless serenity, stared the enigmatic face of the high Peak. Ever and always since his first glimpse of it from far down on the Fontaine-qui-Bouille, its white seamed face had drawn him step by step, without compassion, merciless and compelling, to this insignificant aperture into its unsounded depths. All his vain conjectures, the deceptive glitter of success, and his countless failures he saw now as milestones of a monstrous folly which could have no end but this. He bent his head, leaned over to stare into the velvety blackness of the open shaft.

He was now quite calm, his mind clear. Death for Rogier held no terror. No man of more than superficial perception but has contemplated at some time the voluntary and willing destruction of his faulty, mortal cast. And this deep soft darkness, oozing from the subterranean world that had ever evoked in him the comforting assurance of the mysterious immortal, now seemed to him a cloak of final authority which would at last insure his admittance to the deep unknown. A single movement and to the secret of that mighty Peak he would consign himself forever.

Still he hesitated. For if his mind was lucid enough to confront without trepidation the course before him, it could also clearly perceive the turbulent wake of his carefully considered action. He thought of his family. Mrs. Rogier's quiet disregard of his erratic storms, Ona's obstinate faithfulness even after Cable's death, the children's hushed playing in the yard lest they disturb him in the shop—they all took on for him now a somber beauty enhanced by their family undemonstrativeness. In a blinding flash of reality he saw himself among them through the years, repaying kindness with curtness, and draining them of hopes to fling down this shaft below him. And now this: to reward their enduring faithfulness with an abrupt wordless departure that would inflict upon them the wounds of a lasting cruelty. No! He could not! Secure in his integrity, calmly facing his own fate, he yet was bound to those innocent and unsuspecting loved ones in the shabby old house on Shook's Run—to their trivial follies and childish hopes, to smiles, laughter, sorrow, and discontent, to the eternal sadness that binds us each to the other and all in our loneliness to that of which we are a part.

These quick, searing thoughts roused in him a fire of furious resentment. The devil take them all! They had their own lives to lead, as he had had his. To be free forever from the shame, the poverty, the ignominious narrow life to which he had committed himself! To escape that continual hammering on his head!

It had begun again, driving through his skull with resonant strokes whose vigor he had never experienced before. All his sentiments of the previous moment fled before the blows; he became what he had been, was, and would be always – a man consecrated since birth to a search far below his personal surface. For an instant, confused as he was, the hammering on his skull became synonymous with the blows of the Zebbelins' jack hammers below. One last crack, and he would burst at once through the resistant granite and the walls of his skull to the secret and resplendent heart of the obdurate Peak rising above him, his last ally, his final adversary.

He rose from his knees, threw off his coat, and confronted its dual aspect across the gaping shaft. That great white sentinel of a continent had entranced him, beckoned him, comforted him in his lifelong search. But also it had repulsed him, rejected him, fought him at every turn, because he had not fully, wholeheartedly, sacrificed himself to it without stint. Always from his impassioned search he had held back that fatal modicum of personal egotism remaining from his long inherited past. But not now! If this were all he had left, he would hurl it into the depths of his own granite self and crack open at last its golden heart. This time he would succeed! Crack! Crack! The hammer blows were crashing through his skull now, confirming his resolve. Bathed in sweat from the unendurable pain, he raised both arms, poised on the collar to leap down the shaft. At that moment the blow came, shattering his skull and driving into his brain. There was a terrific explosion of sound and light, of a golden radiance into which both he and the Peak dissolved with a final shriek torn from his bowels.

Inside the cabin, Abe stirred in his bunk. A cold wind was blowing across his bare arm hanging outside the blankets, and fanning into flames the dying fire. He sat up quickly and looked around, his first thought of Rogier. The bunk was empty, the door open.

Abe jumped out, grabbed a burning stick from the fire, and ran outside. There was no need to search for Rogier; Abe knew well enough where to find him. Almost immediately he saw him, a dark huddle on the shaft collar. Lifting the torch above his bald head, he ran forward on bare feet with stark fear. The old man was slumped across the collar, arms outspread, his white head hanging down the gaping shaft. With one hand, Abe pulled him back and turned him over. His tortured face, the frothy white sputum covering his lips, the glassy look of his open and unseeing eyes, were too much for any man to see. Abe flung his burning brand down the shaft. Then he knelt beside Rogier, gently wiping the froth from his mouth and smearing his face with a handful of snow. After a time the old man's body twitched, his eyes flickered with life.

"Colonel! Colonel!"

In the light of the half-moon the stiff lips quivered.

"I know, Colonel! I know!"

Abe's long arms gathered him to his breast in an embrace more tender and less awkward than it had been given him to hold any woman. On his strong and simple face was the profound sadness of a child confronted with something he could not understand but only feel. Faithful, simple Abe, one of the great unsung who in the gloom of the mine, the glare of the furnace, or the isolation of the range does his work unrewarded with but his daily bread—and yet carries forever the unspoken tribute of less humble men.

Mrs. Rogier and Ona were waiting when the Zebbelins and a Victor doctor brought him home to Shook's Run. Rogier was carried up to his own bedroom where he lay like a wasted, wax image in a glass case, insensible to the pain and horror of the last ordeal it was possible for him to withstand.

Just what had happened to him none of the family could understand from Abe's and Jake's confused account. He hadn't fallen down the shaft or been crushed by a rock; nor had he suffered a stroke of paralysis, for he was able to move all his limbs. The family doctor came, replacing the one Jake had roused in Victor. He murmured indecisively something about a seizure, epilepsy, a mental breakdown.

Mrs. Rogier asked abruptly, "You mean—?"

He nodded. "But it may not be permanent. We shall see."

Mrs. Rogier fled to her room to pray. "If only God will spare him that," she murmured repetitiously, remembering his once firm step, his square calm face and steady eyes. Gradually this memory of him aged into the nervous old white-headed man she had known for years. His increasing irritableness, his prolonged abstractions, and lapses of memory took on sudden significance. "Daddy, oh Daddy! If we'd only known!" For though he was more untouchable than ever, his grasp upon her had strengthened. And now, fearful that her prayers might have been misinterpreted, she murmured into her wet pillow the simple request, "Don't let him die, God. No matter what."

Two mornings later Jake and Abe, who had slept in the shop, came in and dawdled over their breakfast until none remained but Ona and Mrs. Rogier.

"I reckon the Colonel will get over it after a long time maybe," said Jake awkwardly. "They ain't much use of our stayin'."

"You know how grateful we are to you both," said Mrs. Rogier.

Both men nodded vehemently. "About the mine," stuttered Jake. "We ain't figurin' on stayin'. She's all played out, like him." He jerked his thumb at the upstairs bedroom.

"We got to find work somewhere's else. The district's playin' out too," Abe said straightforwardly. "We'll just close it up, hey?"

"Of course!" said Ona. "The Sylvanite will never be worked again. If there's anything you can sell, do it before you leave. And God bless you both always, for the way you stuck to Daddy!"

Abe began counting off his calloused fingers. "The plant ain't much, but there's the cable reel and the hoist engine maybe somebody will want. That old boiler we'll have to let rust away. But there's some boxes of powder, the lamps, drills, and all the handtools. And of course the cabin fixin's. A few hundred dollars, all told. We'll send it to you all right."

Ona's eyes flashed. "All these years of working in a no-good, worthless hole when you might have been in a big producer! And I'll bet you haven't been paid regular wages for weeks, have you Jake?"

Jake flushed and hung his head, acutely conscious of that

inward glow provoked when a man's unheeded virtue has finally found him out. "Aw – Miss Ona!"

"No, sir!" went on Ona. "You boys go back up there and sell every bit of steel and timber you can get rid of. Keep the drills to take with you. The money will be little enough. You'll need railroad fare. And let us hear from you, mind. You're Daddy's best and only friends."

Abe rubbed his bald head as he turned to Mrs. Rogier. "It just don't seem fair. We're both strong and powerful well. But him up there – sick in the head, and doctor bills and all – "

"No!" protested Mrs. Rogier decisively but with effort, thinking of her honor fund. "Ona is right. We wish it were a lot more."

The silence was unbearable. Ona broke it by hurling herself in turn against the breasts of the brawny giants before her. "Abe!" – "Jake!" Abashed, each patted her clumsily on the back; then they fled out to the shop, and thence up the back alley to catch the train. It was over, all over at last – the monstrous folly of that stricken man upstairs who was insensible alike to all hope and despair.

Day and night he lay there, not dead nor yet alive, neither immune to light but not yet absorbed by darkness. He was like a man caught between the surface world he had rejected and that subterranean domain which, except for one quick glimpse, had not opened to receive him. And lying in his pellucid dusk, in an unbroken tranquility that was not repose, he moved, breathed, was fed – and seemed conscious of nothing.

The doctor was cheerful but cautious. "He's going to pull through. Rest, care, absolutely no worry. But it'll take time and patience, Mrs. Rogier."

And as Rogier finally began to respond to voices and the touch of familiar hands, Mrs. Rogier braced herself for a glimpse into the inescapable future. It loomed so terrifying before her frail little figure, she snapped the catch on the door and sat down on the bed to confront it with all her courage and resources. Jake had sent a postcard saying he and Abe had been able to sell some five hundred dollars worth of salvage, gutting the mine and cabin of everything to Rogier's boots and wool shirts. They had sent back only his old-fashioned miners' candlestick, the one pathetic reminder of the

Sylvanite which now, like countless others, was gradually being absorbed like a wound into the healing granite flesh of the Peak. Mrs. Rogier sighed as she tore the postcard to bits. That money would have come in mighty handy.

Now on the bed beside her she opened her sugar-bowl, a white Chinese porcelain jar, on which was wreathed a dragon, that Boné had sent her from San Francisco years ago. It was stuffed with bills and envelopes so neatly folded and pressed she had to pry them out. No amount had been too small to add: dollar bills left over as change from her grocery payments, a gold piece received as a Christmas present, portions of the allowances Rogier had given her for household expenses. As the money had accumulated she had changed it into $100 bills, each little stack of ten snapped together with a rubber band and sealed in an envelope. There were five of these, her honor fund. Five thousand dollars—her savings of years, Cable's inheritance, March's education, food taken right out of the children's mouths; a fortune that attested a frugality and duplicity that no one would ever know but her. She had saved the amount at last.

But spread out on the bed in smaller amounts there remained but $180.75 for household expenses, taxes, doctor bills and medicines for Rogier – to last, for all she knew, forever. She did not expect help from Sally Lee, Mary Ann, or Boné. They all had been written of his illness, letters that did not explicitly explain the nature of his illness and the fact that money could be used. They ought to know it! And if they couldn't guess it, Mrs. Rogier would have bit off her tongue before saying more.

Five thousand dollars! And to that man Timothy! Never—no, never!—would she forget him laughing at Daddy that day in front of the Ruxton. For if once she had been impressed by his social prominence, friendship, and waistcoats, she was now more impressed by the five fat envelopes in her lap. If Rogier had lost every cent he owned and his senses besides, Timothy could afford to lose what was to a rich man a measly, speculative investment.

Mrs. Rogier got up and walked to the window where she stood braced against temptation. Always she had imagined evil and dishonor cloaked in the gorgeous raiment of unreality. By their seductive whispers of temptation she would know and be able to flaunt them easily. Now she realized that they, like virtue and honor, were born of the same need, walked side by side, and could be distinguished only by the discerning gaze of one's own integrity. It wasn't fair! A simple thing like doing nothing, just not giving back Timothy the money he didn't expect. Listening to the Devil's promptings, she stuffed the envelopes back in the jar, envisioned it hidden on the top shelf of the closet where she could withdraw money for every need. No bolt of lightning from Heaven seared her hands for their wicked intent, no angel perched on the jar to protect it. Yet a deep quiet voice, peculiarly her own, whispered authoritatively that Daddy might die, they might all starve and the house be sold over their heads, but never would Timothy or any other man be able to say a Rogier had played him false.

If it was to be done, it had to be done now! Resolutely she flung on her coat and bonnet, and walked swiftly uptown with her handbag clutched to her breast. There was just time before the bank closed to change her currency into a draft made out in Timothy's name and enclosed in a manilla envelope. This was more businesslike; currency would never do. Now a new fear beset her. She could not send Timothy the draft by messenger or by mail; a note would have to be enclosed, which she could not write. She owed him the courtesy of delivering it herself.

Stepping into a tourist hack at the curb, she drove to the Ruxton. Prohibited as a lady from entering a gentleman's club, she sent the driver inside with the request that Mr. Timothy step outside a moment. Luckily he was inside. On seeing him approach, faultlessly groomed, Mrs. Rogier remembered how Rogier had looked that rainy afternoon in a porter's hat and coat.

"Mrs. Rogier! How happy I am to see you on any excuse. I do hope that Mr. Rogier, Boné, and the rest of your family are as well and happy as you yourself appear!"

"Forgive my intrusion, Mr. Timothy," she replied, thrusting the envelope into his hands. "I stopped by only to return for Mr. Rogier the money you wished him to invest in his mine."

Timothy took it with a puzzled expression on his face. "That was some time ago. I had almost forgotten it. A sporting venture he agreed to let me in on. Strange he didn't say something if he never intended to use it."

"Not at all," she replied pertly. "You are well aware how

absentminded my husband is. The Sylvanite was never more than a highly speculative venture restricted to his own family members."

Timothy frowned, fiddling with the gold nugget on the watch chain strung across his waistcoat.

"We regret having not accounted for this so long," Mrs. Rogier continued. "It was only on suddenly discovering it that I came up without waiting for Mr. Rogier to fulfill his own obligation."

The phrase illumined for Timothy the careworn look on her face, her rusty bonnet, the cheap tourist hack in which she was sitting instead of a taxicab.

"Mrs. Rogier, no man with the dormant but not dead instincts of a gentleman could possibly refuse to deny the generous prompting of a true lady. A lady of the old South, particularly. Please convey to your husband my sincere thanks and devout congratulations. How is he, by the way?"

"He's had a little upset, Mr. Timothy, but doing quite well. No visitors, of course. But if you will pardon my intrusion – "

Timothy stepped back on the curb, watching the hack drive away.

8

Creeping quietly past his stricken grandfather's room and out of the house each morning at six o'clock, March walked quickly to the Santa Fe railroad depot and into a life as uniquely, indigenously American as that he had known at Shallow Water and Cripple Creek.

Little London was a health resort; manufacturing, with its soot and noise, was prohibited. It was a tourist resort, its mineral springs, bath houses, scenic drives, country estates and summer pavilions modelled upon the pattern of a European spa. It was a college town, a New England seat of learning nestled in the shadow of Pike's Peak. A city of churches—and of five polo fields. A center of classical culture in the crude and vulgar West.

But a railroad town—merciful Heaven! A railroad town of grimy shops and roundhouses with hordes of men carrying lunch buckets and thick Waltham watches and wearing starched blue shirts, and disgorging smoke and grime into the rarefied, mile-high, sparkling champagne air? Never! shrieked the pamphlets and posters and the ladies on the hotel verandas.

And yet Little London had been a railroad town since its

inception. Don't talk of romantic gold rushes. The Pike's Peak Bust had been over a decade and more before Little London sprouted on the plain, and it was a railroad survey that planted its seeds. Johnny-come-lately Cripple Creek, whose gold and sweat created the great mansions flanking its wide avenues, was still discreetly hidden in the mountains and now politely ignored by the best society.

Yes! Little London was a railroad town, as all towns of western America are railroad towns. Where the rails stopped to wait for supplies, a survey farther ahead, the tents went up. Then bunk houses, board shanties, a water tank. It became a junction, and then a town. "Rail-ends!" This was the "Land-ho!" shout of our prairie voyagers. It was as if we sailed across a measureless and unmarked sea, and wherever we made landfall a port of call sprang up. In other lands the market place, town square, or plaza marked the heart of the town anciently grown up around it, and its pulse echoed the beat of the country. But here the railroad depot was the community center, the focal point of life.

Who has not on a dreary Sunday gone down to see the train come in? What do we expect, whom do wait for with a curious and hopeless expectancy on our faces? It is all there in a whistle, a long drawn-out shriek, that sounds round the bend. It tugs at the heart, stirs deep within us that nameless ache and haunting rapture that lies at the bottom of every soul. There is a momentous hush out of all proportion to the event, as if it is imbued with a mystery too profound and too common to be remarked. The train is coming in!

She'll be comin' round the mountain
She'll be comin' round the mountain
She'll be comin' round the mountain
When she comes!

She comes, and here in this vast and lonely hinterland it is always round a mountain's shoulder. And hissing, steaming, a horribly beautiful monster with one glaring eye and a long serpentine body snorts reluctantly to a stop. For what, to where has this monstrous iron sauropod hurtled across prairies and wind-swept plains, spanned gulch and gulley, gorge and ravine, puffed up the grades and rolled drunkenly through smoke-blackened cuts and tunnels, crawled soberly along the mountainside, and swept down twisting and turning from the snowy roof of the world?

Why, to this grimy depot with its crowd of loitering townspeople, its carriages, buckboards, and mud-splattered Tin Lizzies, a row of blanketed squaws squatting with their pots, a horseman engraved against the sky. And behind the dreary grass square, a row of shabby all-night lunch counters, a third-rate hotel, a sinisterly shuttered lodging house, pawnshops, and the street that led uptown.

This is America—all the towns, magnified or miniature, that lie upon its spacious and lonely breast. And to all, for this immortal moment, the arrival of a train assuages their nameless and haunting ache, appeases their hunger for the strange and far-off, lifts the weight of their loneliness under the immense and empty skies.

And when it leaves, pouring sand on the upgrade, and finally cleaving the dusk full stride over the trestle, shrieking once, wildly, at the last crossing, it is as if it has carried out of our lives something that has been there forever—bone of our bone, flesh of our flesh, and the wild and turbulent spirit of our unrest that if it wanders far enough, long enough, must again return home.

So it seemed to March when with papers under his arm he stood on the platform to meet Santa Fe Number 5, northbound, sweeping round the bend of Cheyenne Mountain, that he was standing at the hub of Little London and at the core of whirling time.

Number 5 was a breakfast train. A white-jacketed bus boy was standing beside the door of the Fred Harvey Lunch Room beating a brass gong. To its summons the long train emptied already groomed and toileted ladies from the Pullmans who had reserved seats by telegram a half-hour before; a lazy slattern in a nightcap and purple silk robe who rushed past, haggard women with children, their faces still crinkled by the gritty red plush cushions of the day coaches; well paunched businessmen hungry for ham and eggs; thin, sallow men from the smoker for coffee and a doughnut.

"Get the morning news! *Denver Post* and the *Rocky Mountain News!* Read all about it while you eat! *Pueblo Chieftain!* The *Springs' Gazette!* Git your mornin' PAPer!"

The platform teemed with people. Among them March shouted, his black uniform cap too large even with paper stuffed under the sweatband, his brass buttons glowing conspicuously as red-hot coals. Then suddenly the platform was deserted. Now he shouted himself hoarse outside the coaches to rouse those within, and then posted himself outside the slowly emptying lunch room. People read more on a full stomach. Particularly news and trash.

"All aboar-art!" Highball. And as the train pulled out, he was left alone again on the deserted platform, alone at the core of time, the dead center of the maelstrom whirling about him. That was the everlasting mystery. Trains, crowds, newspapers vanished, only to be replaced by others new and fresh for their brief moment. Nothing varied, nothing changed, yet everything constantly changing. The mystery of movement, this for March was the fascination of railroading.

Quickly he gained friends: the ticket clerks, telegraph operators, and baggagemen, the lunchroom manager and the Fred Harvey girls who smiled at his bashfulness. He began to be brusquely acknowledged by the yardmen, switchmen, and yard clerks, and finally by those lords of the rails themselves, the engineers, firemen, and conductors. They seemed men whose lives of the spirit might never have existed or of which they were never aware. Like the monsters they served, they ran on rails, definite, fixed, punctual to the second. Rain, snow, family, friends – nothing mattered. Their one eternal gesture of prayer to the god that ruled them seven days a week, night and day, was a hand reaching to a watch.

Ghostly flow of time, how far now the sandy Gallegos and those who told time by the first frost and the spring thaw? Number 2 in the block, four minutes late!

After the breakfast train's departure at seven-thirty, March emptied the trash, dusted magazine racks, polished apples with a cloth moistened with olive oil, and cut newspaper heads. Then after coffee and doughnuts, he walked a mile up the tracks and turned east to Columbia School. After school he came back to stay until seven o'clock, helping to ready the newstand in the new station.

There were two railroad depots in Little London: that of the Denver and Rio Grande in the western part of town, below the Antler's Hotel; and that of the Santa Fe to the east, not far from Shook's Run. Both were small grimy stone buildings fronting their exposed yards. But now with the growth of Little London and the booming railroad traffic, a huge new Santa Fe station was being built behind the old one. There was no doubt that it was to be an impressive monument to the prime importance of railroading, and a credit to Little London. Built of red brick and white stone, its huge vaulted waiting room was floored with red tile and furnished with great stained-oak benches, Mission style. In addition, there was a waiting room outside with concrete seats. There was not only a new Fred Harvey lunch room with a horseshoe counter, but a well-appointed dining room. Upstairs were the sleeping rooms of the waitresses; and above the barny baggage room, the telegraph office and private offices.

March, helping Mr. Warren and Mr. Austin to ready the news stand, was impressed. It jutted onto the station platform outside and into the big waiting room inside. There was a little office for Mr. Warren and a checking room for baggage. Also it boasted magazine racks that could be locked at night, eliminating March's chore of emptying and refilling them daily.

"You see now, March, why we wanted to break in a newsboy," said Mr. Warren. "A young man, neat and efficient, who'll be ready when we move into the new station."

The day came when the transfer was made. The grimy old depot was pulled down and the Main Line tracks were re-routed over the site. Between them and the new station a high, iron picket fence was erected, and the subway finished. The first tunnel emerged between Main Line 1 and 2, the second between 3 and 4. Down at the end of the platform were two spurs for the Colorado Midland and the Cripple Creek Short Line. To add to the new station's modern and formal aspect, a Station Master attired in a uniform of golden-tan serge with brass buttons was hired to call the trains.

How proud March was, how he loved it all! Most of the men were now his friends. But there was one exception, an angular, hard-muscled man named Wadkins who worked down in the yards and kept walking up to the station for coffee. His face was long and furrowed, and held a look of furtive cunning and cruelty. Coming up to March, he demanded a paper. March obediently drew one out for him. Wadkins read it through deliberately, his greasy blunt fingers turning each page.

"Please sir, will you pay me now? I can't wait any longer."

The man grinned, "Pay you? You little greenhorn! I work here!"

The newspaper by now was a mass of splotched sheets. He

finally wadded it up, flung it at March, and strode off. March threw it in the trash can and turned in one of his own nickels for it.

A few days later Wadkins again demanded a look at a paper.

"Not till you pay me first," insisted the boy. "I ain't payin' for the ones you spoil!"

Wadkins' thin lips twisted into an angry leer. "You little son-of-a-bitchin' brat! I'm goin' to take the starch out of you right now!"

Some people came up; he turned away and walked quickly into the lunch room.

Ten minutes later the passenger swept in. March, standing entranced as ever by its majestic sweep, was struck violently on his left elbow. His armful of papers splattered on the brick platform, some of them being sucked under the passing wheels. He dropped to his knees, arms outspread to hold the remainder, and flung around. Wadkins was standing behind him, a look of pustulate evil upon his grimy face.

"You big bully! By God, if you ever touch me again, I'll kill you!" the boy shrieked against the roar of the train.

Thereafter he kept a sharp lookout for Wadkins. At sight of him he grew cold and hard, felt his face change to stone. But sometimes the man, passing behind him in a crowd, managed to jerk his papers into the mud or snow, or rip a front page with his thumb. March said nothing to Mr. Warren or Howard Austin of his persecution and the many papers he was obliged to pay for. He shrank into himself, with an intense awareness and silent inscrutability. Wadkins was conscious of it, and became more wary and malicious. It was a strange feud between boy and man, but its strangeness March never questioned. It was as if the hate between them was a chemical fusion that would endure forever.

Through it he saw with preternatural clearness the inherent meanness of the man, the warped and sadistic character whose mirror was Wadkin's deeply-furrowed, thin-lipped face. By it too the boy first glimpsed the depths within himself. He had experienced quick flashes of childish temper, the sudden violent storms that left him weak, frightened, and ashamed hours later. But now it was as if from the bottom of his soul there welled up unceasingly a flood of terrible and savage passion. It filled his thoughts, ran like hot lead through his veins. He absorbed it wholly as he stood grasping his papers, day after day, with a face as blank and set as Cable's.

It was a hate that left him cold and nerveless; a tremendous and formidable fact, a part of his life as ancient and timeless as the earth he trod. In his terrifying aloneness and with a strange awareness, he knew simply that between him and this man stood something that some day must be resolved.

One winter afternoon Number 11 whistled at the bend. Standing at the subway entrace, March could see the black snout nosing through the driving snow. Then suddenly he recognized Wadkins, fifty feet away, plodding up the platform in front of the train. March dodged back hidden from train and man. He was calm, pitiless, resolute. Wadkins would pass him on the narrow platform just as the train would hurtle by. A hand pushed abruptly against him would throw him across the tracks in front of it.

The earth was trembling now. There was a great clanging, the hiss of stream, all the insensate force of a million pounds of iron driving forward on two narrow rails.

In the snow, head down and hands in pockets, Wadkins shuffled by the unseen boy. The next instant the train also rushed past.

March remained crouching in the snow. He was too weak to stand; his face was white and drawn; he gagged until he was unable to cry his papers. An hour later he fled home up the back alley, and knelt in the cold barrenness of Rogier's shop.

"Jesus in Heaven – Blessed Jesus," he prayed inarticulately. "I pretty near killed him. I was goin' to – Oh God, you saved me from bein' a murderer in the nick of time – I don't know what happened, God. But I'm awful glad and don't let it happen again – Save my black wicked soul. Don't let me be bad!"

He could feel the cold, hear the pigeons on the roof. His black hate settled, sediment once more. He emerged as if from a horrible dream. But he knew now, deep in his heart, that within him prowled a strange god whose power he had never dreamed existed.

Now, strangely, he saw Wadkins for what he was; was filled with disgust and pity at the thought of him; and resolved to keep away from him at all costs.

But then a queer thing happened: Wadkins let him alone after weeks of persecution. Why? Had Wadkins seen him, guessed his intention? Had the Lord worked another miracle with Wadkins as He had with March himself? He only knew that the man still ambled up the tracks for coffee, his face evil, cruel, and cunning, but he never jostled nor molested him, never spoke a word.

A month or so later March was standing at his post in front of the subway entrance. A light rain was falling; the brick platform was wet and shiny.

The Cripple Creek Short Line came in slowly: a baggage car, a smoker, and a chair car whose back observation platform, due to the shower, was empty save for one man who clung to the outside railing. March noticed that it was Wadkins, who had jumped on in the yards below for a ride up to the station. As the train rolled past, Wadkins jumped off. His heels slid out from under him on the slippery bricks; he lit flat on his back, then flopped sideways under the rear trucks of the observation car.

March was not twenty feet away. He could hear the sudden jolt and crunch as the wheels passed over the man's legs, the awful greasy swish and a sudden sweetish and nauseating smell, the hollow bumping of his head upon the bricks. Within a second or two the train had passed, leaving the legless trunk of Wadkins flopping in blood and rain on the ties. Then suddenly rose the piercing shrieks of terror and naked fear from a man numbed by the shock of pain, but not yet mercifully blinded by unconsciousness.

The boy did not stir or utter a sound. As if turned to stone in a posture of deathly horror, he stood there until men came rushing with a blanket and the ambulance had come and driven away. Then throwing away his papers, he fled home. All that night as Ona sat beside him pressing wet towels to his head, he could see, as if indelibly engraven in his memory, that searing accusation of his own secret guilt.

"Thoughts are power," Rogier had told him once. "Thoughts are deeds before they take form. Be careful what you think, boy, if you don't want it to happen."

There was no praying now. Nor could he betray his anguishing guilt to his mother. He could only lie there in darkness, frightened by a mystery whose meaning he could not quite fathom. And years later when he tried to piece together this experience as a whole, he still felt something of its hidden meaning – something whose moral, if it could be called a moral, might be no more than an evanescent light cast on a pattern formed in the darkness through which we blindly grope.

9

Rogier was pulling out of his spell, but taking an agonizingly long time. His firmly built, broad shouldered body had wasted away until his clothes hung on him as if on a scarecrow. He had lost some of his hair and the remaining white wisps, after his many days in bed, stuck up above his ears to lend him the aspect of a frightened child. His voice was still gruff and resonant but no longer irritable. He used it only to supplement the mild inquiry of his dull gray eyes, voicing a simple question that might have shamed a child. When he smiled he revealed the emptiness within him. If a smile is always an index of a man's character, his was a grimace that contorted a purposeful face into a foolish mask. Ona and Mrs. Rogier shrank from it, waiting for those instants when his eyes brightened with comprehension like shutters blown open by a draft within. He would be all right! They knew he would! And each look of comprehension and sensible remark they would treasure like mothers elated over a baby's tricks.

It was a joy to them that he was still fastidious in habit and dress; for an hour he would sit carefully smoothing the shawl across his lap. Ona taught him to file his nails, an occupation in which he delighted. Always reassured by the dark, he remained awake to wait for the sound of the Kadles' footsteps. Mrs. Rogier would be aroused by his excited cry and rise to light the lamp. He would be sitting up in bed, bright-eyed as a child who had seen Santa Claus. "The Kadles! They still come to see us!"

"Yes, Daddy! Now get to sleep. They'll come back to see us again tomorrow night."

They never failed to creak up the steps and pause at his door on their nocturnal rounds – those two faithful, family ghosts who had found in the master of the shabby old house on Shook's Run a kindred soul at last.

After a time he was allowed to come down stairs for awhile in the afternoons and evenings. Like a man held in the invisible bondage of a world profound and enigmatic as the one he had envisioned below grass roots, he was always summoned back into it when his visit on this one reached its unpredictable duration. Rogier never minded the abrupt summons which none but he could hear, nor did the ceaseless commuting seem to harm him. A gesture, a flicker of his eyes, a word, and what there was of him that the family could recognize would flit away instantly and silently as a bird from a branch to return again as unbidden and unannounced.

He was getting better! During the long winter evenings he sat before the fireplace in the parlor with Ona and Mrs. Rogier, listening to the three children wrangling noisily over their school books on the dining room table. Mrs. Rogier read her Bible. Her sugar bowl had been emptied, but she managed to sell some of Rogier's contracting machinery: gasoline motors, concrete mixers, winches, and cable reels. Then she had taken a mortgage on the house. It always had been in her name, a hostage given her by Rogier against the time when he would build her a mansion in the impeccable North End. Mrs. Rogier did not worry. When this money gave out, He would provide. Were not they all, like Rogier, in His hands?

Ona sat listening to the children's voices, alert to discern in the wrangle the first let-up of work.

"Mother!" called out March. "We're learning about gold and silver and bronze, what the Greeks made swords from. Shall I say Cripple Creek's got bronze mines too?"

Ona answered sharply. "No, son! It never had a bronze mine,

and it doesn't have much silver and gold any more. The district's all played out. Don't bother about it. Just stick to your ancient history."

At the mention of Cripple Creek, Rogier's head snapped back. His eyes brightened with a look timeless and profound as the face of that immutable Peak which had stood before him and would stand for those to follow, an eternal jest of nature at men whose folly and salvation is the blind perpetuation of a quest that has no truth but this – a flashing vision, darkness, and eternal rest.

Late that spring he suddenly snapped out of it. In the warm sunshine he meandered among the currant bushes, the garden, and the now empty barnyard in back. "What became of those concrete mixers? How do you expect Rawlings to get along without them?" he would demand. "Where's March? Where did you say Abe and Jake went?" Like a man returned from a long absence, he was avid for news, interested in every triviality. The impetus of this miraculous recovery was soon spent. He began to retreat to his shop where he sat for hours at a time, wondering what had happened to him.

The doctor couldn't tell him; he knew the effect but not the cause. You've got to go down into the earth and learn the subtle, mysterious affinity between it and man, the image of his earth.

The crusty shell, what is that? The flesh that warps, erodes, rhythmically reacts to the pull of moon and sun, whose cells like radioactive elements dissipate heat and life. Below, a skeletal bone structure of darker, heavier rock; and within this, a visceral cavity whose central sun radiates psychical energy to all the organs in its constellation.

Doctor! Slip a thermometer down the throat of a volcano. Poke a proctoscope up the hind-end of a mountain, switch on the little electric globe, and take a squint through the tube. What do you see there deep in the bowels of the earth? Slit the epidermis, cut down through flesh and bone. Let's have a look at the liver and lungs and guts of this whirling dervish of a monster. A pretty anatomical puzzle, another smooth machine that runs like a watch. But how? Why? That's the end of all probing. An autopsy on the dead body. You've got to deal with the living soul at the center, its mysterious sun and unknown heart.

We die and rise out of the dead flesh like the phoenix; the

mountains crumble and wash away and rise again in eternal palingenesis; and we all are forever kept in isotatic balance.

But suddenly, from deep within, there is a great displacement. From some focal center the shock travels upward and outward in great undulating, seismic waves. The body trembles with the oscillation; there is a sudden yielding to the strain along a fault, at one or many epicenters; the doctor rushes in: a stroke, a fit, an epileptic seizure. A human earthquake. The diagnosis of the effect is correct. But what about the cause?

A necessary internal readjustment to maintain isotatic equilibrium. But why? A nervous strain, a mental stress, a correction of a displacement at adolescence, or the last organic settling at old age?

Diastrophism, the great earth movements by which continents, ocean basins, and mountains have been continually reformed. That's all his spell had been, decided Rogier. A human diastrophic change. Dom! The earth itself was epileptoidal, its pulse too kept mounting to another crisis. What was he to worry about his own eruption, he felt worn out. Head in hands, his mind suddenly blank, he sat gazing vacantly out the window.

Ona opened the door and stepped inside. "Daddy! I want to talk to you!"

Rogier switched around. "You talkin' to me or a boy you caught stealin' cookies?"

"To you, man to man. Like we have always. What've you been doing out here?"

He blinked his eyes.

"You've been out here brooding. Now Daddy, we're coming to an understanding right now. You've been a sick man and we're all doing our level best to keep you well. But you've got to cooperate. No more brooding on the past, on Cripple Creek, all that stuff."

"Ona, I won't be dictated to!"

"We're past the point of being childish," she went on quietly. "We're down to rock bottom. Neither of us are frightened by your spell, but we can't ignore it. Sitting around brooding's likely to bring on another one. You've got to do something to keep busy."

"Forbidding me to think, by Jove! A half-wit, eh?"

"No more mining. No more contracting. All that's over, Daddy. But you've got to do something, and I've decided what. Raising chickens. This big empty barnyard's just the place for a nice flock. They'll keep us in eggs, and a chicken in the pot once in awhile will taste mighty good. God knows, we need every bite, what with March buying groceries with his paper money."

"Chickens! Almighty God, that you should bring me to this!"

"I've already ordered some hens, a rooster, and baby chicks. You'd better build a coop before they come. We're facing a tough pull, Daddy, all of us."

Rogier began work with hammer, nails, and saw. Never a man with the pride of Mrs. Rogier, he still felt the ignominy of his task. Here he had raised his buggy and carriage horses, his racing trotters and pacers; Pet and Lady-Lou, Dorothy, Tolar, the ornery Little Man, Silver Night, the great Aralee, and the supreme lady of them all, the loved Akeepee. For what? That these magnificent, satin-coated aristocrats, now shadows of the past, be replaced by a straggle of squawking hens! Thoroughly humbled, he drove his nails with methodical precision.

It soon became apparent that Rogier's management of his small flock of sleek white Leghorns, plump and plaid Plymouth Rocks, and Rhode Island Reds was not an unqualified success. True, they kept him busy outside in the sunshine and provided the family with fresh eggs; and he was constantly filling his coat pockets with corn and bread crumbs to feed them. But occasionally they roused him to maniacal fury. He would let them out for an hour to pick among the currant bushes. Then patiently he would endeavor to herd them back into the chicken yard, one at a time, in some strange order of precedence he was trying to teach the whole flock.

The silly hens! He gave up his vain cajoling and bribing, and began throwing dry clods. Always with a quick, underhand snap of the wrist that sent the dirt thudding into wing or tail feathers.

"Not you! Fool!"

Head out and squawking, a slim Leghorn streaked through the open gate, out of turn. Rogier lunged in after her: across the big yard, past the old carriage and ash pit, cornering her finally in the tool house now used for a chicken roost. "There! Dom you!" he screamed, hurling the offender back over the high fence. "Wait for your turn. First the Reds, then you Whites, and the Plymouth Rocks. Now walk in like a lady!"

Order, decorum; a stately marching line of prim hens, beaks up, breasts out, daintily lifting their langorous yellow claws – this was the deep need for order his disorderly mind demanded.

So out he rushed again, tearing his coat on the currant bushes, tripping on the walk, and spilling corn from his pockets. About him and between his legs dashed, flapped, and squawked the fool hens. No matter! Still shouting, bombarding them with clods of dirt, he leaped about, a white-headed old Ichabod brandishing his stick.

"Mr. Rogier! Stop! This very minute!"

The porch steps next door had suddenly sprouted the cadaverous Mr. Pyle. "What did I tell you I'd do the very next time you carried on such a disgraceful scene? Call the Humane Society – that I will! Look at the crippled fowl! I won't have it in this neighborhood!"

By now the righteous Mrs. Pyle was out, as well as the grinning Caseys next door west. The old man let out a mighty howl of rage. "Tend to your own business, Pyle! You sanctimonious Presbyterian plate-passer. You real estate horse thief. You gold-toothed bastard of greed and envy, you tailing from a manure dump, before I take off those striped pants of yours and switch your bony behind to Kingdom Come! Dom me, Pyle, I'll – "

What he did do was to grab the wire netting of the fence between them, lunging back and forth, his white head flung back, uttering piercing shrieks which roused all the neighbors.

"Rah for the Colonel! Tear her down, Crazy Man!" yelled the Casey kids. On the other side Mrs. Kennedy stood on her back step piously fingering her beads.

Rogier by now was oblivious to these customary spectators of his fusses. A peculiar and faint tap-tap-tap was sounding on his head. Increasing in tempo and volume, it was suddenly translated into its visual counterpart: a number of yellowish petals rushing toward a common center to form a golden flower. Before they could assume shape, everything went black. He dropped to his knees, then spread out on the ground.

Aroused by the commotion, Ona and Mrs. Rogier and March at her heels, rushed out of the house to kneel beside him. In a few minutes he quit jerking, his eyes began to clear. "Daddy! Why, Daddy! And your nice hot bath waitin' for you too! Land sakes!"

And he was led into the house.

"March, get those chickens in and close the gate. Mind you, no talkin' back to the neighbors now!"

Then together, wife and daughter got Rogier upstairs for an hour's hot soaking and a nap.

By dark his *petit mal,* his "little absence," was over. Out in the gloomy tool house echoing a muffled cackle from rows of feathered throats, he stood gently stroking a slim white hen. "My little lady! You're not hurt, my child. But we've got to learn. Yes, by Jove, we've all got to learn."

Yes! Colonel Joseph Rogier of the Ca'olinas, Suh, a prominent mine owner of Cripple Creek, and the outstanding contractor and builder of Little London since its founding, was slowly returning to the surface of the earth from depths known only by himself.

10

It was now late May and March's last year at Columbia was drawing to a close. Engrossed in his work at the railroad station, he had seen little of Leslie Shane. But now with the rumor of a class party, he resolved to ask her boldly like a man, and to call for her at her own house. For graduation he had bought new shoes and would have money to carry in his pocket.

Everyone seemed to know about the party. It was to be held in the basement of the unfinished church next door to school. Members of the graduating class, their mothers and teachers were to come. There was to be a Grand March, Virginia Reel, and folk dancing.

Then he discovered that invitations already had been mailed, but one had not come for him. He grew sick with shame that he had been omitted, and a stubborn pride prevented him from inquiring whether it was a school, church, or private party, whether Old Excelsior had perversely forgotten to include him, or whether his own invitation had been lost in the mail or misdirected. He knew only the most horrible suffering of childhood – that of an outcast.

Assidiously he avoided any chance meeting with Leslie; and on the Friday afternoon of the party, immediately after school, he fled down the street. Before he had reached the railroad embankment Will Hapsworth caught up with him. "You goin' to the big party tonight?"

"I'm workin'."

"Well I guess we're the only ones not goin'," said Will, more honest. "I didn't get an invite. They think I ain't good enough to sit watchin' Cecil James show off with the girls. And Leslie Shane's goin' to do a dance all by herself. A real classy party. I'll bet there's lots to eat."

"I wasn't invited either," confessed March.

Miserable and silent they walked home to the Hapsworths' frame house along the dump on Shook's Run. Will's father was a mucker in the coal mines north of town. He had just returned from work, his face black and streaked with sweat, his clothes grimy with coal dust. He was not a dull-witted nor narrow-minded man, but he was a bitter one. "'The *Denver Post* has a heart and a soul', eh?" he was exclaiming. "Why, it's nothin' but a mouthpiece for Capitalism. This ain't America for Americans no more. It's America for the Industrial Lords. Look what happened in Cripple Creek. Remember what they did to us coal miners in southern Colorado. The Battle of Ludlow! Women and children shot down like dogs. Colorado, the richest state in the Union. With your blessed Governor, boughten Senators, and your red-sheet, bull-shittin' *Denver Post* of Tammen and Bonfils – the stinkpot of political intrigue! I tell you, the only hope of common working men, the real Americans, is Eugene V. Debs!"

Will's mother, a plain, scrawny woman, did not reply to his tirade. They were pitifully poor; and to make ends meet, they watched the dump like hawks to salvage uncracked glass, old picture frames, broken furniture, and household articles which they cleverly mended.

"They're common, March! They live on the town dump!" This was Mrs. Rogier's unalterable judgment, though no one was kinder to Will when he came. Yet underneath the Hapsworths' hopeless struggle bubbled a homely warmth, an appetite for life, and a rebellious spirit which March found exciting. It was this that cemented his friendship with Will although they had little time together.

"Let's go," now whispered Will. "Meet me here after your last train. I got something in mind."

That evening at dusk March saw what it was: a big can of thick black grease Will had found on the dump. "The only way they can get out of that church basement is the stairs in front," explained Will. "When the party gets goin' we'll smear every step. They'll have to clean off every one before they can leave. The sons of bitches! That'll teach'em to snoot us! What do you say?"

It was dark and the party was in full swing when they reached the church. The shades on the side windows were drawn, but they could hear shouts, laughter, the tinkle of a piano. Quickly and furtively the boys smeared the steps and the handrail with thick black grease. "Let's hidė and watch, or maybe peek through the window," suggested Will.

"They can all go to hell!" answered March, thinking of Leslie Shane dancing with Cecil James inside. "If I'm not invited I won't stand outside and peek in like a dog!"

"You're right! We might be caught. And we better ditch this grease bucket and the sticks we used. Let's go!"

Back at the dump they hid bucket and sticks, then scrubbed their hands in Shook's Run. "I'd sure like to see Old Excelsior scrapin' off that grease with her lace hanky!" March grinned.

"Swear you won't tell!" muttered Will in a voice already husky with anxiety.

"Wash your hands with soap and don't leave any marks on the towel, Will. And look over your shoes and clothes again." They parted and ran for home.

Now for the two boys began an agonizing two weeks. On Monday morning the school talked of nothing but how the steps had been smeared during the party. A group of boys had been the first to rush out, running for seats in Cecil James' new automobile. In the dark they had slipped and fallen on the greasy stairs. Shirts, pants, and shoes had been ruined. Miss Watrous had brought out a chair and tried to clamber through the railing, spoiling her white gloves and splotching her organdy dress. It had been necessary to telephone the janitors to bring a ladder from outside. Up this and out a window the rest of the party had climbed, snagging more clothes. The place had not been emptied until nearly midnight.

March slunk back and forth from school thoroughly ashamed. He dared not watch the men scrubbing the stone steps of the church next door. He thought of Miss Watrous' spoiled dress, and of Leslie Shane abjectly crawling through the window in her pretty dancing dress. Will still gloated over the news of each spoiled garment. But he was deathly afraid of being caught, and with reason. For Old Excelsior called a meeting of the upper classes.

"You all know about the disgraceful occurrence of last Friday night," she announced curtly. "We have our suspicions who are the culprits. I merely want to announce they will be given another day to confess of their own free will. Otherwise every boy in school will be interviewed separately in my office by the Superintendent of Public Schools and the guilty one will be expelled. If he is present here now, it will be best for him to come to my office immediately to avoid more serious consequences."

Two days dragged by. The church had refused to pay the bill for cleaning the steps, sending it to the school with a curt note that the party had not been a church function. The Superintendent of Schools in turn had referred the matter to the Chief of Police. The following week – the last week of school – the Chief arrived. He questioned without results Schwartz, an overgrown ranch boy; the grocer's clerk who had been in previous scrapes; and a few notoriously "bad" boys. Then another assembly was called, presided over by the Chief, the Superintendent, Old Excelsior, and Miss Watrous. The Chief's announcement was brief. No regular classes would be held, but every student must be present in school to await questioning when called. The inquisition would start next morning. No one would be omitted.

The following morning March, on the way to school, waited vainly for Will on the railroad embankment. Finally he ran down to the Hapsworths' house. Will was sick, said his mother. March went in to find Will dressed, but white with fright.

"You've got to come!" hissed March when they were alone. "They'll know in a minute why you're stayin' out. Face 'em down, like I'm goin' to. What the hell!"

A moment later he told Mrs. Hapsworth calmly, "Will's comin' to school with me. He feels better, and the fresh air will do him good."

They walked slowly along the railroad embankment to certain doom. "I'll tell. I know I'll tell if they get me up there alone," moaned Will.

"They won't. You're in the seventh grade, not the eighth, and you're a new boy. It's me they're after. And I don't give a damn! I'll quit school and work on the railroad." March's face was set, his eyes contracted to wary, dark glass in his impassive face, yet underneath his taut awareness his nerves were stretched to an almost unbearable tension.

All morning they sat in assembly, waiting to be called up in front of the battery of inquisitors. Old Excelsior was figiting, the Chief was growing impatient. Then Miss Watrous stood up.

"This is taking a great deal of time. Graduation day is Friday, as you know, and there's lots to be done. May I offer a few suggestions? Most of those present were at the party, and can be excused from questioning. Nor do I see any need for interviewing the girls and several boys. Leslie, I know, is due at her dancing lesson uptown. Cecil's mother is waiting for him in her car outside. March, as you know, must be down at the Sante Fe station. And Will, as a seventh-grader and new boy at Columbia, certainly was not implicated. I suggest that all of them be excused at present. If you will allow me, I'll answer for all of them personally until they can be interviewed later if necessary."

She spoke quietly, but with a sharp voice. Her casual glance, however, held on March. He, with his stubborn will and nervous strength, might have withstood the probing of the Chief and Superintendent but not that calm, yet searching beam from Miss Watrous' eyes. It flooded his soul, lit up its black guilty sediment, revealed every nook and cranny wherein lay hidden the dream stuff of the hundred myths she had woven for him. She knew! She had forgiven him for her ruined gloves and dress, and was trying to save him from public exposure. If she had spoken the word, he would have risen and made a clean breast of his part in the atrocious crime.

The Chief and Superintendent nodded agreement; and at the imperious wave of her hand, March and Will rose and fled. On Friday school was let out. Each eighth-grade pupil was given at assembly a certificate tied with purple and white ribbons, Columbia's colors, and dismissed. As March accepted his from Miss Watrous, he detected in her eyes a look of ironic amusement. Thus elated at his narrow escape and yet weighed by a sense of guilt, March left Columbia School.

He was growing fast, tall and thin, small-boned like his father, and that summer he bought his first long pants, his "extensions." He had hoped to buy the suit in "The Boys" stylish haberdashery. But the family was so poor Ona prevailed upon him to order it from a large mail-order house.

"A splendid suit, March, really. Look at the picture in the catalogue. Only $7.69. You'd have to pay two or three times more uptown."

"But out of a catalogue! Like ranchers way out of the city!"

"Oh shoot! Who'll know the difference? And you've got to have it to start in high school!"

Late in August the two-piece suit came, a fuzzy brown worsted. To be sure of getting the trousers long enough, March had insisted on stretching the tape an extra two inches. They now dragged on the ground over his shoes, but he turned them up until Ona could cut them off. Very proud, he wore them after dark until school started in order to get used to his strangely mature, long-legged appearance in the mirror.

And now came September: rich Indian Summer, like the lingering mellow glow of blazing summer. The crowds of tourists departed, the trains grew shorter, fewer. Summer cottages and resort cabins were boarded up; great homes were closed while their owners now in turn fled elsewhere with the same unrest that had brought their guests. And now after the first frost up at Cripple Creek the aspen thickets blazed among the pines, and the deer trooped daintily, stiff-legged, down from timberline; and down at Shallow Water the wagons of The People creaked through miles of yellow chamisa. All this the ghostly flow of time had carried behind him. He was entering high school now, grown up, in long pants. But as he lay at night in his grandfather's house listening to the ancient aimless winds prowling along the eaves, he heard the haunting voices of his father and his father's fathers whispering that there is no changing constant change; that all must pass only to come again; for always and forever we are the feather, the flower, the drum, and the mirror of the old gods who never die.

PART II

TAILINGS

1

Often during his first semester Ona asked March how he liked high school. He answered her with a shrug.

High school. What was it, really?

Down from the mines of Cripple Creek came trains of ore to the unloading chutes of the reduction mill. Inside, with faultless precision, the ore was crushed, ground, sent to the roasters and flotation tanks. What gold there was, came out in standard-sized bricks. The waste pulp, the tailings, was sent to the dump. The economic process was simple. It was too expensive to handle low grade and high grade ores separately. They were mixed together and the same treatment was given to the whole run of the mill at once.

The one high school of Little London was no different. So down the chutes went March with all the rest of the ore: a ragged-shirted boy from the West Side; a frightened, handsome Negro girl from Liller; Cecil James sporting a vest and a gold watch chain; Leslie Shane, beautiful and demure; poised children from the North End discussing between classes where they had spent the summer.

"No. You've got to take algebra – Yes, English is required – Here's your card now all filled out. Go get it signed – Next!"

Round and round they went, as if on a moving belt. One room sucked them in and an hour later spewed them out. The teachers regarded them all with the calm scrutiny of gang foremen who had handled ore too long to be surprised at any trivial variations in the run. March wrote on the required notebook paper punched with two holes, learned to use a cheap fountain pen continually leaking. And all this monotonous routine went on with precision to the harsh clanging of the hourly bell.

To escape it he managed to schedule his study periods at mid-morning and mid-afternoon when he could meet the trains at the Sante Fe station instead of being confined in school. A secondhand bicycle which be bought with his savings enabled him to make these quick transitions.

This was March's first impression of high school. It was changed with Will Hapsworth's entrance during the second semester. Then he saw that the high school, like Little London itself, was divided strictly and impassibly as by railroad tracks. Each section of town, each class of society, was as segregated and inviolable within its walls as if the students wore the brand of their social status. Democracy was not a rubber stamp of society which could be imprinted on all men, for no impress could make all men equal. There was nothing in common between boys from the elite North End who drove their own cars and those who came from the West Side with their lunch buckets; between the girls of Liller who wore the gingham of their hard-working mothers and those who spent their summers in Europe. At the bottom of the scale were the poor and orphaned children of the Myron Stratton Home, the charitable institution which had been founded by Stratton, the Croesus of Cripple Creek, for destitute miners' families. The snobbishness involved was creating in them such a hopeless sense of inferiority that the officials of the Home were arranging to remove them from the public high school.

All this was reflected by the two boys' literary societies: the Senate which controlled the weekly school paper, *The Lever;* and the Delphian which controlled the dramatic club. Their functions were primarily social; their parties, dances, and steak fries in the mountains were in reality the school's only social events except one or two farcical school dances which few students attended. The two societies dominated the high school; they were sponsored by the most influential teachers, and their members were invariably drawn only from the North End. Neither March nor Will was admitted.

"God damn their thick hides!" swore Will. "Let's blast the hell out of 'em till they let us in!"

What they would do if they were admitted, they didn't consider. Neither boy owned an automobile, nor could he even drive one. Neither could dance; had no money for outings, even to buy the pearl-encrusted pin denoting membership; and would have been aghast had their fraternal brothers and their girls entered his home. They thought only of the chasm between their poverty-stricken life and their resplendent aspirations.

To bridge it they composed a letter headed "Little Brothers, Big Brothers, and Fathers," a masterpiece of naive candor. Its theme was simple. The Little Brothers of wealthy North End families dominated Little London's grade schools and high school; their Big Brothers dominated The Colorado College in town; and their fathers ran the town with the same selfish arrogance. This whole "un-American" regime should be abolished, beginning with the transformation of the Little Brothers by opening the two literary societies to membership on a purely scholastic basis. They would then, as Big Brothers in college, and later as City Fathers, be more democratic and generous of spirit. The letter was signed "The Well Wishers," and mailed to *The Lever.*

For a week the two boys anxiously awaited the result.

The Lever came out. On the back page was printed a travesty of their letter. Its meaning was mangled and distorted; sentences were cut and replaced by shameful grumblings. It was headed, "Anonymous Socialists Indict School," and signed "The Grumblers." Underneath was a curt paragraph signed by the Principal. It stated sanctimoniously how pained he was that some of his students were so jealous of the popularity of others, warned against the evils of socialism, and lamented the cowardice that had prevented the writers from signing their names.

March and Will were aghast.

"The son of a bitch!" declaimed Will. "Too afraid of the truth to print our letter. The damned coward!"

"No!" answered March. "You forget the Senate Society runs

The Lever. They're the ones who rewrote our letter before they showed it to the Principal."

Unable to endure the accusation of cowardice, they fell headlong into the trap laid for them. They wrote another letter daring the editor to print their first letter just as it was written, and signing their names. Within a week it was obvious that almost everyone in school knew who "The Grumblers" were. Then something happened which brought this trivial occurrence to a disastrous climax.

Late one afternoon Ona, March, and the two girls were sitting on the front porch when Will came walking home from school. Hands in pockets, coat collar up, he was slouching past on the other side of the street as if ashamed of being seen.

"Why, what's the matter with Will?" asked Ona. "You boys haven't quarreled, have you, March?"

"No. He was all right this morning," answered March, giving a shrill whistle.

The two girls yelled, waved their hands. Will turned and slowly, head down, slunk up to the porch. His face was pale and strained; he looked shamed and frightened.

"Oh, Will! Your coat!" Leona's sharp eyes had spotted it first. On the right side of the jacket, directly in front and between shoulder and lapel, the cloth had been burned away to a huge hole. They could see the scorched and ragged lining.

"Will, I'm so sorry!" Nancy's sensitive left eye twitched with pity. "It's the new coat your father bought you to wear to school."

The boy's face constricted. He tried to sneer, to laugh it away; and these pitiful attempts at an unwarranted nonchalance only intensified the pain and fear in his wild, troubled eyes.

"How'd you do it?" demanded March.

"The sons-a-bitches. They done it a-purpose. But my Dad – " Gradually he became coherent. That afternoon in the chemistry class the teacher had asked for an assistant to help demonstrate an experiment in the laboratory. Will volunteered. As he stood bent over the counter with the other students gathered around him, the teacher was called outside. He left them for a few minutes with instructions to handle the acids with care.

"Maybe it was the nitric or maybe the sulphuric acid. But anyway it was them North Enders. Cecil James on the staff of *The*

Lever who rewrote our letter and told everybody who wrote it. He was the one, the rotten, dressed up bastard! He reached around from behind me and poured the nitric in the sulphuric, just what we weren't supposed to do. They mixed like hell-fire and brimstone. The whole mess spouted up like a geyser and burned my coat."

"Now Will!" remonstrated Ona. "He didn't deliberately try to harm you. He's just like other boys and girls."

"What did the teacher say when he came back?" asked Nancy.

"He said he'd told me to be careful, and after this to buy a rubber apron."

"Land alive, boy!" said Ona. "Your face might have been disfigured for life. It's only a coat."

Will's face hardened; a sullen resentment emanated from him. "The whole class was laughing at me fit to kill."

Frightened and ashamed, he crept home to the tawdry frame house on the dump along Shook's Run. The Rogiers had little to say. The coat was irreparably ruined and could never be worn again.

That evening after supper Ona called March aside. "Son, wouldn't you like to run over to Will's a few minutes? I've got the feeling it's going to be a bad evening for him, Mr. Hapsworth and all. You know – Just a cheerful word."

"Why sure, Mother," March reluctantly agreed, knowing Hapsworth better than she.

When March arrived at the Hapsworths' kitchen door, Hapsworth was sitting backwards on a chair, his grimy hands resting on the back and swinging his leather belt. In the corner where he had been flung across the wood box, Will straightened up. March could see he had been whipped badly; a lash of the belt had caught him on one cheek; a welt was rising. Mrs. Hapsworth sat at the kitchen table. Her worn, tear-spotted face wore a look of peculiar hardness.

"I'm sorry," said March, abashed and hesitating at the door. "I guess I won't come in."

"Come in, I said!" thundered Hapsworth without removing his glance from Will. "We got nothing to be ashamed of!"

As March sank upon a chair, Hapsworth stood up in his dirty blue socks and brought his heavy belt down, whistling, across the back of his chair. "I told you those filthy capitalist brats would try to keep you from gettin' an education! And you were fool enough to step up and volunteer. Not them others with two, three, or likely four suits to home. No! When a drift's plugged up and the air's bad, do the rich mine owners in their white collars go down? No! It's a call for volunteers among the workers. And when Hansen gets stretched out, turns yellow, and we haul him up pukin' green slime to stay home for weeks, it's nothin' out of their hides. They try to beat him out of his compensation. And you! The professor ain't buyin' you a new coat, or those rich brats either."

His coarse dirty dungarees had slipped down to his bony hips; his shirt tail crawled out; his black face was beginning to drop beads of sweat thick as shoe polish. "You mind what I'm sayin'. You was sent to school to learn to get what these capitalists have got, and then it'll be us crackin' the whip!"

March stole a look at Will. What he saw filled him with a strange fright and disgust. The boy's fear and resentment over his beating had faded from his face; his eyes were steady upon his father's; he seemed intent upon this vindictive indictment and promise of revenge as if it were already salving his wounds.

Hapsworth, however, was not through. He lifted his foot to the chair and gave his knee a loud whack with the belt. "Now!" he said ominiously. "I'm goin' to see you remember this lesson. Your ma and I saved months for that new coat. And you're goin' to keep on wearin' it, understand?"

Will's eyes widened with new fear and shame. He looked appealingly at his mother wiping away a tear with her apron.

"I can't mend it for him. The hole's too big," she stammered.

"Wear it the way it is, then. Every day!" Hapsworth thundered at the boy. "Let 'em see that hole – the rich brats, the professors, you too. It'll remind you of somethin' you better not forget." He stepped forward, lifted the belt, and stared at the boy shrinking back against the wall. "And if I ever catch you forgettin' it, I'll strap the hide off your bones!"

With this he turned, grabbed up his shoes, and flung into the bedroom.

Will stood up, gazing at his mother with a look March could not bear. March stammered his excuses and fled home.

Next morning he stood at the front window with Mrs. Rogier, Ona, and the two girls, waiting for Will. "Of course he won't come!"

he boasted. "Do you think I would?"

"Never mind," answered Ona. "I'll run over later and talk to Mrs. Hapsworth."

Suddenly Will appeared. He did not stop for March as usual, but walked past stiffly, head up. He was wearing the coat; on it was a huge and glaring patch. The Rogiers dodged back in embarrassed silence. Old clothes, cheap clothes, worn clothes, all cleaned and neatly pressed and mended – but patches never!

March watched him pass by the window, his own face flushed with shame. Then a mighty admiration filled him. Will had a courage greater than he could ever have assumed; and that horrible patch seemed to him now a heraldic symbol of something that the Rogiers with their monstrous false pride could never equal. He ran out quickly and caught up with his chum.

But in the days that followed March saw the difference in Will. For awhile Will kept aloof, a little truculently, until his classmates' glances no longer helplessly strayed to the enormous patch. Then little by little he began to ingratiate himself among the Senate and Delphian boys. March could see him in the halls and on the grounds between classes. His smile seemed open, his pats on their backs spontaneous, his admiration of their society pins profound. And yet with a curious disgust, March divined in his manner a bitter homage, and a sly and eager hunger. Will, seeing him walk by, winked furtively.

"It's like my dad said," he told March later. "You got to get in with them to lick them. I'm goin' to be in a society if it kills me."

How little we know one another! March, confused and disgusted, knew only that he himself was as out of step at high school as he had been at Columbia. But to make up for it, he pedalled furiously back and forth to the Sante Fe station, his one great love.

2

That winter was a crucial one for the Rogiers. The United States had entered the war to make the world safe for democracy, and the wartime rise of prices increased their difficulties. The $30 to $40 a month that March earned selling newspapers helped greatly on the grocery bill, but there were other household expenses too. March came home one night to find the piano moved out of the parlor. The next week another one of the concrete mixers in the back yard was gone. Soon men in a truck came after the great steel safe in the obscure corner of the dining room. Mrs. Rogier was on her knees before it, scraping Rogier's name off the door.

"Daddy's safe that's been in the family all these years. I won't have it carrying his name!" she hissed melodramatically.

"Oh shoot, Mother!" comforted Ona. "The combination lock's broken, and we've only kept the Haviland in it for years!"

Then one day the little cast-iron Nigger-Boy out in front was sold to a wealthy North End family which had long fancied it for their garden. No one said a word while it was being removed. They didn't have to. The Blackamore's outstretched hand had held the reins of Akeepee, Little Man, Aralee, Silver Heels, Tolar, and Silver

Night. From it Sally Lee, Mary Ann, even March when little had clambered upon Rogier's horses. But that night when Mrs. Rogier called the children to table, she was stern, grim-lipped, and deadly serious.

"Now children, before you sit down, I think it's right for you to realize we're having a hard time," she began. "We've eaten up Daddy's concrete mixers, the piano, the safe, and now the Nigger Boy. Where more will come from I don't know, but the Lord will provide. There'll be enough each meal. But only help yourself to what you can eat. Don't leave anything on your plate to be thrown out."

Abashed by her vulgar frankness, the children sat down to a silent meal. Suddenly March blurted out, "Everyone around here goes up to the railroad track with gunny sacks to pick up coal. I don't see why we shouldn't if we're so poor. I know the fireman on Number 6. He'll throw off some coal just where I tell him to. Nobody will see him in the dark, or me when I bring it home."

Mrs. Rogier flung back stiffly in her chair. "Must I point out the difference between poor people and poor white trash? I thought we all instinctively understood!"

"Let the boy bring home all he wants!" growled Rogier. "At the price it is, a good big chunk of anthracite ought to be worn on a watch chain!"

Mrs. Rogier flung down her fork and left the table.

"Never mind, son," cautioned Ona. "We haven't come to that yet. You're helping Mother splendidly with the money you give her. We can pay for what we need; just let's be economical."

Yet in March who sat there, secretly worried as they all were, his grandmother's unhappy spirit roused a savage and uncontrollable shame for the deathless pride and valor of which she was still an untarnished symbol.

The family's usual fare during the winter, with the restrictions on sugar and flour, was corn bread and potatoes covered with "compound gravy." This synthetic spread they all disliked. They ate it for the first taste which vaguely reminded them of the meat they could not afford, and because it hid the absence of butter. Leona could not endure it. Cheerful and light-hearted, she forebore mentioning her disgust at table. But to Nancy and March she had plenty to say.

"Compound gravy! Compound gravy! Isn't it ever going to end? I'll bet it's made of axle grease, it's so yellow and greasy. How do you stand it?"

"Oh, it's not so bad if you squeeze the lumps out flat," murmured Nancy.

"What do you want – T-bone steak and asparagus, with a chocolate cake thrown in?" demanded March.

"Yes!" laughed Leona. "Two helpings please. Mine and yours, since you'd stick up your nose at it!"

That night at supper she was passed the bowl of compound gravy. "No thanks!" she said airily.

March stared down at his plate. In it was a slab of corn bread and two boiled potatoes, all butterless. Abruptly he took the bowl and thrust it at Leona. "Take some!" When she did not move, he grabbed and squeezed her wrist. "Take some, I say!"

Leona took the bowl and rose to her feet. Then without warning she began to fling handsful at him, spattering him from the top of his head to his waist.

"Take some, I say!" she shouted hysterically. "And this and this!" Her light body shaking, her dark face a sickly yellow, she continued to scream. "Tell me what I should eat! Who do you think you are? Compound gravy! Compound gravy! Fill your belly full – Your face – Your ears!"

March, blinded, kicked back his chair, dug out his eyes. What he saw was not a girl's hysteria, but the savage fury and violence of his father when he was finally aroused. She too was a Cable, as well as a Rogier. He stood transfixed, slowly wiping off his face, hair, and clothes.

Leona hurled the bowl at him wildly; it hurtled past his head and crashed against the wall. Then she rushed, wild-eyed and panting, to fling herself kicking on the shabby sofa in the parlor. Ona and Nancy followed to kneel and stroke her hair. "Honey! Quiet down now. It's all over."

Mrs. Rogier, still seated at the table with Rogier, raised a tense white face, and asked calmly, "You'd like some more corn bread, Daddy? A hot piece from the oven?"

The bottom of family misfortune was reached just before

Christmas. The weather was terribly cold and dry; and to conserve coal, they kept only the downstairs rooms heated. In the evening all gathered about the kerosene lamp on the dining room table; it always seemed to be smoking, no matter how often the wick was trimmed. Rogier, years before, had torn out the electrical wiring in a fit of temper because the light bills were so high. He had then installed a carbide gas lighting system at enormous expense. The folly was soon apparent. Great cans of chunk carbide had to be emptied into the plant in the basement. Water was then added to generate the gas. A month later, when the gas was exhausted, the slimy, milky residue had to be carried, bucket by bucket, outside and emptied. Because of the work and expense, the plant was abandoned and kerosene lamps used.

The feeble light of the one on the table was enough to illuminate the family's hopes for Christmas. Mary Ann, bewailing poor business in her Chocolate Shoppe, sent only a box of her bittersweets. Boné sent a lovely card. And Sally Lee from whom they expected a big box of munificent presents, sent a $20 bill to go around. Of this, $15 went for coal.

"I know you're all a little disappointed," said Ona, "but this Christmas we must all be sensible. With the remaining $5 March and I have bought a family present, one we can all use. Guess what it is! A new fangled lamp to use instead of this kerosene one. A Coleman lamp. You pump it up with air, and it's got mantles, and gives the brightest light. Now what do you think of that?"

"What about our Christmas dinner?" asked Nancy.

"Daddy's going to kill that big red rooster he's always chasing with a stick. It'll take two hens if he don't, and we need the eggs."

But Rogier balked at killing his arch enemy, the big red rooster, beginning an argument that lasted till the afternoon before Christmas. It was settled by a ring of the doorbell. Ona and Mrs. Rogier rushed to the door. No one was there, but at their feet lay a grocery basket containing a dressed turkey, celery, and cranberries. The card on top read: "Merry Christmas to my friends and best customers from their groceryman, Mr. Bryce."

"And we've owed him over $50 for two months!" muttered Ona, her eyes misting with tears. "I'm going right over and thank him!"

After a devoutly enjoyed Christmas dinner the Rogiers returned to their meager fare. It was enlivened by one delight – lettuce. Crisp, green lettuce with its crinkly leaves and its reassuring taste of summer and the fertile earth; the great green bunches which lighted up their cheerless winter evenings when the snow whirled against the window panes. The one place where they could buy fresh, cool leaves was Aunt Fanny's jerry-built greenhouse a half-mile up Shook's Run. Almost every evening March and Leona walked up there for the dime purchase.

Shook's Run below the Bijou bridge was a horror of trash and tin cans culminating in the dump along which lived the Hapsworths. Above the bridge, the creek still retained vestiges of its original charm. Cottonwoods lined the steep banks, weeping willows hung over the stream, patches of watercress showed under the ice. Leona loved these evening walks when the yellow lamps in the shanties and small wooden houses on each side seemed lit by the red glare of the sun setting behind the snowy peaks. She tripped along cheerily as the little creek, spurting out her frosty breaths like puffs of tobacco smoke.

She was a head shorter than March. Her hair was lighter than his, and her eyes gray-blue like Ona's, but she had Cable's dark skin which drank up the summer sun and never blistered under the brightest rays. She was sensitive about it, no doubt due to Mrs. Rogier's constant repetition of the family joke. "The stork didn't bring you like all the rest, Leona. A nigger man left you on the doorstep. Or maybe it was old Indian Poe."

March always had seen her as light-hearted and easy-going. Now since her blow-off over compound gravy, he detected in her casual manner the lackadaisical unconcern and deadly fury of his father. But beneath this was also Cable's intense awareness, gentleness, and frightening intuition – qualities which he lacked, possessing instead a black sediment at the bottom of his soul and the fumes of unceasing storm.

As they approached the home-built greenhouse Leona nudged March. "Look at her hair good this time."

March nodded. Aunt Fanny was a Negress. It was said of her that she had become bald because her hair had grown inward instead of upward. She had then bought a wig to cover it. This, Leona insisted, did not stop the ingrowing hair from penetrating her skull and brain. "That's why she's kind of funny at times – like Granddad," explained Leona.

March discounted the explanation. Big and jovial, Aunt Fanny let them select their own lettuce and wrapped it carefully in a newspaper. Also her hair looked perfectly natural to him. "Bosh!" he said as they walked home. "You can't believe everything you hear, Leona." Yet he secretly respected Leona's judgment. She was a strange one, his sister.

As spring ate into winter it became obvious that Rogier was bored with his chickens. They made him too irritable, screwing him up to a pitch of nervous tension that brought on another seizure. Light and infrequent as these were, they still were to be avoided at all costs. Hence Ona suggested that he keep the chickens fenced in the barnyard, and plant a few rows of vegetables in the garden.

Rogier agreed. The work was difficult but he kept on, stooped shoulders and thin back bent over the spade. He overturned the black earth, smoothed it with a rake, laid out rows of lettuce, radishes, green onions. Peace and quiet worked their change. He became calmer, more agreeable. An excellent sign! He was recovering, taking an interest in things, keeping busy!

Then over the high fence sailed his arch enemy, the big red rooster, to scrape up the emerging green shoots in his garden with long sharp claws.

"You cocky little cavalry-spurred Hohenzollern! I'll teach you to strut around and rake up my plants like a Prussian army general!" And grabbing up hoe or rake, Rogier would chase the flapping rooster about the garden till he was cornered. For a minute the old man would stand panting, stroking the rooster's proud arched neck, feeling his sharp spurs. "Next time I'm going to wring your neck, boy, for being so contrary. But now I'll let you off, little William. Get in there and stay there!" And he would toss the rooster over the fence.

One afternoon as he was chasing the squawking bird through the currant bushes, he was overtaken by another spell. His foot caught on a protruding root; he fell full length, arms outspread. After a time he slowly rose out of cloying darkness. As sight and senses cleared, there emerged before him, like something risen from the depths of dreamless sleep to the horizon of wakeful consciousness, a shape without clear outline yet embodying the substance of a hope and meaning that seemed as strangely familiar as it was vague. The Peak! He recognized it now, the face of that high, snowy, massive Peak. And suddenly it all came back to him: its undying challenge and its promise, his years of fruitless search. How could he have forgotten it? For there it still stood as it had stood on that day he had first glimpsed it long ago in timeless time.

He sat looking at it and at the squawking rooster with contrite shame. What had he come to, a seventy-six-year-old man, chasing a dom rooster out of a two-by-four vegetable garden! Spading up eight inches of dirt! He who had spent a lifetime drilling through hard granite into the depths of the immortal earth itself! But let no man say he was yet too old and his faculties worn too thin to take up his search where he had left off. For now suddenly and full formed there leapt into his mind a new plan by which –

"Daddy! Another spell. Just when you were getting along so well. Oh, that damned rooster!"

It was Ona, kneeling on the ground beside him.

"Oh, let him alone!" answered Rogier gruffly, feeling sound as a nut, resolute, and lighthearted. "He won't bother me again. I got something else in mind."

What it was, he explained after he'd had his hot bath and sat down to supper. "The garden's all planted," he began casually. "March can hoe out the weeds after work. Ona, you and the girls can look after those fool hens. I'm tired of them."

"But Daddy – "

Rogier raised his wrinkled hand for silence. "I've got something more important to do. You folks are so all-fired taken with fresh lettuce in the wintertime, I'm goin' to build a little greenhouse where we can raise our own lettuce the year around."

"Fine, Daddy! A good idea!" encouraged Ona. "You can use all those glass window frames stored up in the loft of the shop. And March can help you put it up."

"I'll tend to it," Rogier replied confidently. "The boy's busy enough."

Yes! He was back now, after so many fruitless "little absences" as the doctor called them, to the grass-roots reality of his only meaningful existence.

3

That June March quit his job at the Fred Harvey news stand. He was too big, too old to peddle newspapers; there wasn't any money in it, he thought scornfully. He became a Red Cap.

There had never beeen one at the old depot. But now with the new station's many gates and subways, passengers needed help and Old Lester was granted the concession. Les was an "old" man of thirty-two, a frail, rachitic consumptive who looked fifty-two. He had broken arches and flat feet, most of his thin sandy hair was gone, and his skin was scaly from cheap and insufficient food; his lungs were in such bad shape that after each busy train he had to stretch out on a bench and fight for breath; and he weighed exactly one hundred pounds. He received no salary. His only remuneration was the tips passengers gave him for carrying their bags to and from trains. To earn this privilege he helped at the gate to read tickets and Pullman reservations, and called trains when the Station Master was absent. The importance of these functions had gone to his head. Out of his pitiful savings he bought a French-blue uniform with brass buttons in which he strutted around like a small gamecock. Yet he possessed a courage, a love of life, and the faculty of appraising people at first glance.

It was he who gave March the privilege of working with him. There was need of another boy. The northbound Denver and Rio Grande trains were now being routed through the new Santa Fe station. And now, in the heyday of railroad tourist travel, trains of two or three sections poured in crowds to see the scenic wonders of the Pike's Peak Region. The Santa Fe and the D&RG – the Dirty, Ragged and Greasy – bringing rich people who had wintered in California and were on their way back East; the Colorado and Southern with Pullmans full of sweaty Southerners escaping the baking heat of the Texas plains and Louisiana swamps; the Colorado Midland rattling down the Rockies from Utah; the Midland Terminal and the Short Line from Cripple Creek with its daily Wild Flower Special.

March, tall and thin but wiry, learned the art of carrying six pieces of luggage – two bags in each hand and a suitcase under each arm, the lid against his body so it would not pop open from the pressure. Les taught him to read tickets, the tracks on which each train came in, and the spurs to which the Pullmans were shunted. Now he began to learn the subtle and intuitive art on which every Pullman porter, taxicab driver, hotel flunkey, street urchin, and cardsharp based his livelihood – the knack of reading faces.

To be sure, there was something in clothes that augered the size of a tip, in the cheapness or dearness of a traveller's luggage, whether he came by taxi or street car, whether he occupied a Pullman or a chair car. But who had time to size up all this? The bus drove up to unload fifteen passengers and thirty-five bags. Simultaneously two taxis squealed to a stop behind it.

"Here, boy!" – "Take mine, son, I'm in a hurry!"

The train pulled in. Spot the bags on the platform. Help the Porter to unload the vestibule. There was just time for carrying a quick load out to the taxis, and a dash back to the train to collect tips from outgoing passengers – There wasn't much time to load six parties on, and take two off, staggering heavily loaded in a crowd. You've got to work fast, and you can't pick any duds.

By a quick look at a face – this was the only way you could gauge the size of a tip. Faces that in the busy press of a great railway station dropped their masks and unsuspectingly revealed the open generosity, the spendthrift habit, the strict budgeting, or the miserly selfishness of their souls. If you would know a man, rather than his financial status, observe how much he slips into an open hand in the dark when he is leaving town.

How marvelous they were, these thousands of faces ever swarming the station platform like bees and taking flight again! They became for him symbols of some inner texture of their lives he learned to evaluate instantly but never quite explain: the faces of travelling salesmen whom he hated and avoided; the spoiled and demanding faces of women from the South with their Negro maids; the frank and generous faces of prostitutes whom he always tried to serve; the cunning faces of Little London's political bigwigs; those of gawking Eastern tourists; and above all, the faces of those few men and women, whatever their clothes and baggage, that proclaimed them as true gentlefolk and citizens of the wide earth they trod.

He made his biggest tips from handling a truckload of bags from a large escorted tourist party travelling under the auspices of the Raymond and Whitcomb, Cook's Tours, or other national agencies. Many of these parties were comprised of foreigners, Japanese, Chinese, French, or English. Yet it never seemed strange to him that so many of his own countrymen were so ignorant of the Wild West that they let themselves be herded like sheep to see its scenic wonders.

There were other sources of money: occasional tips given him on the sly by tourist drivers and keepers of third-rate hotels for directing tourists their way. This was against the rules. The transportation company of Diggs and Handel, with whom Rogier had fussed over a mine some years ago, had secured the station franchise. All itinerant baggagemen and tourist drivers of both automobiles and horse-driven hacks were banished to the street where they stood shouting at the curb. Only Diggs and Handel's bus and taxis were allowed to stand at the edge of the station platform. March did his best to chisel the edge off their monopoly. He would hold back his most influential-looking parties till the Diggs and Handel bus had driven away, then call a tourist driver and a baggageman from the street.

The tourist drivers repaid him by taking him with their parties, by carriage or automobile, to the scenic wonders of the Pike's Peak Region: through the Garden of the Gods, up North and South Cheyenne Canyons, to Seven Falls and Helen Hunt Jackson's grave on top; to the Ancient Cliff-Dwellers, the Cave of the Winds, General Palmer's English castle of Glen Eyrie.

There was no doubt about it; America, having saved the world for democracy, was suddenly curious about itself. "See America First" was the thing, at least until Europe was swept up for visitors. And so Little London swarmed and trainloads of the newly rich, war profiteers great and small, hordes of tourists from everywhere. She had mastered at last her environment, stamped out all traces of the little pioneering town at the foot of Pike's Peak. *Little London! The spa of the West with Old World charm.*

Driving around with young Hanlon who had just replaced his carriage with a new automobile, March saw gaudily painted, cast-iron Indian Chiefs on every corner advertising soda water. In Manitou the old street car pavilion was replaced by a huge cement tepee. Hot dog stands boasted imitation log-cabin fronts. A high board fence was erected around Balanced Rock to make sure no one saw it without paying twenty-five cents. Picture show palaces were no longer named the "Majestic," "Princess," or "Odeon," but the "Ute" and the "Chief."

At the end of a trip March complained to Hanlon, "Weren't you ashamed givin' that spiel? The Cliff Dwellers is a fake. It's just copied after the ruins in Mesa Verde. The shards are broken Hopi bowls buried in the sand, brand new. Helen Hunt isn't buried above Seven Falls. It's only an empty grave and the rocks on top are put there for souvenir hunters." Bitterly he went on. "And that Petrified Indian at the Garden of the Gods! You can see he's even got paint and bracelets on. And all that fake Indian jewelry you made people buy. Why, those Ute moccasins were manufactured in Chicago!"

"Hold on!" interrupted Hanlon. "What the hell's the difference what I tell 'em? You can see their mouths gapin' open for flies at anything. That's what they pay their money for. Jesus' underwear! If this town told the truth, nothin' but the truth, most of us would go hungry." He shook his head knowingly. "We only get these suckers three months a year. We've got to make enough out of 'em to last the other nine. That's why everything costs so much. Everything! Every hotel, salt water taffy stand, and souvenir shop's got our number. We get a commission on every dollar they spend. See? Now for God's sake keep your trap shut the next time I haul you around."

A week later Hanlon picked up a party of distinguished visitors, wealthy Chicago meat packers and their wives. Unfortunately he had caught cold on a sunrise trip up the Peak and was too hoarse to deliver his spiel, and asked March to point out the sights as they drove about.

"Really overwhelming. The vastness, I mean," one of the ladies in back remarked, glancing at the folder in her hand. "Now Fraunce does have a chahm. A quiet chahm. Don't you think so, Stella? But here, it's the distances, the sparkling champagne air, the coloration you know, that really gets one, don't you think?"

"Yep!" answered one of the men. "But it's the good ol' U. S. A. for hogs and cattle ever' time. Pork chops and T-bones. But likely scenery hereabouts. Now what do you suppose made them rocks stand up like that?"

March answered bashfully with a remembered bit of Rogier's geology.

"Hummmm. The boy sounds like he knew what he was talking about," growled the other man behind him.

"Yes sir," hoarsely responded Hanlon. "Born and bred of old pioneers. Knows ever' inch of the country. I sometimes bring him along to give the low-down to my smartest customers."

By the time they had reached the Garden of the Gods, March had lost his bashfulness. After dutifully pointing out the post-card-famous Kissing Camels, the Seal and the Bear, he pointed toward a pile of formless rocks. "That's the Shark's Head, lady. See it sticking up against the sky?"

For a moment there was silence.

"Sure, Stella! Look there!" Her husband stretched out his arm.

"Oh yes!" the woman shrieked. "I see it now. Plain as the nose on your face!"

Rapidly now March pointed out more nondescript cliffs and pillars, calling them by any name that jumped into his head: the Two Doves, Lady in White, Manitou's Headdress. He concocted lies that would have choked him with anger had he heard them from another. Here a bear had eaten a child; off this cliff a lovelorn Indian maiden had jumped to her death; there the pioneers had made a last stand against bloodthirsty Utes. "The Massacre of '72 – or was it '73?" he asked with a solemn face.

"It was '73, I believe," spoke up one of the men authoritatively. "I read about it in history. But then," he added modestly, "I'm better at figures than dates."

They bought boxes of ore specimens, glass wampum beads made in Germany, moccasins manufactured in Chicago, souvenir spoons, bows and arrows, salt water taffy, dozens of postcard folders. And when at last they clambered out at their hotel, each shook hands with this all-knowing boy-wonder whose family was among the oldest Pioneer Winners of the Far West.

"And by Gosh, if you ever come to Chicago, son, you look us up. You sure showed us a wonderful time. We were lucky you came along."

Hanlon finally found his voice as the car drove off. "Christ!" he muttered hoarsely. "You told them ignorant meat butchers more lies than there's in all Little Lunnon. How much did they slip you?"

"A five dollar bill," March answered smugly.

Such munificent windfalls came seldom. But March took other rides between trains with Old Dutch, delivering trunks. Old Dutch was a big-boned man, strong as a buffalo but with a squeaky hip, who stood beside his rattletrap truck at the curb soliciting baggage in a bellowing voice. Number 11 from Kansas City, Chicago, and all points east, arriving in two sections at 3:05 p.m., brought him the greatest number of trunks. He delivered them before Number 2 arrived at 5:35, taking March with him.

Panting up a narrow flight of stairs on one end of a big Hartman wardrobe was hard work for the boy, but he was amply rewarded. The Rogiers, penned with their poverty and pride in the shabby old house on Shook's Run, received no visitors and never went calling. Except for the homes of a few schoolmates to which he was occasionally invited to a party, March had never been out. Now, day after day, he saw the nooks and crannies into which flowed the vast streams of people that poured off the trains.

The little summer cottages and cabins with their "cute" names—"Dew Drop In" and "Rancho Costa Plenty"—forty steps up the steep hillside streets of Manitou. The tawdry tourist homes and rooming houses with their florid wallpaper, cigar butts on the dresser, and silk stockings hung over a chair to dry. The Sanitoriums—Star Ranch in the Pines, Cragmor, and the beautiful Woodmen Sanitorium—where the tuberculosis invalids, the "lungers," sat on open porches with their sputum cups, gazing at the mountains which would, of course, restore their health. The hotels he loved to peep inside. Each in some strange manner had a character and an atmosphere all its own: the historic and beloved Antlers fronting Pike's Peak Avenue as if set at the very base of the great Peak itself; the beautiful gray stone Cliff House at the entrance to Williams Canyon; the Mansions with its rose-walled ballroom; the Ruxton, named for the young English explorer who gave his name to the mountain stream it straddled; the sedate Alamo and the family style Alta Vista; even the little Joyce, so cheerful and sprightly.

The great homes of Little London's aristocracy held him spellbound. All his life March had heard his grandmother bewailing the unproductiveness of Rogier's mines that had prevented her from building a proper Rogier domicile in the divine North End. The barny mansions, the rococo palaces, and the enormous brownstone houses on Millionaire Row were impressive enough. But like Cripple Creek gold, they were out of date; their owners had made their piles and settled down to a staid career of preserving them against change. The really showy places were the spacious and luxurious estates in the new Broadmoor section. Each reflected the tastes and whims of its builder: Gothic, Tudor, and Elizabethan houses, Italian villas, Spanish and Mexican ranch houses, Swiss chateaus, even imitation Indian pueblos. Into each one March walked entranced by a spaciousness, cleanliness, and luxury he had never dreamed existed; awed by maids in spotless white uniforms, slipping on smooth polished floors, eating a cookie given him by a cook. And coming out, he stared just as entranced at gardeners tending the great expanses of lawn and garden.

The crowning jewel of this newly developed suburb was the magnificent new Broadmoor Hotel. Built on the site of Count Portales' historic Broadmoor Casino, which March's mother remembered with such an accountable and nostalgic fondness, it upheld with new splendor Little London's tradition of European elegance and luxury. Its multi-storied tiers of white stone gleamed palely from afar against the dark slopes of Cheyenne Mountain. To each side lay the polo fields and nearby a new golf course. The gravelled approach to it lay through a magnificent formal garden and directly behind the hotel a tiny lake boasted on its shore an Italian chapel.

Its setting was so beautiful that the famous artist, Maxfield Parrish, was brought to paint it—the reproductions to advertise a brand of coffee, and the original to hang in the hotel as Little London's most revered work of art. Its artistic integrity no one dared to deny while humbly making obeisance before it; and none ventured to remark that the Master of Blue with an artist's license had moved the lake from behind the hotel to place it in front, so that his masterpiece would conform with all his other paintings.

The Broadmoor was a royal hostelry. Its color was a rich plum-purple, its crest emblazoned in gold. Its own private bus and taxicabs, which met all trains, were so painted and emblazoned. So were all its servants' uniforms, with gold buttons. How wonderful it was, with its beautiful setting, its majestic facade, its luxurious interior with its open terraces, dining rooms, commodious rooms, and a swimming pool whose water was purified by ultra-violet rays!

Madame Jones' parlor with its rubber plant in Cripple Creek, the Palace Hotel, Finn's Folly, were nothing compared to this! All of Cripple Creek's gold had built nothing like it. Times were changing. The perpetual, ever-flowing, constantly changing stream of time. That was what March read in the changing aspect of Little London, in the faces swarming before him on the station platform only to vanish a moment later.

But there came a moment when time stood still, and he stood looking at its unmoving core, remembering his father, the feather, the flower, the drum, and the mirror of the old gods who never die.

4

He saw them one afternoon when Number 11 pulled out, leaving them stranded far down the platform with their bags and bundles. A large group of dark, fat, and dirty Indians, the men wearing ten-gallon Stetsons, ragged trousers and moccasins, the shapeless women wrapped in bright silks. Sullen and bewildered, all squatted under blankets in the blazing summer sun, eating peanuts and bananas.

March watched them with shame and sadness, remembering the proud and arrogant Navajos at Shallow Water. The Indians stared back without moving. And now there began a curious duel, a tug of war, between him and them. "They can't just squat there all day," he thought. "If they want help or to ask directions or something, let 'em yell or wave."

The Indians did neither. They just squatted there, calling him across the tracks with the silent stare of their black, unblinking eyes. Finally March walked over to the undeniable leader of the group, a man big as a hill, dark as new-plowed earth. Inquiringly, March raised both hands to his temples, brushed backward and upward with a light, swift motion in the tribal sign that Cable had taught him signified Osages – "Shave Heads."

Big Hill scowled, "Ho – Hah! – Boy knowin' somethin'. Humph!"

"Where you goin'?" March demanded.

The men around Big Hill found their voices. "Eat. Sleep. Smellin' good air. Drinkin' good water. We goin' somewhere!" Out of their pockets they pulled rolls of bills big enough to choke a cow. Off his, Big Hill peeled a thousand dollars which he handed to March. "Good place! We goin' now!"

March grinned. "Yes sir! Let's go!"

Loading them with all their bags and bundles, rolls of blankets, a stalk of bananas and a case of soda pop, into two yellow tourist Cadillacs and an old red Hudson, he drove them to the Antlers Hotel. The supercilious clerk looked them over, then down at the thousand dollars March laid on the desk, and called the manager.

"Oil-rich Osages from Oklahoma, eh?" he asked. "We're full, but I can let them have the Presidential suite and the bridal suite."

When they were safely installed, March returned to work. But only to be met by a worried Big Hill a few hours later. Their spring had gone dry, he complained. Taking a taxi to the hotel, March discovered the cause of their trouble. They had been drinking out of the toilet bowl, their "spring," which was now empty. He explained its purpose, showed them how to turn on the faucets for water, and returned to the station.

The following day the chief came back. His people were tired of being cooped up in the hotel. "Good air. Good water. Grass. Trees. You find 'em, eh?" He pressed a dollar bill into the boy's hand.

"No!" said March. "No good!"

Big Hill promptly handed out his whole roll. From it March peeled off another thousand dollars. And now in Hanlon's tourist car with a real estate agent, they toured Little London for suitable accomodations. The place they found was a beautiful estate in Broadmoor with a huge lawn threaded by a stream. Here the Osages settled for the summer, learning how to turn on the electric lights and cook on gas, but sleeping under the trees on their blankets.

Occasionally Hanlon drove them to see the sights, their favorite ride being the sunrise trip to the summit of Pike's Peak. And every week or so Big Hill came after March to spend the evening. Over a fire in the garden they cooked huge slabs of steak, then to the beat of a drum they did a stomp dance, finally spreading out to sleep under the stars.

In Little London they became a sensation. Hotels, cafes, and stores refused them nothing. Money to the Osages assumed its only real significance. It was merely green paper. Oil had been struck on their homeland and they had been forced to trade their birthrights for headrights, becoming fabulously rich. But what, wondered March, did they buy with the former slow rhythmic tenor of their days, the awareness of their oneness with their earth? Good air, good water, grass, trees—and with these, a blinded vision, atrophied senses, glutted appetites, an ever-fresh inward life stagnating within them, a putrid decay! Like Indian Poe, like his own father's people, they were lost and alone, restlessly prowling a new America for something they had lost and would not find again.

They oppressed him with a sense of guilt. They annoyed him, irritated him, and laughed at him. And all that summer and the next, when they returned, he kept wondering what drew him back, again and again, to this growing horde of shiftless, ignorant Osages. Big Hill and his band seemed oblivious of their tragedy. Big Hill knew exactly what he was. His rough-hewn face with its jutting big Roman nose paled to anonymity the swarms of transient faces flitting past. His massive body rooted to the earth by his small moccasined feet, he stood like a pillar around which flowed all time and change. Nothing could ever dwindle or change him; he would endure forever. And so to March, caught in the swirling tide of constant change, he loomed up like a monument of something fixed and immutable but which he could not grasp.

March had seen little of Leslie Shane in High School. The family had moved from the top of Bijou Hill to a house in the North End. She was quite popular, becoming a promising dancer who appeared frequently at women's clubs. Now this semester he found her in two of his classes. Sight of her in his geometry class upset him. She had developed quickly. Her small body was strong and firm; her apricot-colored curls glowed like a halo about her pale freckled face; her delicate blue-veined hands were swift in movement. March found it impossible to stand before her in front of the class to prove a theorem on the blackboard with a pointer. Time and again he refused to get up when called.

One day the teacher, a dried-up spinster, held him after class. "March, you have a good, sound mind. Your paper work is excellent. But I won't be dictated to any longer. Unless you get over your bashfulness, or whatever it is, and go to the blackboard like the others when called upon, I shall be forced to fail you at the end of the semester."

"I can't," he replied calmly, with unfounded, unreasonable stubbornness.

Nor did he, even though the teacher failed him as she threatened.

To offset his miserable appearance in the geometry class, he showed off in front of Leslie in their physiography class. The teacher, Mr. Lyle Ross, was a small, wispy-haired, nervously energetic man who reminded March of Rogier with his talk of ancient marine floods and the re-emergence of the earth as the sea retreated, of changing tides and air currents. This was old stuff to March. Already he knew the limestone, sandstone, and granite formations of the region; and brought specimens of ore from Rogier's shop to display.

Wispy, absent-minded Mr. Ross did not restrict himself to books, maps of oceanic currents, U.S. quadrangles, and geology reports. He taught from nature. And so one afternoon the class met at the Busy Corner, rode a streetcar to Adam's Crossing, and walked to a long north-south hogback terminating in an asymmetrical fold where they could see the exposed stratified layers of rock.

"Fossils!" Mr. Ross announced from underneath the umbrella that shielded him from the sun. "Sharks' teeth imbedded in limestone. Let's see how many you can find and dig out with your hammers."

The class spread out to hunt likely spots along the limestone ridge. March and Leslie drifted together as if caught by the same invisible and powerful tide. The sun burned like the heat of an oven; a hawk wheeled overhead; far away sounded the pecking of their companions' little candy hammers. The girl sat quietly before him. She had on a big straw hat, sand-colored with a pinkish weave, to protect her white freckled face from sunburn. The boy worked steadily: cutting away the gray weathered top rock with Rogier's small miner's hammer to expose a small dark speck imbedded in the limestone.

"You've got to be careful," he said, conscious of the steady communion between them. "Sharks' teeth are small and brittle and liable to break." How beautiful she was with her small stub nose, tiny freckles, and soft warm eyes! He remembered the night he had bashfully caressed her cheek with his thumb before he kissed her. Magically now, the mark emerged upon her cheek: broad at the top over her cheekbone and dwindling away down her soft cheek, like a shark's tooth imbedded in white limestone.

"There it is! You chip it out now!" he directed. "Careful!"

With a slight blow of her hammer she exposed it: a beautifully curved shark's tooth, the point imbedded in limestone.

They laughed together with delight. "It's yours. You dug it out," said March.

"No, it's yours. You discovered it," she insisted.

Facing her, looking into her eyes, he suddenly grasped her fine, blue-veined hand. "You're runnin' around with that Cecil James and his crowd."

"He lives near us, he's got a car, and he takes me to dances and parties, March."

He knew now, as every child knows, the tragedy of youth: of mature emotions and longings balked by years of development and attainment that could not be hastened, a barrier that could not be broken through.

"I don't belong to a society. I don't have a car. And besides, I'm too busy at the station for that stuff," he said straightforwardly, without bitterness. "That's the way it is, I guess. But it makes no difference."

Leslie knew it too. Gazing steadily into his eyes, she said just as calmly. "Yes, that's the way it is. But it makes no difference to me, either."

Far up the ridge Mr. Ross was calling. "Fossil hunters! Shark tooth diggers! Boys and girls, one and all! Gather here!"

March and Leslie got up and walked sedately toward him.

A few weeks later she vanished. Shane had sold out his cafe and moved his family away from town—to where, March never learned. He never saw her again.

He also lost Will Hapsworth's friendship. Will had got a job in the "The Boys" haberdashery, sweeping out the store in the morning and selling neckties after school. Immediately he blossomed out in a new two-button, pinch-back suit, striped silk shirts, and brocade ties. Continuing to ingratiate himself with the Delphian Society, he was admitted as a member. His rise to glory was rapid. He brought trade to "The Boys" which promptly made him a clerk; and he in turn became the store's fashion model with his lavish spending. He developed a passion for jewelry, and successively bought a synthetic ruby ring, a tie-clasp mounted with seed pearls, and a silver belt buckle on which was engraven his monogram. Assuming the nonchalant and sophisticated ease of manner of a young-man-about-town, he seemed years removed from March. The two now seldom met. But that winter Will stopped March in the hall.

"You're going to the big school dance at the Antler's Saturday, aren't you? Some of the Delph Boys are taking me in their car. But you show up with your girl, and I'll slide you in our party afterward. Eh?" He winked. "You got to get in with the right people to get along, you know."

March had no girl. He decided to take Leona who had just entered high school. They both were excited, having never been to a dance in the great hotel. Ona, working feverishly, made up a dark brown wool dress for the girl—a simple school dress square cut at the neck and with an embroidered girdle of green yarn.

"It's not quite the thing," she sighed, "but we can't have a fancy party dress now. And besides, you're just a little girl yet."

When March gave Leona four dollars to buy a brown velvet hat with a green feather, her joy knew no bounds. Like Cable, she lived only in the moment, utterly un-selfconscious.

"Now remember," he told her condescendingly, "I'm going on a private party with Will afterward. So don't squawk when we bring you right home from the dance."

Saturday evening after supper they polished their shoes, dressed up, and walked uptown. A wet snow was falling; through it the lights of the hotel, blocking the end of the avenue, glowed softly, warmly. A long line of cars was drawn up at the entrance, disgorging guests. March suffered a pang of shame that he and Leona were walking. Inside the lobby he was more embarrassed. Groups of schoolmates congregated in corners, chatted on lounges, but to his anxious and appealing looks they seemed blind.

He shook loose Leona's arm and took off her coat. "Keep your hat on, it's more grown up," he muttered savagely. "And don't gawk like a ninny!"

After an intolerable wait, they followed the groups downstairs to the ballroom. It was already crowded and in the forefront stood Will with his party. Nervously March walked up to him.

"Why hello, March! What brought you here on such a stormy night? Or rather, what little damsel brought you?"

March reached for Leona's arm and hauled her forward.

"Will!" she exclaimed spontaneously. "How nice you look in that new suit. And how lovely this place is! Do they call it the Rose Room because of the pink walls? And are those the curtains Lon Chaney decorated? It's just like I heard about!"

To Leona's childish exuberance, her sparkling eyes, and rapt face, the group gave a stony indifference. Will fumbled his watch chain, wiped his face with a flourish of his silk handkerchief, and finally mumbled introductions. A boy or two offered a curt "Hello." But Will's partner—the reigning belle of school—set the tone of response. A dreary silence.

Leona did not notice it for looking at the young lady's dress. "What a pretty party dress! All silver! And silver slippers to match, too!"

The young lady arched her eyebrows and backed away. "Really!" she said. Then languidly taking Will's arm, she led him away, followed by the group.

The encounter awoke March to the fact that almost every girl there wore flimsy white, pink, or blue party dresses beside which Leona's plain woolen dress, hat, and brown face seemed suddenly to have sprouted with all the homely familiarity and fresh vigor of the earth itself.

"Take off that hat!" he muttered savagely to Leona. "Can't you see nobody's wearin' hats! And while I'm checking it, wipe off your shoes. They're wet."

"I like my hat. You bought it for me. And I'm going to wear it!" She was a Cable talking to a Rogier, and he could do nothing about it.

The music began. " 'The Beautiful Blue Danube', Brother! This is the way it ought to sound on our phonograph. Oh, I wish Nancy could hear the orchestra too – You can dance this! It's a waltz. But be careful when you turn, you know."

She was small, light, an excellent dancer, and seemed surcharged now with an incandescent joyousness and aliveness. March trudged around the floor with her, his body stiff, his face set in a dark impassive mask. For Will never came up to ask her for a dance.

"The bastard! You taught him how to dance, too!"

Nor did anyone else ask her to dance, or come up to chat with them during intermissions. If this were required or customary, Leona didn't notice it. Questions, ejaculations – "Look at that beautiful girl! Her hair's like gold!" – sly pinches of his arm, her low light laugh – life and enjoyment flowed from her in a bubbling stream. And when at midnight they walked upstairs for their coats, she gripped his arm. "It's been the first dance and best time I ever had, Brother! I hate to leave!"

And he – sullen, shamed, flooded by anger – he too was as much Cable as Rogier. They walked out of the lobby. The snow had left a blanket on the street; the moon was out; the stars gleamed sharp as glass. "I'm glad you wore that hat. Just a match for that brown dress of Mother's. It made those cheesecloth dresses look cheap and flimsy," he said. "Now what do you say, let's stop at one-armed Alex's and get us a hamburger with chile and beans?"

March never had anything to do with Will after that.

Big Hill and the Osages, the loss of Leslie Shane and Will, his obvious failure at high school, all contributed to his delinquency. Abruptly he quit school without saying anything to Ona or to the school authorities, and spent all day at the railroad station. Not until two months later did the Station Master tell him that Mr. Ford wanted to see him.

March walked up the stairs and into the office warily. Mr. Ford was the local agent of the Sante Fe Railroad, managing all its activities and property in Little London. He was a short, rather stout, and benign man who was sitting leisurely at his seldom occupied desk. Across from him sat a truant officer from the school board.

There were no preliminaries. "March," said Mr. Ford, "the

truant officer here tells me you have quit school and are spending all your time here as a Red Cap."

"I'm done with school. I'm going to be a Railroad Man," answered March.

"A laudable goal," answered Mr. Ford. "The Santa Fe needs men with your calibre and ambition. But only after you have satisfied the legal requirements of the school board. March, I'm afraid you've got to go back and finish school."

"Mr. Ford, you can't fire me!" March said boldly. "I'm not on the Sante Fe payroll. All I make is tips."

Mr. Ford looked disconsolate. He uncrossed his legs, smoothed the creases in his trousers. "How right you are. True, so true." Then looking up, he said softly, "There is only one thing I can do. As the Agent of the Santa Fe Railroad, I must forbid you on the property of the Santa Fe for the purpose of gainful occupation."

"Mr. Ford! You couldn't! You can't!"

"I've known you a long time, March. I would like to see you continue in your work till you are old enough to take an official job. But only part-time until you finish the schooling required of you. Do you understand?"

Ona, when March reached home, was in a torrential rage. "So all this time you've been playing hooky! The truant officer told me. Sliding out of the house every morning, staying away all day, while I thought you were in school. Lying, cheating, losing a whole semester!"

"I didn't say I wasn't going to school! I didn't say anything!"

"Don't give me that!" she shouted. "I know your secretiveness. That goddamned Indian business of keeping a straight face and saying nothing. And those dirty, filthy-rich Osages haven't done anything to help it. You'd quit school, give up your chance at an education, being a successful businessman. Now, March, when I'm about to die and leave you as the whole support of Leona and Nancy—God Almighty, son, you're all we got left to carry on! I ought to horsewhip you. And I'm only asking you to show mercy to those who'll depend on you after I'm gone!"

It was a disgraceful scene March left disgusted. But an hour later he went up to the Third Floor to confront her again. "All that talk of dyin'. What'd you mean?" he demanded.

For answer she tore open the bodice of her gingham dress. There on the upper part of her breast, just under the shoulder blade, was a hard red swelling. "That's a breast cancer, March," she said calmly now. "I don't have much time left."

"What's the doctor say?"

She gave him a derisive look. "I didn't ask. We can't afford a hospital, one operation after another as it keeps spreading. No! I've tried ointments, applications, massages. Nothing helps."

And now suddenly compassion gripped him for this incomprehensible woman who happened to be his mother. He could see her washing, mending, cleaning, cooking all day for three children and two failing old people, and saying nothing. And he could see her lying in bed night after night, grim-lipped and silent, feeling that horrible growing lump, and trying to hold back her mounting fear. While he, all these months, was playing hooky from school—and her approaching end.

"Mother!" He dropped to his knees before her and burst into tears. "I didn't know. You can't die! What would we do without you?"

She calmly stroked his head. "Now not a word to anyone, March. Maybe there's a way to do something."

Several days later they walked uptown and boarded a westbound streetcar. Ona in her neat but shabby clothes wore on her square-jawed face a look of determined composure. March beside her squirmed uneasily, staring out at the tawdry buildings and whorehouses of the West Side. Ona patted his hand. "You know, I always liked this ride. 'Member when we all used to ride out this way to Manitou for Sunday picnics in the mountains?"

At Colorado City they got off and trudged to a dilapidated brick building. The doctor's office was up a flight of dusty, creaky stairs. It was crowded with workmen in overalls, shabby housewives, and dirty children. The doctor, they had learned, tended to most of the mill workers, was honest and cheap—and March had the five dollar fee for his examination of Ona. After an hour's wait Ona's turn came. She stood up, thrust a tattered magazine into his hands. "Read the jokes in this. They're real funny. And son, remember that whatever happens is the Lord's will."

A half-hour passed. Then another. Finally she came out, white-faced and shaken. Hand in hand they walked to the corner, boarded a streetcar. Ona, sitting next to the window, began to shake. From this tremor erupted a heart-rending sob. She bent over, stuffing a handkerchief into her mouth, and began an uncontrollable weeping. "I'm going to live! I'm not going to die! It's not malignant, he's sure. He'll treat me or cut it out for twenty dollars."

A fire sprang up within the boy, melting his insides, eating at his brain. Still he sat beside her with a dark, impassive face. The woman flung around, her eyes streaming tears, and gripped his shoulders with hands of steel. "Do you hear me? I'm not going to die! I'm going to live to take care of Granny and watch Granddad build his greenhouse – live to raise Leona and Nancy! Live son, and see you grow into a successful businessman your father would be proud of! Dear sweet God! He's goin' to let me live!"

It was late afternoon. At every stop more mill workers got on. The aisle was crowded with standing passengers. All listening to the hysterical shrieks and sobs of a shabbily dressed woman. "For Pete's sake, mama!" hissed March. "Stop it!"

Ona reared erect, smeared her face with a wet hanky. "For Pete's sake yourself, March! If you don't cut out all your tomfoolery, and help Daddy build his greenhouse, I'm goin' to horsewhip the hide off your bones!"

5

Building a greenhouse by himself was hard work for a man in his late seventies, even though he had been an apprentice, a journeyman, and then a master carpenter in his younger days. There were stout corner posts to anchor, timber wall frames to be squared, glass window frames to be fitted, a door installed. Rogier persisted, with little help from March.

One would have thought that with an enormous shop so completely fitted out any master carpenter would have enjoyed it, the boy would develop into a craftsman. But March had no bent for carpentry. He couldn't drive a nail straight. He was too scatterbrained. So after an hour's work, Rogier dismissed him. "That's fine. You can take off now, son. But if I were you, I'd sneak out the alley. Your mother's a sharp timekeeper, you know."

As the boy gratefully laid down his hammer or saw, Rogier would add, "How about some tenpenny nails? I'm plumb out."

"Sure! I'll buy 'em, Granddad!" And the boy would clamber over the alley fence.

After a time the old man would lay aside his own tools and turn to the Peak watching his indomitable efforts with compassionate understanding. They were great friends again. Rogier had forgiven it for blocking his impassioned search after years of toil. His failure had been his own fault. His human pride, engendered by propensities born in him for generations, had played him false. He had been led astray by the tantalizing promise of mere gold—thrown off balance by the entrancing splendor of the Cresson Vug. And he had paid his debt. Now at last he was consecrated as he had been at first, to the pure and immortal sacredness of his mortal calling.

Winter stopped his work. He couldn't stay in the barny shop while mapping out his campaign; it cost too much to heat. Nor could he spend the evenings in the house. How could he compose his soul in tranquility to the squeak of Mrs. Rogier's rocker or plumb the depths of spirit in a nest of chattering magpies? So after supper he would stamp down into the basement, slamming the kitchen door behind him.

It was a great, warm, clean room. In the far corner sat the unused carbide lighting plant. Next to it was the small wine cellar of more opulent days, empty now save for a few jars of jams and jellies. At the other end was the coal bin filled from the driveway and shut off from the rest of the basement by a plank door. In the center bulked the massive furnace. Through its small door-panes the roaring flames cast a rosy warm glow upon the clean cement floor and walls of rough square-hewn rock.

Something about the room reminded him of a stope deep below grass roots. He would light his candle. It hung to the wall in his old-fashioned miner's candlestick—the simple and ingenious tool which could be thrust into a crevice like an ice pick, hung from an edge like a hook, or set on a level plane. In its glow he sat musing in a chair drawn up before the furnace.

"The Sylvanite was a dud, like the Magpie and all the others before it," he would mutter to himself. "I should have had better sense. 'Whoever needs the earth shall have the earth.' And this time I'm drivin' straight in as soon as I get that lettuce house built."

One cold winter evening when he stamped downstairs, he saw a man sitting in his chair in front of the furnace. The man rose instantly. "Am I taking your chair, sir?"

"Humm. Didn't know you were here. Who let you in?"

"No one, sir. I came down through the coal bin from outside to toast my toes. In fact, I'm toasting my supper too." He nudged with his toe a potato baking under the furnace.

"Humm," Rogier muttered again. "I allow a little bread and jam might go with it." He trudged upstairs and back again, settling on another chair beside his visitor.

The guest slept all night in the basement and was invited upstairs for breakfast. "What are you having?" he asked Leona.

"Shredded Wheat with sliced bananas!" she replied promptly.

"My favorite breakfast!" he replied, sitting down beside her.

There grew up between them a warm intimacy during his two-day visit. The man, slightly built, middle-aged, with uncut sandy hair, was a professional railroad tramp. Year after year he crossed and re-crossed the continent, riding the rods or the blinds, sleeping in off-track jungles with his fellows, splitting wood here and there for a meal. It was a great profession of which he was proud. Every top-notch tramp had his own mark or sign which he inscribed on railroad trestles and the walls of freight stations. The greatest of these tramps was the man whose mark was "A-1." The Rogier guest once had raced him across the continent from New York to San Francisco, losing by only a few hours. Leona related these facts with pride.

"Stop it!" Mrs. Rogier commanded her. "Why, a tramp's liable to cut our throats while we're asleep. What's his precious sign? And pray tell, what's his name?"

Leona shrugged. "You have to be a professional tramp to know his mark. And his name – why, it's 'Shredded Wheat!' He said so!"

Every few months Shredded Wheat would appear, sleeping in the basement or in the shop, then disappearing suddenly as he had come. Leona loved him, making sure he had Shredded Wheat with bananas, wild strawberries, or raspberries every summer morning for breakfast. Everyone else in the family liked him and saved old clothes for him. Rogier especially would permit no criticism of him or his professional career. "Every man's huntin' for somethin' or got some kind of a quirk, I don't care who he is. If every one of us thought just the same, this world would be a mighty dull place to live in!"

Mary Ann returned home. The whole family sighed when she walked in the house that evening, unannounced, with still another gentleman friend. Yet there was a glint in her eyes revealing that this time she meant business. Pulling him into the aura of lamplight, she announced curtly, "This is John, my husband. We were married last week. I know you will all love him. We're going to move in with you and be one happy family together."

John nodded shyly and sat down to table. Unlike big, robust Jim or Sam, he was a rather frail-looking, middle-aged man with graying hair and a gentle sensitive face. Within a few minutes his overwhelming shyness became evident; he didn't talk and could hardly eat.

It was just as evident that Mary Ann could handle all situations. Always brisk and aggressive, she now had a sharp edge honed by adversity. After opening one Chocolate Shoppe after another throughout the mining towns of the Colorado Rockies, all failures perhaps abetted by her shiftless gentlemen friends, she suddenly had come into focus.

"Mining is a bust. The ore's all played out. Mines are closing, camps are shutting down, towns are dwindling. How foolish I was to chase that will-of-the-wisp when home right here is the center of the biggest money-making industry in history!" Pausing to let this conclusion sink in, she continued briskly. "I mean the Pike's Peak Region is drawing more people than the Pike's Peak Rush, Cripple Creek, and all the rest of them put together. Tourists from all over the world. With pocketsfull of money! And so I'm—John and me—are opening a Chocolate Shoppe right here."

"Where?" asked Ona.

"Manitou. Up Ruxton Creek. The center of the mineral springs. I'll wait trade and keep the books. John's going to learn to make candy and manage the candy kitchen. We sign the lease tomorrow."

Within a week the place was open for business. For a chocolate dipping stone Mary Ann carried off the marble slab that graced the ornate hall tree. More changes came. John's overpowering shyness prevented him from eating at the table with a tribe of strange people around him. He began coming home late from work. When he could be induced to sit down with the family, he fled up to his room with a headache immediately afterward. Mary Ann acted promptly. She fitted up the second story back room as a kitchen, reserving the middle room as their bedroom.

The Rogiers downstairs grumbled and stormed at the smell of

cooking above. "A housekeeping apartment in our home!" snorted Ona. "We might as well take in roomers, too!"

Mrs. Rogier sniffled in her hanky.

As the months wore on, their resentment died down. John was a hard worker who soon became adept as a maker of fine candies of every description. He brought home to the children almost every night a big box of the batch of pinoche, fudge, nougat, or peanut brittle he had made that day. It vanished instantly. "If you kids weren't half-starved you wouldn't eat so much!" complained Mary Ann. "I swear, you're all sugar drunks!" Shy as John was, he was gentle, patient, and forgiving; and he eventually won over the family. The children began to call him "Uncle John."

And the Chocolate Shoppe was making money.

There was no doubt about it when Mary Ann ordered the house rewired for electricity. Then a team of men showed up with her to measure the living room and dining room, the size of the front windows, and to shake the sofa loose from its broken leg. "The place is so run down and worn out, it's disgraceful! Downright shabby!" she complained. "Those old-fashioned lace curtains are a joke. The rug's been threadbare for years. And look at that tottering sofa. The whole place looks like a shanty of poor white trash. I'm going to freshen it up!"

March, in his last year at high school, had become self-conscious and just as ashamed of the run-down house. With Mary Ann's announcement, a glow of pride suffused him. He could envision a thick Oriental rug on the floor, tasteful draperies at the windows, a modern couch and a few excellent "occasional" chairs, all softly glowing under electric lamps.

Instead, there was laid on the floor stiff, rubberized, imitation rugs made of linoleum with a blatant design of roses. On these was set an array of furniture stiff as iron, shiny as shoe-polish. At the windows were hung curtains screaming with violent purple iris. There were no lamps; a white porcelain lighting fixture was hung from the ceiling.

That evening when Mary Ann came home to proudly survey her "freshening up," all March's outraged sense of good taste, his rejection of vulgarity, erupted. "What do you mean sending down this trash? Our home was shabby and old-fashioned maybe, but in good taste. Now it looks like the parlor of a whorehouse on Myers

Avenue! An imitation rug of linoleum. It would look bad enough in the dark, without those ghastly white lights shinin' on it!"

"Hold on!" interrupted Mary Ann. "Not linoleum. Congoleum. The latest thing. The edges'll soon flatten down! And what, may I ask, do you know of whorehouses on Myers Avenue?"

"The furniture! Grand Rapids veneer. Not even honest wood. Purple flags screaming from the curtains at the roses on the floor. And that picture. It makes me sick at my stomach to walk in here!"

"And who are you, smarty, to put up your nose at your own home?" shouted Mary Ann. "I took down that old landscape over the fireplace because we're all tired of staring at it after fifty years. This print of the Master of Blue with a beautiful Greek temple and a bunch of grapes is his most popular masterpiece. It hangs in the window of every furniture store in town!"

It was a stormy disgraceful row from which March stalked out in fury. "The lad's at an impressionable stage," observed Rogier mildly, not too enthusiastic about Mary Ann's changes himself. Uncle John fled upstairs with a headache. Mrs. Rogier sniffled.

"And this is the thanks I get for trying to improve our happy home!" Mary Ann flounced upstairs.

Ona glanced sharply at Mrs. Rogier. "Mother! Quit sniffling! And make it plain to Mary Ann she's not to do any interior decorating of the Third Floor!" Then she too trudged tiredly up to bed with the two girls in that cavernous attic where she lay feeling the scar on her breast, listening for the steps of the faithful Kadles, and waiting perchance for another appearance of that mysterious, frightening light. Listening too, sleeplessly, for the sound of March's footsteps—that strange son of his strange father whom she loved most and understood least of all the persons given her to meet in her narrow but mysterious life.

Rawlings came to call. "Mr. Rogier—Joe!" He rushed up to his former employer of uncounted years, shook him by the shoulders, gave him a hearty hug. "When I saw you last I thought the game was up. You was in bed, your eyes blank as a hoot owl's, you didn't know me for nothin'. And now I see you sound as a nut, still kickin', hey! Joe!"

"Thought I'd gone crazy or was dyin', or both, hey? You old son-of-a-gun. Finally got up enough backbone to open an office as a building contractor on your own. Well, match this!"

Rogier led him out to see his greenhouse. It was set a safe distance from the house. The building was about the size of an average room, running east to west so that it would get the full swing of the sun by day. On winter nights buckets of hot ashes and coals would keep the plants from freezing. Rawlings looked it over carefully. "Just the thing for a retired businessman, Joe! I'm right proud of you. But that roof's a little out of plumb if I can see straight." He squinted along a timber. "What you need's a couple of two-by-tens or two-by-twelves laid straight and set solid. But what's this?"

He walked to the west end closed off from the rest of the glass room by a wooden partition in which was set a solid door locked by a huge padlock. Over it hung a sign, "Private."

"A tool house or a storage room? Mighty funny in a greenhouse. Why don't you use the big shop in back instead of cluttering up this nice glass buildin'? What's it for, anyway?"

"The sign says 'Private,' " muttered Rogier.

Rawlings shrugged. "Well anyway Joe, I'm goin' to send down a couple of men and a load of timber to help you out."

"Rawlings! I'll build that myself just the way I want it, without your help!" His voice was sharp and decisive.

Rawlings' embarrassment was eased when Ona called him into the house for tea. His hands still horny and his clothes ill-fitting, he grinned at her. "I ain't no Britisher yet, to be drinkin' tea in the middle of the afternoon. Just a plain old American cup of coffee'll suit me fine."

When they had settled down Ona said casually, "Mr. Rawlings, we're all proud of you for getting into business for yourself after all these years. Without your help Daddy could never have finished those last jobs of his. Now I hope you're contracting for some fine big buildings of your own."

"As a matter of fact I ain't, Miss Ona. I'm tearin' down. More money in it." He turned to Rogier. "Yep, Joe. Been up to your old stampin' ground, Cripple Creek." Rogier sat up straight as Rawlings continued. "The whole district's on the toboggan. Hardly 5,000 people up there now. The High Line and Low Line cars ain't runnin' no more. Nobody to ride 'em. The mines are closin' down. And most of the towns – Elkton, Anaconda, Arequa, Mound City – are plumb deserted. And that's where I'm making my money."

"How's that you say?" asked Rogier, a dangerous glint in his eyes.

"Why, it's simple man. Why should contractin' firms in Little London here buy timber from mill yards when there's all kinds of it in Cripple Creek for the takin'—big seasoned timbers from gallows frames, lumber galore from abandoned houses, window frames and doors too. That's what I'm doin'. Runnin' a wreckin' crew instead of a construction crew. And cartin' it all down by truck."

Rogier's face seemed to have turned to stone, a faint pallor showing through his stubble of beard.

"It might surprise you to learn I tore out that stout cribbing you built. The logs was still sound," continued Rawlings. "I even got some good brick from that little hotel in Goldfield."

Rogier leapt to his feet, his face distorted with anger. "Stop it, damn you, Rawlings! I went up there when it was still a barren cowpasture. With my naked hands I helped to build it up, log on log, stone on stone. The very cornerstones of some of those buildings you've torn down carried my name. That earth, that granite, is the soil of my flesh. And now, blast your soul, you come here—in my house—and think to tell me this!"

"Joe!"

"Daddy, please!"

Rogier could not be stopped. "You've betrayed me. Everything I stand for. A man's a builder or a destroyer. And you—I know you now. You've gone rotten. Get out of my home! Keep out of my sight!" he howled, lunging toward his old foreman.

It was all Ona could do to hold him. Rawlings, who had witnessed too many of Rogier's ungovernable rages before his breakdown, fearfully backed away; and with a look of sadness and forgiveness on his mild face, hastily pressed Ona's hand and slipped out the door.

Rogier sank down on a chair, still shaking. Ona stood before him. "Daddy, do you know who that was? Your construction foreman for thirty years or more. Your most loyal and faithful friend."

"Rawlings is the name," Rogier said imperturbably. "A man who's turned traitor. It was high time I found him out."

6

The June when March finally graduated from high school, Boné came home for another visit. The reason for his coming was the "Pike's Peak Carnival." Not for years had the traditional Shan Kive been held, when Buckskin Charlie and his Utes were brought home from their reservation to pitch their lodges on the mesa west of town; when in feathers and buckskins they paraded the street with prospectors, miners, hunters, old pioneers; when a downtown block was roped off for their last night's dance. But with the tremendous influx of tourists it behooved Little London to put on a show of sorts. A few Utes had been brought in. Dressed in dirty blue denims, they disconsolately roamed the streets between iron casts of noble Indian chiefs advertising soda water. Fat-bellied bankers and thin store clerks boasted two-color boots and ten-gallon hats; loyal Rotarians grew beards; society women descended from limousines to shop in sunbonnets and silk plaid dresses; polo ponies sported Western stock saddles.

The grand climax of the carnival was to be a "Pageant of the Past" in the Garden of the Gods. Boné, "our own famous Colorado composer," had been engaged to write the music for it. Boné had not written the family, but the details were fully reported in the *Gazette*. All the Rogiers titillated with excitement and anticipation except March.

He was now almost six feet tall, slim and wiry like his father. He had given up his work as a Red Cap, considering it too menial to accept gratuities, and had been given a job by Mr. Ford as a baggage clerk with a regular salary. The conviction of Will Hapsworth for stealing clothes from "The Boys," and his internment in the reformatory school, had made March suspicious. And his continuing friendship with Big Hill and his Osages inclined him to view the approaching carnival as merely an exploitation to ensnare tourists.

Continuing newspaper reportage of his famous uncle did not allay his doubts. If Boné's first recognition had come with his "Indian Suite" written under Lockhart at Shallow Water, his first success was the lyrical "Song of the Willows." He had then achieved national fame as a song writer with his popular ragtime "Ching, Ching, Chinaman," and "Our Old Family Ghosts." These nonsensical tunes followed by others had recouped the nest egg wheedled from him by Rogier for his mine. During a trip to Europe he had written an opera, a few sonatas, and a string quartette which had been competent enough to give him some small reputation. But they were not popular. And so he had returned to write "Songs from Plain and Prairie," "Tepee Tales," and "Melodies in Red," for which he was best known throughout Europe and America. Perhaps he realized that he had great talent but not greatness; that America's music was not Indian melodies, Negro spirituals, or folk songs; but that these pure and full-throated voices must be absorbed, built up, and combined in one symphonic peal of passionate avowal from the great integrated soul of all America. He had set his heart on such symphonic structure. Yet driven from coast to coast by the economic necessity for concert tours, weakened by ill-health, and consumed by an ambition perhaps too great for his strength, he had relapsed into security. In Oklahoma he had picked up a talented Indian soprano, Princess Bluebird, with whom he was touring the country. For two weeks now they had been appearing in Denver, from where they had been brought to Little London.

Princess Bluebird was an Osage, a half-breed, Big Hill told March at sight of her photograph. But there were no Indian "princesses" among the Osages or any Plains tribes. The beaded headband supporting an eagle feather, which she wore, had been an indication of sacredness or high rank restricted to warriors. Not until recently had it been adopted by women for so-called "Indian Princess" contests sponsored by whites.

Two days before the Pageant they arrived at the house. Hardly had they got out of the taxi before the whole family was on the porch to greet them.

" Boné, my dear boy!"

"Aunt Martha! The finest mother a boy ever had!" Hugging her with one arm, he reached out the other to Rogier. "And Ona!"

"This is Leona and Nancy, Boné. Not little any longer. Do you recognize March, this big man? You've been his inspiration all these years!"

"And my Princess – My family, Bluebird."

Kissed and hugged, they were finally led into the house. March thought he had never seen a woman more beautiful than Princess Bluebird, dressed in full buckskin and beaded moccasins, wearing the band on her dark hair. Boné had changed little, but seemed smaller. He had the round head of a musician, his black hair turning gray above his ears; and the thin, big knuckled hands of a pianist which he began at once to drum on the arm of his chair. March knew he had contracted phthisis – although Boné called it asthma, and was so high strung and nervous it was impossible to hold him on one subject for a full minute. He gave the impression of great talent and assurance, but not the wholesome soundness of a great artist, the strange completeness of a world within himself.

There was so much to talk about, and so little time for it! "We've got to go," Boné said, rising. "The Brown Palace sent me to the Broadmoor. I'm always at the mercy of hotels, you know. Have to make a few changes in the score before the rehearsal tomorrow. You're all coming, of course?"

"We wouldn't miss it for the world." said Ona.

March expected Boné to take or to provide tickets for the family. Instead, he winked as he left. "Come up in back afterwards. It'll help swell the crowd. Tricks in every trade, you know!"

The Rogiers stood on the porch, watching his taxi drive away. The cost of the long drive and keeping it waiting, thought March, would have bought all of their tickets.

Ona was disappointed too, she told March when she drew him aside after supper. "But that doesn't mean we're not all going – except Mary Ann and Uncle John who have to keep their shop open. We'd never forgive ourselves if we didn't."

"At two dollars apiece? Hell with it! Boné's too rattle-brained to think of anybody but himself."

"For shame, March! He's a great artist. Your own uncle, absentminded or not." Her voice grew stern. "You're going to take us out of your Saturday pay check. If need be we can take it out of the grocery money later. But we're going! Understand?"

"Twelve dollars! And how're you going to get there and back? It's too far for Granny and Grandad to walk from the streetcar line. Am I hiring a taxi too?"

"That will arrange itself," she said calmly, putting her arm around him. "He was like yourself once, son. Poor and perplexed, not knowing what the future would hold. Be inspired by what he has achieved – our own Boné. I know you will, son!"

They went, all six of them: Rogier and Mrs. Rogier, Ona and the three children. Their next door neighbor, Kennedy, took them in his car on his way to work in Colorado City; they would have to find their own way home.

They walked into the roped enclosure, spread a blanket on the ground. The summer night was warm and fragrant; the high sandstone cliffs stood out like a painted background behind the raised stage covered with sod and dried grass; off to the side peanut and popcorn stands littered the grounds under flickering gasoline flares.

Nancy's somber face with her drawn left eye twitched into a smile. "It's pretty as a circus. Thank you for bringing us, March!"

"Dom!" said Rogier. "I haven't seen a show for years!"

Their obvious delight in this unusual outing did not melt the hard core of curious resentment within March. He sat sullenly chewing a blade of grass.

The lights went out. There was suddenly a high pitched yell. An Indian brave bounded across the stage in a spotlight, paused with a hand to forehead in the immemorial gesture of all calendar Indians, and leaped behind a piñon. There came a burst of music.

The Pageant of the Past had begun.

It lasted almost two hours and consisted primarily of three processions across the stage: a group of feathered and painted Indians; a covered wagon containing red-shirted miners and their wives; and finally, with a screech of a fire siren, a train, painted on a screen, propelled across the stage.

Each of the processions stopped on the stage for its act. The Indians deplored the vanishing game; made a treaty with an Explorer; and finally sang a dirge to the Great Spirit lamenting the Passing of the Red Man.

In Act Two some of them came back and tomahawked a woman who fell across a wagon tongue, showing a beautiful silk-stockinged leg. But the miners struck pay dirt – a nugget big as a fist. "Pike's Peak or Bust!" they shouted. "By God, boys, we got the Ransom of an Empire!"

The third act portrayed "The Founding of the West – The Dawn of the Future." From the painted train poured the Empire Builders. They hammered on anvils, revolved spinning wheels, hoisted cardboard masonry into high walls; and eventually Little London was wheeled into view, painted on a beaverboard screen with Pike's Peak in the background. The West Was Won!

"But to us in the future," a frock-coated orator recited to soft music, "this legacy of beauty and courage must forever be our bulwark. Let us not forget the unlettered but noble Pioneer Fathers who opened the gates of this free and unsullied America. Let us lift our eyes unto the hills, and be ever renewed by the pure and serene mountains, the cloudless skies of Colorado" –

Finale. "The Red Rock Garden March." Writer, composer, singer, actors on the platform. Then the pudgy, tuxedoed Little Londoner who had promised to make up any deficit in the budget.

It was a ghastly travesty: colorful but empty, all form and no substance, expensively produced but cheap and sentimental. March sat through it appalled, listening to the tremendous applause with bewilderment. Those miners in squeaky new cowboy boots! That gold nugget! March knew nothing of music, but it seemed to him that Boné's was but little better than its vehicle. Only Princess Bluebird's clear soprano lifted a few songs out of their uninspired melodies. The short prelude he liked, and in the "Red Rock Garden March" he felt the youthful vigor he remembered in Boné. For the rest, it was a dull accompaniment. He got up at the end feeling done out of twelve dollars.

"Brother! Wasn't those colored lights pretty at the end? Red, white, and blue! And did you see the Indian waving the American flag?"

"We've got to go down and congratulate Boné," persisted Nancy. "He told us to. He did!"

They walked up to the edge of the crowd around Boné. He was dressed up, his cheeks were rouged, he was laughing and shaking hands.

"A marvellous touch, sir! I recognized your hands at the piano!"

"Authenticity in every note – so – so commanding! Our foremost native composer. He lived his early life among the savages, I hear."

"The scope, the vastness – the sweep of history, I mean. I tell you drama here is just emerging." –

There was no getting to him. March herded his little flock out of the enclosure to the road. It was impossible for the two elderly Rogiers to walk two miles in the dark to the streetcar line. Nor was there a taxi in sight. Standing at the edge of the road, beclouded with swirling dust, March yapped angrily, "I told you, Mother –"

At that instant there sounded a high-pitched yell as a Cadillac limousine stopped beside them. Out of it leaned Big Hill. "Boy walkin'. No good! Ridin' better!"

"I've got my family!" March shouted back.

Big Hill imperiously waved his hand toward the car in back. It was Hanlon's tourist car with still more Osages, and in back of it was still another. Big Hill was in no hurry. Keeping the long line of cars waiting, he moved Osages from car to car to make room for his new passengers. Leona and Nancy were put in one, Ona in another, and March with his grandparents in Big Hill's limousine. It was a little crowded, of course; Mrs. Rogier had to sit on the lap of a blanketed gentleman three times her size.

"Mr. Hill," she exclaimed. "Your Indian Princess was beautiful! She sang like a bird!"

"Bluebird. Good song."

"And it was my boy who wrote the music, Mr. Hill."

"Good boy."

Big Hill was in high humor. His broad face and great body exuded pleasure, contentment, and approval. "Good show! Seven shots shootin' from a six-gun. I count 'em. Ai. Ai. Some gun!" There was nothing ironic in his acute observation. He was as pleasurably excited by the performance as were the Rogiers.

If it seemed his driver was taking the Rogiers the long way home, they were more surprised when the limousine rolled into the driveway of Big Hill's house. "But Mr. Hill," began Mrs. Rogier. Imperiously he waved them across the lawn to a barbecue pit where a huge chunk of beef was roasting. Two Osage women took it off, throwing on the fire armloads of fresh wood. A man came out of the house with a suspiciously-shaped bottle and a box of tin cups which he set on wooden table.

"Mr. Hill! Meat at midnight! Why!" Mrs. Rogier was more shocked at the size of that mammoth roast.

"Good meat. Eat 'em anytime. We dancin' first," answered their host.

The stomp dance around the fire began, one Osage at a time flinging off his blanket or shawl and moving into the circle. The big men lifting their knees high, bending low, then jerking erect, eyes to the sky. The women hardly raising their feet, dancing demurely but in perfect rhythm.

Another car rolled up. Out of it jumped Princess Bluebird, still in costume, to join in. "Boy sick?" asked Big Hill. March got up and moved into the circle. Then Leona. The Princess grabbed Nancy by the hand. "Come on, honey! Use your hips, not your feet!"

At last Big Hill sank down on the grass beside Rogier. "Good time! We eatin' now!"

"Dom!" said Rogier. "I'm hungry!"

They all ate, sitting on the grass in the light of the leaping flames. Paper plates filled with thick slices of roast beef and chunks of bread. Tin cups of strong black coffee. Apples and bananas. Mrs. Rogier began to figit. "Why, it must be almost two o'clock in the morning!"

"Catchin' train?" Big Hill inquired. "Got all night, all mornin'." But finally he sent them home with his driver.

When had all the family been out together? Long after Big Hill's hired car had taken them home, they laughed and prattled about the Pageant and Big Hill's party; Ona could hardly get them off to bed. March, who worked the morning shift from three o'clock till noon, stayed up. He dressed in his work clothes, laid out his bowl of cold breakfast cereal. Then he made a cup of coffee and carried it out on the porch.

He was not aware of a taxi slowly cruising down the street, lights out, until it had stopped in front. Then he noticed a man sitting on the running board. He rose as March walked toward him. It was Boné. His breath smelled faintly of whisky. "What're you doing here this time of night?" demanded March.

"Big reception at the Broadmoor. Bluebird skipped out early to hunt up some Osages nearby. These Indians! Wanted to take you all to the reception, but you didn't come up on stage. You saw the show?"

"Of course. An went up to see you, but you were too busy."

"My God, boy!" The man shook him by the shoulders. "Never too busy for all of you. Damnation! I've spanked your little bottom, March. This is my home. I couldn't leave it – for years perhaps – without one more look at it. Why, I remember Sister Molly's old elm, when Shook's Run had a wooden bridge –"

"Ssh!" cautioned March. "You'll wake up Mother and the girls."

They sat down on the grass in front of the dark waiting taxi.

"You liked the Pageant?" inquired Boné.

March hesitated a moment. "No! It was cheap and trashy, something a real artist wouldn't have stooped to. No! It was a tinhorn show!"

Boné hiccoughed. "Boy! You're bitter and intolerant, and it takes the sting out of the little truth in your words. Do you think every composer is a Beethoven, every pianist a Liszt? Oh, you're so young, so idealistic!"

He moistened his hands on the damp grass and wiped his face. "Don't you realize, you young fool, we musicians have to live? How do you suppose I make my money – on my best work? Hah! By being a monkey at the piano in Chicago, New York, Denver, Oshkosh! By dressing in Indian feathers in Vienna and Stockholm. By writing scores like this tonight. It took me only two days! March, forget it. Before long you'll be up against the same problem. Then you'll remember your uncle more charitably. You'll think of the old days at Shallow Water. And we'll have a good laugh together, eh!"

He leaned forward, flung his arms around the boy, stooped to kiss him on the cheek. At that instant it happened – a sudden fright and revulsion whose cause March could not explain. But whatever it was, Boné's rouged cheeks, delicate hands, and effeminate sensitiveness immediately translated March's feelings into action. Roughly he pushed Boné away. "Don't you ever lay your hands on me again!"

Boné recoiled as if struck. A tear rolled down his cheek. "March!"

The boy rose. "Three o'clock. Time for me to go to work." He strode quickly down the street.

At noon when he returned home, the family was bubbling with excitement. Boné last night had sneaked into the house, slept on the sofa, and taken breakfast with them. He had bought all kinds of good things at the grocery store and given each of them a souvenir program. "The kind that cost a dollar!" said Nancy. "And he wrote something on them for us too, about our being the inspiration for the 'Red Rock Garden March'!"

The big surprise came when Ona took March upstairs and showed him a check for $100 that Boné had left before he drove back to Denver. "For you, son. To start to college on. It'll pay for the first semester's tuition, and if you make good, he'll send more!"

And now the talk began, lengthening into days and weeks; a wrangle in which every member of the family participated. March had no intention of going to college; he hated school. He wanted to be a Railroad Man, and already he had a job. But everyone insisted: Rogier in his baggy trousers, Mary Ann and Uncle John, Ona, even the two girls. What were they, wondered March: a tribunal, a group of seers laying out his life, assuming the prerogative of God and Chance, or merely one of a million families striving in ignorance, poverty, and pride to advance a son one step farther than any of them had taken?

"No Rogier has ever been to college," added Mrs. Rogier. "All you have to do is go one day to set a new record for the family."

Reluctantly March walked up to the registrar to find out if he could meet the entrance requirements. Despite his poor high school grades, he was allowed to register and given a catalogue of the courses offered. To Ona it was the menu of a delectable feast over whose *entrees* she smacked her lips. "Medieval European history – Greek drama – Calculus – Political science! Me, oh my!" But if all the plums of the world's knowledge lay at her boy's feet, she was childish and shrewd enough to see that he picked up the right ones. Doctor, Merchant, Lawyer, Chief: what career was he to follow?

The college offered three basic curricula: classics with a major in Latin and Greek, business administration and banking, and science. It was obvious to Ona that March was not cut out for a Professor of Greek. "Business, banking, finance. That's the thing for nowadays! You have to be a business man, March, in any line."

Rogier objected. "Why stuff that down the boy's gullet? Business is money-grubbin', pinchin' pennies, figurin' how to skin your neighbor before he skins you. Call it Economics, Business Law, or anything else, that's all it is. By Jove, he ought to take engineerin' and learn somethin' about his own earth and Natural Laws!"

The disgraceful scene that followed brought out at last Ona's resentment of a lifetime and the family's secret grudge against Rogier for his failure to strike it rich. She jumped to her feet, hands clenched, shouting. "Stop it! I know what you mean by engineering – mining! My boy won't be saddled with your crazy ideas. I won't have him ruined like Tom, Jonathan, you and all the rest! I tell you, I won't!" She flung around to face March. "You're going to take Business or I'm going to tear up this check!"

March trudged back to the campus, miserable and confused. Here he signed up for the four subjects required of every freshman. The family's mighty discussions had come to nought. And in September, on Boné's $100, he entered college.

7

Rogier's greenhouse was finished, a tolerable job of which the family was proud. On each side of the center aisle were banks and shelves and boxes of growing green: not only crinkly leaves of "pickin" lettuce, but onions and chives and herbs, and potted flowers of every kind. None of the family questioned the windowless plank room adjoining it on the west end, undoubtedly a tool house. The stout door, locked with a big padlock and marked "Private," was enough to proclaim it one of Rogier's foibles.

That the old man was working himself to the bone was evident. All day long he was outdoors or in the greenhouse: digging fresh earth, weeding, nursing, and in the winter carrying out coals and hot ashes to keep his plants from freezing at night. He was thin and shrunken, a mere skeleton inside his baggy trousers and sagging coat. But the family rejoiced. He had found something peaceful to do. His spells were less frequent. He ate heartily, slept soundly at night, and he had developed a peculiar humor.

It was the custom of Mrs. Pyle next door to whistle from the back door whenever she wanted Pyle. He then tripped to the house in a ludicrously dainty fashion from the yard. Leona and Nancy for fun often whistled for Roger to come to dinner. He would grin slyly, spread his arms, rise on his toes, and come prancing down the back walk in imitation of Pyle – and often under his very eyes.

Yet Ona began to grow suspicious. He insisted on emptying the ashes from the furnace and fireplace without March's help, lugging bucketsful out to the alley. Even in the winter he spent hours locked within the closed tool house at the end of the greenhouse. And during the evenings he sat down in the basement in front of the furnace, his miners' candle flickering on a scratch pad upon his knee.

"Daddy's up to something!" Ona exploded one evening to Mrs. Rogier. "What in God's name is it?"

"All that Cripple Creek business is out of his mind. Rawlings put the kibosh on that," Mrs. Rogier answered smugly. "Let him alone."

Downstairs in the basement, Rogier continued to figure the obstacles and advantages of the tremendous plan that had leaped into his mind, full grown. Up in Cripple Creek, at the Sylvanite, he had begun work at an elevation of almost 11,000 feet. He had sunk his shaft to five levels through solid granite in his prolonged effort to bore into the very heart of the Peak. He was wise enough to realize that a man's failure is due to causes hidden within himself rather than to outward circumstances. Yet despite these intangible factors in the mysterious equation of a man's fate, he knew that mere lack of money had stopped him from driving deeper. There was no need to recall the details of his abysmal failure.

No, by Jove! Not when his new plan illuminated success with all the bright glory of a promise fulfilled at last. Here in Little London he was at an elevation of only 6,000 feet – a mile below the collar of the Sylvanite. What a head start! He had only to dig a lateral tunnel into the base of the Peak to achieve his objective.

He was quite sensible. There were great difficulties. The base of the Peak was six miles away, a long distance for one man his age to dig. He would have to bore underneath Little London and Colorado City; there were water mains, sewage pipes, and underground conduits to avoid. And above all, he must preserve utmost secrecy.

Yet the advantages were reasonably greater. The tunnel would not have to be too deep – a mere fifty feet; and what was that to a hard-rock man! Moreover, the ground rose swiftly, and by maintaining the same level he would gradually be sinking. The farther he got, the firmer the earth – gravel, shale, sandstone; he would not need cribbing. In any case, the digging on an average would be neglible compared to driving through solid granite.

Scratching away with his pencil in the flickering light of the candle above him, Rogier compared the vertical and horizontal approaches to the glowing golden heart of the Peak. Driving a mile straight down from the portal of the Sylvanite through hard granite at a cost of $40 a foot or more, would have cost him dom near a quarter-million dollars – a fortune he never could have made from the profits on his contracting business. But a lateral tunnel, while six times longer, would have to be dug only through soft earth at little expense. A man could do it with a pick and shovel, given time. And when it was finished – Rogier could have let out a shout of triumph! He would be 5,000 feet below the Sylvanite. Three thousand feet below the bottom of the district's mines and the thousands of men working above. Rogier laughed and slapped his leg. What would Cripple Creek stockbrokers and mining engineers think, the townspeople of Little London, when they found he'd burrowed beneath them! And Pyle, the sanctimonious hypocrite! He'd never guess what had gone on under his very nose.

For then, after years of toil and frustration, after a lifetime of devout concentration, Rogier would feel like Atlas the weight of the mighty snow-covered Peak above him; hear the breathing pulse and rhythmic throb of the great heart of the continent. And suddenly, with one last stroke of his pick, he would break through to the brightness and the glory, the incandescent mystery of that secret and immortal Self which had forever hovered in his mind like something risen from the depths of dreamless sleep to the horizon of wakeful consciousness.

Elated and disturbed, Rogier climbed upstairs and walked out into the snowy back garden. It was nearly midnight. The moon was in its first quarter. In its glow the Peak stood clear in the cloudless sky. Rogier stared at it a long time. Something between them still remained unresolved, friends and enemies though they had been; but this time, old as they both had grown, their synonymity would be established.

March was too relieved to get out of helping Rogier empty ashes to notice how often the old man trudged with his loads to the ash pit in the alley. One afternoon when he was in the shop, the dump man called to him. "What's goin' on here, son? I'm gittin' mighty tired of emptying this pit of yours so often. Half of it's dirt. Not ashes."

"Can't you see we've got a greenhouse?" March answered just as testily. "Dirt's got to be changed!"

Promptly he forgot the incident; he had his own troubles.

Already disgruntled, he found his first year at college a continual horror of disillusionment. Little London's college since its founding had been "A New England Seat of Learning Nestled in the Shadow of Pike's Peak." Popularly known as an outpost of Boston, its large and beautiful campus lay in the heart of the North End and was called "New Massachusetts." Most of its professors, benefactors, and donators of buildings were staunch New England Congregationalists whose eyes like General Palmer's looked back to Mother England.

The present Administration Building formerly had been the ornate home of a Cripple Creek tycoon. Yet all the other buildings, from the first historic Cutler Hall, whether built of gray stone or peachblow sandstone, reflected in some measure New England architecture. Their crowning glory, and the first addition in twenty years, was the new memorial chapel being built at a cost of $350,000. Not a single stone from the granite mountains shut off from sight by its stained glass windows rooted it to its own earth. Romanesque style, its stone had been shipped from Indiana. Its pretentious cornerstones, however, had been brought all the way from Merrie England. There were four of them. One from Winchester to symbolize "the relation between Church and State which has been the peculiar characteristic of England's history." One each from Oxford and Cambridge. And one from Gatton Surrey which "speaks to us of the parish churches of England, where the people who really count received their training. For it is characteristic of the Gospel that it makes little account of influential people." The speeches made when they were laid embroidered the theme to relate the history of the donor's ancestors who came from the localities.

An expensive mausoleum of England's past, and with no roots

in its own living earth, it and the school epitomized to March Little London itself. A college located at the mouth of the Pass that had led to two of the world's greatest mining booms, it no longer taught mining and metallurgy. The historic assay furnace in the basement of Cutler Hall which had been made and used by Stratton, founder of Cripple Creek, had been knocked to pieces and sold for junk. In a region where the great open pages of geological structure were visible from the campus, the school had no major course in geology. The few courses in engineering leading to a degree in general science were pathetically inadequate and attended by a mere handful of students. The school of business and banking was no more than a concession to the times. The college in short emphasized the classical arts, and its faculty ran to type.

Mostly from New England, they were old, unimaginative, passionately conservative. They were like cloistered monks who had reduced life to a symbol, named it truth, and now proclaimed its formula. They were agreeable and dull. They were dead.

There was every excuse for the hopeless stagnation and stupefying conservatism which March found infecting the school. Unlike a state university, the college depended upon subscriptions and endowments. This limited its size and growth. There were just over 400 students in school. For them were seven national fraternities, and three girls' societies pledged to national sororities. In all, one house for every forty of the total enrolled students.

Most of the students, March found, were from well-to-do families. They had to be: tuition and living expenses in the fraternity and sorority houses were high, and there were no industries in Little London to provide jobs for working students. With little engineering and science in the curriculum, demanding long hours of laboratory work, the students were usually through classes by noon. And Little London, a tourist playground with its mild weather, mountain trails, golf courses, polo fields, dining rooms, dance floors, and mineral springs, provided them an indolent and delightful sojourn.

Little wonder that the college was commonly known throughout the state as "The Country Club," and was even a bit proud of its nickname.

There was no place March could have gone more unsuited to his needs and temperament. Nineteen years old, he had all the failings and good qualities of his breeding: he was proud and timid, reserved in action and bold in thought, stubborn, sensitive, passionate in feeling, but appearing cold when most aroused. His high school companions like Cecil James had merely moved from their literary societies to the fraternities. March was not pledged to a fraternity. As a "town boy" he found himself as isolated and alone as he had been farther down the street in high school. For him "College" as the Rogiers regarded it did not exist.

To add to his discontent, Boné did not send the additional $100 he had promised for the second semester. Nor did Ona know where to write him. Mr. Ford, the Santa Fe agent, came to his rescue by giving March a job as a "number grabber" on the "Graveyard" – the third shift Yard Clerk, working in the railroad yards from eleven at night until seven in the morning.

Carrying a lantern and a packet of Switch Lists, one for each track in the yards, he was required to keep record of every car on every track every hour of the night. To accomplish this he had to know the yards so well that when he swung off a yard engine – a goat – anywhere on the darkest night, he knew immediately where he was. What a maze of tracks there were: Main Lines 1, 2, 3, 4, 5, 6; Pass 1, 2, 3, 4; Main Line Pocket, Pass Pocket; the Spurs, Stubs, Warehouses, and Terminals. Below the station the yards flowed south and west around town – a great river of steel whose tributaries crept along warehouses, into coal and lumber yards, between grain elevators. Old frame houses, a night watchman's shack, a grimy all-night lunch counter, nigger shanties, and decrepit whorehouses flanked the right-of-way. Then the river of tracks thinned out, creeping on west to Colorado City and the big Golden Cycle mill on the mesa. It was nearly four miles long, a world known best by the people of the night. In it March was still alone and lonely.

Then at seven o'clock in the morning he had barely time to rush home on his bicycle, clean up and eat breakfast, and pedal furiously up to the Country Club for an eight o'clock class. How dull, dead, and impractical it seemed!

Ona couldn't sleep at night for worrying about him down there in the yards, prowling around with a lantern, jumping on and off freight trains in the dark. She would go to bed early in the cavernous Third Floor with Leona and Nancy in their beds across the room. In a little while she could hear Rogier come up from the basement to join Mrs. Rogier in the big master bedroom on the second floor. Business was good in the Chocolate Shoppe in Manitou; Mary Ann and Uncle John worked late. Ona could hear the streetcar squeak to a stop on Kiowa, their steps coming down Bijou. She listened to them enter the house and climb the stairs to the middle room below. Soon the murmur of their voices ceased. Now there was silence, and Ona lay gripping the sides of her bed.

She had not been able to keep her fears to herself, and had told the family about that strange, ghostly, and malevolent light. It kept appearing intermittently despite Rogier's grumbling efforts to ascertain the cause. She had then angrily confronted March. "You're in college now! What with takin' physics, electricity, chemistry, and all, *you* ought to be smart enough to do something about it!"

So for days and nights March investigated lights and shadows, measured angles of reflection, traced all possible causes to no avail. Then, angry himself, he had on three different nights off, slept in Ona's room with a loaded twenty-two rifle beside him. On the third night it appeared again, a narrow beam of light shining on the closet door at the head of the landing. Ona silently reached over to grip March's shoulder. He awoke instantly, picking up his rifle. Together they watched the light swing slowly, hesitantly, across the wall. When it reached the knob on the door of March's room, he rose up in bed, shouted "Stop!" and fired. The light disappeared instantly.

All of them – Ona, March, and the awakened girls – rushed to the landing. The bullet had torn a hole through the door. Nothing else was to be seen; nor was there any reasonable explanation to offer the rest of the family when they came running upstairs.

So Ona lay gripping the sides of her bed, dreading its appearance. Instead, long after it was due, she heard the reassuring steps of the Kadles making their nocturnal round of inspection. The dual mystery of all existence, the perpetual unseen battle between good and evil, the comforting Kadles and the malevolent light.

After a cat nap she was awakened by the milk man rumbling by and the scrawny red rooster crowing out in back. It was nearly dawn. Time for her son—that strange son of his strange father—to blow out his lantern. She rose on one elbow and in the graying light looked at the faces of the sleeping girls. Leona's was dark on the pillow, a happy face. In her make-up was none of March's brooding sullenness and tragic intensity. Alert, intuitive, all light, she was tripping through high school on her toes, the most popular girl in her class. Despite made-over dresses and shoes which she shined herself, she was taken to parties and picnics by both high school and college boys.

Nancy was cut from another cloth. An old soul in a young body, she was quiet, compassionate, humble. Perhaps it was her left eyelid that made her so unpopular. Heavy and without reflex, it drooped over her eye. Sometimes when she was happy and laughing in a crowd it would be all right. Then suddenly it would droop down again as if in a solemn wink that refuted her gaiety. She became content to stay home, sitting in the rocker up in the front second-story bedroom.

"What's the matter, dear?" Ona had asked her once. "I thought you were going out on the picnic party with the rest."

"They didn't ask me," Nancy said with a somber smile. "I guess they don't want me with my droopy eye. They want girls like Leona, she's so pretty and lively."

"Don'd you worry, dear." Ona gave her a hug. "Business and running around isn't for homebodies like you and me. We'll keep the home fires burning and be the happiest of all, won't we? When are you going to have your Sunday school class of little boys down again?"

Now in the gray dawn Nancy's pale face was somber on its pillow. Ona sighed. In that chair downstairs her grandmother had rocked away the last years of her unbelievable life, chewing at the wart on her diamond-covered finger. Sister Molly had died while waiting there with hopeless abandon for Tom who had never returned; and Mrs. Rogier, forever sitting out Rogier's absences at Cripple Creek. Here too she herself had waited, unloved and ignored, until Jonathan had caught her up for a brief and passionate interlude; and now, in empty dawn, she was still waiting for March. Suddenly and intuitively she knew that it would fall to Nancy to sit at a window bearing in turn their burden of hope and courage, of folly and futility.

"What is this strange pattern stamped upon our lives?" she wondered, blindly seeking the thread that bound them all together in the mysterious life swirling around the passionless stability of this shabby old house on Shook's Run. "Why, you'd think it was all laid out for us from the start, and we had no choice!"

Rogier, Tom, Cable, March – the men were all alike, vibrating to far horizons, ever restless and uprooted. But in each of three generations, in each of these men's lives, had appeared a woman loved, left, and forgotten, to bear for them trivial burdens with strength and uncomplaining patience.

Who will ever understand a woman, she thought. We are sweethearts and wives, we are daughters and mothers of men. Yet our fathers forget us and the passion that begot us; the touch of our husbands' hands grows cold and falls away. The fruit of our wombs is severed so soon from the bough. By our sons we are forgotten.

And still and forever we endure. We are the red lips smiling through parted lilac blossoms in spring, the passion of summer storms when the lightning crackles around the granite peaks, the ripe fruit of the harvest. Toothless and wrinkled we huddle against the winter storm, beside the dying embers, sewing moccasins for the long trail. And still and forever we endure – greater than the promise, the passion, the harvest of our flesh.

We are women but there is something in us greater than any woman. How then can we be understood? Men seek gold and silver, the riches of the earth, and yet it is the common flesh of that earth they tread underfoot which is the most precious of all. How then shall women be understood, when their riches are the most precious and secret of all?

We are the Earth Mother, our flesh is her flesh, we are the womb of all life. So still and forever we endure.

My father, my brother, my husband, my son – all these have plumbed and are plumbing the depths of the earth. Yet in their daughter, their sister, their wife, their mother lies the mystery they sought and will seek forever. Like the earth, I am the secret of life and I shall never be known.

And so she sat, heavy with the mystery, gazing out the window at the earth-heaped mountains rising into the dawn as endurable and unknowable as she. All things pass. But in her secret oneness Nancy would endure as had she.

8

It was inevitable after his first year in college that March drifted into engineering. The small group of science and engineering students contained a few older men who had returned to school to brush up on theory with the hope of advancing in their technical work.

Professor Thomason, because of ill health, on loan to the college from his permanent post in New England, was the head of the department. He was a tall, sandy haired man about fifty. His aversion was Art; his religion Theoretical Physics; his creed the Electron Theory. In his way he was brilliant; a hard worker and a tyrant. But without any knowledge of men, industry, or practical engineering, he was a hot-blooded theorist.

It was his aim to reduce his students gradually to a select group, for each of whom upon graduation he would secure a teaching fellowship in an Eastern university where he could obtain his doctorate. To achieve it, he supervised the selection of all their courses; saw to it they took no more English, history, economics, and language than was barely necessary; laid out all their outside reading; and gave them keys to the basement laboratory where they had to work nights, Saturdays, and sometimes on Sundays to keep up. The effect of all this was to divorce his small department from the mainstream of college life. His students were further alienated by being quartered in old Cutler Hall across the campus.

March found himself perched on a high stool at a drafting table in the historic old building his grandfather had erected. The place reminded him so much of the shop at home that he had the uncanny feeling Rogier was perched on the stool beside him, sharpening his own pencil by pushing the knifeblade outward with his thumb.

Professor Thomason insisted that his students sit with their slide rules in hands during his lectures. He would abruptly, stop talking, scribble an equation on the blackboard, and demand they finish the computation "within one-tenth of one percent – the accuracy of your slide-rules! Who's the first to give me an answer?"

He had another irritating idiocyncrasy. He would whip around at any time, point his bony finger at a boy, and ask out of context, "What causes the Aurora Borealis? The rainbow?"– "Jameson, what is thunder?–lightning?"

Oh, it is the red forked tongue of the great serpent when the white-bellied clouds gather over the parched desert of the Navajos, over the shrivelled little corn patches below the cliffs of Oraibi. In the dusty plaza the dancing Snake priests shake louder their rattles; the resonant stamp of their moccasined feet on the *pochta,* the sounding board, sounds like the faint rumble of thunder. And with writhing rattlesnakes firmly but gently clenched in their mouths, they lift their horribly painted faces upward to the darkening sky. Oh yes, it is the red forked tongue of the great serpent whose image is wrapped around the mouths of the huge water jars, the fertility serpent, the feathered serpent who summons the tall walking rain majestically striding sky and desert, bringing life to shrivelled corn and shrivelled people.

"Lightning, sir," said Jameson, "is an electrical discharge caused by an electrical potential set up as a result of rising air currents blowing off the edges of the larger water drops in the cloud, and carrying away the smaller drops of spray which remain. Thunder, following the flash, is caused by the vibrations set up by the sudden heating and expansion of air along the path of lightning."

March's gaze strayed outside to the sun gleaming through a

haze of autumnal gold rich with the ripeness of Indian Summer. He was suddenly recalled by a young lady saying, "Indian Summer is only a figment of a poet's fancy. It does not exist as a meteorological entity. The haze is simply composed of collected and suspended smoke and particles of vegetation, and is caused by a stagnated high pressure area."

"Correct!" The professor rapped the desk. "Cable! What is this? This desk, the chair you're sitting on?"

March sat up. "All matter, sir, is nothing but an elemental charge of electricity, you might say. The molecules of all substances are broken down into atoms, and these atoms are composed of electrons with their satellite protons – positive and negative charges of electricity whose numbers and arrangements determine the outward form of matter which we call by different names. We will eventually break down this ultimate unit, and release its locked-up energy for the industrial uses of man."

"It will do. It will do," said Professor Thomason. "What I'm trying to get all of you to do is to regard even simple phenomena in terms of your calling. Clear your minds of old beliefs. Think freely. All nature, everything that exists, is nothing in itself. It has no life, no meaning. We have reduced all to its simple expression in scientific laws. Now, by learning to apply them, we will at last be masters of the universe, of life itself."

This was his interpretation of the mysterious, all-pervading life force flowing through interstellar space, a stone, a blade of grass, ourselves; the mysterious flow of undifferentiated and unlimited power informing the great breathing mountains, the rutting deer, the passions and thoughts of man. It was clear, mathematically precise, but it denied the mystery of creation, the secret unknown gods who whisper in all men.

Some of the students were amazed and amused, like children robbed of Santa Claus. "Murder – social subtraction, eh?" they joked.

But March sat through these lectures as if Professor Thomason had him by the throat. He was inarticulate, unable to voice his misery. It was not as if he did not understand. His mind worked well enough, but something within him passionately refuted the view of life that science held out before him. Rogier, for all his queer ideas, had at least an appreciation of life's mysterious profundity, its torment and beauty. Thomason, never.

Perhaps his opinion of the professor was not entirely unjust. For there was one aspect of life Thomason's rigid theory did not include – sex. And this was the strange god within him now crying with a voice at once terrifying and compelling. During high school he had attended a compulsory lecture and movie on the evils of unsanctified and promiscuous sex. The preliminary lecture was innocuous enough. But the movie was disastrous. It showed in a few brief scenes a man meeting a woman of ill repute and their casual courtship ending with an embrace in her bedroom. Then followed in tedious medical detail his trips to the doctor, the spread of a horrible venereal disease as he was taken to the hospital. Shots of other patients in the ward, faces distorted, bodies covered with sores. Finally a close-up of the hero, the victim of his passions: legs spread and held up by ropes, screaming with agony. March could stand no more. Dripping sweat, unable to breathe, he reeled up the aisle. A nurse caught him before he fainted, squeezed an ammonia capsule under his nose, and finally let him stagger outside, frightened, revolted, and ashamed.

The movie accomplished more than its purpose. It brought out the Puritanical streak in March that proclaimed sex and sin as synonymous. And it buried deep within him the first faint urgings of his developing maturity.

But now for some cause he could not understand, he became aware of women's smiles and women's shapes. Madame Jones' parlor on Myers Avenue in Cripple Creek, the women in their cheap lodging houses near the Santa Fe station, the whorehouses west of town, became meaningful. The lewd jokes of taxicab drivers took on new significance. Whenever he thought of them his mind grew cold, and at the same time his body seemed to leap into flame. Lying in bed at night he thought ceaselessly of thousands of naked women in their beds, in narrow Pullman berths; of beautiful nymphs with long hair and pink-tipped breasts floating in the sea of desire, calling, calling.

Evidently many of his campus friends were not as tortured with secret longings. There were too many girls and young summer widows vacationing in Little London while their husbands slaved in the heat at home.

"I never seen such a place!" Hanlon cried enthusiastically to him one day. "The hotels, cabins, and streets are full of hot-breathin' hussies pinin' for somebody to take 'em out. Seems like you young bucks at college have got a hell of a harem to work over!"

Indeed several students with cars openly boasted of the women who had paid their expenses all summer for their sturdy favors.

The Country Club at Stud for Visiting Tourists.

March wondered if he were going mad; he had no doubt his mind was diseased. His feeling was intensified one morning in chapel when Valeria Constance's hand fell on his knee.

Seats in the chapel were assigned to students alphabetically. For more than two years he had been sitting beside Valeria during the compulsory chapel period each morning. This was the only time they ever met, and they never talked. March had taken a dislike to her from the start. Valeria's father was a well-to-do editor of one of the Denver newspapers. Even as a freshman she put on airs. She had a room of her own in one of the halls, dressed well, and became immensely popular. In her second year she sported a bright red roadster. Then the girls began to edge away from her. She became known as a sweetheart of Sigma Chi, then of every other fraternity in turn. In her junior year she dropped everyone, refused all dates, got rid of her car. Whether her father had lost his money or she had taken up philosophy, no one knew. Valeria kept them all guessing and went her way alone.

She was good looking, tall, and thin; but aside from a chance word to her, March ignored her. Yet more and more often of late he felt a hot and quickening throb of desire when near her. Outside, the spell passed.

He cursed himself for a fool. "She's getting skinnier every day," he thought. "I don't know what's worse – the smell of her perfume or the smell of the cigarettes she's always smoking."

To crave her while near, and to hate her while absent – this was the paradox that baffled him. Until that morning when she casually dropped her hand on his knee. March jerked erect with embarrassment. It was an important day: a noted speaker had come to address them and the faculty were dressed in their black robes. March had put on his old brown suit. The knees of the trousers were threadbare, and Ona had reinforced them on the inside with slabs of mending tissue. They looked excellent when pressed, but were stiff as a board.

Valeria appeared not to notice the knife-edge crease on which her hand dropped. "Meet me outside when this farce is over," she whispered.

She was waiting for him when the talk was over. "I see you had to dress up today like all the other sheep. I thought better of you than that."

They took a side path to Palmer Hall. Valeria continued, "We've been sitting together now for over two years. You've never asked me for a date, hardly been civil. Are you bashful, a grind, or got an inferiority complex? Let's call off the feud. Ask me for a date and see what I'll say."

"What fraternity house are you trying to spite now? Why pick on me?"

"Because you're so damned blunt and rude. At least you're not like these simpering idiots. What do you say—tomorrow night at seven-thirty? I'll get my leave till eleven-thirty."

"Dinner?" asked March.

"Don't be a fool!" Without another word she ran up the steps of Palmer Hall, leaving him feeling exactly that.

Next evening March dressed up as best he could and sought out Hanlon. He was positive Valeria would want to go to a hotel to dance. "I'm in a hole," he explained. "You can't take a girl to a dance on the street car – not this one. The drug store clowns on the corner would laugh us out of school."

"Oh hell, jump in my car!" replied Hanlon. "I'll take you there at least."

Valeria was waiting in the hall when March got out of the car. "What's that for?" she asked.

March explained.

"You're trying to run to form, but you're out of character," she said sharply. "Tell him to go on. I want to walk and talk."

They walked down to the creek and up the long park to Third Lake. The moon was coming up, reflected on the water like a floating silver dollar. A beaver slapped his flat tail, a fish splashed noisily. Sitting beside her, March could see the outline of her long thin legs, the shape of her small firm breasts as she leaned forward to light a cigarette. March shuddered. He put his arm around her, leaned back and clasped her breast.

"Never mind," she said listlessly. "I don't have to be loved. Every time I go out with a boy, he seems to think it's only an excuse to neck. I like to get out. That's all."

The simple assertion, with the friendly pressure of her body, instantly quenched the flame within him. For a moment he was angry, frustrated, then he relaxed and listened to her talk.

She seemed to have had everything: an excellent home, friends, three summers in Europe, every wish fulfilled. Nothing mattered. She hungered for something she had never known. She was like those strange insects of night that live but a few hours, beating their wings in a mad flight of ecstasy, and expiring at dawn. But if this explained her actions during her first two years in college, what had happened now to change her so completely?

Valeria didn't know. "You've seen me in the college plays?" – she always took the vampire part. "Well, that's the way I feel. As if I were born to be a prostitute or something. Never 'good.' I feel that if I were married, settled down for an easy existence in the house my father bought for me, it would kill me. But I can't be 'bad.' Not with my family. So I'm at the end of my rope. Already!"

"Oh, you just want to sow a few wild oats. All women are like that," he said knowingly. "You'll snap out of that when you're married."

"I'm engaged," she answered abruptly. "A fellow in Yale. Nice but dull. He's coming to help my father. I can't hurt either of them. But it will mean the death of me. I have a premonition."

March laughed, but nervously. There was something horribly real and bitterly sincere in her listless tone that belied her melodramatic assertion.

"I've got one year more!" she cried. "And everything is stale. I've slept with a dozen boys. Nothing matters. I feel alone always. And all I care for now is to lie and look at the mountains. Something's happened to me. I don't know what."

And so that night March went home from his first date in college having spent ten cents for two cups of coffee, feeling somehow thwarted and taken in.

He was now working at the Santa Fe station only in the summer, leaving him free during the school year to get up into the mountains on weekends. Valeria took long hikes with him often. He grew to know her quick and brilliant mind; she was an honor student. If he resented the quick hot wave of desire the first sight of her aroused in him, he also appreciated the casual sympathy between them that took its place. But they seemed never really to meet as he had met Leslie Shane. There was something that did not fuse between them. She was like a vampire greedy to suck from him the warm blood of intuitive understanding which she sensed in his dark brooding face. He too was as selfish. Resenting the animal desire in him which she throttled by her quick mind, he drew back deep within himself against her.

How unsatisfying it was for them both, this constant attraction and repulsion. We all desire the passion of the flesh, the understanding of the mind, and the intuition of the spirit, all in one. So we refuse the priceless gifts that come to us singly.

Late that fall March, who had been up the mountains, caught a ride down on a freight. Snow was beginning to fall, yet the air was warm and vibrant. It was nearly dusk when the train rolled across the high trestle above the upper end of North Cheyenne Canyon. March could see a group of cabins, the falls below, and Bruin Inn. From here he could walk down the canyon and catch a streetcar to town. Waving back to the conductor, he swung free with his duffle bag, and slid down the gravel slope.

As he walked down the narrow trail, he suddenly met Valeria sauntering along in walking shoes and fur coat. "Hello, Figure meetin' you!"

She answered surlily, in one of her moods. "You look dirty as a miner, an Indian," she said eyeing his boots, corduroys, and leather jacket. "What's in the bag?"

"A slab of bacon and some cans, coffee, bread. Want to eat 'em up?" he asked jokingly.

"Why not?" she assented listlessly. "Down at the Inn a crowd of fools would ruin supper by playing that squeaky phonograph." She stared at him steadily. "Go down to Lavely's and get us a cabin for the night. Just tell them you've got a friend. I don't want to go back to that stuffy dorm."

He walked down to the cabins. The caretaker nodded. "Two of yeh? You can have that little one-room cabin across the creek. No need of my goin' up there with you. There's wood. Just pay now and leave the key here in the mornin'."

It was done. In abashed silence March lit the lamp, built fires in the fireplace and small cook-stove while Valeria huddled on the bed, smoking. They ate hungrily. Then March heated water, washed the dishes, repacked his duffle bag. Valeria watched his rhythmical, capable hands with amusement. "How neat and methodical you are!"

"In the moutains it's a good habit to be ready for whatever comes," he said simply.

The room had warmed up now. In the ruddy glow of the fire the oilcloth covered table seemed less shiny; the smooth log walls took on a mellow tone. Valeria took off all her clothes except her brassiere and silk panties. Then putting back on her mink coat, she sat down on the bed.

"I suppose you feel righteously wicked. A man always does. Even Professor Enderly, for all his philosophy."

At the boy's start of surprise, she went on obdurately. "Oh yes. I first thought him the freest, most intelligent man on the campus. I took every course he gave. I joined the group meeting in his apartment – Agh! It was just talk. All in his head. He made love like a silly schoolboy – That's philosophy for you. Words!"

She pulled him down to sit beside her. "You're not like that, March. You're strange, somehow. Different. You don't think, really. You've got a sense-intuition that'll be stronger, truer than your mind will ever be. But I'm afraid you'll take it on yourself to think your way instead of feeling it."

She lit another of her interminable cigarettes. "Be yourself, always. Remember me, who can't. Oh, remember me, March, when I'm lost and gone!"

March shuddered. A terrible conviction that she would really die–soon, so soon!–swept over him. He put his arms around her but without desire, as if he were embracing the fleshless voice of a truth he had never known till now. He perceived now what had kept them apart. His flow of life, except for a spurt of passion when always he first met her, had sunk down to coagulate deep within him. And yet he was afraid.

Valeria rose and threw off her coat. "Unsnap my bra, will you?"

Fumblingly he unfastened the snap, watched her step out of her panties and walk up to the fire. He had thought her thin and bony. Now he saw how full and rounded were her thighs and hips, how firm and pointed were her small breasts. And yet he was shocked by the whiteness of her smooth skin; it was like that of a candle, a candle that was swiftly burning out. He hastily flung off his clothes, walked up behind her, and put his arms around her.

She leaned back her head and smiled reprovingly. "Now March. You're in a hurry because you're shy. Or do you think I'll run away? Let's get good and warm before we get into bed."

Even till then he had misjudged her, with her cold and analytical mind. Then suddenly he found himself immersed in a mindless passion that endowed her long frail body with a physical strength and inward power beyond his comprehension. Out of it he emerged weak and spent to lie quietly beside her. Valeria snuggled up close to him. "How cosy you feel. Now don't talk. You might say something."

Would he ever forget her he wondered when he awoke next morning: this haunting face so childlike now in sleep, her narrow mouth curved slightly in a smile, her yellow hair sprawled over the pillow? Would he ever forget her who for the first time had eased the misery of his pent-up passion, and forever laid the Puritanical ghost of sin and sex which had haunted him?

It was still early. He rose quietly so as not to disturb her, and bounded to the window. The sky was cloudless; the thin fall of snow was soggy already. The storm, and that within him, was spent. He felt cleansed and whole, buoyantly alive. Stretching on his toes, he flung wide his arms, arched his chest, and gulped great breaths of air.

"Shut that window and light a fire!" Valeria's petulant voice demanded behind him.

He ran back, knelt and kissed her eyes, stroked the hair back from her eyes. "Oh, Valeria! I never felt like this before!"

"Light that stove too. I want some coffee," she demanded sharply. then, when he'd put the pot on, she said in a soft voice, "Now come back here and lie with me. We've got all morning, haven't we?"

How different it was now, holding her slim full body against him, feeling the warm moth-like texture of her lips! He had no more inhibitions. They were strangers no more. They had met at last.

9

Glancing out of the Third Floor window one morning, Ona happened to see Rogier across the street. He was squatting on the high bank of Shook's Run, one hand shading his eyes, and staring intently toward the house. A moment later he moved west, kneeling on the ground and squinting along his outstretched arm. She immediately stalked downstairs and across the street to confront him.

"What are you up to now, Daddy?" she demanded. "I know it's something!"

The old man looked her steadily in the eyes. "There's some people in that big three-story house there tryin' to spy on me! I aim to find out who!" Indignantly he strutted across the street and into his greenhouse.

Yes, Rogier had encountered an unforseen difficulty in digging his tunnel into the base of Pike's Peak. Closing the plank door behind him, he had only to walk a few steps down into the passage to see it: a pool of water, a shallow well filling up with underground water. Dom! He should have known better, digging so close to Shook's Run! Hence he had gone across the street to the bank of the creek to ascertain, without benefit of surveying instruments, if there were a slight rise in altitude behind the house where he could avoid the seepage. There was not. He would have to make out where he was.

Indomitably he installed a small hand pump, running the hose out into the currant bushes where it would not be noticed, and pumping most of the night. Next day seepage water filled up the hole again.

Well, he'd have to bridge it and extend his tunnel through the slightly higher properties of the Pyles and the Caseys next door. So over the well he constructed a footbridge of planks. Beyond this he dug an inclined plane cleated with slats from apple boxes to keep him from slipping on the wet earth, and resumed driving his lateral tunnel.

The hard work with pick and shovel he didn't mind. Getting rid of the excavated dirt was the difficulty. Some of it he could mix with ashes and dump in the ash pit. The rest of it he would have to trundle up the alley in a wheelbarrow and dump in a vacant lot. If sometimes his thin back gave out, or the muscles of his skinny shanks knotted with cramps, he had only to sit and stare at the Peak. Its compassionate face condoned his efforts. It encouraged him "Time!" it said. "All anything takes is time!" And Rogier knew his tunnel was getting along. Already it was through Pyle's lot and beginning to burrow under the Casey's backyard. Digging now would be easy.

March was not as satisfied with his own progress. Professor Thomason's picked group had dwindled to a sparse dozen under his tyranny. Stuffed with theory and mathematics, they clamored for something concrete.

"We're not a technical trade school like a state university or the Colorado School of Mines," Thomason reminded them. "Basic principles, the principles underlying every field of science and engineering. That is what we're after."

But under their prodding, and without technical facilities, he arranged for them to obtain field work. He sent them separately to make detailed reports on the old steam power plant east of town, the hydroelectric plant at Manitou, and the new power plant at the Broadmoor Hotel. For high voltage, X-ray, and ultra-violet work, he sent others to hospitals and tuberculosis sanitariums. Another was sent with a railroad division lineman to learn how to locate grounds and crosses. To March, whom he understood had a mining background, he suggested some field studies in Cripple Creek.

"I hate mining!" answered March.

"No mining or geology. Just a look at the new electrical plants supplanting the old steam hoists. A report on the proposed new drainage tunnel," Thomason said imperturbably. "No industrial applications. Just the underlying principles, mind. Take your time. You'll be excused from class work. And we can pay you laboratory assistant fees to defray your expenses."

So early that spring March packed his bag and announced to Ona he was going up to Cripple Creek.

"Up to the district? Mining!" she shouted. "Like Tom, Daddy, your own father! And now you, son! Is this what you've been doing to me all this time in college while I thought you were learning to be a successful businessman? Betraying me! Behind my back!"

Her childish ignorance and distorted image of his purpose made him furious, but her real anguish clawed at his heart. She looked so old and tired today—a wash day; her hair was turning gray, the crows' feet growing deeper around her eyes.

"Mother! Don't be so dumb!" he pleaded. "I'm not taking up mining. I'm just going up there to see the electrical plants as part of my outside laboratory work in physics. Lord, you'd think I was leavin' with a pick on my back!"

"Well, don't tell Daddy where you're going," she cried despairingly. "It might bring it all back. Or even bring on another spell." She began straightening the room, a woman's only answer to success, failure, and hope alike.

It was just daybreak when March swung off the freight caboose and walked down into the district. There was no fault in the vein of his memory as he stared through a light stinging snow into that vast granite cup which held so precious a part of his childhood.

Above him a seamed, mute, and impassive face stared back at him through the gray and ghastly morning light. In a wrinkle up its cheek lay what had been the Sylvanite, still manned by the ghosts of Abe and Jake, his father, and the undying spirit of his grandfather whose outworn body still puttered like a mechanical robot in a makeshift greenhouse far below. Around him rose the old familiar hills: Bull Hill, Squaw Mountain, Tenderfoot and Globe Hills,

Mount Pisgah, Big Bull, and the Nipple. And cutting below them the deep arroyos: Arequa Gulch, Poverty Gulch, and Grassy Gulch. A dreary landscape scarred and pitted with gallows frames, smoke-stacks, shaft houses, glory holes, ore dumps, and squalid miners' shanties; the features unchanged, but their expression lifeless. A world gone dead.

Down the slope huddled a clump of apparently abandoned cabins. From one a slatternly woman came out, stared at him sullenly from a pinched blue face, then gathered up a dishpan of snow to melt for the morning coffee. March turned up his coat collar, lit the new pipe he was affecting, and trudged on.

From Victor, once proud "City of Mines," a scarce dozen chimneys were sending up their streams of smoke. Stores and houses were deserted or torn down, their gaping excavations filled with snow. Scores of shaggy half-wild burros roamed the empty streets even though the town council had appointed a man to keep them off the sidewalks—sidewalks with weeds growing in the cracks. He peered into a deserted saloon. The mahogany bar was gray with dust, an empty whisky bottle was standing on the shelf behind it. But as the end of Fourth Street, a block from the central downtown corner, he ran into a few miners coming down from the working on the hill. The lamps were still burning on the front of their caps. Their dirty faces were pinched with cold.

He followed them to a narrow brick building whose lower front had housed the Opera House, and climbed upstairs to what he remembered as the Gold Coin Hotel. Here he entered a small drab parlor containing a stove surrounded by rows of stiff chairs. Soon Mrs. Okerstrom came in. She was a fine, fat old Swedish woman with a brogue thick as pea soup, one of the old-timers of the district. She was the landlady of the place — the Gold Coin Boarding House.

"Vat it iss you want?" she demanded.

March explained timidly, mentioning his grandfather. Her stern weathered face, flushed like a drunk's from cooking over the kitchen stove, broke into blossom. She grabbed him by the shoulders. "Ya! Vy don't you say who it iss you are? Old man's Rogier's boy! Vell, vell. I don't know how to belieff you have grown!"

A clock struck six. From their rooms around the dreary parlor miners in stiff muck-smeared clothes and boots clumped in, carrying the chairs into the long dining room. March had breakfast with them: oatmeal with canned milk, hot biscuits, eggs, bacon, fried mush, stewed prunes. They ate silently and ravenously, raising their stony white faces from their plates only to call Mrs. Okerstrom from the kitchen with another heaping platter.

While she washed dishes, March watched the men off to work. From the window he could see them trudging up the trail from the end of the street to the working on top of the hill. It was beginning to snow again. The seven o'clock whistles were blowing. The sun was not yet up.

In back of the boarding house lay the long disused corridors of the Gold Coin Hotel. Cold and dark, they were strung with cobwebs. On each side lay the honeycombed cells, heaped with old dusty furniture. From one of these rooms Mrs. Okerstrom pulled two chairs and a small table. In the kitchen she gave him a bucket of soapy water to wash them off with.

"No empty rooms have I," she explained. "So few boarders. Ah, so bad these mines!" But up the slope of Squaw Mountain there was a log cabin March could use.

They set off through the snow with the three pieces. The cabin was not far away. The road led past the great brick shaft house of the famous Gold Coin. The walls had caved; the machinery lay broken and rusted under the debris. Nearby stood a group of weathered shanties. Only one family lived in the best and was gradually knocking down the others for firewood.

Farther up the slope stood the cabin he was to use. It was of good sound logs, and contained a bed, cook stove, and a gunny sack of blankets hanging from the rafters. When Mrs. Okerstrom left him, he cleaned up, made the bed and fire. He bought an axe, borrowed a lamp and a few dishes. His near neighbor loaned him a bucket, showed him where to get water, and cautioned him against the open, unprotected shaft that gaped downward a hundred feet just outside his door. He was settled. And during the weeks he returned to it for days at a time, the little cabin became the first home of his own.

To save money, he cooked most of his simple meals. But sometimes he gorged at Mrs. Okerstrom's table. He loved to listen to the hard clipped talk of the miners, especially the old-timers. In manner, speech, and appearance they seemed to have taken on the hard-rock durability of the earth in which they spent their lives. One evening a writing woman from Denver came for supper. She wanted a story: not the usual thing, she insisted, but "a true tale of glamorous Cripple Creek."

A sudden hush fell on the long table. The men coughed, scraped their boots, looked down at their plates. March himself felt embarrassed. Then abruptly a former old faro dealer and bartender named Bill Rankin spoke up.

"Hell yes, lady! Damned if I can't deal you one right off the top of the deck: how Cunningham Mountain got its name of the Nipple!"

Mrs. Okerstrom hastily retreated to the kitchen. March squirmed as he stole a look at the speaker. Rankin's rheumy blue eyes were dead serious. He rubbed his white whiskers reflectively, then lit his stub pipe with a flourish.

"You can place the Nipple right likely, Ma'am," he began. "It sticks up just south of town here. A tolerable bit outside the porphry spread, but in them days ever' hill and gulch was worth a look.

"Well up there in its granite side Cunningham sunk his shaft. He put her down and didn't hit a speck of color. Now Cunningham was a mite on the stubborn side. He couldn't believe that hole of his wouldn't pan out sometime. So he stuck there in his shanty. But ever' Sat'day he come into town, got roarin' drunk and paraded up Myers Avenue to see the girls, a-shoutin' and a-cussin' the purtiest you ever heard. Oh, but he was a likely man with his curly yellow hair and his way with a wench!

"Now I'll be damned if Mrs. Hancock didn't take a fancy to him. She was a widow woman, rich, right good-lookin', and lively as a plump young mare what with her husband bein' dead a good year. But she was stuck up and proud as all get-out, one of the High Society.

"Now nature, lady, is a fickle hussy. And when Mrs. Hancock got that ace-deuce look in her eyes, and the nipples on them plump breasts of hers got to stickin' out her fancy shirtwaist, and she panted like a lizard on a hot rock—well, Cunningham was a mighty likely man as I been sayin'.

"Before long ever-body knew what was goin' on. Hell's fire! The whole town missed his paradin' up Myers Avenue ever'

Sat'day, shoutin' and cussin', slappin' the girls across the bottom and snappin' their red garters till he found one to suit him. Instead, he rode in quiet like, and hitched his horse in front of Mrs. Hancock's big house.

"You can bet she was still persnickety. She marched to the Ladies Club carryin' her nose higher'n ever. 'Really', she would say, 'I do believe Mr. Cunningham's claim on Cunningham Mountain has excellent prospects. I'm doing everything possible to encourage him to develop it.' That's what she was lettin' on: that they was talkin' business, them two.

"Well, Ma'am, one of them fine Sat'days when Cunningham come in for some of that tall encouragin', he bit off one of her nipples – plumb off, slick as a whistle!"

March saw the Denver lady's face redden; involuntarily she drew her coat across her bosom. Mrs. Okerstrom, listening in the doorway, ducked back into her kitchen. March grinned slyly. Yes indeed, Madam, Glamorous Cripple Creek abounds in legend. The staunch spirit of its Pioneer Fathers and Winners of the West should awaken us to their valor and unimpeachable idealism. But withal, we must remember that they were human.

Rankin refilled his pipe and continued. "Now I ain't sayin' Cunningham carried that pink nipple of hers back to his mountain. But I am sayin' that Mrs. Hancock didn't have it no more. She went around swishin' her skirts, trippin' in to the Ladies Club with her nose up just the same—but with one of her nipples gone. It didn't phase her a good God-damn. But all the ladies in the club got to sniggerin' when they saw one side of her shirtwaist flat as a pancake, and wonderin' what had become of the nipple that used to stick out. But nobody said a word. She was that uppish.

"Now there was a kleptomaniac woman in town who went callin' on all the ladies regular, but couldn't help herself from sneakin' out of their parlors some little doo-dad or somethin'. She didn't mean to steal none, and she was ashamed to bring them back. So they kept pilin' up—and gettin' scarcer and scarcer in all the other ladies' parlors.

"Finally they got together to give her a lesson. They made her bring all the what-nots and doo-dads to the Ladies Club, so they could pick out what was theirs. About four o'clock in come Mrs.

Hancock. Nose up, hoity-toity like, she ambled around lookin' at the sea-shells, hair brushes, paper roses, and flower vases and all, to see if anything was hers.

"By this time the kleptomaniac woman was mad and tired of bein' rawhided. She rose up on her hindquarters, looked Mrs. Hancock up and down, then spoke up sharp and loud for ever'body to hear:

" 'Mrs. Hancock! Don't you go snoopin' around here any more for that nipple of yours. I certainly didn't steal it. You just better go look for it on Mr. Cunningham's Mountain!"

"Now blast my soul to hell, Ma'am! If that ain't why Cunningham Mountain's called the Nipple, I hope the livin' God strikes me dead on the spot!"

Glamouous Cripple Creek! With its 475 mines producing from an area of six square miles more gold than the Mother Lode of California and the Klondike combined; three railroads hauling ore down and empties back, with thousands of passengers; the High Line and the Low Line whizzing through its dozen towns and innumerable camps; the great houses on Myers Avenue, "The Homestead," "Old Faithful," and "Sunnyrest" and the swarming cribs behind. Madame Jones and Charlotte, oh sweet Charlotte! Abe and Jake, the tall dark man coughing on the dump who was his father, and the indomitable master of the Sylvanite, his grandfather. God Almighty! And the columbines among the pines, the red hawk sailing above, and the mousy burros trotting down the trail with twinkling feet. Always and forever it would still exist, throbbing with vitality, rich with wonder and magic, the mystery of the last of £10,000 sterling. But not here, where from a cabin on Squaw Mountain he stared out upon a frost-shattered world dreary and lifeless, oppressive with its high remoteness and capitulation to decay.

Making friends with Bill Rankin, who took him around, March presented his letter of introduction from Professor Thomason to the superintendents of the largest mines and continued his studies.

Statistics bore out his observations. There were now only forty-eight mines working: production had dropped to a bare $4,000,000 a year; and there remained less than 5,000 people in the entire District. Of course there were new modern plants and methods of operation. Immense syndicates and powerful corporations controlled the mines, mills, railroads. The few miners worked on a royalty or split-check basis, merely operating a single level, one stope or drift. They supplied the work and tools; the company supplied the pneumatic air and operated the hoist. If there were no pay ore, the company was out little but the men were out their work and time, and without bacon and beans. If there were a strike of sorts, the discoverers got only their stipulated royalty.

Of course there was a little hope; the most barren desert and desolate heart is not without it. There was talk of another drainage tunnel to be built. Five miles long, it would drain the district down to 3,000 feet on the premise that ore would be found to continue at depth. But what good would that do, wondered March; the big corporations would reap the profit.

"No industrial applications, mind!" Professor Thomason had told March. "Just the underlying principles!" And the underlying principle, March found, was that the days of independent mining, when a man relied on his own initiative, strength, and love of life, were over. A corporational profit of six percent was squeezing out here, as it was in the beet fields, the cotton and wheat fields, the juices of the living earth. He found himself staring at a huge industrial machine. And he knew that if he became a successful engineer he would be no more than one of its inconsequential cogs.

Why he kept coming back long after his report was finished, March didn't know. Maybe it was just to get away from the deadening constriction of the Country Club; from the more oppressive miasma of defeat and decay that permeated the shabby old house on Shook's Run and all his crazy tribe; from the constant clatter and rumble of goats and freights in the railroad yards. Or to simply sit here high above them all, feeling the snowcap melting on his head and running in rivulets down his cheeks, the avalanches ripping great hunks out of his winter-fat sides, the columbines and anemones springing up between his rooted toes – Perhaps, after all, it was the wedges of wild geese flying past overhead, tearing a wordless cry of longing from his heart. The strange and haunting cry of the tormenting unrest that was the legacy of his father and of his own mixed blood, of America itself.

10

Walking down Bijou Hill one afternoon on his return from Cripple Creek, March was disturbed to see an unusual commotion in the street ahead of him. Mrs. Jackson was dashing down the walk, dish towel in hand; the grocer Mr. Bryce in his white apron ran frantically across the road; swarms of children came flocking across Shook's Run. Good Lord! They all were making for his own home! With a premonition of disaster he broke into a run.

At the entrance to the driveway he halted and dropped his duffle bag. A throng of people swarmed before him shouting, crawling up on the fence, pushing forward. Mrs. Pyle next door was leaning out of her upper window, hands over her face, but peeking between her fingers.

"Granddad!" The cry seemed torn from his bowels as he suddenly went sick with fear and compassion. He dashed forward, brutally cleaving his way through the packed neighbors.

A devastating sight flashed before him. The west end of Rogier's greenhouse had collapsed; broken panes of glass were strewn over the back walk. In the middle of the driveway loomed a gaping hole. Farther west the earth had caved in under Pyle's fence, leaving a post sticking up with a flag of chicken wire. Even as he looked, Pyle's freshly planted garden caved in. Then he noticed the flimsy wooden garage in back of the Casey house. It was ominously tilted to one side as if upset by an earthquake.

"Stand back!" someone shouted. "The whole ground's undermined!"

Now March saw Leona and Nancy standing with arms around each other, stiff and frightened. Mrs. Rogier was waiting in broken glass and lettuce leaves, her hands clasped over her breast. March pushed on. Six feet down in a hole crouched Ona and Mr. Kennedy, tugging at a protruding foot.

"Here he is!" shouted Kennedy. "Help us get him out!"

Two men dropped down, clawing back the earth and prying off with a crow-bar a timber fallen across Rogier. March helped to drag him out as a car rolled in the driveway. A man hopped out, carrying a respirator. Rogier lay on the ground in front of the collapsed end of his greenhouse, his head in Ona's lap. He was unconscious. A thin trickle of blood oozed through his white hair. He was covered with dirt: his ears, mouth, and nose were full; his hands clenched it; damp earth stuck to his clothes, his shoes. It was as if he had been buried alive and yanked out like a fishworm. As the doctor worked on him with the respirator, March noticed the clipping tacked on the lintel of his greenhouse door: "Whoever needs the earth, shall have the earth."

Around him swarmed the crowd, looking down at him who had fallen the lowest a man can fall this side of the grave, his talents quenched, his dream besmirched.

"Look at them holes! Ain't it a scream? Boy, he was headin' straight for China!"

" 'Spose he was a German spy, goin' to blow up the town?"

"Look at my garden!" shrieked Pyle. "My radishes and spring peas! MY garden!"

"Aw, that old codger was batty as a hoot owl! But what in the name of God was he up to?"

No one knew except Rogier, and he was still unconscious though breathing when he was driven to the hospital.

It really had been very simple. Elated though he was by the progress of his tunnel, Rogier had been alert to the difficulties. The ever-continuing problem, of course, was getting rid of excavated dirt. With the coming of spring, he could no longer mix it with furnace ashes to dump in the ash pit. The vacant lot up the alley, to which he trundled it, was covered. There remained only two more locations for disposal: the banks of Shook's Run across the street, and the dump almost two blocks away. While he was debating these alternatives, another problem posed itself to his practical mind.

The base of Pike's Peak was some distance away. A declination of a degree or two to the north would bring his tunnel under Ute Pass; or a few degrees to the south, under the Cheyenne Canyons. No! He would have to hit it square, full on! To achieve this accuracy of aim, he mounted on a board an old mariner's compass bought at a pawnshop on Huerfano Street. Taking a reading on this as he sighted the Peak from outside, he carried it inside the greenhouse to mount at the entrance of his tunnel.

Then he became aware of another difficulty. How was he, deep in darkness below grass roots, to know whether he was driving at a level instead of inclining or declining his tunnel? He strung a plumb line from the entrance of his tunnel to its farthest end; and as he progressed he took readings with a carpenter's level.

A man had to think of these things, he reminded himself.

What he did not worry about—being a mining man who for thirty years had blasted and drilled tunnels, drifts, and crosscuts through hard granite without the need for cribbing—was the soft black loam, soggy with spring moisture, through which he was digging. Occasionally a clump fell in from wall or ceiling. No matter! Adequate cribbing, with stout pine A-frames and two-inch lagging boards, was beyond his means. It was enough to plant a two-by-four here and there, with a protective sheath of slats from discarded apple boxes.

Yet aside from these practical considerations of an alert, professional mining man, Rogier was screwed up to a high nervous tension. His mind felt like an alarm clock about to go off. Something was driving him to greater and greater haste. Hurry! He was getting old. Hurry! His pulse beat faster, his hands trembled. When he got up that morning he stumbled on the bathroom step. At breakfast he gobbled down his bowl of mush and ran out to his greenhouse. He could hardly force himself to putter at his shelves and boxes in plain view of family and neighbors before opening the padlocked door.

Loosening a chunk of the black loam, he carried it into the light for a better look. How richly black, finely textured, and fragrant it was! Crumbling the clod on a plank, he picked out a couple of fish-worms to look at their translucent amber bodies against the light. Then a snail, another fellow-creature who lived unnoticed in these depths. There came to view a small arrowhead beautifully flaked. Yes, the people who chipped it knew their Mother! But exactly what was it?

He sat down to look at the earth through a magnifying glass. There was no need to send it to an assayer. It was a composite unity of miniscule particles bound together by almost invisible threads of vegetable matter. Living roots and trunks and branches duplicating in miniature the great giants of the forests. He looked closer: at the infinitesmal specks of multicolored stone, the granicular texture of fine clay mortared with salts and minerals in solution, the almost invisible interstices which breathed in air. How beautifully composed and integrated it was—this organic cornerstone of all continents, of a small planet that whirled through interstellar space. No wonder it gave life to his lettuce and radishes, to whole civilizations of mankind.

But what was the ultimate secret of its fertility, the source of the life it engendered? That, not fools' gold, was what he sought. The subterranean sun. So he returned to the mouth of his shaft, lifted the hatch, and lit his miner's candle. For a moment he stood there before his mariner's compass and carpenter's level, like a pilot about to embark on a subterranean voyage no man had ever charted. Ahead of him in the flickering light stretched the long and narrow passage like a vulva into the hidden recesses of living flesh. Hurry! He walked in, and resumed digging. His pick was dull. He seemed short-winded; his legs trembled. He was getting old. There was no time to be lost.

Suddenly the earth caved in. He retreated, but only to confront another avalanche. A serious miscalculation, no doubt. He dug his way through. Then a rush of falling dirt blew out his candle. A clump of dirt dropping on his head knocked out his wind, made him weak and dizzy. Staggering forward, he dropped into the pool of water. Cussing, he clawed his way up. His efforts dislodged another stream of heavy black dirt. As he reached the entrance of the tunnel, the daylight seemed suddenly cut off. Simultaneously the alarm clock in his head went off. In explosive darkness he lurched forward, grabbed at a support and locked his hands around it. He did not feel the flimsy two-by-four give way as he fell backward. A few faintly colored, fish-shaped petals had already begun to whirl around a yellow-bright spot before his eyes as if trying to arrange themselves in a pattern he had never seen but which he seemed to know would be that of a great golden flower. He did not see it take shape. There was a tremendous crash as the timbers came down, followed by the shattering of glass. Then he was flooded with darkness and silence.

PART III

DUST

1

Rogier, back home from the hospital, lay silent and unmoving in his darkened room. Coincident with his seizure, he had suffered a serious blow on his head, a deep cut over his left eye whose scar gave him a sly and sinister look, and a rupture which necessitated his wearing a tin and leather truss – injuries enough to have killed a dray horse. It was miraculous that he pulled through. But he had come to the end of his tether. The greatest gift to which he might look forward now was a peaceful death. So thought the family.

"It might have been a mercy," began March, "but good Lord! Won't anything stop him? Fits, ruptures, cracked head, cut eye, old age! He's worse than a gopher." Yet humbled to the dust as his grandfather was, March saw in the flicker of his eyes the glimmer of an inner fire that could never be wholly estinguished; the imperishable, eternally groping spirit of man that made him invincible to success and ease, failure and shame.

His last pitiful folly was at once the pride and disgrace of the neighborhood. Pyle stormed, threatened suit, and finally paid to have his hole filled in and the fence rebuilt. The Caseys propped up their leaning garage, joyfully shouting insults as they worked. March boarded up the remnant of the greenhouse, filled in the collapsed tunnel under the driveway. Yet long after the scars of the crazy old man's backyard digging had been obliterated, neighbors brought visitors to view the scene. The Shook's Run Gold Mine had become as locally famous as its Cripple Creek prototype, the Sylvanite.

The Rogiers retreated into the decrepit old house as if sealing themselves up in a tomb. Over them all had come a change. They were exhausted and numbed by years of work and worry. Rogier had outworn them all. Lying upstairs like a lump of decomposed granite held together by tin and leather, he was still a man of stone.

"Hasn't that pampered pip-squeak in Memphis answered your letter yet?" Mary Ann demanded of Mrs. Rogier when the hospital and doctor bills arrived. "You wrote her a stiff one, didn't you?"

Mrs. Rogier had written Sally Lee indeed; a hasty note saying that Rogier was quite ill, a delicate reminder that a check would be accepted. A month later an answer came, a postcard from Paris. Sally Lee was in Europe, showing dear little Sugar Lump at her impressionable age the scenic wonders across the sea. Sally Lee was saddened to hear of Daddy's illness, hoped he was now recovering, and wished he were with her on tour.

"What about Boné?" asked Mary Ann sharply.

Mrs. Rogier spread out her hands emptily. Boné had not sent his current address.

Mary Ann, disgruntled, settled down with Uncle John to pay off the mounting debts.

March too had come to the end of his rope. The miasma of defeat and decay that penetrated every pore of the house roused him to fury. It was like a cancer; he was afraid lest it fasten on him and eat into his own flesh. Little London he abhorred. At the Country Club he saw Valeria seldom. They were like stars, each in its separate orbit, which had touched in a moment of truth and passed. Neither would forget the other, but there was nothing that permanently bound them together. He began cutting chapel, lying outside on the grass watching the clouds and listening to the pipe organ wheezing inside. The departing professors passed him with angry looks. He did not notice them, but lay drawn tight within himself, impenetrable. Through the daily class lectures he sat quietly but uninterested. His afternoon laboratory work he did lackadaisically and left early for home to read. Summer was coming, but he did not ask Mr. Ford to save him a job in the Santa Fe yards. In a mindless calm he wondered vaguely what had come upon him. Spring fever, he thought, unable to overcome his lassitude. Something was coming to a crisis.

Early one Friday morning in May he walked to school to take an important examination. Only the six major students of Dr. Thomason were taking it. The end of the school year was some weeks away; yet the students passing this test were promised immunity from the final examinations and approved applications to larger technical schools for teaching fellowships.

"Bring your slide rules and all the notes you want," Thomason had told them the day before. "It won't be necessary to write anything on your cuffs. Only don't talk among yourselves."

The professor was in his office when March arrived, and did not come out. He merely handed March a notebook as he walked into the basement laboratory. March sat down on a chair below a window. The other five students were scattered around him. The short, solid pillars of brick topped with immense slabs of slate had been cleared of apparatus. On them lay textbooks and lecture notes, engineering handbooks, and logarithm tables.

Where were the examination questions?

There were none. One of the men turned around to March. "Professor Thomason said we were simply to solve the circuit on the blackboard." It was the only word spoken.

The blackboard on two sides of the room was covered with a drawing of one vast compound electrical circuit. At first glance it seemed to begin with a generating plant, run to a main switchboard through several circuit-breakers, and thence to an amazing network that seemed to contain every problem March had encountered during his three years' work. A devil of a mess!

March leaned back in his chair. There was no hurry; they had four hours. He was not sure, but he believed that he could work it out. Still, he did not begin.

Staring at the generator diagram, he remembered the old steam plant east of town he had visited, the whirling drums cutting the lines of force in the magnetized rims to generate the power drawn off from the plant to supply the town. Was this the source of power? No, because the drums had to be set whirling by steam from the old boiler. What made it go? Coal. What was the nature of coal, the inherent power of fuel itself, deriving from the enormous pressures of earth and time? The beds of coal were simply great forests that had been washed out upon the plains and covered with sediment from crumbled, vanished mountains. And the life of these forests – It all went back to a beginning no one knew. This was merely an industrial application of the one sacred power of life that flowed through everything that lived and breathed, the stone, the blade of grass, beast and bird and man. The Great Spirit, stripped of its divinity and mechanically employed only for monetary gain in a materialistic civilization.

Lazing in his chair, March could see the bleak future spreading out before him. A big technical school. Years of work in more basement laboratories. Degrees. Then with a doctorate his priestly initiation into the cult of Science. Why, in time he might concoct a tidy little theory himself and be acclaimed a genius. March was vaguely aware that just as there were but few true artists, there were also pitifully few real scientists. Like Thomason the rest of them were merely industrial engineers. Their consciousness did not deepen with the perception of nature and her laws; they were mastered by their own machines. They believed they were geniuses, forgetting that genius is the power of evoking life, not throttling it. It was the love of truth, the love of life, that led to pure science. But these men were interested only in the application of science to commercial ends. They were industrialists.

March felt this strongly enough, if not clearly, to realize fully for the first time he could never give up life for industry. He was on the wrong trail, and spring was pounding in his blood an aching restlessness that no longer could be denied. He could see out the window, on a level with his head, a single clump of grass sticking up against the cloudless blue and shouting all the mystery of his youth.

Spring, the wanton hussy! Who has not smelled the perfume of her passing, heard the rustle of her skirts when the apple blossoms flutter to the ground and the rain flicks against the window pane, seen her steps in the long black furrows behind the plow? But who knows her? In all of vast America she is never twice the same.

It is Corpus Cristi in the little Mexican settlements, when the people stream out from Mass and kneel chanting in the rock street before doorways hung with evergreens. Good Friday and Easter, the time when the *Penitentes* come out from a *morada* and straggle up a remote arroyo, lashing their naked backs with whips of cactus, to hang a limp member on a cross. It is San Juan Day when all the waters of the world are blessed, and old grandmothers creep out in the dawn to bathe their flabby, wrinkled bodies in the muddy creek; when exactly at four o'clock it rains.

It is Holy Cross Day at Taos when the Indian races are run, the men and boys giving back with bursts of speed their energy to the sun who will return it again to mankind; when at San Felipe the green corn dance is held on the bank of the swollen Rio Grande, a hundred old men singing to the beat of a belly drum while 300 dancers stomp the dusty plaza from sunup till sundown. Over Cochiti and Zuni, cliff-high Acoma, the white-bellied clouds gather, and the thunder cracks open the gates of sky.

Here in the high hinterland of America the snowcaps shrink on the peaks, the water pours down canyons to three seas, the anemones push sturdily erect through snow. But now come the late and heavy snows. The freshly budded lilacs bend and break. Paper ice forms over lake and pond. Wild ducks drop from the mists into the marshes. A lone robin chirps disconsolately underneath a bush. The running sap congeals on the spruce bark into hard globules of chewing gum.

Fickle spring! A blizzard one day and a dry gritty wind the next. A vast and slow birth with horrible travail. All aboard behind the snowplow for the first ride to the summit of Pike's Peak! The high passes begin to open: La Veta, Hoosier, Rabbit Ear, Monarch, Tennessee, Whiskey, Slumgullion, and Mosquito. The little mining towns watch for the first train in, muttering incoherently of fresh vegetables. Now the road crews hit the ball. Avalanches make all trains late. The D&RG is stuck again.

The shaggy bear leaves his den, the deer climb higher and rub the moss-growth from their prongs. Who sees the wild geese, hears the woodpecker, for the bitterness, the sweetness, the wracking birth pangs of spring?

It is a state of mind, a wordless cry, a resurrection, misery and hope sharped and flatted by the wailing winds. Above all, it is a tormenting unrest, a wild passion to hit the lonely trail over the last horizon into the forever unknown and unknowable, wearing a single upright feather – not defiantly as men flaunt the faded cockades of their decadent heritage, but proudly, like the everlasting insignia of the wild earth's nobility.

An hour had passed. March rose, wrote his name in the empty notebook and laid it on the table. Without stopping at Dr. Thomason's office, he walked out and crossed the campus to the Administration Building. At the cashier's window he collected twenty-two dollars due him for work as a laboratory assistant. He was supposed to turn it in at the next window as payment on his tuition. Instead, he jammed the money in his pocket and walked slowly home.

The two girls were in school. Ona was over at the grocery store. Rogier was lying on the sofa, and Mrs. Rogier was dusting. March went upstairs and packed his leather-rimmed canvas duffle bag. Before long his mother came hurriedly up the stairs.

"What's the matter, son? Home this time of day! Are you sick?" She suddenly saw the duffle bag. Her glance swept the bare top of his dresser and the empty hooks inside the closet, flew back wildly to his face.

"Don't get upset, Mother," he said quietly, standing before her. "I've quit school, and I'm leaving home. Sit down, Mother."

He pushed her down gently on the bed, sat beside her and put his arm over her shoulders.

"You're mad, son. Mad!" she gasped. And yet there was something in his quiet tone, assurance and unusual gentleness that sent a chill up her spine.

He explained patiently as best he could. "And so you see, Mother, it's no place for me. I'd got all I could out of it a year ago, but never knew it till now – Don't look so! Wouldn't I be leaving soon anyway to go to work? We're poorer now than ever with Grandad the way he is. You'll be needing the money I can send you."

"But where are you going? God in Heaven, boy!"

"The Wyoming oil fields, Mother. There's a big boom on. Work for everyone."

"What kind? What can a boy do? It's a wild goose chase, son.

Be sensible. Don't leave yet."

She knew it was futile talk. The moment had come that she had dreaded and waited for, day by day, ever since he had gone to Cripple Creek. Tom, Rogier, Cable, and now her son, her only son! How could she repeat now the pain and anguish, her protestations of love and affirmations of faith, go through that scene of parting in which she had participated nights on end? It was like a play she had rehearsed for years, and now at the rise of the curtain she found herself tongue-tied and frozen. Only the pain stabbing her heart was real.

Indomitably she stood up and wiped away a tear as if ashamed of that single priceless pearl formed within her years before by the tiny grit of her first fear. "Well, son!" She grasped him sturdily by the shoulders, her big heavy body hard as stone, her square jaws clenched. "So you're really goin'. Well!"

If she'd only wept or stormed or something! Anything but this slow fusing of despair and strength, a tear and a smile – this Rogier undemonstrativeness! It was more than the boy could bear. He flung his arms around her, stroked back her graying hair, kissed her beautifully white, girlish smooth face.

"I'll be comin' back soon. Hell! Sure I will!"

"I'll be fixin' up a few things for you," she answered simply and walked head up into her room.

March told Leona and Nancy good-bye when they came home for lunch, answering their joshing with quiet grins. Mrs. Rogier was perplexed but loyal. "It beats all how things happen. But I count on my boys every time. Just remember you're a Rogier, March!"

For Mary Ann and Uncle John he left a note. But when he went to bid his grandfather farewell, something hard and bitter within him dissolved in a sudden glow of pride and compassion. Rogier, lying on the sofa, stood up: bent over, both hands clutching his truss.

"Don't stand up for me Grandad!" March cried, cut to the quick.

Rogier, wincing with pain, adjusted his contraption and straightened up to grasp the boy by the arms. His white head barely reached March's shoulder.

"I just want to tell you I'm leavin'," March stammered.

The old man had snapped out of his usual haze; his eyes were clear, his voice resolute. "I heard you at the table. And boy, I think it's good. Every tub's got to stand on its own bottom." He paused, as if trying to dig out from the shaft of a collapsed memory at least a specimen of pay dirt. "Minin' you say? No, not minin'. But you're diggin' in, hey!" He dug futilely in his empty pants pockets. "Dom, boy! I hate to see you leavin' without a cent. If things had panned out different –"

"Grandad!" The boy caught him to breast, this shrunken bag of bones, and over his head cried to all the years behind and those ahead, "Grandad, everything I know about mining, construction, geology, and all that, I got from you. I won't forget it, ever. Or you, Grandad! Ever!"

He grabbed up his duffle bag, kissed Ona for the last time, and ran out the door. Walking swiftly to the station, he felt the sadness lifting from him. He was alone and free at last! The world lay immense and naked before him.

He had turned his back forever upon college without gratitude, shame, or regret for his wasted opportunities and the unlocked doors he'd never entered. But when he stood for the last time in the Santa Fe railroad station, he knew this would always be his Alma Mater. These were the classrooms where he had learned the lessons of life: the great waiting room in which he had shouted his newspapers, the Fred Harvey newsstand in which he had polished apples, the huge baggage room where he had wrestled loads of trunks, the grimy little freight office down in the yards. It was a coeducational institution, of course. Look at the Misses Fred Harvey majoring in – should we say home economics? – or coffee and pie? Dining Room juniors and seniors in starched all-white. Not a frowsy head among them at six a.m.

He could remember his campus in starlight: the Upper Yards and Middle Pass Pocket and the Lower Yards. He knew it instinctively as on the dark night he was caught between Lower Four and Main Two, with twenty seconds to reach, unlock, and throw the switch for a cattle train. And the hot steam spouting like geysers, the red-bellied furnaces of the 4400's and the shriek of the great steel cats racing around the bend. The slippery roofs of jolting freights on a rainy night and the cold grab irons – these were his athletic field and gymnasium. "By God, you made it! I thought when she hit the turn you was a goner!"

His Technical Advisor, the Yard Master, knew both practice and theory; in a pinch he could replace a broken driving rod, swearing with the best. His Dean of Men, the Station Master, spouted no sanctimonious quotations from the Bible, but he knew the vagaries of men and women. And his President, the Station Agent, Mr. Ford, had fired him twice but still slapped him on the back.

Change, change, change. The constant, ever-flowing movement of life that changes all things. This was what he had learned here, the stage and the institution created by the phenomenon of the great American unrest. Just as he had learned at Shallow Water and Cripple Creek its dual counterpoint: the verities that lay embodied within the hub of time, the core of life itself. And there came over him again the mystery of his own being: Am I the leaf that falls into the flow or the leaf that sprouts anew; the rock disintegrated by time or the timeless dust within the rock?

A whistle sounded. The train swept round the bend, clanged in with hissing jets. "Come on, Mister Cable, before you miss it."

"Aw, say, Les!" he protested, grabbing futilely at his duffle bag. "I'll tote this damn thing, Quit your kiddin'!"

But it was Old Les who stuffed it aboard the smoker and came back to join the men gathered around March, joshing, shaking his hand.

"He'll never get away! From force of habit he'll be jumpin' off at the water tower!"

"Don't spend all your money on the girls!"

Behind all the rude jocularity March could sense a deep good will, the farewell of men to one who could never outgrow them, succeed to a niche higher than it was their lot to attain, but always remain, as he once was, a comrade of their stature, no better and sometimes less than they.

But now the stop was up; the platform was almost empty. The Station Master left the gate.

"Well, son," he said simply and directly, sticking out his hand. "I'm wishin' you good luck. We've had our squabbles and they're forgotten. When you get to sittin' in a fine big office with secretaries and such, or somethin' else, don't forgit us and how you used to bust through these gates bulgin' with suitcases. And when you come back, big and important, remember us boys will be glad to see you."

With this baccalaureate sermon echoing in his ears and heart, March swung on board. He found his seat. And pressing his nose and clouded eyes against the window pane, he saw dimly from the high trestle over Bijou that Shook's Run and the ramshackle old house were passing irretrievably by.

In the middle of the street stood an old white-headed man with his arm upraised, and beside him a woman waving her handkerchief.

Behind them, their eternal background and his, stood Pike's Peak.

2

Rogier, still wearing his truss to hold his rupture in place but vehemently refusing to carry a cane, limped around house and yard like a man bound by invisible hobbles. His white hair, thin as corn silk, hung down in sparse strands to his stiff white collar – still fastened by his diamond button and worn without a necktie. His powerful body had shrunk to a bag of sticks draped in coat and pants that hung on him in folds; he looked like a scarecrow. He had lost most of his teeth and lived on mush, French toast, and sweet potatoes. His spells were infrequent and mild, often lasting but a few minutes. He did not read, being content to sit out in the sunshine or on the high stool in his shop. He gave no trouble at all.

This was the pathetic and sometimes ludicrous caricature to which had been reduced the proud yet humble and always indomitable "Colonel" Joseph Rogier as viewed by his family, the neighbors, and the children who occasionally jeered at him and his backyard mine across the fence.

Rogier did not mind if he ever noticed them. For after a lifetime of work and worry, success and abysmal failures, and the loss of his few old friends, he had come at last to the threshold of his greatest discovery.

Like something risen from the depths of dreamless sleep to the horizon of wakeful consciousness, without clear outline yet embodying the substance of a hope and meaning as strangely familiar as it was vague – thus had he first glimpsed it years before, believing it was that high snowy Peak which had drawn and held him like a lodestone he could not escape. Into its granite depths he had drilled and blasted toward its glowing heart, the luminescent sun, the golden flower of life. But now, sitting in the afternoon sun, he stared at the Peak without seeming to see it objectively manifested before him. It was where it had always been – inside him.

He could see it when he sat in the shop on rainy days, down in the basement on winter evenings, in bed at night. Daylight and darkness meant little to him now. For if at intervals he was consciously bright as a silver dollar just struck from the Denver mint, most of the time he lived in that curious realm between dreamless sleep and wakeful consciousness; as if becalmed in that immeasurable interval between two breaths when the mind is stilled and the mysterious faculty of intuition bridges the gap between the tyrannical reasoning of the finite mind and the all-embracing comprehension of an infinite and universal consciousness. In that pellucid dusk everything was all one to him now; success and failure, sloth and ambition, poverty and riches, acclaim and derision, all merged into one indivisible whole. The great snowy Peak itself was no longer a friend to be coerced, an enemy to be combatted. It was like himself, a material shell, a transient symbol. What its purpose and meaning was, or his own, he could not yet read clearly. He no longer anticipated its taking shape as faintly colored, fish-shaped petals slowly revolving around a yellow-bright center as if trying to arrange themselves into the pattern of a great golden flower. Being timeless it was also formless; and he was content to accept it as it was.

No, Rogier gave no trouble at all. Ona did not worry about him. But in bed at night she worried about March. Leona she loved and understood. But always at sight of March's dark, sensitive, and stubborn face, her soul had streamed out to him as if she had been pierced with a knife. And yet she had never been able to touch him. There was between them a curious and imperceptible barrier. In him the ghost of Cable prowled. Not the careless, gentle husband, the casual companion of her days. But the lover, the soft sensuous flow that had enshrouded her in a mindless passion, the subtle awareness her analytical mind could never fathom. He was the wildness of the night to which she succumbed so completely, but from which next morning she shrank as if in terror. In him was intuition, not reason; cruelty, not coldness. He was the eternal stranger who had appeared from nowhere, made her his, and departed swiftly, silently, still unknown.

He is my son, my only son, she thought, and yet to me he is a stranger. It is a strange thing and a bitter thing, but true. Boné of my bone, flesh of my flesh, he is closer to me than was my husband. And yet I cannot touch him. For in the immense and lasting loneliness of their separate selves, it is given to a man and woman to meet, to touch, and break away. And a woman ever after would reach out her hand to her son and draw her husband back again, who is forever gone. And this cannot be. So he is a stranger.

Why this strange and bitter thing? she wondered, listening for the comforting steps of the Kadles in the darkness. He is his father's coarse straight hair, his black bottomless eyes, and his slim straight body and strange living awareness. But he is also the fruit of my womb. To him I was the tree of life; my sap runs in his veins, he is a limb torn from me, whole. I know my son! I know him as no woman, no man will, ever. But because I see myself in him, and no one can believe it is herself she sees, I see him always a stranger.

"Damn him! He treats me like a squaw!" she cried to herself in bitter loneliness, knowing that it was the shame and hurt, the pride and glory of every mother to be treated like a squaw by her son.

"But where is he, and what in God's name can he be doing all this time?" she cried to the Kadles making their nocturnal rounds.

Infrequent, short, scrawled notes from him began to arrive. He was in the Salt Creek oil fields of Wyoming, working as a roustabout or day laborer in a gang laying six miles of eight-inch pipe. Like Cripple Creek, Salt Creek was a place-name for an immense oil structure that included many fields: Big Muddy, Poison Spider, Lost Soldier, Crook's Gap, Teapot, and Salt Creek. He himself lived in a construction camp not far from Lavoye, a squatter camp that reminded him of early Cripple Creek with its squatters' shanties, drab wooden stores, company commissaries, and dance halls. The work was hard, but the food was good and the pay fair: fifty cents an hour, with a dollar and a half subtracted for meals and the use of a bunk. Enclosed was a money order.

Mary Ann sniffed at the small amount. "At least he's showing a sense of responsibility!" Next day she mailed him a box of candy.

That fall postcards came from Malott and Okanogan, Washington in the Columbia River valley, where March was picking apples. One weekend he had gone up to Canada. The immense valley did not appeal to him. It had been formed by glacial action; he was a Leo, a sun-child, preferring a country of volcanic origin.

Ona sighed. "A sun-child! Of all things! Where could he have got that zodiacal notion except from Daddy?!" She settled down for a long wait, knowing that he was heading south.

His Christmas card came from Oregon, where he was working at a timber mill. Ona did not know just where; the postmark was blurred.

And now came no word from him at all.

March, still working slowly through the vast immensities and lonely little towns heaving gently on the back of the sleeping earth-monster of America, felt his mind go numb, his soul expand into space. There rushed through him again the rich flow of life he had known as a child — a tempestuous rush of sensory impressions undefined and unconstrained. And ever he could hear the aimless ancient winds cry hauntingly to him with the voices of his father's people:

Brother, where do you go now in the new moccasins of manhood, with a brave heart, and a lean and hungry look?

Brothers, his heart answered, I do not know. I have known the short-grass plains of my father's people, the Cheyennes, the Kiowas, the Blue Cloud Arapahoes. I have seen the great male Rockies where Buckskin Charley and his Utes pitched their smoke-gray lodges, the cold campfires of the mighty Sioux, the buffalo grounds of the Crows, the sacred Wallowa of the people with pierced noses, the Nez Perce. Old and familiar are the *hogans* of the Navajos, the mud-brown terraced towns of the Pueblos, and cliff-high Acoma with those of the mesa-top Hopis. New to my moccasins are the deserts of the Shoshones and Piutes, the baking river valley of the Cocopahs and those giant, naked war-clubbers, the Mojaves. Now I am come to *Apacheria,* the barren parched rock mountains of the Apaches. Where my trail leads I do not know. I have forgotten what I seek.

And around his solitary campfires the ancient aimless winds cried back derisively: Break your own trail, brother! We work for no man nor people!

That spring March reached the Mexican border. It was a separate country unmarked on any map. On one side the United States with its rabid commercialism and industrialization, its plumbing and stock markets. On the other, Old Mexico with its pride and poverty, its obduracy to change. The border was neither, but a world between; the last frontier. It was a chasm a thousand miles long, whose deepest sink-holes were the towns – Tia Juana, Tecate, Mexicali, Algodones, Nogales, Naco, Agua Prieta, Juarez – into which poured all the vices and perversions, the brutality and cruelty, the tailings of both races.

Bars and cabarets, *cantinas* and *casinos.* Chinese lottery counters, *refresqueria* stands on the corners, *taco* venders carrying their tables on their heads. Phonographs blasting from every doorway, stacks of sugar cane, strips of drying meat, and tubs of guts in open meat stalls beclouded with flies. A Packard limousine and a burro loaded with firewood; brown bare feet and high French heels treading the dust of Mexico's infinite dryness. Ragged *pelados,* somber old señoras wrapped to the eyes in black *rebozos.* Forty dollar panama hats and silver braided, high peaked *sombreros.* French champagne, Spanish sherry, and Portuguese port; and in the mud floor drinking dens raw *mezcal* and cheap *tequila.* Pigs rooting in the *plaza;* a guitar whining "La Paloma." The stench of beer, the acrid smell of urine in the dry dust – A thousand screaming contradictions resolved into the harmonic whole.

And the faces he saw! The arrogant faces of strutting fat Mexican generals and their scrawny mistresses, the red faces of bluff Anglo cattle ranchers and rustlers, the white anemic faces of American politicians and those of obsequiously polite Mexicans who aped with equal greed and cunning their American neighbors' "Beeg Business" methods. And in the sputter of *ocote* torches the evil faces of petty criminals of both countries, the cruel masks of the half-breeds, the disintegrated faces of the *peones* deprived of their land, the yellow faces of Chinese long run out of Arizona and now being driven from Sonora, the cheap powdered faces of prostitutes from rows of open cribs, the pock-marked diseased faces of beggars, the hopeless faces of decadent Indians sprawled in a stupor in the gutters or asleep on the steps of the cathedral.

And all these faces, so dark and haunting by night and so timelessly imprinted in his memory by the hard glitter of the sun, resolved into one face in which he glimpsed the mystery and howling terror of its single soul. It was the savage fusion of two blood streams, the white and the red. It was the clamorous cry of the mixed-blood – the *mestizos, ladinos, creoles, coyotes*. Here he was staring into the racial soul of mixed-blood America. And as if in a mirror, he saw the violence, the mystery, the dark beauty of his own soul. He too was a mixed-blood. He loved it and hated it, and he felt at home.

Wandering from town to town in crowded auto stages, sleeping in lodging houses and four-bit throws, and eating where he could, March wound up at Nogales. Here he became friends with John Bratling, head bartender of the "Cave" on the south side of the Line. The Cave was a new *cantina* built into the rocky side of the hill. It formerly had been the Mexican jail, and the small rocky cells from which the iron latticed doors had been removed now served as private dining rooms. The cabaret was large and beautiful, boasting the finest food and wines available. The barroom in front was long and narrow, with a sawdust floor. Despite its tacky appearance, it was a famous rendezvous.

Bratling was a suave, polished Englishman ruined by the war, who had put to work his knowledge of wines and liquors, and was obliged to live in this dry desert climate for his health. He knew every man worth knowing on both sides of the Line – Mexican generals, immigration and railroad officials, engineers, bankers, politicians, gamblers, and owners of the big ranches south. He also knew their first names and their favorite drinks, a memory worth a fortune to the Cave. He had only one failing. For months he neither smoked nor drank, he kept reasonable hours, and he saved money for his one wish – a walking trip through Italy. Then one day, without warning, he would go on a "high lonesome:" locking himself in his room and drinking himself into a delirium until he was carried to the hospital.

He lived in a ramshackle hotel, the Santa Caterina, where most of the dealers and entertainers had rooms. Off duty at midnight they gathered in his room to talk until morning. March visited with them often. It was a strange Bohemia that flowered then for once and always, and which was to remain with March as a never-to-be-forgotten fantasy of his youth.

One night Bratling asked him abruptly, "March, what kind of work are you doing down here?"

"I'm a malaria control engineer."

Jose, an ecarte dealer, laughed. "A mosquito chaser!"

March nodded glumly. He knew his payroll title merely glossed the job of draining irrigation ditches and swampy fields of stagnant water.

Bratling said simply, "We ought to be able to do better than that for you, March. Eh, Jose?"

Jose eloquently spread out his beautiful, narrow hands. He was a *mestizo*. His face was the color of *café con leche*, with high cheek bones and full lobed ears from which dangled long turquoise ear-drops. He wore gray gaberdine shirts with mother-of-pearl buttons, and black string ties. He was on duty from five until midnight, and was paid twenty-five dollars a day. While dealing he never recognized a friend, never spoke. When March came to his table to place his $2 bet, Jose allowed him to play until he had won enough to buy a good dinner. If March persisted in playing, Jose broke him flat.

Now for a month Jose in his room had been trying to teach him to deal. Jose was a born dealer. He could shuffle a deck with either hand; deal six hands of poker rapidly face down, and then call out each card in each hand; he could deal from top and bottom too adroitly for March to observe; could palm a card; and lay down any hand March could order, as if it came out naturally from the deck. That the cards were marked seemed impossible until Jose showed him how they came so in sealed packages from the manufacturers. Yet there was more to it than craftsmanship; something that made Jose one of the best dealers along the border and that prevented March from ever becoming the worst.

Jose had put it bluntly at last. "It just ain't in you, kid. You got guts although you're too stubborn. You got a flat face, and you could get your hands in shape with glycerine. But you just ain't got the feel of cards in your bones. So lay off. You ain't cut out that way."

Three days later Bratling sent word to March to come to the Cave that evening. When March arrived, he saw a party of Americans celebrating in the cabaret. Heading the group was a portly man named James Finnerty – Vice-President in Charge of Operations of Western Mines, Incorporated. At least once a year, said Bratling, Finnery came down for a spree, leaving it to him to provide food, liquor, entertainment, and plenty of girls. "We're good friends," added Bratling, "so speak up when you meet him."

A few minutes later when Finnerty came out to the bar, Bratling introduced March. "This is the young man I was telling you about, Mr. Finnerty. It seems to me that Western Mines ought to have a place somewhere for an ambitious young fellow."

"Shurtinly!" mumbled the Vice-President, putting down his fourth Martini. "Lots of mines, good mines, all over the worl' – I want some more lil' onions, John, on lil' sticks – What'd I say, sir?"

"You were telling me what an extended corporation Western Mines is sir," answered March, "and how you needed trained men all over the world."

Finnerty blinked. "Technical school trainin'? Minin'?"

"Colorado. Cripple Creek."

"Hmm." Finnerty's small eyes steadied. He was worth his salt, for despite the flush suffusing his face and his thick tongue, he was wary and cautious. "I don't hire men. No shure! Got an Employment Supervisor. College professors send him their kids. You go to him. Maybe he can use a young engineer in one of our copper pits on the Sonora boundary. Hey? Tell him Finnerty sent you."

"Perhaps a note from you would help, Mr. Finnerty," said Bratling, laying a pencil and paper in front of him. "And here's another Martini. Not quite so dry, sir; you mustn't spoil your dinner."

When Finnerty had ambled back to his crowd, Bratling winked at March. "Hold on to that note, boy! It's a ticket right into the payroll of Western Mines. How much railroad fare are you going to need?"

3

Familiar only with the deep hard-rock mines of Cripple Creek, March thought the Copper Boy the damndest looking hole he'd ever seen. It wasn't a mine, really. Western Mines had simply sliced off the top of a hill with a butter knife and was dipping out spoonsful of reddish sugar rich in copper. But the spoons were huge steam-driven buckets that travelled on railway tracks around and around the great open pit in concentric circles which descended deeper year by year.

This immense pit, surrounded by company offices, shops, tool-houses, and railroad sheds, lay on the backbone of a narrow parched-brown range which rose out of the desert like an immense gila-monster turned into stone.

To the south, on the barren dove-gray plain from which rose the smoke-blue Sierra Madre, lay the Mexican town of Dos Ritos – a single dusty street lined with *cantinas, casinos,* cribs, and squalid adobes.

To the north, lining a narrow steep-walled gulch, sprawled the American town of Piedras Blancas. About desert mining camps there was always the feeling of hopeless, hard dreariness, as if the land had gone dead. So it was with Piedras Blancas. Even the big Copper Boy Hotel, built by Western Mines to accommodate its occasional guests, held a look of careless abandon despite its old-fashioned, ornate architecture. The one lively spot in town was Mother Brenet's boarding house, where March roomed and boarded. The dining room sat fifty men at a meal. The long oilcloth table at night supported huge bowls of vegetable soup, platters of roast beef, loaves of French sour bread, vegetables, stewed fruit, two kinds of pie, and gingerbread cake. The charge per meal was forty cents.

At work March found that a junior engineer was a jack-of-all-trades who did everything but fill his superior's pipe. He trudged along with the timekeeper and crew bosses, was ordered out of the shops and roundhouses, was found in the way of the assayers, tried to check car loadings and compute tonnage. His little successes were attributed to "fool's luck" and his inexperience was the excuse for loading him with a thousand distasteful jobs.

"Here, Cable, work out these figures for me, will you? It'll give you good experience."

"It might pay you, March, to come back on your own time and spend a few evenings on this. I feel you ought to know what these reports include."

Jackson, the superintendent of the camp, was a typical company official. He wore shiny boots, whipcord trousers, and a large Stetson. He and his wife lived at the hotel and spent their evenings playing bridge.

The chief engineer was an old bowlegged Scotchman named MacGregor. He was a bachelor, and despite his large salary lived in a small company cottage which he kept neat as a pin. Mac wore an old wrinkled suit, flannel shirt, and a black bow tie sewed on a rubber band.

Between them existed an unexpressed antipathy. The cause for it March understood one evening when he had dinner with the Morrels in their cottage. They were plain, homey people. Morrel was the chief clerk, an excellent man but without the technical training and personality that might have made him outstanding in the company.

"Yep, that's what it takes to get along in this company —

politics and personality," he explained. "Take the boss, Jackson. He runs the whole camp—payroll, production, all that. But he doesn't know a whoop about mining. He doesn't have to. Just look at our reports, the same standard forms for every one of Western Mines' holdings. And the mines are no different. Look at the Copper Boy. The old-timers took all the chances. And when the thing proved good, the ore all blocked out, Western Mines bought it for a song. All they had to do then was haul out ore according to its market price. It might be a factory, a chain grocerystore – anything. It just happens that it's ore the company deals in.

"All the selling, buying, transportation, milling, hiring is done for all mines in the General Office. The superintendents are like store managers: men who know the company policies and routines, and see they're followed to a T. And the fellow that gets the job is the politician.

"But on every job technical problems come up. Too expensive for the General Engineering Office to send out a man each time. So they have an old-time mining man directly handling the removal of ore – Mac here, for instance. He knows his stuff and gets a good salary, but he reports to Jackson and will never get any higher.

"Do you catch on? Imagine Mac dressed up, playing bridge, entertaining company directors and visiting stockholders at the hotel! So the Office has Jackson. He's got personality. Look at those boots and hat! The Romantic Engineer in the Wilds of Arizona. Do the New Yorkers eat that up? You ought to hear the ladies!"

"Now, now!" remonstrated Mrs. Morrel.

Morrel laughed and refilled his pipe. "Keep all this under your hat, March. You're a bright young chap and I'd like to see you get along. I've seen too many young engineers just out from school, thinking that technical training is all they need. It isn't. So here's my advice. Forget all this stuff about the brave engineer conquering nature. Mining is a business now, like any other. It's the stock market that rules the game. Learn all you can from Mac; he thinks a lot of you. But for Pete's sake, boy, play up to the Boss. Jackson's the man who'll make or break you. Drop over to the hotel where the officials stay and make yourself agreeable. And when Finnerty brings down a big party for another 'inspection' trip across the Line, you bust a gut to be included!"

March walked home slowly in the moonlight. Below him, like a sea beating against a rock, lay the unbroken chaparral desert. What would that ruined old man, his grandfather, have thought of Morrel's exposition on mining? And how strange it was, March thought, that he was now caught in what he had tried to escape.

Months later he was reminded of it when Finnerty arrived with a large group of company officials and stockholders on a tour of inspection. Piedras Blancas drew a deep breath and stood at attention. The hotel was scrubbed and polished, the Copper Boy put in apple-pie order. Jackson stalked around with a fixed and oily grin on his face.

For two days the party went over plant and pit. On the third day, during which the men held conferences and read reports, the women were driven on a sight-seeing tour over the Border to Dos Ritos. March was one of the drivers of the company cars. He had shined his own boots, put on a necktie, and did his best to be agreeable.

"Now, Mr. Cable, be sure and stop when we get to the border. I want to say I stood with one foot in America and the other in Mexico – No? Isn't there a line drawn on the ground or something? Well, I declare! All the country looks the same. It ought to be different!"

"So you can speak Spanish, Big Boy! You gay young dog! Now I know where you spend your time. How about showing me a Place – you know, the kind our husbands hit for when we're not along? I'll bet these little Mexican cuties can really shake it up!"

March managed to get them back to the hotel in time for the banquet to which all of the engineers, clerks, and their wives were invited, the laborers having been given the afternoon off. Finnerty and Jackson were talking on the front steps when he drove up.

"Oh, James!" screamed Mrs. Finnerty who had been in the party. "We've had the loveliest time. We had Lombardi cocktails at the Foreign Club. Pink. In tall glasses. Young Mr. Cable here ordered them for us. Do you know him?"

Finnerty blinked.

"You probably don't remember me, Mr. Finnerty," said March, "but you gave me a note in Nogales during your last business trip."

"Yes, yes," recollected Finnerty. "I see you got your job.

How's he doing, Jackson?"

"Developing nicely, sir!" spoke up Jackson, turning to March with a sudden air of cordiality. "I didn't know you had met our Vice-President, March."

The boy detected a sting in his remark. "Mr. Jackson has given me the run of the place, Mr. Finnerty. I appreciate his changing me about."

Both smiled; Jackson in a peevish temper had lately handed him over to Mac.

Politics! March grinned as he drove off.

After the banquet Finnerty and Jackson drew him aside. "Ah - March - ah," began Jackson. "I've told Mr. Finnerty you might be the one to do us a great favor. Your wide acquaintance across the Line – escapades one might say – Tut, tut! my boy. Only natural. And they have never interfered with your work."

"Hell!" said Finnerty. "Speak out! We're all grown up, eh, Cable?"

"In short," went on Jackson, "Mr. Finnerty wants to give his guests a stag party before they return to New York. A touch of the border, of Mexico."

"You know John in Nogales, Cable. That's the kind of a party I want. The real stuff!" demanded Finnerty. "A hell of a good meal with lots to drink, entertaining, and plenty of girls. Get me?"

March nodded.

Jackson resumed. "Mrs. Jackson and I, with my staff members and their wives, are entertaining the ladies at bridge while their husbands are away. Mr. Finnerty gives you a clean bill as far as expense goes. If you can arrange it, take tomorrow off and the next day also."

"I'll do what I can," March replied soberly.

"Fine!" said Jackson. "We trust you implicitly. I'll have a voucher cashed for you tomorrow morning, and meet all bills beyond that."

The party began at nine o'clock in *El Zorro Azul* on the single dusty street of Dos Ritos. When Finnerty and his men arrived the bar was empty save for a group of Mexican army officers March had invited. The night was warm, the stars hung low over the chaparral, and down the street they could hear the hoof beats of an occasional horse. The men drank as most Americans drink across the border: hastily, gulping one after another. Then, faces flushed, they gathered in the back room.

The table was already set on the polished dance floor, lighted candles glowing on the white cloth. On a plank dais behind, four musicians dressed in gaudy *charro* costumes were thumbing their guitars. On one side of the room stood a long buffet stacked with liquor bottles, trays, and glasses. Around it stood a group of Mexican girls dressed in cheap evening gowns, their black hair freshly oiled, and their dark faces splotched with white powder. The Mexican officers nodded to them casually without showing undue familiarity, but Finnerty stopped at the door in amazement.

"Jesus Christ! What's this – a formal dinner? I told you I wanted a stag party."

March nodded at Lola, who had supplied the girls for him. She grabbed Finnerty by the arm. "Come weeth me. A leetle drink, *verdad*? I show you!"

She sprinkled some salt on her left hand in the hollow between thumb and forefinger, and with one quick motion adeptly smeared it over her gums. Then she tossed down a jigger of white liquor, and noisily sucked a slice of lemon. "*Puro Mexicano, no?*"

"Tequila! That's how you drink it, boys! Watch me!" shouted Finnerty.

Now they all stood poking salt in their mouths and sucking lemons like children. The strong cactus brandy, on top of the many cocktails they had taken out front, was beginning to shake them loose from their shamefaced air of restraint. Even the corpulent, uniformed *generales* began to unbend. The girls, observed March, were behaving nicely. Their full breasts shook as they laughed, and they took no offense when a hand negligently slapped them across the bottoms.

Ceferino announced dinner. But there were chairs only for the men.

"Dinner without the ladies? It isn't fair!" sputtered one of the men, who had his arm around one of the girls. "What're you going to do, honey?"

For answer she undid a button, drew down her dress. A laugh went up. She stood before them in dancing trunks, shoes, and stockings. "Damn me! They're entertainers. Here, Cutie, let me help you out of yours!"

The dinner, served to music and dancing, was superb; fresh shrimp from Guaymas, *guaycamole* salad, venison cutlets surrounded by quail; and scattered along the table by way of novelty, fried beans, *enchiladas,* and *tortillas.* Wines of course, Spanish and Portuguese, duty free.

All restraint ebbed. The *generales* were gorging on the free feast, cursing fluently in Spanish the waiter who did not keep their plates and glasses filled. The New Yorkers clapped and yelled for the girls, pulling them on laps to feed tidbits while feeling a knee or breast.

Finnerty, seated at the head of the table with March on his right, kept slapping the boy on the back. "By God, boy! As good a party as John ever got up, and at half the expense. Western Mines won't forget you. No shure!" On his lap sat a girl in a worn black velvet dress, to whom he was giving champagne. She had slapped on his head an orchestra player's huge sombrero. Whenever he tried to kiss her, she yanked the brim down over his eyes and punched him jokingly in the ribs.

Now the fun began. More men jumped up from table and ran to join a group surrounding a girl in the far corner. "Hot damn! *Carramba!* Give us the works!" Someone tossed a dollar at her feet. She took off her shoes. With a clatter of more silver on the floor, she took off stockings and brassiere. The men went wild.

A fat general sitting next to March said quietly, *"Estan hecho los zorrillos, no?"*

March was not too drunk on wine and Finnerty's praise to appreciate the play on words. *El Zorro Azul* meant in English "The Blue Fox," and its drunken and drowsy guests could rightly be regarded as acting like *zorros* or foxes. The general instead had changed the word to *zorillos,* skunks. March could not resent the insult to his own countrymen, nor could he ignore it. He mumbled quietly, *"Me hace uno el zorro"* — "I am pretending to be a fox and not to hear, *mi General."*

The tenor of the room began to change. It was now after midnight and drawn by the noise all the *pelados* and beggars of Dos Ritos were crowding into the bar hoping for a scrap of something to eat, a drink, or a piece of silver. Most of the Mexican officers had slipped out with their girls. Finnerty and his American guests were demanding from the remaining girls an all-nude chorus. The girls did not object to stripping, but were greedy for money and demanding $10 apiece.

In the midst of the hubbub March raised his eyes to see framed in the open window a face he would never forget. It was dark, somber, hard as flint, with a few black whiskers on the chin. The man's steady reptilian eyes were black as obsidian, timeless and fixed as the sierras themselves. His tattered straw hat was pushed back, a ragged splinter of coarse black hair lying on his forehead. Below his brown muscular throat his wrinkled dark hand was holding the corner of a *serape* up to his shoulder.

March knew the intent awareness that held the man there, unmoving. The smell of food and spilled wine, the sound of shouts, and the sight of naked flesh did not disturb him. His flinty eyes refuted them all with a blank indifference that held neither envy nor contempt, but was only a fixed negation.

Sight of him sobered March instantly. Once again he felt himself set between two worlds incomprehensible to each other.

But now there was another commotion. One of Finnerty's guests, a director of the company, was missing. March hurried out in back to a long courtyard lined on each side with cribs—narrow cell-like rooms above which were crudely lettered the girls' names, and in front of which were hammocks strung from a few tamarisks. In back stood an open sheet-iron *mingitorio* rankly smelling of urine.

Here, as he suspected, he found the bespectacled director shouting for help. He was backed against a wall, surrounded by a pack of *putas* clad only in dirty shifts. One of them, with a sweep of her hand, had jerked open his fly, tearing off the buttons. Another had yanked out his shirttail. The others were now massed to tear off his clothes and ransack his pockets.

March strode forward, jerked the man free by his collar, and flung the girls all the silver in his pocket. Then they fled out front.

The night was nearly spent. Down the dusty street pattered a burro laden with firewood. A coyote yapped from the hills. Dos Ritos seemed desolate and dwarfed as a scatter of ant hills on the plain. And against all this, enduring and unchanged under the glitter of the desert stars, only the few lights of the Blue Fox glared pitifully. In their glow a man was puking on the portal. The party

4

Something was happening behind carved mahogany desks in a great spider city that shook Piedras Blancas in its far flung web. Stocks were falling on the New York Exchange, prices were tumbling, the bottom was dropping out of copper.

Jackson called March into his office. "March, there's no need to tell you what's going on. We've all been following it in the papers. Western Mines is letting men out all over the country. We're not going to close the Copper Boy. But we've got to shut down to a skeleton force until this Depression is over."

"I understand," said March.

"Not yet!" contradicted Jackson. "You're one of the youngest engineers on the payroll, and we're letting out others with more experience. But Mr. Finnerty—and myself!—think you're very promising material. So he offers you an alternative. Western Mines has an undeveloped silver property in the Mexican back country. One of our men is down there blocking out ore in case we can use Mexican silver. It's an out-of-the-way place. But if you want you can go down there and help him until we make a decision as to what should be done about it. My advice is to take it. It's an opportunity."

March agreed heartily and went home to get ready.

Next day Morrel took him to the auto stage that was to carry him to the train junction. "You're lucky, boy! The axe is chopping off everybody here. You know what your new job, is, don't you? A sentimental sop because you threw that drunken brawl for Finnerty. That's what you get for following my advice. Good luck! And when you get laid up with maleria, dysentery, and God knows what else, don't say I didn't warn you!"

Two mornings later March boarded the slow mix-train that crawled twice a week down the west coast of Mexico. He wore short boots, corduroy trousers, leather jacket, and a gray Stetson. All else he owned was packed in his duffle bag, chained and padlocked to the arm of his seat against the ever-present *rateros*.

The grimy plush seats were jammed with people, bags, and bundles. Dust blew in the windows; the toilet was a horror; and the aisles stank of green orange peelings, pink banana skins, and pomegranate rinds. The rank smell of spilled tequila mingled with the acrid smoke of hand-rolled cigarettes.

In the second-class coach rode the peons and the Indians, sitting immovable on the hard plank seats and in the aisle, wrapped in their *serapes* and *rebozos,* and holding babies, great clumps of pomegranates, and crates of chickens.

Behind was a Pullman carrying four passengers. Up front were three boxcars and a flat car on which sat a guard of scrawny little soldiers in pinkish cotton uniforms with half the buttons gone; there had been another Yaqui uprising.

All day the train crawled southward over the cactus-covered plain. The blue mountains following on the left. To the right the fetid jungle and the slimy rivers running down to the sea. Mountain, plain, and jungle on a sloping shelf: all of Mexico at once. And Indian country. The last "Far West."

The train stopped beside a water tank and boxcar station. An Indian boy got on carrying a small spotted fawn all eyes and legs. "*Cinco pesos,*" he whined, staggering down the aisle. Outside March saw a man sitting on the ground beside his horse. He wore leather chaps and held a rifle across his knees. After a time the boy appeared; he had sold his fawn. The man hoisted him to the horse's rump. Then he swung into the saddle and they vanished into the chaparral.

At dark the train stopped for another hour. The town was not to be seen. But in the flare of ocote torches March saw the platform crowded with people noisily greeting each other, the men clasping each other in an *embrazo,* cheek to cheek. Friendliness with a revolver on the hip.

"*Cafe con leche! Granadas mejores!*"

March got out.

Women in black *rebozos* squatted beside charcoal brasiers warming pieces of meat smothered in red sauce. Others shuffled up to him, barefooted, offering *tortillas,* huge red pomegranates strung on twisted vines, *tamales,* and earthen mugs of muddy coffee which might have been dipped from the river. Mangy dogs ran yelping from pot to pot; an old woman on the edge of the crowd squatted down like a hen to urinate.

A group of *Indios,* Mayas, stood haughtily aloof, blankets drawn up to their hard glittering eyes. One had blankets to sell: pure white, with borders of black or blue. "*Serapes! Serapes de Mayo!* he called softly. But always the hard glitter of eyes and an intense awareness.

A people like a black obsidian knife sheathed in soft adobe, thought March. Who will draw it from the land?

But now from the darkness he could see the four passengers in the Pullman. An American businessman and his wife, and a fat Mexican general and his scrawny mistress splattering her pock-marked face with more white powder.

Here, as everywhere, was all Mexico with its proud poverty and rapacious aristocracy, its unplumbed past and unfulfilled future. Mexico, the motherland of western America as England was that of the east. The meeting place of time and timelessness. March felt a wriggle up his spine. He was coming home at last.

In the dark and ghostly flow the train moved on.

The catch on the vestibule door was broken; all night it kept banging back and forth. The paper drinking cups were used up and scattered in the aisle. A woman stood at the empty container wailing, "*No hay tazas . . . no hay!*" until somebody loaned her an earthen mug. The little pink-clad soldiers had come in for the night, stacking their rifles; the train was now out of Yaqui territory. There were no seats. They squatted in the aisles, gnawing open little green oranges and spitting out the pulp.

And still the train crawled on in the dark still night with a subdued apprehension; no longer a train, but the spirit of the boy's own unrest drawn effortlessly into the imperturbable stillness, the infinite mystery and wildness of the earth.

At daybreak March awoke. Outside in the dawn-dusk he saw a plodding burro loaded with a jag of wood. Behind followed a man in *huaraches* and *serape,* his full white cotton pants flopping about his sturdy Indian legs. He did not look up. Then, flooded by sunlight, the earth emerged with all its nascent wonder, its timeless visage and indestructible freshness.

That afternoon at a boxcar junction March transferred to a weekly train which chugged up into the sierras. It comprised a donkey-engine, a boxcar, and a coach with eight seats, the rest of the car being used for freight. The rails followed a brown river up a rocky gorge. The heat was oppressive; the dense green growth gave off a sickly smell.

A *pueblocito* appeared, Las Minas, said to be the site of some mines which had been worked soon after the Conquest and then abandoned. Here a few passengers got on with baskets of watermelons hardly bigger than two fists. They did not talk as the train moved on, but sat clutching their fruit and staring out at the steadily rising hills.

It was nearly eight o'clock and still light when the train reached the end of the line. There was no one to meet it save the driver of a rattletrap *arrana.* March clambered into it with his four companions. The driver lashed his team with that inherent hate for horses March sensed in all Mexicans, and the coach bumped away.

They reached the town plaza before dark. March got out and looked about him. A crippled peon was lighting the few lamps with a torch. Dusty oleander and bougainvilleas, *seda* and *alamo* trees lined the square. From a forbidding black-walled cathedral a mellow bell rang softly in the warm, dark silence. A few men stood on the corner, indifferent, sterile, and sullen as the rough stones paving the plaza. A beautiful town, dead and indifferent, but still resisting the pressure of the encircling mountains. El Tazon de las Montanas. A Mexican Acropolis in the Sierra Madres.

Picking up his duffle bag, March walked to an enormous inn on one side of the plaza and was given a room. It had a lofty ceiling, stone floor, and walls two feet thick. Lost in it was a bed, chair, and a washstand. He was glad to come out for a miserable meal of greasy chicken, beans, and tortillas in a tiny dining room. He did not join the man at the other table. A distant politeness: it expressed the wary aloofness of Mexico. They nodded, warily observing each other. March saw a well-built man of about forty-five, sloppily dressed in boots, baggy trousers, and khaki shirt. He was strangely youthful looking despite a scar over his left eye, thin brown hair barely covering his flat-topped head, and stony blue eyes that held the fatalistic indifference of one who had been too long in the lonely places. Not until March leaned back and lit a cigarette did the man speak.

"*Ja!* American cigarettes I have not smoked for eighteen months!"

March handed over the package. "Here, keep these. My name's March Cable."

His companion rose quickly, clicked his heels together, and bowed. "Von Ratlube, at your service," he said curtly but pleasantly.

He was March's new boss: Baron Klaus von Ratlube.

March rose, stuck out his hand, and gave him his letter from Western Mines. "How lucky I am. Or you were awfully good to come here and meet me."

"That hat. Klaus knows when you come in, here is a young American mining engineer who will have some cigarettes." Von Ratlube read the letter, crumpled it, and threw it under the table. "Klaus will call you March, and you will call him Klaus. We shall get along, the only two white men here."

Klaus was in no hurry to get back to his mine, *La Mina Nueva,* forty kilometers back in the sierra. Hearing that he might soon have an assistant, he had come into town a week ago to drink beer while waiting. Now with a companion he still waited, drinking beer. An undeveloped mine and a man awaiting instructions to open it up, forgotten in a timeless country where there was no alarm clock, no calendar.

The immense old hotel, run by a shiftless couple, they had to themselves. It had a strange hard deadness, these great, empty, and formal rooms, and the messy kitchen where the woman squatted smoking among her blackened pots. In back lay a garden overgrown with vivid blue morning glories and bougainvillea blossoms dripping magenta and purple, and with brilliant birds flashing through papery banana trees. In it was a bath: a hut containing a stone basin where one stood up to the knees and splashed cold water in the darkness. There was no *excusado;* one went in the fallen-down shed in the corral.

March and Klaus rose early while it was still cool. They fried their own breakfast eggs, the meals were so distasteful. Then they strolled down to the market, an open courtyard with a roof. Men and woman squatted before their earthen pots, wicker baskets, peanuts, fruits, vegetables. Little melons, bristly *tunas,* limes, green oranges, always stacked so neatly in small pyramids. There was no attempt to sell, to brush away the flies swarming on the hanging meat in the bright hot silence.

From noon till midafternoon they slept. March really wanted to be alone. For afterward Klaus came out to drink beer and talk some more.

At dusk bats began flying out of the cathedral tower. Black chips from black stone walls. Women came to the water fountain to fill their jars and then stalked back, eyes down, through the dark. The crippled lamp-lighter went the rounds with his torch. Big doors slammed shut and were locked with keys nearly a foot long. Iron grillwork barred all windows. And all around the mountains drew closer with oppressive silence. So Moorish really. And Spanish. But holding a down-pressing Indian negation of both.

There were five musicians in town who played for weddings, fiestas, and funerals. They paid their tax by playing twice a week in the plaza. Coronet, flute, trombone, guitars—anything. It all sounded the same. Tax music. No one minded. The people strolled around and around the park. The women on the inside going one way, the men the other. Laughs, greetings, bold stares from the men at the young girls, suspicious looks from the women. All in a subdued key: muted voices, furtive looks. Really two silent, slow, opposite-flowing streams that never mingled, seldom touched. But always with an intense awareness of the other. Then suddenly—slap

— bang! — the musicians put away their instruments, and everyone vanished as if warned of a coming storm.

Late one night March was awakened by a couple singing outside.

Zamboa navajoa cumuripa corral,
Santini pitahaya balmoa algodal!

The man's deep voice was a dark curtain against which the woman's rose leaping and quivering like a brilliant flame; one living flame in the dead, oppressive night. One of the haunting, timeless *aires de la tierra.*

March jumped up and ran to the window. Through the iron grillwork he glimpsed the faint glow of a charcoal brasier, and around it some of the *serranos*, the small quick Indians of the hills, who had come down into town that day. But by the time he had jumped into his pants, unbarred and unlocked the great wooden door, and run outside they were gone.

March was growing sick of Klaus' constant talk. From morning till night, he talked about himself, third person. It was the disease of a man's loneliness. But the death it brought was silence. So March endured it.

The von Ratlube family ranked high in the German aristocracy. Klaus' education at the University of Göttingen was of the best: geology, English and French, with a neat saber-cut scar as a decorative reminder of his days in the Studenter Corps. During the war he joined Richthofen's flying squadron and became one of the leading German aces. His three brothers were killed. He himself cracked up badly.

"Klaus' head was broken like an egg-shell," he said. "Feel his head. It has a flat metal cap on top of the skull. Skin and hair were grafted over it."

At the end of the war he went to Rumania, thence to some remote Russian mines. In Amsterdam he next obtained a contract to work in a group of mines in Belgian East Africa. After three years he caught maleria, and was transferred to Alaska. The sudden change almost killed him. Stricken with pneumonia, he was shipped to a hospital in California. A year later he obtained work with Western Mines in their holdings in Arizona, whence he had been sent down here in Mexico eighteen months ago. Every month his salary check came. Every month he sent in his report. He had blocked out 75,000 tons of silver ore in La Mina Nueva. But still no orders, no money came to develop it into a working property.

"Pagh! The whole country is lousy with silver. Here, Klaus has 75,000 tons blocked out. Who wants it? Nobody. Your country once said it was worth $1.29 an ounce. Now it is worth only the price of a bottle of beer. So Klaus stays here. He is forgotten. Nobody remembers him. It is best so." Leaning over, he slapped March on the knee. "Klaus tells you these things because you are like his little brother."

They were sitting after the *siesta* hour at a table in front of the *Cantina El Club* fronting the plaza. In the hot bright stillness of the afternoon a horse clattered slowly into sight. The rider, the town's policeman, was sitting lazily in the saddle. Attached to the horn was a long taut rope which stretched behind him. Then March saw what was attached to the other end. A *peon*. The rope was looped about his neck. His hat was gone, he was choked with heat and dust. His hands were tied behind his back, his bare feet bloody from stumbling through cactus and over stones. Nobody on the plaza paid him any attention. And in the stifling heat, his head stretched forward like a running rooster's, the prisoner was yanked along.

March felt a little sick at seeing the naked fear in his eyes and his swollen protruding tongue.

"Pancho! Another bottle!" ordered Klaus.

5

Klaus had the German sentimentality; also the German belly for beer, however lean he looked. He drank the excellent bottled beer being promoted by the government to replace the fiery native cactus liquors. It was expensive so far up here. But March too preferred it to the brutal, greenish-white *mezcal* that came so cheaply.

"Klaus can drink more beer than you! Want to see?" Klaus said abruptly one afternoon on the plaza.

It was the day March had received a letter from Ona, enclosing a page of the little college weekly with a paragraph marked in pencil. Valeria Constance, married the week after her graduation, had died while giving birth to a still-born son.

March shrugged assent and drained his bottle.

By evening they were both pleasantly drunk. A light supper of cold greasy chicken had no effect. They returned to their table to sip a bottle of *mezcal. "Ja! Der gute, trockene brand!"* said Klaus. But at ten o'clock Pancho closed the *cantina.*

With a fresh bottle under Klaus' arm, they sat in the plaza. Three white shadows gathered around them. The bottle made the rounds. Then Klaus took out another from his hip pocket. One of the *pelados* began to sing.

"Musica! Musica para todos. Eh, amigos?" demanded Klaus.

"*Como no?*" They grinned. In Mexico it was the answer to everything, even death and revolutions. "Why not?" So two of them went to round up the village musicians while the singer roused Pancho for more bottles.

Now they all paraded around the plaza singing to guitars. "*Borrachita, me voy*"... It was all very beautiful, most touching. But no one answered the serenade from the iron-barred windows. And the dark heavy night smothered voices and whining strings.

They straggled down to the market place. Off in the darkness gleamed the tiny fires of a mule train down from the hills. Soon the *serranos* came over, sturdy little Indians in tattered *serapes*. They stood heavy with negation and silence, their black eyes fixed on the *pelados* lounging on a bench.

March retched violently. The clear, greenish liquor had brought out a sweat that ran down his cheeks. Now he felt better. Klaus led him apart from the others. He was very drunk and babbling in his German-tinged English.

"Nobody remembers Klaus. Nobody remembers March. He is like Klaus' little brother. *Blutsbruderschaft!* We shall be blood brothers, no?"

He had already drawn out his clasp knife, opened the blade. Before March could guess his intention, Klaus grabbed the boy's left arm and slashed the inside of his wrist. Quickly now Klaus cut his own left wrist. With his other hand he held their cut wrists together.

"Blutsbruderschaft schwören!" Staggering, he flung his arm over March's shoulder. *"Brüder – auf immer und immer!"*

And so they stood there in the dark circle of trees, wrists still held together, the warm blood beginning to trickle down the finger tips. March was aware of Klaus' proud dignity that drunkenness did not mar, the sincere comradeship he gave with his blood. And yet the rite seemed somehow false and sentimental. Blood communion but not of the blood, he thought hazily. A German schoolboy trick. He remembered the only evening he had spent at a college fraternity house in Little London: the songs, the beer mugs, the theatrically fraternal spirit that was dissipated instantly once the members were off the campus. And he felt a little ashamed and very foolish as he stood wiping off his bloody wrist with a dirty handkerchief. It was just a surface cut; not into a vein, luckily.

One of the *serranos* came up in his thin-soled *huaraches,* his dark brilliant eyes showing an intense awareness. March gave him a cigarette, watching his mobile face as he bent to the cupped flame of a match. And he sensed that between him and this unknown dark little Indian from the hills was more than between him and a lonely uprooted German aristocrat. For we here in Indian America are the feather, the flower, the drum, and the mirror of the old gods who have never died.

"Come, *Brüderlein!*" said Klaus, laying his hand on March's shoulder to accentuate that word of endearment so rarely used. *"Jetzt muss getrunken werden!"*

In the silvery moonlight they drifted back to the white ghosts across the plaza. But the bottles were empty and the musicians had gone. Only two *pelados* and the *Indios* remained. All straggled down the cobblestone street to an adobe hut near the bend of the river. There the *pelados* vanished. Klaus pounded on the door. An old woman looking like a witch opened it and held up a lighted candle.

"Menudo, mi madre! We want *menudo!"*

Her seamed brown face searched each of them in turn. March gave her some *pesos.* She bit each of them, then let them in. Across the threshold, sleeping on a *petate,* lay a young boy. Klaus awakened him with a kick, ordering him to rouse Pancho for more *mezcal.*

"No hay dinero!" the boy whined sullenly. *"No hay!"*

"Klaus will pay. To Pancho tomorrow, Klaus will pay!"

The hut was one dirt-floored room. But because the old woman was known as the maker of the best *menudo* in the mountains, there was a long table and two benches. On these crowded the two white men and the Indians. The old woman roused the fire in a stove in the corner, put on her pots. The boy came back with more *mezcal,* rolled up in his *serape* on the floor, and instantly fell asleep. The dreamless dog-sleep of Indians that comes so instantly and easily any time, any place.

An hour passed, perhaps two. The hut was steamy from boiling tripe and smoky from cigarettes: cheap packaged "Faros" and *punche* rolled in corn leaves. The raw liquor was bringing out sweat to the men's bodies, and with it the peculiar racial smell. One of them threw back his *serape,* and in the light of the guttering candle March saw his smooth brown chest. Not muscular, but heavy and soft like a woman's. Like adobe. But powerful.

They were singing, talking in their own *idioma.* Klaus began to whistle in two keys a theme from Wagner. When they did not still, he lost his temper. *"Verfluchte Mexikaner!"* he shouted. *"Himmel, Donnerwetter noch einmal! Verfluchte Mexikaner! Maul halten wahrend ich musiziere!"*

His angry demand could not be mistaken. The *serranos* hushed, drew into themselves. Klaus slumped down again at the head of the table. In a conciliating tone he muttered, *"Le gustan Klaus, no? Porque Alemán, sí?"*

"Sí. We like Germans, *Señor.* Mexico likes Germans." It had a flat emptiness. They went on drinking.

"Hermanocito, my little brother! *Alemán tambien, amigos!"* Klaus affirmed, slapping March on the shoulder.

They knew he lied; and March could see their flinty black eyes sweeping him with veiled glances. A dead silence had gathered around them and now endured, unbroken. It was heavy and yet electric, like the air before a storm.

The old woman brought over her pot of *menudo,* a greasy thick soup of tripe with scraps of onions and hominy, ladling it out in earthenware bowls with a dirty iron spoon. Then she brought *cabeza,* the boiled head of a cow. The stuff was horrible. It made March feel sick, but more *mezcal* settled his stomach. He leaned back, fighting against nausea.

Klaus he saw go suddenly pale, his face greenish white and slimy with sweat. He had to go out. March went with him, and the Indians followed. A faint breeze rustled through the papery banana leaves. Down the clearing the river sucked at the stones. Klaus let water, turned toward town. But the Indians stood in front of him, immovable, silent.

"Himmel! Was ist das!" Then contemptuously, with a stiff bow, *"Meine Herren, ich bin ihr Gefangener!"* He stumbled back inside the hut with March at his heels.

Once more Klaus staggered to his feet and lurched out into the clearing with March. No farther. The Indians stopped them again, tried to lead them down to the river. *"Verfluchte Mexikaner!* They want to kill us. Klaus doesn't care!"

March yanked him back inside the hut where, head on his arms, Klaus sat huddled at the table. The old woman had gone to bed, her bare feet sticking out from a blanket. The boy lay snoring on the floor. The only sound was the soft *idioma* of the *serranos* talking among themselves, and it was part of the oppressive silence. Two rows of powerful brown bodies, walls of soft warm flesh hemming in the two white men in the corner.

"You are his little brother, German too?" someone asked March.

"No!" he answered with a quick stubborn pride. *"Yanqui!"*

A little tension rippled around the table although the faces did not change. A foreigner, an Americano, an *Imperialísimo Yanqui.* March felt for the first time the sullen brooding hate of the Indian for his white master. It had always been there, not in the conscious individual mind, but deep in the blood; the subterranean hate of a race whose flowering had been frustrated by another. The brutal liquor had brought it out. He filled his glass again, shoved the bottle across the table.

Beside him, on his left, sat a young *serrano.* Over his bare torso he wore a tattered *serape.* As was the custom, it had a narrow slit in the center called *la boca,* "the mouth," through which protruded his head with its fell of black uncut hair. *"Amigo? Simpático?"* he kept asking in a taunting, malicious tone.

"Como no? Amigo. Simpático," March answered patiently, recognizing the persistent attempts to intimidate him, and feeling grow within him a hard streak of granite.

Once more the Indian asked his interminable question, this time taking March's right hand and inserting it under his *serape,* on his sweaty belly, to feel the bone haft of a knife protruding from his trousers.

March suddenly jerked out the knife, flung his arm backward and upward, and drove the blade with all his strength into the lintel of the window behind him. "Yes! As long as my friend's knife remains there above us!"

The blade quivered in the rotting wood like a reed trembling in the wind. Underneath the table March planted his feet firmly. He pushed back his glass on the table. Drunkenly alert, he gathered himself to turn and lunge for the man's throat at his first move for the knife, sinking his thumbs into the hollows below the ears. "If it's going to come, let it come now," he thought savagely. The Indian did not move, nor did March. A faint flicker, like a ripple, passed over the black eyes across the table. No one spoke.

"There is the power of the blood," March thought hazily with drunken determination, "but there is the power of the will, too. I am my father and I am also my grandfather."

One of the men took another swig. So did March. The edge of the tension dulled. Still the Indians waited with inexhaustible patience. Yet March knew that in his weakness lay his strength: to maintain an unceasing awareness, to give like soft adobe, but to feel within him a core of granite. So he gathered himself in his drunkenness to endure, to out-drink his companions.

They all kept getting drunker, more sullen. March, possessed by a savage exultation, felt as if he were walking a tightrope high above them; a taut line suspended across a deep chasm a thousand miles long.

One by one the *serranos* relaxed, falling back against the wall or lying down on the floor already spotted with vomit. But the candle was almost burnt; he could not trust darkness. He rose. His legs were numb, his mind a roaring furnace. He managed to rouse Klaus and they staggered outside. No one followed them.

Klaus weakly raised March's hand to the flat top of his head. The boy could feel a pulse beating under the platinum cap. "My head," said Klaus.

"Hell with your head! Mind your feet!" muttered March.

The German was too heavy to carry up the narrow cobbled streets. Then the old lamplighter appeared, and together they dragged him to the plaza. The sky was greenish-grey above the *sierras;* it was almost dawn.

The huge door of the hotel was bolted shut. Sandoval let them in, muttering, *"Borrachos!"*

March lurched past him alone, stumbling to his room. Everything suddenly gave way within him. He hit the side of the bed, clutched for the blanket, and fell on the floor dragging it over him.

In the morning his cracked lips were covered with a black scale like soot. His heart was pounding terribly. He could hardly walk across the room. Klaus was even weaker. Neither man could eat.

For two days they sat with drawn faces, suffering mutely in the heat. Perhaps, after all, it was time to return to the mine.

6

La Mina Nueva was a long ride by muleback up in the sierras.

The working was really very old, one of the mines opened by the early Spaniards, perhaps by the Indians before them, said Klaus. He had found in one of the old tunnels a joint of wooden ladder bound with a rawhide which crumpled when he picked it up, and on the walls a few half-obliterated Aztec markings. One needn't believe an engineer when he talked of his own mine, especially in Mexico where all mines are said to have been Moctezuma's. Anyhow it was very old. A dim trail now overgrown led from it across the sierra, a *Camino Real* over which the silver had been carried by mule *conductas* to the coast and thence by ship to Spain. This original working was called *La Mina Antigua*.

It had been reached by an inclined tunnel along the footwall of the vein, big enough to accomodate the little burros laden with sacks of ore. But Klaus, when he had come, had moved east of the opening to a new site on the hillside. Here he had cleared the chaparral and sunk a shaft from which he ran a few discovery tunnels. The hoist was a dangerous make-shift: a small wooden platform without sides, lowered by a wheezing gasoline engine taken out of an American automobile. Gasoline for it was brought up in huge square tins, two to a burro. At the bottom of the hill was a clump of miserable huts with thatched roofs occupied by the *peons* working for him. This was *La Mina Nueva*.

It was early Cripple Creek in the days of the Sylvanite, thought March when he saw it; not the corporation era of huge modern plants operated by Western Mines.

The work was hard but simple; Klaus was a top-notch man with a nose for ore. The two men puttered below, taking samples which Klaus assayed above. Then they ran narrow tunnels and drifts. The blocks of ore between they measured and computed tonnage. Once a month Klaus or March, taking turns, would ride down the trail to the village and take the train to the nearest town. Here letters and a report to Western Mines were mailed. Their checks were always waiting at the bank. Two leather sacks were filled with silver pesos to pay the laborers; supplies were bought; and with a new shipment of gasoline tins, he would ride home with a dozen loaded burros.

Klaus and March did not go together. For then March found he could not pry Klaus loose from the village. He would stay a week or two drinking beer. And when they returned, it was to find most of the workers gone. So the work went on, unhurried, to no end at all.

They climbed one day farther back into the high sierras. Two men walked ahead of their mules, clearing the overgrown trail with their huge steel *machetes*. Wicked-looking knives, thought March; a blow would halve a man like a cucumber. In a clearing lay an adobe ruin: the mill or mint, said Klaus, where the silver from *La Mina Antigua* had been prepared for the long mule *conductas* crossing the mountains. Nearby, fronting a weed-grown plaza, stood a large, magnificent church. Really a cathedral, its stone walls blackened with age and weather.

As they stared at it, a woman came out from a hovel behind it. "*Pobres! Indios!* We have nothing, *Señores!*" The dread, the haunting fear of strangers.

For a *peso* she unlocked the massive carved doors and let them in. The immense nave, lit only by a tiny window high in the thick walls, was empty. There were no seats, no benches of course; in all churches the people kneeled on the hard bare floors. The altar long had been stripped of *reredos* and *santos*. But in front stood a withered stalk of corn, at whose foot lay some withered flowers and the dark stain of turkey blood left by Indians who still came here upon occasion. March was glad to get out into the bright sunlight and rise again on the twisting trail.

On a high ridgetop they left the two men to hobble the mules and sleep in the grass. Klaus now showed March why they had come, tracing across the truncated summit reappearing outcrops in the decomposed granite. They found the fault, followed it down to a steep rocky gorge. Midway across the western wall March could see an exposed jadeite-green vein nearly twenty feet wide.

"Pure copper, Klaus! You've found a deposit that'll beat the Copper Boy!"

"Not pure, but copper. And Klaus thinks it will run to silver at depth." He pointed to the talus slope at the bottom of the gorge. "Down there is lime. A site for a mill where a railroad could reach it from across the plains." He began to whistle, then broke off. "But at first the run would have to be taken out by burros. Why not? Klaus and March could see to it all."

The hot sun was flooding the gorge with a pool of heat. By the time the two men reached the mules they were wet with sweat, their eyes glazed, their throats like rasps. Klaus' flat, platinum-covered head was throbbing like a pulse.

Back at *La Mina Nueva* that night Klaus' enthusiasm had evaporated. "Bah! Klaus has a silver mine here bursting with ore to be taken out. He has found another deposit. The whole mountains are full of silver. What is that? Nobody wants it. And Klaus is kept here, forgotten."

March looked up bleakly from the newspapers Ona had sent him. Back in the States history was repeating itself. Another panic, like that of '93 which had written the doom of the booming silver camps of the Colorado Rockies, was spreading over the country. Prices were tumbling. Industrial plants were closing, men were being thrown out of jobs, a wave of unrest was sweeping the rich heaven of gringoland. And here, sitting on top of 90,000 tons of silver ore while other men stood patiently waiting in ever-lengthening bread lines in all the large cities, March felt the awry balance between the rich abundant earth and men who could not learn how to use it.

Klaus at last had run out of talk. In the adobe where the two men lived together, he would sit after supper reading newspapers over and over, and whistling through his teeth. March could stand it no longer.

"For Christ's sake, stop that eternal whistling!" he shouted, jumping to his feet.

Klaus rose, clicked his heels together, and bowed coldly. "Klaus von Ratlube is disturbing the young American with his odious presence?"

They got along badly. Klaus had forgotten the midnight ritual of blood communion which had made them brothers. He sat glowering across the table at March sewing up a tear in his shirt. Neither spoke. And in their silence grew the strange hate which comes to two men alone in the wilderness. "Cabin fever," thought March.

So one night he said abruptly, "Klaus, I'm not going to bunk here with you any more. It's bad for both of us. Serafina is moving my stuff into the little adobe tomorrow morning."

"*Ja!* Get out then!"

Serafina did their cooking and washing. She was old, fat, and shapeless. But she had been with Klaus two years now and had begun to learn a little cleanliness and to give the pots a good scrubbing. The quarrel between the two men delighted her. Oh, it was good, very good! Soon they would fight. Maybe they would cut each other with knives or shoot off guns. This would be better. There had not been so much excitement for months.

Nothing happened. At night March went home to his little adobe below the bigger one Klaus occupied. In one corner stood a small stove and a packing-case china closet for his few dishes. And he had made a table and chair. A bare little place, but it soon took on warmth. His one distasteful chore was cooking his own suppers, for Klaus had kept Serafina.

Up above, Klaus watched the old woman pattering around in her floppy *huaraches,* looking out the window and murmuring, "*Probrecito!* He is all alone. He misses Serafina, no?"

Klaus got a little ashamed "*Chinga tu madre!* Stop moaning, old pig of a woman. Hurry up with my supper and then go down and get *Señor* Cable's. Every night. *Sabe?*"

So sullenly, every twilight, Serafina scraped together Klaus' supper and then plodded down the trail to fix March's. "It is twice as much work. It is ten times the work," she grumbled.

"*Ándale!* Get on with you!" cried March sharply. "You know you get twice as much money and have two places to steal from."

The old woman grinned. She was devoted to both men.

After supper March carried his chair outside. Klaus above him was already sitting out on his wider *portal*. March could see in the dusk the tiny red glow of his cigarette. To his right the plank hoist house of the mine faded into darkness.

One night, through the velvety blackness, came the sound of Klaus whistling in two keys a bar from Verdi. "How'd you like that one?" his shout came down.

March in turn whistled back a few bars from "Carry Me Back to Old Virginny."

Their relationship smoothed out. Occasionally March took supper with Klaus, or the German came down to spend the evening with him. There was about these "social calls" an air of warmth and hospitality, a faint formality too, which broke the old monotony. Yet March held on fiercely to his quiet aloneness against Klaus' repeated attempts to break it. So they got along better.

The dozen workmen and their families lived down along the stream. In the darkness their cooking fires gleamed red. Sometimes a group of *serranos* spent the night with them, or a burro train on its way to market in the village. A guitar began to whine and voices broke into song. Perhaps there would sound a drum beaten with the heel of a hand to accompany the singers. The deep rich voices, soft and powerful in their maleness, came welling up as if from the earth itself. And from above, Klaus' whistle.

March sat alone in darkness between them, belonging to both and yet of neither. He sat, as had his grandfather, in the lamplight of a single lonely mine in the mountains; and outside he saw, as his father had seen, the red campfires of his fathers' fathers. And it seemed to him that in some curious fashion he had completed a mysterious cycle. Something was beginning to take shape within him. What it was, he did not know, but he felt that he was coming to a verge.

His feeling was manifested by outward events on his next trip for money, mail, and supplies.

Finishing his chores in El Tazon, he made ready to return to the mine. Dawn was scarcely an hour away as he crossed the empty plaza. Behind him the sierras heaved into the violet sky and the black tower of the cathedral began to loom out of the darkness. Demetrio and the *arrieros* were waiting in the corral. They had packed the burros with supplies and gasoline tins, two to an animal, had saddled the mules. Already they had eaten, and now sat smoking around the dying embers of a small fire.

"Esta bien, Jefé," said Demetrio, rising.

March nodded. He tightened the girth of his saddle; went over the pack fastenings—one of the ropes, last trip, had worked loose and spilled a sack of flour; then counted the gasoline tins. Two were missing.

"You brought all the gasoline, Demetrio?" he asked casually.

"Sin dudo, Jéfe. Cómo no?"

"Get the other two! Quickly!"

Demetrio's dark face assumed a dumb, expressionless look. He counted the gasoline tins; he counted his fingers. *"Madre!* Can it really be that two are missing? What eyes the *Señor* has even in darkness!"

"Only to see that Demetrio and his men no longer wish presents of the empty cans. Their woman prefer to carry their water in little jars."

Demetrio peered into the darkness. "Sons of the devil! Cursed *rateros!* Where are you who have stolen the *Jefé's gasolina?* My knife will find the guilty one!"

"Demetrio! Find those tins!"

The men rose quietly and began puttering around. It was Demetrio who awkwardly discovered them hidden under some straw in the corral. "Look! My sharp eyes have found the hiding place of the thieves!" And bullingly, he saw to it that they were lashed on a burro.

In single file they rode slowly out of the corral, past the empty market, and across the river. Dawn was already breaking. March was forever grateful for the delay in starting.

As he splashed across the ford, reined up and waited for the heavily laden burros to pass, he heard a whinny off to the side. He turned quickly into the chaparral. A horse was grazing quietly, a man sprawled limply in the saddle. "Klaus! Here!" He dismounted, grabbed the mare's bridle. Klaus did not stir. Face down, he was lying with his hands twisted in the loose reins wrapped about her neck. When March lowered him to the ground, he let out a low moan. His face and head were dark with clotted blood.

March turned the pack train back to town, carrying Klaus on his mule as gently as possible. Demetrio beside him talked constantly. "The mare brought him safely down the trail. But always she is afraid of water. Remember, *Jéfe?* In the brush she would have stayed. We would have missed her in the dark. Aye! It was the will of God those *rateros* hid our *gasolina*. No?"

"It is as you say — the will of God that we were delayed to find him and not pass by in darkness," assented March. "And the will of God will surely lead me to the guilty if you fail again to guard all animals and packs in the corral."

"I solemnly swear, *Jéfe*. By Our Lady!"

"It is well. There will be many temptations. Chiefly *mezcal*," answered March drily.

He carried Klaus into the hotel, washed off the blood, and sent for the local herb doctor who left poultices and emetics which March tossed out into the garden as soon as the man left.

A gash in Klaus' head had torn loose a piece of the skin and hair grafted over his platinum plate. This could be washed with iodine and plastered back with adhesive—with a prayer his skull had not been cracked. His left arm was broken and beginning to swell. The worst injury seemed to be in his side. Whenever he moved he moaned with pain. From exposure, he also had caught a touch of his old fever. His face by noon was flushed, and he had begun to sweat and chill alternately.

March sat by him, wiping off his face, giving him sips of boiled water with lime juice and quinine to hold his fever down. There was only one thing to do: take him to the train and get him to a competent doctor. "It won't do to wait, Klaus. There's only one train a week, remember? Klaus!"

Klaus did not reply. He was still delirious.

That afternoon March sent Demetrio with the pack train back to the mine, and in the evening loaded Klaus into the ramshackle coach which jolted over the rough road to the train. The tedious journey that night was a nightmare. Klaus was stretched out on a double seat, the other passengers inquiring every few minutes. "He is dead yet, *Señor?* No? But surely soon. See? His breath comes ever shorter."

Klaus was a brave man one minute and a child the next. He lay gritting his teeth to still his moans against pain. Then he would relapse into a petulant whine. "Little brother! You are still angry at Klaus. You won't give Klaus any more water."

They got to town, doctor, and a small hospital. Klaus' lacerated scalp was resewn, his broken arm set, his fever brought down. But something was terribly wrong with his side; he was to be sent to Guadalajara.

The two men joked. "So the mine fell in on you! How do I know you didn't arrange it on purpose?" asked March. "The pretty girls in Guadalajara!"

"*Ja!* And you, little brother, will be sleeping with Serafina! It is what you need to improve your Spanish—a sleeping dictionary!"

He really looked like a ghost. Insisting that he would be back in a couple of weeks, he ordered March to keep the mine open without notifying Western Mines of his accident. "Send another report of 5,000 more tons of ore blocked out. It goes into the waste basket with the others. Klaus is forgotten. But he wants his pay. Eh?"

Next day March set off alone for *La Mina Nueva*.

7

The place was in a devil of a mess. Demetrio finally had stolen his two tins of gasoline – to buy *mezcal* in town, March surmised. Several of the workers had left, as he had known they would. They had to have their silver *pesos* at the end of each day's work, even though they couldn't spend them for a week. At the mine itself the steel drum hung suspended across the top of the shaft; the cable was torn loose; the gasoline engine looked like it had a cracked block. The cribbing of the shaft was loose. Dirt and stones kept falling. And the new tunnel had caved in.

From Serafina he gradually learned what had happened the afternoon of the accident.

Klaus had needed a few more big timbers in a tunnel leading off from the bottom of the shaft. These were usually lowered by the hoist, with either Klaus or March operating the gasoline engine. Now with March gone, Klaus foolishly decided to have someone else lower the timbers instead of dragging them down the old inclined tunnel – an hour's work apiece.

Juan de Dios was selected to sit at the engine above. Klaus showed him how to run it. It was very simple: a hand here, a hand there, and when the little mark appeared on the unwinding cable, this.

"Qué bonito! It is nothing, *Señor.* So carefully I watch. Every *momentito!"*

So he did at first after Klaus went down. Then something happened to Juan de Dios. His body straightened, his strong simple face grew stern, his soul expanded. He had learned the white men's secret of the *máquina. Pues!* Juan de Dios, poor Indian, was now *Señor Ingeniero.* In the wink of an eye, the flash of a butterfly's wing, he had crossed the chasm of centuries.

So he straightened his *sombrero,* stuck an unlit cigarette behind his ear, and called for spectators. They came running: women, children, an old man or two in ragged *serapes.* The two helpers attached the cable hooks to the timber chains, carefully swung the log slantwise to the shaft where it could straighten and drop down slowly. Now they stood back respectfully.

Juan de Dios rang his bell. *Qué bonito!* The motor churned, the exhaust popped, the fumes ran out. As if serenely unconscious of the adulation in their dark eyes, *Señor Ingeniero* Juan de Dios put his hand here, his hand there, and when the little mark appeared on the slowly unwinding cable, did this. So simple! Like a miracle almost.

Down below Klaus unhooked the timber, snaked it with a burro into the tunnel, rang his bell for another.

As the spectators grew braver, venturing a look down the shaft, Juan de Dios grew more important. He whizzed up the engine, retarded the spark to make the exhaust pop, and wound up the cable at high speed.

Another timber was lowered until the tip barely stuck up above the shaft collar. Now it descended out of sight. Now it popped up again, half a length out, to drop again. A woman made a sly, obscene remark. Everyone laughed. An old man clapped his hands. "What a mighty man is Juan de Dios! His wife has never seen such plunging!

Señor Ingeniero affected not to notice them. Power flowed from him. The great log did just as he willed. Dignified and important, he sat up straight, *huarache*-clad feet stuck out before him, bare toes protruding from the leather thongs. His hat, however, needed straightening. He removed his hand and straightened it, of course.

There was a sudden bang and clatter. The cable jerked loose from the drum, whipping round and round like an unwinding snake. *Santísima!* A hand here, a hand there. So simple a moment before. But now in his confusion Juan de Dios had forgotten which was which.

"*Madre mía!*" he wailed, releasing all controls. Jumping to his feet, he stared wildly down the shaft. The huge log was dropping, banging against the sides of the shaft, tearing loose stones and dirt. The drum creaked and rolled. Then the pulleys were torn loose; the cable yanked the drum over; the rocking gasoline engine pulled at the plank platform.

"*Jesu Cristo!*" With a frightened cry he fled with the spectators. And not too soon. The drum, yanked loose, caught across the shaft collar. The cable snapped loose like a thread from a spool. The great log plunged downward.

Juan de Dios, hiding behind a bush, heard a mighty crash and yell. A puff of dust rose out of the shaft. Then silence.

Slowly the people came forth. "It was the devil in the *máquina* which broke loose," explained Juan de Dios authoritatively, his composure restored. "Did you not hear the whistles, the shrieks, the moans?"

But with the Aleman there had been two men and a burro. Lighting candles and torches they trooped down the old inclined tunnel. The two workers they found safe. The burro was crushed. And the *Ingeniero,* the Aleman, was caught like a *tigre* in a pit. They dug him out, administered hot soup and advice. Klaus refused both, insisting he be put on his horse. They hoisted him to the saddle, tied one boot to the stirrups. Alone, he rode off into the darkness. No one accompanied him. There was too much to talk about. Juan de Dios had vanished into the hills: to escape the devil of the *máquina,* he said, and to compose his soul in tranquality –

Resolutely March cleaned up the mine as best he could and wrote Klaus in Guadalajara, asking whether he should order new hoisting machinery. Klaus replied in a shaky hand. Western Mines would have to authorize the expenditure. The company would not do so if it knew he were away and laid up. It might suspend all activity and stop his pay. He advised March to close the mine, keeping an eye on it from town until Klaus returned.

March shut down *La Mina Nueva,* dismissed the few remaining workers, and returned to El Tazón. To avoid the wretched cooking in the hotel, he rented a house. It was really very lovely: faded pink adobe walls, big rooms with a few pieces of furniture, and an overgrown garden through which ran a faint trail to the toilet. The dusty road in front was filled with people going to town. Down the slope in back the curving river glimmered silver between thick growths of mangos.

The house, like most Mexican houses, had a family attached to it as caretakers. They lived in a *barrio,* neighborhood or compound of many families, along the river. Maria Rita Campos was the matriarchal head of the large family. With unbelievable assurance she would come walking down the road and into the house: head up, swinging her hips with a slight *meneo,* in the walk of a queen which blindness had never altered.

Saturnino, one of her sons, was a stocky man who patched the walls, brought wood, and did chores. Then humbly holding his hat to his breast, he would stand around in his quiet heaviness, his eyes alert as an animal's. It was he who occasionally accompanied March back to the mine.

Late one afternoon March walked down to the river. All the women had been washing their clothes and spreading them out on the bank to dry. Now they were bathing in the river with the men who had come to join them. All were naked. Their blue-black hair shone in the setting sun; full breasts, mighty buttocks and strong Indian legs gleamed redly; white teeth flashed. Two children were scrubbing their mother's back, laughing and splashing each other. A man called to him, waving. It was Saturnino. March slipped off his clothes and waded into the river.

It was then he saw her as she rose from a ducking, facing him. A girl and a woman too: her face a child's, her beautifully formed body a woman's. And seeing her ripe breasts so small and pointed, her young vigorous shoulders and iodine-colored arms, March felt a shock as if he had stepped on an electric cable.

The girl swept back the hair from her face. On her toes, she kept bounding up and down in the waist-high water, smiling at him. Who she was, he did not know. And a little abashed, he swam away toward Saturnino.

Early next morning he went to the market for the day's shopping. The place was crowded; in Mexico all life, like the flowers, opened with the sun. Some men from the hills had brought down goat cheeses, big as millstones, two to a burro. March wanted some, but that offered him smelled of burro. While he stood there complaining, the girl he had seen the evening before stepped up. "Burro! Burro! It smells!" With a staccato burst of the *idioma,* she demanded two slices cut from the center and neatly wrapped in a newspaper, which she handed to March. Without more ado, she took over his marketing. Eggs, tomatoes, *aguacates.* Helplessly he followed her from stall to stall, watching her pinch vegetables and fruit, listening to her angry dickering for a squawking fowl. "Bones and feathers! Thief! Where is one with meat?"

When the *bolsa* was full, she took it from him, walking beside him but an appropriate step behind. As they entered his house, a cockroach ran out from the kitchen. He stepped on it, kicked it outside.

"No! Never!" the girl protested. "Where there are *cucaraches* there are no *alacranes!*" He nodded, afraid of the deadly little scorpions.

The girl looked over the house with a peculiar air of proprietorship. Then hands on hip, she asked forthrightly, *"No hay mujer?"*

"No hay mujer. Soltero."

She cleaned the house, cooked supper for him and that night as a matter of course she slept with him.

Her name was Conchita; and as he might have suspected, she was a granddaughter of Maria Rita Campos. The Indian in her gave her at times a sullen, brooding heaviness. This was overlaid with a cheerful brightness, an immense ambition. Most of the year she lived away from home teaching in a small rural school somewhere down along the railroad. Here she had learned to speak English, wear squeaky shoes upon occasion, and splash talcum powder on her dark ruddy cheeks. These railroad-junction airs, as March called them, she seldom affected; she went around in bare feet and *rebozo,* with the submissive meekness and timeless anonymity of the earth itself. But someday she would be *gente de razón* and wear beautiful clothes all day, every day.

That she became his mistress raised the status of them both. March was no longer regarded as a suspicious *gringo* foreigner, and

Conchita was viewed with respect as a woman who had a household of her own to boss. There was no doubt she enjoyed her role. She liked the command of the household money, and to lord it over the big family in back. She did all the shopping in the market. What she saved by merciless haggling, she made up for with what she took home.

"This chicken – you only ate half of it. So I shall take this old tasteless meat to my toothless grandmother. And these *aguacates*. See? Black spots already."

If at times March suspected he was feeding the whole family, he was paying less than before and he liked the life Conchita gave the house. Their relationship lent both of their lives a substance, but it did not alter the form. There was no sentimental love making between them. She was direct and honest, without pretense. When he lay down beside her at night it was as if a secret key shut off his consciousness of self. He remembered at times his childish love for Leslie Shane. It too was mindless but nebulous, a flicker of the pure spirit. Of Valeria Constance he thought also: the queer cold clutch of their two minds, ever wary of the other even in his passionate yearning. How different this! It was without spiritual essence perhaps, yet it was more than physical. It created a world in which sex was master, but in it was much more – timeless and engulfing, beyond analysis.

So they lay together under the open window. Moonlight washed across the stone floor. The leaves of the banana tree scraped against the patio wall with a paperish sound. And over them, heavy with the weight of centuries, pressed down the sierras. In the deep dark flow, in the ghostly flow, he felt himself sink and drift, and sink again.

At sunrise she leaped up to build the morning fire and to half-fill a tin tub with lukewarm water. Every morning March took a bath. Imagine! Conchita preferred the river and lots of company. He ate breakfast alone in the sunlit patio. Inside, she rattled pots and pans. Lord, what a racket! Then off she went to the market to haggle and gossip till noon.

March really wanted the mornings to himself out here in the sun and flowers to work on a report of the mine. For Finnerty, "in view of the alarming state of affairs increasing in this country," was finally evaluating all of Western Mines' holdings in Mexico and elsewhere.

March sent his lengthy report to Klaus, and he with corrections forwarded it to Finnerty. On it Western Mines was to base its final decision whether to open up the mine for production or abandon it until times got better. But Klaus was apprehensive. His crushed side required surgery; there was no telling when he could get back to work. So with the report on the mine he finally sent in an account of his own accident with his doctor's statement, affirming that he had left March in charge of *La Mina Nueva.* March received copies of the report and correspondence, and continued his weeks of waiting.

Conchita at last made ready to leave; she was going to teach this year in a big school in a big town on the main railroad line. For days she talked excitedly of nothing else, but March sensed her reluctance. The family did not approve of her leaving such a fine *casa* and a rich man who had money whether he worked or not. Saturnino especially objected, forseeing his silver for *mezcal* cut off. Only blind old Maria Rita Campos was sympathetic to them both. "*Que lástima.* Perhaps the *Señor* will understand. Girls now-a-days —But we will take care of you. All will be as before."

March was touched. He put his arms around this splendid old woman. "*Mi madre,* I understand. She goes with God. And here all will be as before."

The last night he and Conchita spent together was an ordeal for them both. Conchita wept and stormed, swearing she would never leave. Between deluges of tears she gave way to gusts of passion that exhausted them both of all feeling. Next day, bright-eyed and cheerful, she held court to bid everyone goodbye. March then drove with her in the old *arraña* to catch the train. She was dressed in her squeaky shoes, pink dress, and pancake hat, with more new clothes in two new leather suitcases. She was still waving to him, hat askew, when the train rattled out of sight.

This was the vision of her that plagued him as he lay alone in an empty bed in an empty house night after night. Conchita as he had known her had vanished. Conchita with her ripe, warm, and red-brown body cloaked in a *rebozo,* trudging barefoot in the dust to town. Kneeling on the stone floor, beating out *tortillas.* Clap-clap-clap! An economic fact. Also the heartbeat of Mexico. Yet something within this passionate child of the earth had drawn her away in squeaky shoes, pink dress, and pancake hat; the same mysterious life-force that impelled the leaves of a plant to forever grow upward toward the sun. The same overpowering restlessness that had drawn him here to these remote sierras. A strange unfathomable destiny neither could resist with drawing her upward into the light of consciousness, and him downward into the shadowy realm of the unconscious. But here for a moment they had met and fused, briefly but fully as life allowed. Conchita! She had been his, and would always be his. He loved her. And now she was gone.

Outside, the lightning flashed. Thunder shook the sierras. The lashing rain whipped the banana trees all night. And in the morning, still grieving, he got up to fry his own eggs in an empty, lifeless house. What was happening within him? He did not know. So he kept waiting like a man whose only destiny was to touch bottom before he could rise again.

Eventually a letter came from the Vice-President in Charge of Operations of Western Mines. Finnerty remembered him well. He complimented March for having taken full responsibility for *La Mina Nueva* and submitting such an excellent report. Western Mines, however, could not at this time undertake development of the mine. March was to close it at once. A bonus of three months' salary was enclosed, terminating his services. "Keep in touch with me, however," he requested. "At the first opportunity we want to place you elsewhere." To this he added a pithy statement to the effect that Western Mines always assumed full responsibility for the welfare of its engineers. All of Von Ratlube's medical expenses would be borne by the company, and he would be transferred to a hospital in the States as soon as expedient.

March felt relieved. He closed up his house and for the last time held old blind Maria in a close embrace. *"Mi madre. Mi madre!"* Whom was he ever to call "Mother" besides Ona?

"It will always be your home when you return. Go with God and in the peace, Senor."

Saturnino rode with him to the mine. The shaft still gaped open. March closed the wound in Mother Earth with a blast of dynamite, and turned his back on 100,000 tons of undeveloped silver ore. Saturnino, dumb as he was, understood. They shook hands formally, and Saturnino turned back toward town. March, his duffle bag slung on the back of his mule, began climbing the dim trail up into the sierras.

8

No, nothing now troubled Rogier, who had weathered more storms than ever beset most men. He existed in a dusky limbo between two worlds, the silent darkness of the unconscious and the clamorous light of reason; to both he gave allegiance. He ate and slept well, pruned the currant bushes, interjected pithy comments into the conversation at the dinner table. He took pride in wearing clean shirts, although his trousers were always baggy. He trimmed his nails. And yet beyond these humble confines of his mortal existence in a shabby old house on Shook's Run, he was always aware of that other nebulous, timeless domain of which he was also a part.

If at times he was conscious of teetering on the hairline boundary between these two states of existence, either of which might claim him wholly, Rogier did not care. He felt himself beyond the tyranny of time and circumstance, like the majestic Peak which rose before him. It had suffered cataclysms and submergences only to rise again. So would he.

One afternoon in early spring the two halves of his being began to separate, each world claiming its own. He hobbled upstairs and went into the bathroom. Ona, sitting in Sister Molly's big room at the end of the hall, heard him go in and lock the door. Five minutes passed, then ten. She walked down the hall, knocked on the door. "Daddy! Are you still there?"

He angrily unlocked the door and burst out. The flap of his trousers was open. His face was gray. Without answering, he clumped down the stairs and hobbled through the yard to the chicken house. Here he squared off again and tried to urinate. The effort brought out drops of sweat to his blanched face.

Dom! What was the matter? Fighting against his fear, he buttoned up his pants and strolled out into the sunshine to compose himself. The sky was a stainless blue, the mountains clear and white. Yet all this, the unheeding world about him, seemed suspended in the tranquility of fearful suspense.

Driven by his necessity, he hurried around the shop to stand at the back fence. This time he was wracked by a pain that seemed to rip his groin and bowels with a saw-toothed knife.

"God Almighty!" he groaned. "I can't let water!"

The magnitude of this absurdity burst upon him like a thunderclap. Legs spread, he stood in a strained posture of micturition. His head was thrown back, and with wild beseeching eyes he searched the vast palimpsest of the sky for the faintest trace of help, of hope. There was neither. He howled his anguish; and fly still open, he ran out into the alley to stand at a telephone pole, and thence to the ash pit—to all the familiar spots where he had urinated in years past when too busy on his mining speculations to take time to go into the house. One was no more effective than the last. His every futile effort brought a resurgence of the terrible pain, and with it a mounting horror of what had befallen him. Howling his despair, he ran back into the house, bent over, clutching his groin with both hands.

Ona saw him coming. "Daddy! What's the matter? Your rupture?"

"I can't let my water! God Almighty, girl! I can't!" Doubling up as if caught by cramps, he let out another wild howl.

"Get on the bed and keep quiet. Quick! I'll get the doctor!"

Ona ran across the street to telephone from the grocery store. The doctor—the young one—was in; and fifteen minutes later he drove up in his car. With a catheter he drew Rogier's water and left the old man relieved.

Two hours later Rogier sneaked into the bathroom and came out shouting as before. He was bound up tighter than ever.

A second time the doctor came and relieved him, but now in the bedroom he handed Ona a small package. "A new catheter for you, Mrs. Cable. You'll have to learn how to use it from now on."

"What's that?" Rogier on the bed lifted a face suddenly transfixed.

"Just this," replied the young doctor flatly. "I can't be driving down here a dozen times a day to catheterize you. Mrs. Cable here seems to be the only one who can do it for you—unless you want a full-time nurse or to go to the hospital."

Rogier, unable to reply, turned first to the doctor and then to his daughter a look of unfathomable horror. Ona flinched. Too well she knew his fastidiousness, the monstrous restraint and courtesy of his Southern breeding which prevented him from discussing the facts of life even with his own family. In all his many illnesses he could hardly abide the touch of hands to his person. And now this! To have the secret parts of his body – his water drawn by his own daughter! Ona could read on his face how vile and degrading it seemed to him.

Father and daughter stared at each other without speaking. Then suddenly through his eyes she saw crack and burst asunder the fastnesses of Rogier's granite core. What misfortune and worry, old age and the threat of insanity had never accomplished, shame did in a single moment. His square jaw dropped heavily and hung in defeat. He seemed to crumble, inside, before her eyes.

"Daddy! Don' take it like that!" She flung her arms around him. "We've been through everything together, you and I. And what's this? Nothin'! It'll only take a minute. And besides, what else is there to do?"

"Come, come," spoke up the doctor with professional curtness. "I'll show Mrs. Cable right now how to use this new catheter."

Rogier did not answer. In a hypnosis of acquiescent horror he was led into the bathroom. A few minutes later he stumbled into his bedroom and undressed while Ona showed the doctor out. When she came back upstairs, the old man was in bed with his face turned to the wall. He never left it.

His sufferings increased. Drawing water from him became an increasingly difficult task for Ona and a more painful one for him. He could not masticate, and liquid food had to be forced down him. His feet were cold, even with a hot water bottle in bed. Soon his legs were numb to the knees. All the worn out parts of his body were ceasing to function. He was turning to stone. The earth, of which he had always felt himself a part, was reclaiming it own.

Leona and Nancy kept out of his room, yet the whole house seemed permeated by a miasma of death and decay. Mary Ann, rying to be efficient, stalled the doctor on every possible occasion. 'What is his condition? Is he making progress? What are you going to try now? Perhaps a consultation—"

"My dear madame! There is nothing to try. Your father is a worn-out watch. Old age is something we cannot mend. I'm only doing what I can to make easier his last days. Please!"

Mrs. Rogier accepted defeat the best of all. Something in him precious to her had died years ago; this was but a physical anticlimax. She became aware of this one afternoon while sitting at his bedside. Awakening from a nap, Rogier turned his head toward the open window and brushed back a wisp of white hair. "What's that—Akeepee? Didn't Sally Lee give her her sugar?"

"Land alive!" Mrs. Rogier turned her good ear toward the window. "That's some chickens outside, not a horse nosin' for sugar. Akeepee's been dead for nearly thirty years. You been dreamin', Daddy!"

"I reckon," Rogier assented listlessly.

"Why, I bet my bottom dollar you been dreamin' of all them pacers and trotters of yours," she went on cheerfully. "'Member the day Aralee won from Taffy Lass, and how Little Man tried to climb the telegraph pole? You was mighty proud of them horses, Daddy! Take Silver Night!"

She rambled on, trying to comfort the thin wasted mummy in its sarcophagus of blankets—he who for more than half a century had been the sturdy tree of life to which she had clung as a parasitic mistletoe, frail as she was. "B. N." — "Big Nigger" — that had been her nickname for him long ago, when she married him at sixteen, because he was to her a faithful protector, abundant provider, and unobtrusive master like that big Negro body servant who still lingered in the magnolia-frail memories of her earliest childhood.

Rogier roused, eyes clearing. "Marthy, those mines were no good. None of 'em ever panned out. A wild goose chase, like you always said. I guess you never knew —"

And suddenly she realized there was in him something she had never known. For sixty years she had known him — her own husband: his weaknesses and his strength, his idiocyncrasies, his confounded stubborness and splendid folly. But a secret something in him always had kept them apart. It was not her illness, his busy professional life; not their own children, Boné, or Sister Molly's two boys whom they had reared, the many other mouths he had fed; not even his inborn aloofness, his undemonstrativeness, aristocratic restraint, and independence. It was something more chimerical and hence more powerful, like a star to which his life had been dedicated at birth. It had led him across the wilderness of a continent, to the ridgepole of the Rockies, to a single snowy peak—a star which had gleamed and faded, but to which alone he had been wholly faithful. Not knowing it, she had never really known him. It frightened her.

"Never mind those old mines, Daddy! Who cares?"

Rogier clumsily laid his hand on hers. "You never got away from Shook's Run. To that big house in the North End."

Her slim body rose erect on its straight chair at the bedside. Involuntarily she withdrew her hand from his unaccustomed caress, then quickly clutched it again. This frank avowal coming from him after so many years was more than she could bear.

"Oh shoot, Daddy! I haven't been rememberin' that foolishness for years! Why, this old house has always been a mighty lovin' nest to us and ours!"

Her embarrassed voice dwindled away. Rogier was not to be stopped. "Marthy, I been pigheaded, but not blind. You've missed a lot. Maybe we both have."

His voice, welling up thickly from the granitic stopes of his congealing body, caught and held her. A film was gathering over his eyes again, yet through it blazed a flicker of his indomitable spirit. Mrs. Rogier went stiff. To acknowledge the mystery of their lives, the unbearable truth of their essential separateness through their years together, was something she had no strength to endure.

From the depths of her body she wanted to shriek, "Stop! Let it pass unknown! Let this familiar stranger pass in the loved guise I knew always!" And she silently prayed Heaven to prevent him from unmasking his naked soul at last. With effort she controlled herself, seeking refuge behind the barrier of the plausible.

"We've had a fine, full life together, Daddy," she said, tenderly stroking his head. "You've had ever'thing happen to you and you pulled through. This is a tough time, no escapin' that. But you're goin' to come through with flyin' colors. You're on the stretch, Daddy! Come on, rest and sleep and get strong. I'll be here at the finish."

He did not reply. She gave him a sip of water and leaned back, holding his hand.

Rogier awoke in a heavy darkness, blacker than the space between the midnight stars. All around him pressed walls of rock. They squeezed his body, forced the air out of his lungs. A drop of sweat rolled down his cheek. Still he lay there, unmoving, feeling his flesh congealing and adhering to the granite. Now he knew where he was. In a dark stope in the depths of the Peak. There was the drip of subterranean water, the slow pulse of living stone. He was down — way down. Then up from the blackness rose a faint light.

"Reynolds! Hey Reynolds!" he cried out in a hoarse whisper.

The light swelled like a halo, approached swiftly.

It was Ona setting a lamp on the table.

"You're not worrying about Old Man Reynolds? He's been gone for years," she said softly but resolutely. "Here." She wiped off his face with a warm wet cloth.

"What time is it?" articulated Rogier.

"Maybe midnight. No matter. I'll sit here as always."

He was profoundly grateful. Dom everybody else! Only she comforted him. Cut of a piece, they were more than father and daughter. She understood him.

"Cable had no business bein' in the Sylvanite," he muttered hoarsely. "You're not holdin' it against me, girl?"

"No, Daddy," she answered without subterfuge. "It just happened. He had no place anywhere except with us for the time he was here."

"Good girl, Ona." The old man closed his eyes. Then suddenly, from a wide mouth opened by his unhung jaw, he began breathing great gasps which seemed to tear his chest apart.

Ona stared at him, clenching her fists, then flung herself on the cot across the room. Rogier was dying as he had lived, boring down, ever down. In the last days of his grass roots waking state, he had paid off with pain his mortal debts to the surface world which had borne him. The earth had claimed him. And as he sank into its depths in a dream state, its drifts and stopes of living flesh kept closing on his own, constricting his breathing, pressing out in dreams and memories the last residue of experiences and impressions collected in his mortal lifetime.He was quite aware, in his conscious moments, of the joy and guilt they contained. But these were only momentary judgments and evaluations of the surface world above to which he had never wholly subscribed, irascible and independent as he had been. If for the moment he acknowledged them, it was only to get rid of them. For now, unencumbered, he could sink down more often for longer intervals to a third and deeper level. In this state of dreamless sleep all his bodily aches and pains, his conscious worries, and the memories, dreams, and fantasies squeezed out of his unconscious, were obliterated. He knew nothing. Yet he knew all without knowing from this deepest level of his being—all that he had subtly felt throughout his life, all that he had blasted and drilled for through hard granite into the depths of a mountain peak. A mere lump of fleshy earth like his own, whose heart and meaning were coincident with his own. Rogier at last had reached his deepest, richest stope. And when more and more infrequently he shot up the shaft to surface, blinking at rational daylight, he fuzzily resented these interruptions in his true existence.

Still he did not die. It was taking the earth a long time to claim him, a man made of granite. How horrible, indecent, revolting, this dying man who was denied the grace of an easy death as he had denied an easy life. The family was exhausted; even Mrs. Rogier prayed for him a quick and easy end. But it was Ona who fought the doctor for it.

"I fail to see just what you're hinting at, Mrs. Cable," he said after a long conversation.

"Good God!" she flung back, at the limit of her endurance. "Have you no understanding, no human sympathy? Look at him lying there with his sufferings, his intolerable stench! And yet you stand there like a fool asking what I want, what he wants. Death, I tell you! A quick and compassionate death!" She leaned back against the wall, panting for breath. "A pill under the tongue. Something to put in his drinking water tonight. Anything!"

The young doctor for once had lost his composure. He flushed, gasped, yanked a finger under his collar. "Mrs. Cable! I understand your feelings. But such a thing is unethical in my profession. I cannot countenance it!" He caught up his medicine kit and plunged down the stairs in hasty retreat.

"You cowardly wretch! You poor excuse of nothin'!" Ona shrieked after him. "Don't you ever come here again!"

"I'll stop by in the morning!" he shouted back. "Perhaps I can do something!"

The following night, after an absence in a coma which had lasted some twelve hours, Rogier returned and flicked open his eyes. It was nearly two o'clock. The night lamp was smoking on the table beside Ona across the room She was sound asleep in her chair, completely exhausted.

"Ona!" he called in a tearing gasp no louder than a whisper.

The woman stirred gently, her head wobbling sleepily on its full neck, then limply falling back with a dull thud against the wall. All again was smothered in silence.

It was suddenly broken by the sound as of steps coming up the creaking stairs. Rogier struggled up an inch or two against the head of the bed. His clouded gray eyes lighted with a resurgence of life like that of dying embers before they were wholly consumed. The steps halted on the landing, came down the hall, and stopped in front of his open bedroom door. Rogier could not see his callers in the murky light of the smoking lamp. There was no need to. He reared up with eyes blazing recognition of the presence of those two invisible, faithful, old family retainers. His lips contorted in a silent shriek. He flung up his hand in a synonymous gesture of hail and farewell.

Then it dropped heavily. His head fell back. Something thick and warm rose and clogged his throat—the last organic something not yet congealed into stone within him. He gave one more rending gasp, one last cry to Ona and the Kadles, to all that was human and ghostly in that old house which had been his home.

It was this that roused Ona. She leaped to her feet, fell on her knees at his bedside, clutching his shoulders.

Rogier had already passed—a man who had died as he had lived, alone.

The funeral was held in the house three days later. There was a mass of flowers: enormous wreaths from Sally Lee and Boné, a profusion of bouquets from friends and neighbors, and a small token of white roses fashioned into the shape of a miner's pick. Attached to it was an unsigned card that read: "In memory of a hard-rock man from some of his old workers."

This anonymous offering from a group of men who sometime had worked for Rogier brought tears to Ona's eyes for the first time. It was the one sincere tribute she acknowledged. Stonily she had watched Mrs. Rogier's childish pride at receiving so many flowers: the splendid tributes to the dead from those who had ignored the living; from those whose flower-money would have eased a few moments of his years of suffering; from those who had been too ashamed of him to call upon him during his affliction.

The funeral seemed to her a travesty. The notice of Rogier's death brought a few old-timers more fortunate in Cripple Creek than he. Their big cars made an impressive showing in front of the drab old house. But if their greetings to Mrs. Rogier glowed with sweet memories of their early life in Little London, they discreetly avoided any mention of the years between.

For the most part the house was filled with curious neighbors. The big sliding redwood doors between the front room and dining room had been rolled back; the glass cabinets of ore specimens had been dusted; the Victrola was covered with a moth-eaten Confederate flag. Both rooms and the hall were crowded with those who had hooted at the crazy old man from their stoops, jeered at him across the back fences, thrown stones at him, and slapped each other hilariously as they recounted on street corners his latest fraility. Yet now that he had gone they suddenly felt the absence of a man whose infuriating idiocyncrasies had isolated and made him an individual in their midst—an uncomprehended stranger whose awry and indomitable life yet had echoed something of each one there. So they had flocked here to pay him homage with their final curiosity.

Ona, moving about, could hear snatches of their whispers.

"A fine old man, eh, Mr. Johnson? I won't forget the way he used to chase them chickens with a club, yellin' at the top of his voice."

"Didn't nobody ever find out about that there backyard mine of his? You know, the old man used to be richer'n all get-out. Had race horses and all that. Look at them flowers and the North Enders sittin' up front! What I mean is did the old codger think there was gold in his back yard, or had he buried some there and was tryin' to find where he'd put it? Do you suppose we could get leave to dig out there ourselves?"

There was a sudden stir in the hall.

"Mr. Pyle! And Mrs. Pyle! Well!" Mrs. Rogier exclaimed in a delighted voice. "We been savin' you seats."

"Tut, tut! No trouble to come at all," the Rogiers' cadaverous next-door neighbor declared pompously. And then in a quick whisper to Ona, "You might be sellin'. Or need a new mortgage. Let me know first. I – "

"Sit down!" Ona said curtly, and turned away.

The master of ceremonies arrived: an old friend of Rogier's for forty years or so, the preacher who had married Ona and Cable and who now, after his retirement from the ministry, was eking out an existence as a librarian. Old and somewhat infirm, he took his place up front. Now silence filled the house. Rogier no longer held the principal role in this reenactment of the drama of all humanity; an invisible presence had replaced him. The audience subtly changed into participants. Not now were they curious and gossiping spectators, but people of simple hearts, slow to understand and slower to forgive what they could not understand, but recognizing now as all must recognize the simple dignity of death.

The service, as Rogier would have wished and as Ona had insisted, was very brief: a few words about Rogier's fifty-six years in Little London and Cripple Creek, a prayer, and a hymn sung to the accompaniment of a borrowed piano. Then all filed past to look at the dead man in his simple, sturdy casket. A fairly good job had been done on the corpse. His black broadcloth suit hid his wasted form. He still wore a starched white collar fastened with his diamond collar-button, and without a necktie. His square face, whose cheeks were stuffed with cotton and rouged too redly, looked broad and resolute. Synthetically freed from the ravages of illness and old age, the old man looked better than he had for ten years. And as his indomitable spirit had retreated from his granite body, it seemed to have left it something of its dignity.

Now it was over.

Ona watched the cars roll away with their few occupants. Mr. Pyle, freed at last from the thorn in his flesh, scuttled off quickly. Mr. Bryce had to get back to his grocery store. There were no cars for the crowd in such a run-down neighborhood. Ona and the rest of the family rode in young Dutch's tourist car behind the hearse; behind it followed a couple of others.

The burial place was the family lot in the cemetery southeast of town. It lay on a ridge of the bluffs covered with pine and spruce. The road curved past the great Stratton monument, marble crypts, bronze-door mausoleums, rows of impressive tombstones. The short cavalcade stopped in front of the huge pine which marked the Rogier lot. Ona dug her fist into her mouth. Unable to afford proper care, she saw that the graves of Mrs. White, Sister Molly, and Cable were sunken under their rotting wooden headboards and covered with weeds. On the opposite slope of the ridge one of her childhood playmates had been scalped by Indians while herding sheep. In the gulch between lay an accumulation of refuse and tin cans.

Mrs. Rogier wept into her lace hanky at the sight. "I don't care — I don't care — It's still got one more place."

Between the wide tawny prairies and the high blue mountains surmounted by their sentinel Peak, Ona stonily watched the coffin being lowered into the grave. It had been dug through adobe and loose country rock into hard granite. Here Rogier was finally laid to rest — into that mysterious and eternal earth which at last accepted as its due that dust within the rock with a hospitality it had never accorded the stubborn and futile gropings of his outrageous spirit.

9

Just where he was going and for what, March didn t know. Perhaps, on the surface, to see Klaus in Guadalajara before their lives separated. He could have taken the weekly stub train to the main line and traveled comfortably by railroad. But this would have been only trying to rationalize the irrational. There was still in him an unspent residue of his tormenting unrest. Somewhere, sometime, he had to touch bottom before he could begin his long climb upward. And so alone he crept into the mysterious wrinkled Sierras Madres, the naked profundity of the mother mountains of Mexico.

There kept rising before him a sunlit wilderness of parched brown rock. Jagged sierras studded with chaparral and cactus, and seamed with stupendous gorges and canyons. Suddenly from a high rimrock he looked down into the *Barranca* – that vast chasm with its maze of canyons cut through the backbone of a continent. Far below him he glimpsed the river threading its way through clumps of lemon, orange, and mango trees. And in between, on the steep rocky slopes of the canyons, the Tarahumaras, said to be the least known, wildest, and most primitive of all tribes.

All through the sierras March had glimpsed them. A single man, naked except for a breechclout and with long uncombed hair, appearing for an instant and then vanishing like an animal wary of human contact. Or a couple standing forlornly on a street corner. Little people, with the wonder and the mystery in their dark eyes. This was their homeland, but where were they?

Occasionally he came upon a rock hut beside a tiny *milpa* of corn on a rocky hillside, or a cave in the cliffs. A glimpse inside revealed their life: raising a few stalks of corn, grinding the kernels on a stone *metate;* herding a little band of goats, and weaving the hair into *serapes, cobijas,* and belts on a crude horizontal loom; carrying a bag of tropical fruit to sell in a remote settlement.

But how wary the Tarahumaras were! On the steep hillsides he caught glimpses only of their browsing goats, and heard the shrill plaintive wail of their reed flutes warning of his approach. Thousands of them scattered throughout this vast uncharted maze, but without villages and tribal unity, hiding in these isolate gorges, these uterine folds and cavern wombs of their eternal earth mother.

His encounter with them came unexpectedly. Rounding the end of a cliff wall, he rode into a large encampment on the level floor of a pocket canyon. Sight and sound hit him simultaneously. A *fiesta* of sorts was going on, and many of the Tarahumaras were dressed for the occasion. In the fading afternoon light he could see men in ragged *pantalones* and shirts, with feathers stuck in their straw hats; women dressed in voluminous skirts and red kerchiefs, all packing babies on their backs. Behind them sat others who had come from their isolate huts and caves in the far canyons wearing only breechclouts, *serapes,* and red kerchiefs twisted around their long tangled hair. A few men were shuffling in a dance to the hoarse beat of a small drum, the *kampora,* and the shrill whistle of the *baka,* a reed flute. Across the circle a man was squeaking on a hand-carved violin.

March reined up his old mule at once, and dismounted. A tremor of excitement, perhaps alarm, passed through the crowd. Always the fear of intrusion by strangers. Patiently and politely, March kept waiting. Finally the *Seligame,* carrying the lance which showed him to be their head man or chief, came up to him with two other men. In simple Spanish he invited March to the fiesta, and conducted him to the gathering. As March approached, the dance and music stopped. The people rose to greet him. They slithered up to him softly on bare feet, eyes demurely lowered. Then they raised both hands and gently touched their palms or the tips of their fingers to his own, sometimes murmuring a soft "Kevira." Always this softness of voice, gesture, and manner. Then as they looked up, he could see in the blackness of their eyes the remoteness of the *barranca* itself, the withdrawn look of a people who had never emerged from its dark depths.

Next morning the races began, the men runners kicking a wooden ball over the long course and the women using a small hoop and stick. These races, March learned, were features of all their infrequent gatherings. For the Tarahumaras were famed long-distance runners, accustomed to running down a deer, and able to jog a hundred miles without stopping. Their own name for themselves was *Raramuri,* compounded of the words *rara* for "foot" and *juma,* "to run." There was need for their unbelievable endurance in this rugged wilderness. They were too poor to afford guns, and the sparse game was too wild to approach with bow and arrows. So doggedly they would run down a deer until it was exhausted and then cut its throat with a knife.

What a pitiful *fiesta* it was, compelled by the people's need for communion after months of isolation in their far canyons. Little half-starved men toughened to hardship, women suffering from syphillis and intestinal ailments, rachitic children. Dressed in the pitiful finery of their red kerchiefs, ragged pants and skirts, and feathers. Dancing their *dutuburi* to chanting and rattling. Eating a few scraps of meat and corn, and drinking the little coffee March was able to contribute. A people with the humility of a great pride, the gentleness of a great strength, and a great passion for their freedom. Yet a people who had never broken free of the earth serpent, their mother. March could see in their eyes the perpetual darkness of their deep barrancas.

But if there was little food, there was at last *tesguino,* a strong liquor brewed from the corn they had contributed. Up the canyon the *hechizero,* the shaman or medicine man, had built a fire surrounded by a magic ring of earth. Into it he was dancing, shaking his little bells. Calling forth the powers of the *peyote* taken by the watchers squatting around the ring.

The tinkle of the bells. The reflection of the leaping flames against the cliffs. The puking of men around him. The whole eerie ritual of a people trying to surmount the limits of their earth-bound existence. All this, with the nauseating effect of the few peyote buttons he had chewed on top of the strong *tesguino*, made March deathly ill. He puked into the little hole dug before him. Then he crawled weakly back to the encampment. And here, sunk deep into a shadowy world unlit by the light of reason, he remained.

Now it was over. The sun rising over the rimrock was flooding the canyon with brightness. The encampment was breaking up. He could see the Raramuri straggling off, climbing the steep hillsides, returning to their far canyons. And it seemed that he was watching all humanity streaming out from its common womb of the unconscious, beginning its slow climb into the light and freedom of consciousness. Nothing could stop it, even here among this last great tribe of the Raramuri.

Something had happened to him he could not yet see clearly. But he knew at last he had touched bottom.

The perpetually starved Raramuri of course had killed and eaten his old spavined mule. But one of the young men slung his duffle bag to his shoulders, holding it steady with a tumpline passed across his forehead. He guided March out of the barranca to a small village.

A couple of days later he found a boy to guide him to the next one, each riding a burro. And so he kept climbing.

The villages were few and small. Tiny *ranchitos* of a few adobes or thatched *jacales* in a remote valley or clinging to a hillside beside their corn *milpas*. In one of them he might be marooned for two or three days, even a week. The boy who had brought him had returned to his own village with his two burros.

"Let us go on to the next village," March had urged. "It is only one day further. *Favór!*"

"No, *Jéfe*." The boy's black deer-eyes refused the offered silver. "Already I am one day from *mi tierra*. I must go back."

Mi tierra! Mi tierra! It always waits, this earth mother, for her son. The umbilical cord which binds him to it can be stretched no farther than a day.

And so March waited until he could find someone to guide him to the next *ranchito*. The trail, old as it was, he could never have found himself. March found a man. But first the *Señor* must wait; the earth is crying for its seed. A single day, *Señor!* But the tattered fellow spent a week stubbornly plowing his scrubby little hillside *milpa* with the crotch of a tree. "It is *mi tierra, Señor.*"

And so March waited: sleeping in an adobe, rolled up in his *serape* on a *petate* on the earthen floor with the rest of the family stretched out beside him, a dog and a goat stepping on his legs. Sometimes there would be a sliver of wild pig or scrawny chicken to eat, usually no more than beans, a bit of goat cheese, and a leathery *tortilla*.

He came back to the hut one evening to find the *Señora* in great distress. A terrible thing had happened. March was carrying with him a leather bag of silver *pesos* with which he was paying his expenses. That day while he was gone the naked children had undone the bag, rolling the silver cartwheels across the floor in play. To the old woman the money was an unbelievable treasure, more than she would see during the rest of her life. Yet she was down on her knees patiently hunting lest a *peso* might be lost. "*Señor!*" she wailed. "Tell me there is not one missing! I cannot count!"

He continued on, climbing higher and higher, yet sinking deeper and deeper into the ghostly flow of time, in an aimless journey whose details were always to remain clear but without fixed continuity, like the dream-flow of time itself.

He was in high country now, crossing the crest of the continental divide. Great bulks of heaving mountains dark with spruce and pine. Little patches of paper ice on the streams each morning, and once in awhile a thin sprinkle of snow. March found himself thinking of home, of the glistening silver peaks of the Rockies –

Winter! Who knows winter except the mountain-bred northerner who then comes into his own? Like all seasons it is a world apart, and he who has once known its white and haunting silence feels elsewhere an outcast.

At the first frost the land changes tone, gives out a deeper note. The heaving earth subsides, sleeps under its thickening blanket. The lakes glass over like frosted mirrors; the last mallards and long-legged herons rise from the freezing marshes; the muskrats slide out of the ponds. Long slender aspen trunks turn white. Through the gelid gloom of the forests flap great arctic owls like ghostly white bats. Bears grumble sleepily in their lairs. From timberline deer wind down daintily out of the drifts.

The deep snows come. Softness alternates harshness. The tall peaks rear whiter, clearer, sharper against the amethyst sky; stupendous stalagmites reaching toward heaven from the earth below.

Winter wears the year's most precious jewels. Necklaces of snowbirds are strung between fence posts. Diamong dust glitters upon the fields. Glacé spruce branches droop *lavallieres* of metallic cones. Snowflakes are designs in the abstract, frosted window panes cut glass and rock crystal. The evening sun is a ruby in a platinum setting. Lakes are chunk turquoise mounted in hand-beaten Navajo silver.

But a single, bare, wind-warped juniper hangs to the sheer side of a snowy cliff. This is winter's real beauty, a stark nakedness of line with which nothing can compare.

Now all vibrates to a higher pitch: the hunger howl of cruising. wolves muted by the shrieking winds; the music of the wintry stars; the pale sea-green, deep blue, and purple of the spectrum's cold end. Deep winter! It is a metaphysical phrase. For in winter, deep winter, the blood sinks down into its homeland, the hearth is its enduring symbol, and the wanderer yearns for his old seat.

You can smell the buckwheat cake batter souring on the back porches all winter long. It thickens the blood; you can tell in early March when it is time to stop, by the rash coming out on the skin. Then sassafras tea tonight, children, to thin the blood.

Up in Cripple Creek the bare granite boulders crack open like pistol shots. Miners' wives warm up frozen dynamite in their kitchen ovens, and from a carcass hack off chips of meat with a hand-axe. Along the narrow-gauge hay is thrown off to elk, starving, up to their bellies in snow and resting their antlers on the frozen crust. Abe and Jake are splicing a steel cable with frozen mittens. Rogier is damning the delay. And a dark, hawk-faced man is coughing beside the fireplace.

Spectral blue-white winter. In the winter the soul sinks home. It is rest for renewal, a gathering of life for another period of gestation. Oh, the year around I shall restlessly wander space. But in winter I seek depth. In winter my soul sinks home –

So March kept thinking of an old white-headed man and of those with him on Shook's Run, of the ghost of his father and his father's fathers. Yet he could not turn back. There was something, somewhere, he had to find that would tell him who and what he was: the leaf that falls into the flow or the leaf that sprouts anew; the rock shattered by frost and disintegrated by time, or the timeless dust within the rock. So from the top of one high ridge he climbed down into a deeper canyon, into the mindless depths of a timeless land and people.

The Yaquis in the mountain fastnesses of their turbulent river he had left behind. The broader-faced, docile Mayas had disappeared. He no longer glimpsed solitary Tarahumares. Who these Chinipas and Oleros were he did not know. The tribal idiomas kept changing. March was hard put to understand the people in the simple Spanish they both spoke. It did not matter. They were all little hills Indians with soft mobile bodies, arched chests, sturdy legs, and quick poetic hands. The soul image of an old dark race that time had never altered, men in whom the old gods were still strong.

It was difficult to find guides. March discovered that it was easier to obtain a small boy or an old man; they could be better spared from home and persuaded to talk. To induce conversation he made little pencil drawings of plants and herbs, asking their names and uses. The old men knew them all: *herba romero* to place on a cross when the owl cried at night; *guarapio* to put on the stomach for *cholerico;* the spear-leaved *amargosa* which could be crushed and applied to a knife cut; *tepusa* to bind on face and feet; and the small white flower of the *barablanca* for headache. He saw also the small *peyote* cactus which induced strange visions when chewed, and the devil's weed used by *diableros.* Even his boy guides knew the old trails, the sentinel peaks, the hidden shrines. The earth became alive, rich with new meanings.

He came one morning to a rocky hill on whose summit lay a bunch of fresh flowers and a turkey cock with its throat cut. The boy with him answered his questions by simply holding aside the brush to reveal the side of a cut-stone pyramid. *Aye, aye, aye. We are the feather, the flower, the drum, and the mirror of the old gods who will never die.*

A charcoal maker led him down into a village late one afternoon. A spermy white mist hung over the mountains. Water ran down his blackened face, soaked his *serape*. He gave his burro to March. The little beast had no bridle, and for a saddle only two flat sticks tied together with rawhide to keep his rider off the backbone. On this March sat holding his duffle bag, his long legs hanging nearly to the ground. The narrow trail wound downward along the bed of a swollen stream. The water swirled up his knees, rain streamed from his battered hat. The man in front splashed on. He had rolled up his white cotton pants, and at every step emerged his beautiful Indian legs. How smooth and round, never knotted with muscle, but so powerful! There was a strange strength and beauty in these men, thought March, but you've got to see their legs.

It was nearly dusk when from the rimrock of a teacup valley they saw below a great blackened-stone cathedral surrounded by a cluster of squat adobes. The milky white mist was lifting from the sheer wall of cliffs on the opposite side. On top of a crag March glimpsed a crumpled, truncated pyramid of weathered rock, an ancient Aztec *teocalli*.

They jogged down swiftly now to the first stub streets below. The charcoal maker stopped. "My house is off there," he said, nodding to the left.

March slid off the burro. *"Mil gracias.* How much is owing my friend?"

The man regarded him silently. "Fifty cents perhaps? I do not know."

"It is not enough. Will you accept a *peso?"*

The man took it proudly without thanks and turned away.

Darkness had fallen and with it an oppressive deadness. The people of the village, the man had said, still spoke Nahuatl; and like their Aztec forefathers, like the very stones, had sunk back down into the earth at dark. There was no inn for muleteers, no *casa de huespedes* where a chance stranger could find lodging. Not even a light. Wet and hungry, March stumbled around the dark, empty plaza.

A man appeared and led him home to a small adobe. Over a charcoal brasier huddled a woman and three half-naked children. March gratefully sank down in a corner, huddling in his *serape*.

Man and wife talked a long time together in the old tongue.

Then the man turned to March "We would be honored to have you, *Señor,*" he said in Spanish, in a soft proud voice. "But in town there is a bed. You will come, please?"

March followed him across the plaza, in front of the huge empty cathedral. The town was dark and dead as midnight. Not even a torch glimmered. The man pounded on a door. A voice sounded a whimpering, muffled fear. More talk. Then the door opened to show a wrinkled old crone holding up a cup of tallow with a lighted wick.

"This it is, the house which has a bed," explained March's companion. "Peace, *Señor.*"

"Go with God," replied March. "I shall come tomorrow with my thanks."

He followed the old woman through the *zaguan* to an immense, windowless storage room heaped with corn. Two more women came and laboriously moved the corn to one side. Then they brought pails of water, mops, brooms.

"Señoras! Ya esta limpia!"

Against his protests, they swept and washed the floor. Out again they went, leaving him squatting in the doorway, dead tired, soaking wet, hungry, and heavy with sleep. Soon they returned with the bed: a rude wooden frame, chest high, with a bottom of woven hemp cords. Over this they put a *petate* to lie on, and a dry *serape* to cover him.

"Gracias! Mil gracias! Buenas noches, Señoras!"

Their laborious preparations had taken an hour or more. The floor had dried, leaving only puddles on the worn stones. Yet this was not yet enough to do the stranger honor. The old crone returned with a yellowed shawl that had a long silk fringe; a descendant of one of the Chinese shawls lodged here on its way from China to Spain, and now called "Spanish." This she spread smoothly on the bed. At last she left him. "Peace, *Señor.*"

Peace. Always a dead sterile peace. A dark brooding heaviness impregnated with fear—of light and air, of strangers intruding with the clatter of horses' hoofs or the quick dull thud of a knife striking home. Peace. So March could hear them bolting the doors, whispering outside. But always honor and hospitality, despite the fear of betrayal. Warm with gratitude, March slept.

These were the *ranchitos,* the tiny villages, the centuries-old towns he found lost and forgotten in the waves of the heaving earth he breasted. Places having names in a strange tongue, fading into timeless time as one place, one name, the name of the bitter briefness of man's days, his hunger for the ever-beyond, and the haunting loneliness of one who saw on every face the enduring soul of a people rooted to their earth. In each a church, a crumbling mission, a great cathedral whose blackened stone walls would have held twice or ten times the population of the village. The monuments of a race which had impressed upon another a religion and a culture which had not sprung from its own soil. The tombs of *Senor Jesu Cristo,* a limp image of death in every church, gory with clotted red paint, pierced with cactus thorns. And outside, the weed-grown pyramids, the shrines along the mountain trails with fresh flowers and fresh blood, the little stone idols buried in the corn *milpas.* All proclaiming still the dark goddess with all the fertility of the earth itself. Tonantzin, ancient earth mother, in her mantle of sweeping rain. The new Guadalupana clad in the robe of heaven, in a blue mantle dotted with stars like toasted maize grains. Beat the tall drum *huehuetl,* the flat drum *teponaztle,* for the feather, the flower, the drum, and mirror of the old gods who had never died. But neither had they come to full flower, March thought; they too were entombed in walls of living flesh.

10

Eventually he came to a town, a *camion,* a railroad junction, and so reached Guadalajara. His uncut hair hung down his neck, his beard had grown, his clothes were tattered. He went to a barber shop, cleaned up as best he might. Possessed by an insane craving for sugar, he sat in the *plaza mayor* gorging on sticky sweet potatoes baked and smeared with *peloncillo,* on *dulces* bought from street-corner vendors. His duffle bag had fallen into a river while he was crossing on a raft; the old suit inside it was ruined; but in the lining of the trousers under the belt he had hidden a few *Banco de Mexico* paper notes. These he ripped out and went to the Hotel Imperial.

It was an enormous mausoleum of white marble full of over-stuffed furniture and decorated with scrolls, doodads, and whatnots. Yet it was modern enough to boast showers and a good dining room in which he feasted on a *biftek* followed by *mole de guajalote.* Then clean and content he slept between sheets.

Next day, while waiting for changes to be made in a cheap new suit, he sat in the *plaza,* almost deafened by church bells: a resonant, deep-toned booming from the Byzantine towers of the 16th century cathedral, chiming, ringing, clanging from a dozen churches. After months of solitude in the wilderness he could not accustom himself to this second largest city in Mexico. Trains, trams, sleek limousines, and beautiful old carriages; men in tidy business suits, well-groomed women, children accompanied by *duenas;* filthy beggars, ragged *pelados,* Indians in their white cotton shirts and *pantalones.* They all swarmed by, faces white, dark, and *café-con-leche* which gradually merged into one face, the face of modern *mestizo* Mexico.

Every continent, March thought, had its own great spirit of place, its own polarity, its own terrestrial magnetism, whatever you chose to call it. The white Europeans who swarmed into this old New World with those two miracles, gunpowder and the horse, were not in tune with the land as were the indigenous Indians; they couldn't root themselves in a new homeland, conforming to its spiritual laws. So up in March's America they killed off the Indians, penning in reservations the pitiful remnants of the great tribes to deteriorate like buffalo in a zoo. But down here, cruel and rapacious as they were, the conquerors were gradually swallowed in the blood they had shed. A fusion took place between the white and the Indian, resulting in a new race, the *mestizo.*

White talcum powder splattered on dark cheeks, high French heels under barefoot Indian feet, the very skulls of the whites gradually tending to conform to the head type of the Indians. One face, one people, growing from the same soil.

A gradual amalgamation of races was an inevitable necessity, March thought. No tribe – not even the Tarahumaras, no race, could forever escape it. In one vast stream all humanity kept welling up from its common cavern womb, the dark unconscious, into the light of consciousness. Nothing could dam its flow; it would eventually wipe out all differences of race, creed, and culture in one great blending of all.

An amalgamation that would not be a scientific mixture of customs, beliefs, and wills, that would not be an economic trade, but which would gather these in its flow. A fusion that would be the death of each, the white and the Indian, as he was today. A death and a great rebirth. And from them, together, the new American – a new continental soul reborn, with new spiritual conceptions and moving to a more profound rhythm than either had ever known.

The shops were closing. The street lights were coming on. The church bells were still ringing. Still March sat there in the gathering dusk.

Mexico! The motherland of his western America, whose remote sierras and faint trails had led him from space to depth, the only answer to the flow of time. Mother Mexico which had settled forever the spirit of his tormenting unrest and given him the answer to himself.

Finally, late next afternoon, he went to see Klaus. The German was living in an old residential hotel with a little private patio where he could be waited upon. His head, broken arm and ribs had long healed; the surgery on his side had been successful; the hospital had discharged him to recuperate.

"*Himmel!* It was nothing!" roared Klaus, giving March the *embrazo*. "Klaus loafs like a gentleman on company expenses! Little brother! Tonight we will drink much beer and see the beautiful girls of Guadalajara together! That suit does not fit. Klaus shall take you to his tailor tomorrow!"

They dined regally at the Fenix, got a little drunk together, and dozed through the antics of an all-blond, nude chorus at the expensive La Azteca cabaret. Then they drove home in a carriage to Klaus' hotel to come awake again on French brandy.

Klaus was eager to get to work again. Finnerty had written him of two possible openings. "Pachuga! Who does not know the mines of Pachuga? So close to Mexico City! But Guanajuato, little brother! The Veta Madre is the richest silver lode in the world. It will not be exhausted in another 500 years. We will be kings together, *cómo no?*"

Stimulated by brandy, he talked on. Suddenly he broke off, slapped his leg. "*Mein Gott!* The *telegrama*. Where is it?" He rummaged through a desk, a stack of papers on the table, and finally passed to March a dirty wrinkled envelope.

March slit it open and glanced at the date, nearly three weeks back. It was from his mother. For an instant he hesitated before reading the terse message. His presentiment of its meaning changed to a certitude that filled him with a tearing pain and anguish such as he had never known – Then suddenly the words gleamed and blurred before him with the evanescent brilliance of the one and only truth of all men's lives – the gleam of a rising star which lights up for each our loneliness, our grandeur, and despair, then fades and dies without leaving a mark of its passage on the eternal skies of night.

Klaus had poured himself another brandy and was still talking. "Guanajuato. *Ja!* That is the place for us, *Bruderlein!* A 500-year-old Spanish colonial citadel high in the hills, like a castle on the Rhine. Great old houses. Good food. And the girls! Ripe little peaches hanging on old family trees. Just waiting for Klaus and March to squeeze out their juice. Eh, little brother? And the silver. Mountains of silver. Klaus will write Finnerty tomorrow."

March stood up, sobered, cold, and resolute. "No Klaus. No more mining. I'm through with Mexico. I'm going home." He lunged out the door.

Klaus went with him to the station next evening. They clasped hands, then Klaus laid his arm over March's shoulder. "We shall not forget, eh *Bruderlein?*" And March, looking into his friend's face, knew suddenly what he had meant to him. The train pulled slowly out of the station, the dusty valley, into the darkness of his own thoughts.

To March that long and tiresome journey home seemed not a matter of spanning space, but of decreasing depth.

Grieving over Rogier's death, irritated at himself for receiving Ona's telegram so late, and ashamed of missing the funeral, he felt like a man slowly lifting from the bottom of a mine. The slow train rocked like an ascending hoist, his ears plugged, he yearned for light. But he was rising, ever rising. The sierras dwindled, muddy rivers slid by, the swampy lowlands fell behind with their matted jungle growth and cloying heat. He felt the rush of cool air. And then one morning he saw what every miner sees with a leaping heart – the source of all beauty, light. It was sunrise over a vast tawny desert hirsute with cactus, the high Sonoran mesa stretching into Arizona. He had emerged at last.

He got off the train at the end of the railroad line and was cleared across the International Line by customs officials. The little border town was hauntingly familiar. *Cantina* lights were beginning to blaze forth, *taco* vendors were lighting their kerosene lamps, Ford *camiones* loaded with big-hipped men and scrawny little *Señoras* rushed past him. The border had not changed, but it seemed different. The brutal pock-marked faces of the half-breeds, the hopeless faces of the decadent Indians, the hard cunning faces of the whites, all seemed to him curiously blended and subdued. That deep dark chasm seemed inexplicably to have flattened out. The border was no longer a depthless pit between two races. It was a bridge. March felt a nameless ecstasy beginning to well from his heart. Neither space nor depth held now for him any fear. He had bridged them both.

He was in his own country. Everybody was talking English. English slang! He stopped at a neon-lit "Cut Rate" drug store. Colored placards swung on strings from the ceiling, decorated the shelves. A raucous voice shrieked from a microphone "Two for a quarter!"—"Ninety-eight cents while they last!"—"One cent sale today only!" He saw thirty-nine brands of tooth-brushes, sixty-two kinds of tooth-paste, rubber gloves, patent medicines, vaginal douches, pure ivory back-scratchers, colored postcards, rayon panties, tobacco, cigarettes, candy, stewing pans, chewing gum, miniature turtles, Siamese fish, electric frying pans, and at the soda fountain signs advertising nut sundaes, banana splits, and Lovers' Delight. All Reduced for Today Only. Mechanistic, materialistic *Estados Unidos* of the *Imperialisimo Yanqui* selling its soul for the good old American Dollar, its standard of culture. But who could buy it? Everybody else was after the dollar too.

How vulgar it was. But it seemed to March the naive vulgarity of children, of a nation, a people who had not yet grown up. This was his country; he loved it all. Imagine! Cellophane-packaged handerchiefs, a dime apiece! He bought three for a quarter, on sale for today only, and hurried out like a thief.

He caught the north-bound train. He had watched the lofty peaks of Ixtaccihuatl and Popocatepetl fade into the turquoise with a sense of irrevocable loss. Now, like a man who must have a snowy peak on the horizon to give his life meaning and direction, he watched for another even more familiar. It began to rise north of the Sangre de Cristos, the slow uplift of a range long and blue as that of a great fish rising out of the pelagic plain. And then he saw it, a great snowy peak too high for any mortal man to climb. Pike's Peak!

March knew now he had come to home.

It was late afternoon when he got off the train and walked through Little London, still carrying his duffle bag. The lilacs were out; the warm sunshine was redolent with spring; tourist cars whizzed past into the canyons. How he had hated his town's smugness and choking conservatism, its gaudy make-believe, and pretentious air. But all this he saw now only as a cosmetic mask. It would crack and wear away as all superimposed cultures must fade and pass away. And he remembered the great pyramids he had seen, the crumbling cathedrals, the haunting look in the eyes of the Tarahumaras. From this Little London with its false ideals he saw rising the Little London of tomorrow—a town rooted to its own *tierra*, with its own traditions, and proudly conscious of its own integral uniqueness.

From the top of Bijou Hill he saw Shook's Run with its new bridge, the haunted old house. *Mi tierra. Mi casa.*

Ona met him in the hall.

"*Mi madre!* Mother! Oh, Mother!"

Blinded, dazed, he heard a rush of feet, felt Leona and Nancy poking him in the ribs, Mary Ann and Uncle John wringing his hand. And then he saw and grabbed the little frail figure of Mrs. Rogier.

"Granny! Why, Granny—"

But deep in his heart was an emptiness that could not be filled. Helplessly he stared into the rickety empty chair in the corner. He had returned to his grandfather's house, but it would never be quite the same.

March had missed Rogier's funeral, but he had arrived in plenty of time for something as distressing—the dissolution of a family that during three generations had endured in this haunted old house on Shook's Run.

The big question had been what to do with the house. Mary Ann had answered it at a family conference shortly before March arrived. "I saw Mr. Pyle yesterday," she announced abruptly. "I told him he could handle the house. There's a mortgage on it which must be met. It might as well be sold."

Ona's face flushed with anger. "Pyle! That shyster! Never! Daddy would turn over in his grave if Pyle ever laid his sticky hand on this house. Who gave you permission to boss this affair, anyway?

It's Mother's own house, in her own name, and she's going to live here as long as she pleases."

"Now, Ona, be practical for once in your life," remonstrated Mary Ann. "Look at it. A ramshackle old barn of three stories and nine big rooms, and the shop in back. No paint for years. No garage. And set in a neighborhood that soon will be really a slum. Besides, it's already been done. I gave Pyle the go-ahead, with Mother's signed power of attorney."

"The devil you say!" ejaculated Ona, jumping to her feet and staring down accusingly at Mrs. Rogier.

"I don't know. I don't understand," wailed Mrs. Rogier. "I just signed the paper like she said."

Mary Ann efficiently took over. When March arrived he observed that a junk dealer already had cleaned out the back yard of the last of the old winches and rusty cable reels which Rogier had held on to so indomitably. His prized hand tools in the shop had been sold in one pile. Ona had rescued for March only his miner's candlestick and a polished bird's-eye maple T-square Rogier had made in Maryland and with which he had drawn all his plans.

"What's become of that big trunk of Indian stuff on the Third Floor?" he asked Ona. In it had been packed Cable's fringed buckskin shirt with its panels of stained porcupine quills, the huge Cheyenne war bonnet of eagle feathers tipped with red yarn buckskin leggings, Arapaho moccasins, a bundle of sacred arrows, and a prized medicine pouch; and with these, the Navajo and Pueblo collection Cable had brought back from Shallow Water. A man's simple and priceless heritage bequeathed to his son.

Ona sighed. "It was gone before I knew it. I don't know where. A museum man or somebody took it. Shall we try to get it back?"

"Let it go!" he said harshly.

Then suddenly one morning a second-hand book dealer arrived with two trucks. A pair of scales was set up in front of the shop. One after another the men came out with armloads of books. They were stuffed in gunny sacks, weighed, and thrown in the trucks: Rogier's library of a lifetime which had lined two walls of his shop. The *Bhagavad Gita, Gilgamesh Epic, Tel-El-Amarna Letters of Babylonia and Egypt,* the *Book of the Breaths of Life,* the *Kabbalah* and *Lament of Lamech,* the *Koran* from Arabia and the *Shah Nameh* from Persia, the Egyptian and the Tibetan *Book of the Dead*, the *Upanishads* and *Suttas*, *Analects of Confucius*, "New Thought" books and books of cheap mysticism, the Masonic plates for which he had paid a hundred dollars apiece, and the pamphlets he could never refuse at a dime; his shelves of mathematics, engineering dynamics, and geology; of philosophy, art, and history; and lastly his countless rolls of maps.

Mrs. Rogier, Ona, and March stood helplessly beside Mary Ann. A book fell out of a sack and split open to reveal a yellowed slip of paper. It was an old signed check made out to Rogier by Stratton at the time he was worth ten million dollars, and the amount was not filled in. March handed it to Ona. "Here. Put this in your family Bible."

"I can't stand it!" moaned Mrs. Rogier. "Next to his mines and horses Daddy loved his books. Almost as much as his children. He spent more time with them."

"Don't be foolish!" Mary Ann answered sensibly. "Books are the most useless commodity in the world. It costs more to cart them around than to buy new ones. And where'd you put 'em?"

March stood watching in silence. There had been the day when he would have regarded this disgraceful scene as a sacrilege. But now, he thought, Mary Ann was right. Forty pounds of religion. Sixty pounds of philosophy. A hundredweight of science, art, and history. Throw on the *Divine Comedy*—that'll tip the scales. Dead weight all of it. Four thousand years of knowledge—and a woman's song on a deserted *plaza* at midnight, the pleading look in the eyes of a primitive Tarahumara refuted it all. It is not dead knowledge we need, but the intuition of the living moment.

So he stood there, raising his eyes to the snowy Peak towering in the blue. In it lay Rogier's life, his triumph, his folly and despair. It was not books that Rogier had plumbed, but the earth itself.

More trucks came to empty the house of nonessential furniture, doodads and whatnots. Pyle stood at the fence rubbing his hands in approbation. He had great plans for the house, he said. Its three stories and many rooms could easily be converted into a lodging house of several flats and separate rooms for individual lodgers; maybe even a boarding house. Also the huge shop in back would make an excellent apartment when adequately partitioned. The family was too shocked to say a word.

That evening at dinner March turned casually toward Mary Ann. "You haven't forgotten a thing. Now tell me, what disposition have you and Pyle made for the Kadles?"

"They can go to hell with their everlasting squeaking—or with you to Patagonia or wherever you traipse off to next!"

It was an unwarranted disapproval of those two invisible but faithful members of the family that shocked everyone at the table, but which revealed to them that even Mary Ann was upset.

11

Where all of them were going became the constant subject of conversation between Ona and March when they sat alone up in the Third Floor. Mary Ann's and Uncle John's Chocolate Shoppe in Manitou had been quite successful, but of course there was always the winter slump. They now intended to move it to Denver. "Little towns have always been my big mistake," she maintained. "For high class confectionery you've got to have a year-round trade that appreciates quality." Mrs. Rogier and Ona, with the money left from the sale of the house, were going to move into a small flat away from this part of town where they wouldn't be troubled by heartaches. In fact, they had looked at one in the North End. "Not too far up, and a bit west," Ona added quickly. "It won't spoil us, and we can see the mountains across the creek. A pretty view. You know it was up in the North End where we first lived. In a house built like a Maltese cross, near the Big Ditch the Indians used to splash across on their ponies."

She was silent a moment. "We haven't told you before, son, but Leona won't be with us. She wants to get married and I guess we ought to let her. A nice young man. You'll meet him soon. And they'll be living here in town where we can see them often."

"And Nancy will be moving to Denver?"

"No, she's not going with Mary Ann and Uncle John. They'll have too much to do, getting a new business started, to give her much company. Besides, Nancy's always been with us. And she's going to stay with Mother and me, still workin' downtown in the ten cent store, pots and pans department. With her droopy eye she doesn't get out often, you know. So like I told her, we'll be three homebodies together, like we always been."

It was this yet unbroken pattern of their lives that was in Ona's mind several days later as she sat at the window waiting for March to return from Cripple Creek. A letter had come to him from the Vice-President in Charge of Operations of Western Mines. Finnerty remembered him well; he had done excellent work for the company in Mexico. Conditions were such that Western Mines had no opening for him at present in the United States, but Finnerty had taken the liberty of recommending him to a large company contracting for a drainage tunnel in Cripple Creek. Would Mr. Cable please follow up and advise? So March had taken the early morning train.

Late that afternoon Ona saw him coming down the street. Her heart beat with pride at seeing his rangy body dressed in new clothes, his lean dark face tanned darker by long exposure to the Mexican sun, the long swinging stride that reminded her of Cable. She jumped up, met him at the door. "Did you see him, son? Have you got a job?"

"Let's go upstairs, Mother," he said quietly.

They climbed the stairs to the Third Floor and sat down to talk undisturbed. March tersely explained the substance of his interview. All Colorado was mining about $20,000,000 worth of gold a year—what Cripple Creek alone was putting out when it led the world in the production of gold. The district's output now had dropped to less than $3,000,000. But the price of gold had just been raised from $21 to $35 an ounce. Old dumps were being reworked, old mines being reopened. Now things looked bright for the district. Its present bottom had been lowered to 8,000 feet altitude by two early drainage tunnels. Now the long proposed third tunnel was going through. It would lower the bottom to 7,000 feet, draining the whole district of thirty square miles. It would cost nearly $1,500,000 but it would open up at least $6,000,000 worth of ore. Who knew how much more lay at even greater depth? Anyway, the firm Finnerty had sent him to had contracted to drive the tunnel and the engineer who had interviewed March had offered him a job.

"You took it?" Ona exclaimed, beaming. "It's a compliment to you, being recommended by the vice-president of a big outfit like Western Mines. You've worked hard for it. I'm proud of you! You're a young man yet. Times are hard now. You likely couldn't find anything else. It won't last long—three or four years at the most. And you can be studyin' for somethin' better."

She patted his hand. "Just think son! I'll have you here with me awhile yet! We'll have an extra room or a bed for you in our new flat. They say in these new-fangled places there's beds in the front rooms. They just pull down from the wall, easy as anything. There you can stay on weekends when you come down from Cripple Creek. Just like Daddy comin' down from the Sylvanite in the old days. Like your own father, son. And we'll be watchin' from the window, Mother and Nancy and me, to see you come down the street puffin' on a black cigar or pipe, like as not."

"Mother!"

With bright eyes, she prattled on. "Why, shoot! Times haven't changed at all. Only you'll be on a regular salary—and a whopping big one too or I miss my reckon, what with your college education and bein' to Mexico and all. No worries about the vein peterin' out. Money in the bank pretty soon, I fancy. A good name as a smart and reliable young man growin' up with the country. Good clothes you look good in—you sure do, son! No dirty old boots or mules to cuss at; you'll be ridin' the cushions. And when I see my son a-stridin' down the street on his way back from Cripple Creek, I'll say to myself, 'That's my boy. He's a Rogier and a Cable too. A regular first rate minin' man, born with the feelin' in his blood!' "

So she went on, sitting in the ghostly emptiness of the barny Third Floor bedroom, clutching at the tattered remnants of an almost forgotten dream of happiness with the invincible and undaunted belief in her son that she had so stoutly and futilely maintained for her father, her husband, and Tom.

March rose, heavy with an intolerable anguish, to stare down at her who all her life had fought tooth-and-nail against their involvement in Cripple Creek. We want so little, at the end, to justify our monstrous faith in others! How could he fail her now?

Disconsolately, guiltily, he stared out the window upon Shook's Run. Then abruptly he turned to face her. "Mother! I turned down that job. I'm through with Cripple Creek and Mexico. I'm done with mining, anywhere!"

A look of blank incomprehension froze on Ona's face.

"No mining in any shape or form," he repeated. "I'm not a hard-rock man, an engineer. I don't want to dig in the ground for gold or silver or anything else. People are more important than places. I'll do my diggin' in them."

"How?" she asked dully.

"I don't know, Mother. I don't know yet how they're put together. Maybe I'll take some premedical courses and then psychology. These new depth psychologists and psychiatrists are going way down below grass roots, opening up new levels of understanding, discovering ore bodies we never knew existed. Just what I'll wind up doing, I don't know, but that's the vein I'm after."

He could see her hackles rise. "Psychiatrists! Doctors to raving mad men! God Almighty! You're out of your own head!" She fixed on him a shrewd accusing look. "Some foreign woman in Mexico hooked you and changed your normal view of life, didn't she? Or did you catch one of those tropical diseases that water the brain?"

"Don't bait me. I just want to find out what people really are, who I am."

She was angry now. "I know who you are, if you don't! You're a young Smart Alec who's forgetting he comes from a fine normal family with a proud background. Rogiers, every one of them!"

"Stop it!" he shouted himself now. "I can't stand that everlasting song of the Old South any more. Let me tell you who we are! We're a decadent family gone to pot! Wastrels, failures, shams, epileptics, homosexuals, half-breeds! What happened? Why? How?"

Ona could not withstand his outburst. She lowered her head, began to twist the handkerchief in her lap. Then she raised her anguished face. "Son! We're no different than any family in the whole wide world. We've had our backsliders. We've made our mistakes. And we've forgiven those who made them. But in us all beats the same warm heart. We all want the same thing, not knowing what it is. We try and fail, and try again. There's somethin' in us that can't be put down. We're people, son, just people the world over!"

She began to sniffle, but her voice was clear and resolute. "Would you be like God, tryin' to know why He put us here, what makes us feel and act the way we do? Let well enough alone, boy. We Rogiers and North Enders, the Hottentots and the heathen Chinese, all of us, are goin' to make out in the end, just give us time. You're young and impatient, boy. Just try to understand without knowin' so much."

The storm was over. March felt contrite and humble as he stared out the window at the Peak rising above Bijou Hill. Yet still there hovered something above it, whatever it was, that committed him to its search. He turned and put his arms around Ona. "Let's don't quarrel, Mother. Things will work out like you say. I'll be stayin' with you all winter while I finish up some courses in school and find out what to do next. No need to worry about money, with all I saved from my salary in Mexico and a whopping big bonus to boot."

"Well, that's something anyway," she said, pressing her tear-stained face against his.

Upset, March left the house for a walk. On a sudden impulse he boarded a streetcar to the south part of town and on foot struck across the prairies to the cemetery. It was sentimental nonsense, this going to gawk at Rogier's grave, he thought; for like Cable he had an aversion to burial places. Mrs. Rogier, however, had been after him ever since he had returned. "Now March, you ought to go out to the cemetery. You wasn't there for the funeral and Daddy missed you. You ought to go, really you ought."

Walking along, he grumbled to himself, "I'll bet two-bits against a buffalo nickel she asks me when I get back if I took flowers." For of course he had been the only one who had not sent a wreath. And yet carting out now a bouquet of hothouse roses would have been incongruous. Rogier would have sat up in his grave and blurted out, "Dom, boy! What's all this? Don't clutter me up with such stuff. Just hand me down a cigar. By Jove, there's nothin' like a good smoke when a man's restin'!"

Still March was a little ashamed, walking along so empty-handed. It was June, the solstitial turn of the year when our Father Sun reaches the northernmost end of his journey. Summer, when full-breasted, full-bottomed Mother Earth comes into her own.

Down in Old Mexico the white glare is blinding, the heat is like an oven's blast. The lush tropical growth along the trails gives off the green sickening odor of chlorophyl. In front of thatched *ramadas,* in the clearings, fires are built, not so much for cooking as to keep away swarms of insects. Delicious pearls of sweat cling to the bottles of *Carta Blanca* beer pushed over the bars of every *cantina.* And from the ground outside arises the distinctive smell of all Mexico, the acrid stench of dust impregnanted with urine. The rivers run soap-green, frothing into white suds around the rocks. In them every evening splash the *Indios* of the *pueblocito,* naked bodies reddened by the sinking sun. The moon rises high over rustling banana leaves and pale white orchids, shines in the open window upon the damp full breasts of a woman of the earth waiting passionately for her due. She shall have it! now in summer when the gently gushing female rain and the hard male rain unite to fructify the sterile earth of human flesh.

But here in High Country end all roads, all trails. From the baking plains and stinking lowlands they lead upward to cottages in the canyons, cabins in the pines. Long-legged colts and velvet-coated calves frisk in mountain meadows. A lone eagle screams from the crag. Magpies and chipmunks follow the smoke of picnic fires. Down from the peaks tumble rivers and rivulets. Trout streams: rainbow, native brook, and the big browns. Kids have got the trick. They load your supper table with butter-fried trout stacked up like cordwood. At the little railroad depots, when a train comes in, they hold up to dining car chefs more basketsfull packed in layers of green leaves. And in every remote Saddle Rock Grill, Sentinel Rock Cafe, and other eating joint a sign hangs at the window: "Fresh Trout—All You Can Eat for Fifty Cents—Spuds Incl."

Summer too is the time for the big rodeos when the broncs come busting out of the chutes, and forty-a-month waddies ride to fame by sticking eight seconds on Five-Minutes-to-Midnight or Old Steamboat, or ride down upon, rope, and tie a plunging steer in seventeen seconds.

Up in Cripple Creek the last big mines open up for tourists, displaying specimens of ore they haven't mined for ages. While in a forgotten gulch a gray-bearded old-timer gives his old working hell while the ground is thawed—for the last time, Mister!

Little London is at the topside of her hour. Crowds throng the hotel verandas, fill the rooming houses and flimsy cottages. Rich people return to open up their Broadmoor mansions. Up the narrow trails from Manitou burros climb with jolting tourists. Everyone wears khaki pants and hiking boots. At the Iron Springs Pavillion they buy saltwater taffy by the ton, dished out in little colored-stripe paper bags. Tourist drivers shout from their hacks and jalopies: "Throw snowballs from the top of Pike's Peak on the Fourth of July!" And the blunt-nosed little engine snorts up the Cog Road pushing its tiny car.

You don't have to look at the calendar. You can tell it's summer by looking at the prices for a bed, a hamburger, and a postcard. Or even at signs posted along the dusty roads a hundred miles away: "Detour here around the Tourist Trap of the Rockies." Who cares? For this is the opulent, full-blossomed season of the year when Little London makes hay while the sun shines—

No, thought March, it wouldn't do to go to his grandfather's grave empty-handed. In the flare of the sinking sun the prairie was a brilliant blanket of white wild onions, bluebells, scarlet Indian paintbrushes, sand daisies, columbines, lupines. He remembered the hundreds of flower stalls in Guadalajara, the remote altars in the sierras covered with fresh flowers. Fresh flowers and fresh blood. His grandfather would have liked that! The old pagan!

March could not resist stooping for an armful. But when he reached the cemetery he had some difficulty finding the family lot. It was unmarked, Cable's sunken grave and Rogier's fresh one devoid of headboards pending the erection of small stone markers which March had ordered. He flashed a look down the gulch. It was filled with tin cans. The pines soughed faintly, a magpie screamed. He knelt and self-consciously but carefully spread the crimson flowers over Rogier's and Cable's graves, side by side. And now as he stood looking down at that patch of earth which held them both, he heard above him the muted whisper of the aimless ancient winds.

Remember what the Indians said of your grandfather's people, that it was the destiny of white men to turn into stone. Remember too your grandfather's square hewn face and figure, his granite will. Look now at the massive granite Peak, son; do you no longer recognize your grandfather's flesh?

Did not your father's fathers and their sons rise out of soft adobe? Out of it and its rich abundance they built the walls of their soft warm-colored bodies. Into it they have returned. Do you no longer recognize your father's flesh? Look down at your feet, son.

And now they both lie before you, intermingled, even as the rising plains merge into the rocky mountains. Here where the chamisa blooms brightest, the sage smells sharpest — who knows which is buried here? Over them both the tall rain walks, the ghost buffalo sweep past, and we, the ancient aimless ones, whisper in the pines. What is adobe and what is granite but the mingled flesh of all flesh, the earth eternal? Look closer, son.

He could feel their cool fingers lifting from him his pride, sorrow, and regret. Their voices comforted him. Yet his inner self cried back, You talk so glibly of the flesh of the earth and the earth of the flesh over whose surface you pass so aimlessly and eternally! But what is the mystery that imbues this flesh with life? Just what am I? That is what I ask!

The aimless ancient winds did not answer; they had passed by already. In their stead answered the resonant voice of the earth, the cruel and immense, the deep and forgiving earth of a continent timelessly spanning the seas 3,000 miles apart.

You are them both, adobe and granite, indivisible and intermingled. You are the flesh of their flesh, and their flesh is of my flesh. We are all one earth. Together, undivided and eternal, we echo the pulse which throbs through stone; the same isotatic equilibrium holds you and the frosty peaks in place; you crumble and wash away, and rise ever again in eternal palingenesis.

You sound like my grandfather! he cried. Flesh and earth! Is there nothing more?

You are the pieces of a broken arrow rejoined. The hand of Quetzalcoatl returned on his raft of snakes to reach forth and lift a people out of their pit. You are the earth of all America out of which shall spring a new and unknown flower — the flower of this mighty, unknown continent risen so soon from the blue depths of time. The flower, the feather, the drum, and the mirror of old gods who have never died. The voice of new gods yet to be heard.

I have heard this before! was his curiously stubborn response. It echoes the voice of my father and my father's people, the wail of the Raramuri you hold in abject bondage!

And once again the mighty earth thundered forth, *Take care, son! Don't be in such a hurry. For in the ghostly flow of time which seems to move and yet never moves, you are the leaf that falls and the leaf that sprouts anew. The rock disintegrated by time, and the timeless dust within the rock. The false pride, crumbled magnolia leaves, and moth-rotted Confederate flag of your grandfather's people. And your father's dark hawk face and the smoke of a thousand strange campfires in his blood. You are all that ever has been and all that ever will be, and from me you are ever reborn.*

For a moment he was silent, feeling a strange resoluteness gathering within him. Maybe I'm all that, flattering as it seems, he admitted. Likely I'm less than that, yet more in a way you neglect to mention. For you sound like my lesser mother, Mother Earth, and I would have you know too I'm not a hard-rock man. I'm done with mining in your bowels for what I seek. And so I must break the umbilical cord with which you also would hold me. Great as you are, there is something greater. What about heaven, Mother Earth, under which you lie so supinely, that fructifies and lashes even you into meek submission?

Oh! You would not only exhaust the meaning of your mother and of your father too, but supersede the duality of all mortal existence! What big boots you think to wear, tadpole that you are! grumbled the earth warningly. *Such impertinence can't question my power. There is in you something that is always mine. Take care! Someday I'll collect my due!*

Your threats don't frighten me, Mother Earth! he cried back with a burst of new self-confidence, staring upward above the western horizon. There is in me something that will escape you. What is the mystery that impregnates your flesh, imbues all earth with life? That is what I'm still asking. The one secret self hidden in the dark stopes deep within our lesser selves. That is what I seek!

The earth gave one last rumble and was still. It did not answer. Perhaps it could not, being itself, like countless other earths in interstellar space, but a part of that vast mystery of all creation informed with life for its own duration.

The sun had set. In the luminous purity of the twilight March could see the pale silvery sheen of the great Peak majestic and immense above the purpling wall of mountains to the west. He stared at it as if at an imperishable monument to a faith he had finally surmounted. And now silence spoke with the voice that outspeaks all. Listening, he saw it before him, like something risen from the depths of dreamless sleep to the horizon of wakeful consciousness, without clear outline yet embodying the substance of a hope and meaning that seemed strangely familiar as it was vague. Toward it he began his long and resolute journey.